# ROOKIE OF THE YEAR

## (THE UNDERDOG SERIES #2)

### BREA BROWN

WAYZGOOSE PRESS

# CONTENTS

Edited by Maggie Sokolik

Cover design by Keri Knutson at alchemybookcovers.com

(Note: An earlier, slightly modified edition of this novel, with the same title, was originally published in 2016, 9871520278001).

*For the Kansas City Chiefs, who have made this fan extremely proud (and sometimes hairless).*

*You're winners in my book, no matter what!*

## ONE

## CRUSHING DEFEAT

*"Jet Knox has been running for his life all night, Jim."*

*"Yeah, Bob. You're not kidding. The offensive line has been deci-mated by injuries, meaning Knox has had zero pass protection, and the Chargers' defense knows it."*

*"The blitz has been relentless. Knox has no time to look downfield for a receiver, so his choices are hand it off or run it himself. He's chosen the latter more often than he has all season, putting all of his faith in his own legs."*

*"He has, by far, the team's most rushing yards tonight. That's usually an indication the offense isn't clicking, which is never a good thing."*

*"In this case, it's not necessarily a bad thing, though. Here at the two-minute warning, the Chiefs are still in this game, thanks to those legs."*

*"Yeah, like some sort of late Christmas miracle."*

"Shut up!" I yell-groan at the TV, jabbing at the mute button and springing from the couch.

Watching our final regular season game, a home game that could determine our Playoffs fate, has been torture. Solitary torture. Despite considerable pressure from both my brother, Greg, and best bud, Colin, I insisted on going it alone at Jet's house.

Well, not completely alone. Quatorze, Jet's intrepid Bichon Frisé, hung in there with me for part of the first quarter. But my shouting, clapping, hair-pulling, and general theatrics scared him off early. When I nearly flipped the leather recliner with one of my exasperated backward flops, he ran for the stairs, and I haven't seen him since. I did move to the couch, though, to save me from death by La-Z-Boy.

I can't sit still. Since I'm engaged to be married to the galloping team quarterback (yeah, it's totally surreal), every game this season has been difficult to watch, but this one, with its postseason implications, is more than personal. We win, we're in. We lose, we have to rely on another team in our division, led by one of the best QBs of all time, to lose their game tomorrow—against one of the worst teams in the league. I don't like those odds. Putting your destiny in someone else's hands sucks, especially when those hands belong to Hall-of-Fame shoo-in Pete Jay.

Our opponents today, the Chargers, might not be playing for a spot in the postseason, but this is definitely a revenge match. We beat them in Jet's first game back after recovering from a hand injury, and what a sweet victory that was. The chance to play spoiler and kill our Playoff dreams would be a satisfying consolation prize for one of our biggest rivals. They want this win almost as badly as we do. Almost. But not quite.

And as annoying as the announcers' commentary is, it's spot-on. Jet *is* trying to carry the entire team on his back (or legs, in this case), and while he's been successful, we're still trailing by a touchdown and an extra point with only two minutes left in the game and no time-outs. Plus, we're pinned all the way back on our own ten-yard line. We have a long way to go. Ninety yards, to be precise.

Now, while I wait through the two-minute warning commercial break, I whistle softly at the bottom of the staircase and coo, "Torzi-boy. C'mere, sweetie." I hear his tags jingle but after several seconds, he fails to appear. "I'm sorry, buddy!" Still nothing.

Retreating to the living room, I see the game is back on. We have the ball. Reflexively, I snatch the remote from the sofa cushion. My finger hovers over the mute button, then slides up to the "power" button. While Jet and the rest of the team break from the huddle to line up for the next play, I seriously consider turning off the television. But I can't do it. No matter how hard it is to watch every play, I can't *not* watch. And I'd keep the sound off, so I don't have to listen to the analysts' nattering, but then I can't hear Jet's voice, either. And I need to hear his voice.

Steeling myself, I restore the volume and press the gigantic remote to my nose. I remain standing while I peek around the device.

Cozied up to the backside of the center at the line of scrimmage, Jet booms, "Kill, kill, kill!" signifying that he's changing the original plan at the last second. The play clock creeps toward zero.

"Eep!" I close my eyes and press the remote harder to my forehead.

*"NOW FOR THE LOW, LOW PRICE OF $19.99. BUT WAIT! THERE'S MORE! START OFF THE NEW YEAR WITH A BONUS DOUBLE-ORDER FOR THE PRICE OF ONE!"*

"No, no, no, no, no!" I chant, thumbing at the soft keys to

get me away from the infomercial for shoe inserts and back to the right station.

By the time I get there, the play is over, and the network is showing a slow-motion replay of a low hit on Jet. The dirty tackle results in a penalty against the other team, which means we get to move farther down the field and closer to the end zone, but the game is suddenly secondary. I cringe while watching Jet's right knee hyperextend under the crushing blow from the opposing player. When they cut back to live TV, I study my fiancé as he limps off the abuse and receives the next play through his helmet speaker.

"Bully!" I yell at the next shot of the defensive end, who's shaking his head as if to protest the call. "Nasty, rotten bully!" As soon as I get another visual of Jet, I point to the television. "Stop changing the play at the line! And hand it off, why don't ya? You're killin' me, Knox!"

Of course, my pleas are futile. And after the center hikes the ball to him, Jet drops back for a pass that will never happen, because nobody's open downfield. For the umpteenth time today, he sees a gap and runs for it before sliding for the first down. Pumped, he leaps to his feet and regroups with the team to quickly relay the next play, just as likely not to occur, depending on how badly his protection breaks down.

"Ohmygosh, ohmygosh, ohmygosh." Knees feeling like I've been chased around a field all afternoon, I lower myself to the sofa and perch on the edge, bracing my elbows on my thighs and my head in my hands. "C'mon, you big, beautiful beast."

He fakes a hand-off to a teammate and keeps the ball, not even hesitating this time as he makes a break for the center of the field before cutting over to the sideline.

I rocket into the sort of extreme posture reserved for ballerinas and punch the air. "Go! Go! Go! Go!"

Forty-nine yards later, he scampers out of bounds before a barreling three-hundred pounder can push him there—or worse.

"Stop doing that!" I whimper, perversely proud and terrified and angry, all at the same time. "But good job, going out of bounds to stop the clock. You're so smart. But also so dumb."

Now we're in the other team's territory, definitely within Schoengert's field goal range, but a field goal isn't going to cut it. We have to get a touchdown and an extra point to tie it. Or a two-point conversion to win it. Surely, they won't go for two, though. No, they'll do the safe thing and tie it, taking their chances in overtime. Right? Yes.

We have to get in the end zone first, though. And it's still thirty-four yards away. Seems like miles.

The guys break the huddle with a synchronized clap and return to the line. Miraculously, Jet hands it off for real this time, and the running back gains eight more yards. But that eats up plenty of clock, so with less than a minute to go, it's time to start passing. The Chargers defense knows it and brings the full-on blitz, relentlessly rushing Jet on the next play. That puts the burly, knee-killing bully and a couple of his friends in Jet's face again, but it leaves some guys open downfield. Our tight end, Mr. Tight End Keaton Busch's replacement, Kent "Tiff" Tiffenauer, pulls the pass down but is immediately tackled, still right outside the red zone, that magical twenty yards in front of the goal line. Time keeps ticking.

The guys hurry to line up. Jet yells something unintelligible (to us at home), and the center hikes the ball. But it's too soon. Jet isn't ready for it, so it bounces off his hands and lands on the turf. A pile of sweaty men falls on top of it and each other, kicking and clawing for the brown ball.

"No!" I'm not sure if I'm more upset about the fumbled snap or the fact that Jet's at the bottom of that pile. Maybe it's best not to think too much about it. The answer may not reflect well on me.

After much shoving and whistle-blowing, the refs give the ball back to us. Somehow, Jet managed to fall on it and keep it. When everyone else stands to walk away, he pops up and flips the ball to the nearest ref, like it's no big deal.

"Pull it together out there, guys!" I yell. "Sonofa—!"

The ref calls for the clock to be reset to a measly thirty-two seconds after reviewing and confirming the play as a Chiefs fumble and recovery. Everyone lines up once more and tries to shake off the drama. But before the next snap, the Chargers call time-out.

"Dang it!" I slap the sofa cushion and wince at the sting in my palm.

The cameras follow Jet to the sideline, where he waves off the water-squirting attendant, slides his helmet halfway up his forehead so we can see his full face, and leans in to listen to Coach Dick Bauer's latest instructions. Lips: white, drawn-in. Eyes: wide, staring. He opens his mouth to speak, but the offensive coordinator cuts him off with a raised hand, so he yanks his helmet back down and fastens the chin strap with a tetchy snap. The ref blows the whistle to signal the end of the time-out, and the shot cuts away to the players returning to the field.

Oh, boy. That looked… tense. Now the question is, will Jet follow orders, despite his obvious disagreement. Or will he go rogue, with possibly disastrous—or heroic—results?

I can't watch. I can't look away. I can't watch. I can't look away.

The game resumes during a can't-look-away moment, so I'm committed to seeing the drama unfold. Jet falls back several long strides, his eyes focused on the end zone. Nobody's open, and it doesn't look like they'll be getting that way any time soon. The offensive line is holding, holding, holding… not holding! Two defenders break away from their opponents and stagger toward Jet. He spins away from one and scrambles from the other, running as fast as he can toward the sideline, still looking toward the end zone for an open receiver to magically appear. He pulls back his arm to throw the ball away and stop the clock, but Low-Hit Meanie has caught up to him.

"Look out!" I screech as the defender's huge paw slaps down on the vulnerable pigskin. Before Jet's arm can rock forward, the ball falls from his hand and rolls to the turf. Meanie scoops it up and runs. And runs. And runs. All the way to the other end zone, nearly eighty yards away.

I cover my mouth and nose, waiting for a whistle, a yellow flag, anything to signify the defensive touchdown won't count. The rest of the stadium must be doing the same thing, because the usually deafening crowd silences. The camera finds Jet, who gave chase until his enemy crossed the goal line. With the clock at zero and the officiating crew all signaling "touchdown," the defeated warrior stands at midfield, his hands on his hips, his head back as he stares unseeing at the cold, gray sky. He drops his chin and spews an expletive that requires the television production crew to quickly cut to another shot, which happens to be of the Chargers congregating in the end zone and celebrating their crushing victory.

A fan close to a live mic yells, "Knox, you suck!"

"No, he doesn't!" I mumble.

Within seconds, the fumble, recovery, and run-back are confirmed. Game over. We lose.

———

"There were three things I couldn't let happen," Jet says hours later, sitting shell-shocked in the same huge chair that almost killed me. "A sack, a fumble, or an interception."

I sit sideways in his lap and kiss his smooth, post-game shaved chin. "Shhh. You don't have to—"

"No, Maura. I do. I owe you—and this whole damn city—an explanation."

"And we got one. At the presser."

He snorts. "No. I gave the answers I was *told* to give. Nobody wanted me to take the blame."

"Because it wasn't your fault. Entirely. Where was the O-line today?"

"On the bench. Hurt."

"Ha! And their backups?"

"Out-matched. They held up better than I thought they would. Damn Hissler. That guy! He was in my grille all damn day."

"You were amazing. You had the most rushing yards of any other player on the team!"

He laughs sadly and rubs his eyes. "It's not supposed to be like that. At all. That's not a cool stat."

"Okay, but—"

"My job is to *throw* the ball."

"Nobody was open!"

"Yeah. And when that happens, my job is to throw it away."

"You tried."

"And failed. And fumbled. *I* fumbled. When we had a real chance of tying it up."

"Who called that play, anyway? The passing game was dead all afternoon. Who decided a pass play would be the game winner? Idiot!"

He fidgets under me. "Uh, well…"

"No! Please, tell me *you* didn't make that decision."

"Not entirely. The play call was 'pass,' but I called it different at the line. The bootleg the coaches wanted us to run would have been dead in the water."

I nibble my thumbnail. "Yeah, that would have been disastrous." *Like the play he chose wasn't?* "They would have been all over it."

"Anyway, it's my call if I see the defense lined up a certain way, and they were, so I adjusted."

"But pass? Jet!"

To his credit, he looks more sheepish than defensive when he says, "I guess I didn't want to change it up too much, because we didn't have a lot of time. I wanted to lob it into the end zone and be done with it."

"Only seconds before, you had run almost fifty yards! Why not try it again?"

He shakes his head. "It's different on a short field. Everything is too compressed."

I sigh. "Whatever. Listen. I don't think we should dwell on it. We should move forward and think about the next step. Looking back and regretting every mistake isn't healthy."

He nods. "Right. But looking forward means waiting to see

what happens in tomorrow night's game. Denver is going to cream the Raiders."

"You don't know that."

"Pete Jay? He's on fire. And they have the hottest tight end in the league."

I nudge my lips against his. "I disagree."

He laughs. "Be serious."

"I *am*. I'd take your tight end over Denver's any day."

"We *are* talking about my ass, right? Not the team's tight end. Or the tight end's tight end."

"Correct. Tiff doesn't do it for me."

"Oh, good. Because you used to have a thing for tight ends."

"Still do. But only yours." I nibble his bottom lip. Nibbling leads to pecking.

He half-heartedly returns my kiss but stares into space, past my face. "If I'd brought my arm forward a half-second sooner, it would have been ruled an incomplete pass. Or if I'd run faster for the sideline."

I groan and roll off his lap. He doesn't object. Instead he exhales loudly and gripes, "This season has been a disaster! Which would be fine—well, not fine, but you know what I mean—if we didn't have such high hopes."

Stifling my impatience, I remain silent and let him talk it out. He obviously needs to vent more than I need to stop thinking about it.

"Going into the season, our power rankings were amazing. We had Busch, we had a stout O-line, and we had one of the best wide receivers in the league. Then Busch had to screw it all up with that Bedroom Bowl shit. And I got hurt. And half the O-line went down. Then there's O'Doyle. I don't know what his problem was this season. Brick hands. It's been one disaster after another. I heard a fan yell for Wilcox today. *Before* I screwed up. What the hell?"

I collect my water glass from the coffee table. Over my shoulder on my way to the kitchen, I toss, "You're the one who says you're either the hero or the zero."

"But I was running my ass off out there! Without me, we wouldn't have even been in it on that last drive."

I shrug. "I didn't say it made sense. I'm only repeating what you've told me a hundred times."

"Great. I love having my own words thrown back in my face."

I halt, close my eyes, count to ten, and chant silently, *I love him, I love him, I love him,* before smiling tightly and continuing on my way.

It's not like this is unexpected. It would have been weird if he'd come home in a good mood after that game. In fact, I'm prepared for an extremely rough week. Because he's right that unless an absolute miracle happens—and we seem short on those lately—Denver *will* beat the Raiders. And the Chiefs' season will be over.

Worse, Jet's fumble will stand as the last play of their season. It will be replayed *ad nauseum*. Fans will be hard-pressed to remember the numerous highlights of a year that included more wins than losses, by a lot. Instead, they'll focus on the scandal and the injuries and the questionable decisions made under impossible pressure. That's how they are. That's how *I* was, until I met and fell in love with Jet, making me much more than your average fan.

Now I have to be super-fiancée-fan. It's as daunting as it sounds.

I return from the kitchen with a beer for each of us and find him in the exact same position, staring at the dormant fireplace, no doubt playing back a mental highlight reel that only contains the season's worst moments. Before I can take a stab at distracting him, though, his cell phone rings on the end table next to him.

He glances at it and moans. "Oh, geez. My mom."

I figure he's going to let it go to voicemail, but he surprises me by thrusting the device toward me while he takes the beer I'm offering. "Can you...?"

"Can I, what? Talk to your mom?" *Oh, Lord, no. I foolishly thought this day couldn't get worse. But talking to my future mother-in-law right now? That could make things infinitely worse.*

"C'mon. Please?" He bats his lashes. "She'll keep calling if we don't answer."

Dang it to hell. Stupid, stupid weak me. I snatch the phone from his hand and tap the green button, answering brightly, "Hey, Gloria!"

"Oh. Maura. I thought—I'm almost positive I called my son's phone." Her fake chuckle grates against my eardrum.

"You did. I'm answering because..."

I seek guidance from Jet, who mimes a peeing motion that makes me snort back a giggle.

"Jet's in the bathroom."

"I see. Well, I could have left a message. I didn't realize you answered his phone when he was indisposed."

I gulp at the implied disapproval. "I don't, normally. But he specifically asked me to pick up a call from you. Because he wants to talk to you."

He slaps his forehead and mouths, *What? No!*

Delighting in his panic, I wait a second before adding, "But he can't." He slumps back into his chair and gives me a thumbs-up as he swigs his beer.

"Why not?" Gloria asks, her tone wary. "Other than the obvious reason right this second."

I lower my voice, as if worried I might be overheard. "He's distraught about the game."

Jet freezes, mid-drink.

Gloria clicks her tongue. "Poor guy. That's precisely why I'm calling. I want to make sure he's okay."

"He'll be fine. Eventually. But he didn't want you to hear him crying."

Her sharp inhale is almost as comical as the mist of beer that sprays from Jet's mouth. He pops from his chair and reaches for the phone with dripping hands, but thanks to his stiff knees, I evade him much more successfully than he avoided Matt Hissler at the end of the game.

"Maura!" he hisses, wiping his hands on the front of his post-game dress shirt and limping after me.

I turn my back to him and plug a finger in my exposed ear so I can focus on what Gloria's saying. "Crying? Oh, dear! He's taking it worse than I thought. Is it the media? Are they saying horrible things?"

"Not yet, but you can be sure they will."

"He's usually so good about tuning that stuff out. He must blame himself. But it was only one play!"

"I've been trying to convince him of that, but— Oh, here he is now."

"Put him on. I need to talk to my poor baby."

I whirl on Jet and hold the device out to him. He narrows his eyes at me and tries to suppress his grin while he takes the phone, covering the mouthpiece. "You're pure evil," he says with more than a hint of admiration in his voice.

"Bet you'll never make me screen your calls for you again, though. I'm not your secretary."

I step past him, but he snags my elbow and murmurs down at me, "Don't leave me."

Ignoring the more serious meaning to those words, I say glibly, "Wouldn't dream of it. Beau stocked your freezer with my favorite ice cream today."

As I exit the room to give him some privacy, I smile at his side of the conversation. "No, Mom. I swear, I'm fine. Yeah, it sucks, but it'll be okay. My knees are sore, but I'll ice them in a minute. Yes, I promise!"

## THE FALLOUT

My office door swings open after only the most perfunctory warning knock. Hiding in here, eating my lunch like the pariah-by-association I suddenly am, I pause mid-chew, slapping for the napkin on my desk to wipe the chicken salad from the corner of my mouth. Looking more professional becomes less critical when I see that my guest is one of my besties, Colin, holding up a brown paper lunch sack in greeting.

"Cheers. The self-important bloke at the front desk said you were between appointments. Hope you don't mind a bit of company."

Swiping at my face, I smile. "Oh, thank God. I thought you were one of my co-workers. Sit down."

He closes the door and pulls up a guest chair to the other side of the desk, where he unpacks his lunch, a tuna sandwich, boiled egg, and bottle of water.

"Dude. How do you manage to subsist on that?"

He looks down at his meal. "What? It's plenty. I sit all day."

I raise an eyebrow at him while gesturing to my own food.

I've already eaten most of my sandwich, but a bag of chips, an apple, stick of string cheese, a container of yogurt, and a bottle of iced tea remain. "Yeah, so do I."

He chuckles. "I've never been a big eater. But beer, I can drink massive quantities of that."

I can attest to that. The guy never gets drunk, either.

"A beer sounds great right now," I say wistfully.

"I bet. Rough going today, Lady Maura?"

Returning to my meal, I focus on poking into submission the chunk of chicken about to fall from between the two slices of bread in my hands. "In some ways, yes. But not as overtly ugly as I thought. Most people have been treating me like I have the plague. Lots of conversations hastily aborted when I walk into the room."

He chews and swallows a bite of sandwich. After a drink of water, he picks up his boiled egg but says before biting into it, "Tossers."

"Yeah. 'Her boyfriend has...'" I drop to a whisper. "'The fumbles.'"

His shoulders shake, and he covers his mouth to avoid spraying yolk. Having recovered with the help of another drink, he sets down his half-eaten egg and leans back in the chair, rubbing his belly as if he's recently devoured a four-course meal. "Ah, yes. I'm no stranger to those pitying looks and whispered asides. Awful."

"But this is only football!"

He looks around to make sure we're still alone. "Shhh! Don't let anyone else hear you say that. It'll be all over the Internet that Jet Knox's beloved hates football. We can't have that."

I roll my eyes. "Anyone who knows me knows that's not

true. The opposite is the case, in fact. But seriously. Nobody is going to die if we don't make it into the Playoffs."

"And there's still a shot, as I understand it, correct?"

"Infinitesimal, but yes."

"There you have it." He sits forward once more and finishes his lunch in a few swift bites.

I push aside my remaining food and slump with my cheek on my fist, my elbow on my desk. "If only someone else had screwed up at the end of the game. Why did it have to be Jet?"

Crumpling his paper sack, Colin shrugs. "He took a shot. That's what leaders do. Sometimes it pays off, sometimes it doesn't. If he hadn't at least tried, people would have criticized him for that. He was in a no-win situation."

"And now I find myself feeling like I have to walk around, defending that decision."

"Which is ludicrous."

"But goes with the territory. This is my life now, Colin."

"All the more reason not to be an apologist. Give 'em the ol'..." He jabs his first two fingers skyward with the back of his hand facing me.

I giggle at his quintessentially British obscene gesture. "Not sure many people around here would know what that means."

"Better still. But I don't mean for you to literally do it. Symbolically do it by holding your head high and refusing to make excuses or explain anything to them. At the end of the day, you and Jet are both winners, not because of what he does on the field, but by how you conduct yourselves as everyday citizens. If people can't appreciate that, they're not worth the effort, anyway."

I sigh. "I guess."

"Do you love him any less because of that play?"

I pretend to think about it, then smile while reaching for my yogurt and peeling off the lid. "Of course, not."

"Then everyone else can sod off."

I lick the foil and toss it into the trash. "Yeah! Sod off, people!"

"That's the badger!"

"You're so weird."

But he's made me laugh, a nearly impossible feat today. Judging by his smug smile, he's accomplished exactly what he hoped on his lunch break. If only I could keep him in my back pocket the rest of the day.

———

Three hours later, I receive a text from my other best friend, Rae, one of the team's trainers and a late-to-the-game fan of Jet's.

*Don't watch ESPN today. Or any news.*

*Hadn't planned on it.*

*Liar.*

*Okay. Considered it. Stayed strong. What's the worst of it?*

*Not telling.*

A glance at the time tells me I have a few minutes before my next client, a master plumber who shouldn't have any trouble finding a placement and will likely have his pick of any of the three referrals I give him. I stare at the last two words Rae's sent as I consider taking a peek for myself on social media or any of the dozen sports sites I've diligently avoided for most of the season. But I made a pact with Jet: no seeking out stress on the Internet. After all, stress does an efficient enough job of finding us by itself.

Before I can decide if it's worth the raised blood pressure, much less breaking my promise, another message comes through: *Idiots, all of 'em.*

*Goes without saying.*

*Make sure Knox keeps ice on those knees. That's your biggest worry.*

*Ha! I wish.*

The device rings in my hands almost immediately after I've sent that last text. Although Derek in reception still hasn't buzzed me to tell me my appointment is here, I hesitate to answer Rae's call. Things still aren't the same between my oldest friend and me after our disagreements last fall. She's trying, and I'm trying, but that's exactly it. It's obvious we are. We do okay in text messages and emails, where we can take time to compose responses and weigh our words. Verbal encounters tend to be stilted.

Then again, things will never improve if we don't work on them, and if this particular conversation gets weird, I can always cut it short and blame work.

"How bad is it in the locker room? What's the general mood?" I ask without preamble after accepting her call.

She snorts. "What do you think? The guys are bummed. It's like someone told them they aren't allowed to eat red meat ever again."

I laugh in spite of my glum mood. "No. I mean, Jet feels like everyone blames him and hates him for what happened."

"What? Nobody hates him. That guy! He has the most warped perception sometimes. If anything, the guys on the O-line are the outcasts. They're keeping their heads down for sure. They know they let everyone down yesterday."

I slump in my chair. "Oh, good. Well, not *good*. But I was worried when I left for work this morning that Jet was going to have a miserable day."

"His day's been miserable in other ways. But these bone-heads get that he did his best out there. Sometimes it's not your day. Most of them have been doing this long enough to know that. And those who are still too green to know it got the message from Coach Bauer. Loud and clear. He's not going to tolerate anyone pinning that loss on Knox."

Stinging tears herald my relief. "I worry about him, that's all."

"Instead of wringing your hands like a timid old lady, why don't you *do* something?"

And... there's my familiar friend. Never one to mince words for the sake of feelings, she can always be counted on to tell it straight. Still, I don't often think the same way she does, and this is one of those times, so I grunt, "Huh?"

"How are you going to keep Jet occupied during the Denver game tonight? No, wait! Don't answer that out loud; I don't need to know any graphic details. I'm just saying, you better have a plan."

*Oh, sheesh.*

At my silence, she clicks her tongue. "I know, 'plan' is a dirty word for you."

I swallow.

She groans. "Tell me Knox isn't going to watch tonight's game. I was proud of him for turning down Jackson's stupid watch party invitation and assumed it meant he wasn't going to tune in at all."

"Uh..."

"Did you tell him self-flagellation would be less painful?"

"He doesn't do that during the season." More seriously, after her satisfying chuckle, I answer, "He's determined to suffer the consequences of what he's calling his 'choke moment.'"

She sighs. "No, no, no. Keep his mind on Hawaii. You're going with him to the Pro Bowl, right?"

"You bet I am! I've earned it! This season has been Hell. And I still haven't been rewarded for skipping the San Diego game."

She laughs. "I'm pretty sure Knox thinks you guys are square there."

I look down at my ring and smile, remembering how he proposed to me afterward on national television. "Oh, that. Well, that took the sting out of it somewhat, but I'm still waiting for my make-up vacation. To be honest, now that the disappointment has faded a bit and the reality has sunk in, I'm relieved the season is over."

"It's not over 'til the linebacker sings, girl."

"You know it's over."

Before she can admit I'm right, Derek announces my next client.

"Gotta go."

"Chin up. Hawaii."

Yeah. Hawaii!

———

It doesn't surprise me, but it does dismay me to discover my brother waiting for me in my driveway when I swing by my house to change my clothes, choose an outfit for tomorrow, and replenish my overnight bag in preparation for another night at Jet's. Greg has tried to call several times today, but even if I'd been amenable to talking to him (not likely), I was with clients every time. Therefore, he resorted to texting me. Which I also ignored.

It would be different if he were trying to get in touch to

show his support or say something inspirational. But he's not. He only wants to say...

"What was he thinking?" He slams the door to his luxury SUV and trails me to the front door, where I wordlessly insert my key and let us in with a curt nod to Jason Bourne.

"Did you greet that poster?" Greg asks, suddenly willing to put his third degree grilling about the game on hold to harass me about something else.

"I always acknowledge him," I answer. "It's only polite."

Greg snorts. "You're not right."

"No, what's not right is you ambushing me on my driveway after work so you can trash my boyfriend."

"Matt Damon is not your—"

"I'm talking about Jet, you idiot." I toss my keys on the nearest end table on my way through the living room to the kitchen, where I pull out the beer I've been craving all afternoon.

I hold one out to Greg, but he shakes his head. "We're not drinking."

"'We'? Because I sure as heck am."

"Deirdre and me. She can't drink, so I abstain too."

"That's the dumbest thing I've ever heard," I say with a smirk. My brother and his wife are the pregnant couple everyone else makes fun of. Completely over-the-top and not at all ashamed of it.

"Dumber than that play call last night? I don't think so. The offensive coordinator should be fired."

I'd rather volunteer to be Deirdre's birthing coach than admit to Greg that the final play call was Jet's. Instead, I swig my beer and shrug one shoulder toward my ear. After swallowing, I belch to let my older brother know exactly how much stock I put in his opinion. On anything.

"Nice." Based on his tone, I can't tell if he's being sarcastic or sincere. Again, I don't care. "And then Jet. Everyone knows he's my future brother-in-law. Do you realize how horrible work was today? I took so much shit."

"You have to take the good with the bad, when you're a shameless name-dropper." With a loud clank, I drop my empty bottle in the recycling bin and stick out my tongue at him.

He returns the gesture and follows me down the hall to my bedroom, standing in the doorway while I flip through the clothes in my closet. I search for something that won't require ironing in the morning.

"What they should have done is run the wildcat. I wish we'd go back to calling that once in a while, to keep other teams on their toes."

I toss a pair of brown trousers and an off-white cashmere sweater on my bed. Digging through the shoes on my closet floor, I search for my favorite booties. "I'll be sure to pass along your request."

"No, you won't."

"You're right, I won't. I'm totally humoring you."

"And you're going to watch the game at Jet's tonight?"

"Yeppers."

"That sounds depressing."

"It's part of the gig." I come up with the booties and toss them in my duffel, looking up at him with a tight smile. "When I'm on a beach in Hawaii in a couple of weeks, none of this will matter. There's always next season."

"That's what we said last season. And the one before that. *This* was supposed to be our year, Mo!"

"Well, I guess we were wrong."

"We'll always be wrong, if we don't start making better choices in the draft and on the field."

"And you call yourself a fan."

"You call *yourself* a fan, sitting back and taking this like it's no big deal? If your fiancé's not careful, he could find himself sitting on a bench as the backup in some frozen hole like Buffalo."

With precision, I roll my wool trousers and sweater, placing them on top of my shoes. I toss in a pair of panties and a tan bra and zip the bag. Shouldering the strap, I step up to Greg and poke him in the chest. "Why don't you worry about your own life and let Jet worry about his?"

"Chiefs football is a big part of my life, though."

"I suggest you get more of a life."

Clenching his jaw, he blinks down at me.

"Now, if you don't mind, I need to get going. I promised Jet I'd be at his place for dinner. And I'm sure Deirdre's wondering where the heck you are."

I slide past him and into the hallway, suddenly more interested in getting the heck out of here than changing into something more comfortable. I'll find something at Jet's.

## THREE

## MILE-HIGH MIRACLE

While the rest of his teammates gather at defensive end Demarcus Jackson's house to watch the Broncos play (uh, beat) the Raiders tonight, Jet and I settle in for what promises to be a gloomy evening.

When I asked him during dinner why he didn't want the moral support of his teammates, he shrugged and mumbled something at his plate that basically amounted to, "Nobody's going to want to see my face when that game is over, and so is our season."

I relayed what Rae told me earlier today, but he wasn't buying it. "Nobody's stupid enough to say anything negative where a trainer or coach would hear it. But they're thinking it. And they're saying it to each other, in safe places. Trust me."

"Would you be dogging a teammate in a similar position?"

"No. Shit happens. And every game is more than one play, one turnover, one bad officiating call. But when you're mad and disappointed…"

"In other words, you're better than everyone else and able to rise above."

"What? No! That's not what I—"

"That's basically what you're saying. *You* wouldn't make one guy a scapegoat for an entire game or season, but your teammates would. Because they're not as good a guy as you are."

He set his fork on his plate and wiped his mouth. "I don't feel like being around a bunch of people tonight."

Satisfied with that answer, I kissed his head while picking up his plate on my way into the kitchen. "Please, stop beating yourself up."

Who knows if I got through to him? He didn't reply. He sat alone at the table for several more minutes while I put away the leftovers. Then he disappeared into the basement until the Monday night pre-game show started.

Now, in his baggy workout shorts and faded t-shirt, he arranges himself in his chair, his feet elevated, one family-sized package of frozen peas resting on each knee.

I eye the enormous tumbler of dark liquid he's placed on the table within reach. "Uh, Jet? Sweetie?"

"Hmm?"

"You're not on any painkillers, are you?"

"Nope. Unless you count Bengay, which I don't. Why?"

"No reason. Except..." When I pause, he looks at me and notices me staring at his drink.

"It's mostly ice and Coke."

Having watched him pour half a bottle of Jack into the cup, I'm aware he's fibbing. But watching this game isn't going to be easy for him, and the last thing I want to do is pick another fight by being a nag, so I drop it. As long as he's not mixing Vicodin with that booze, I'm good. I'd like him to live long enough to say that "till death do us part" line in a few months. And then some, if that's not too greedy.

"Great. Sounds delicious."

Torzi hops into his master's lap, generating a grimace from Jet, who then flashes me a sweet smile. "You want some?" He lifts the glass toward me, but I shake my head. One of us should stay sober, although I have a feeling I might regret this rare urge to be the responsible one.

"Nope. It's all yours. Get comfortable and don't think about me at all."

He grins while scratching his furry friend behind the ears. "Not possible. But I'll try to get comfortable." After a long swallow, he smacks his lips. "Mmm. That's damn good. The only thing that'd make it better is if you were sitting here with me."

I laugh. "I'd hate to upset your delicate balance of frozen produce and fur baby. Maybe later, when it's not so crowded over there."

"I'd choose you over the Jolly Green Giant and Torzi any day."

"Nice to know. Really comforting."

"But I promised my mom and Rae I'd keep ice on these bad boys for the next few days."

"It's cute that Rae cares so much."

"She likes having an excuse to boss me around. If I wasn't in so much pain, I'd totally ignore her. Gonna make Hissler pay for my double knee replacement surgery when I need it." He gulps again and crunches ice between his teeth. "The guy's an animal."

"He's not one of my favorite people right now."

"Aw, babe, 'sokay. I'm a strong, tough guy."

And... it starts. Beer is on his list of no-no's during the season, so other than that one wimpy beer yesterday, Jet hasn't touched a drop of alcohol in months. I'm not surprised by how quickly "babe" has emerged tonight. That doesn't mean I have to like it.

I sigh but turn my attention to the game, which is finally starting. In a few hours, we'll have a definitive end to the season, and then it's, "Aloha!"

Where I can get some decent new swimsuits in mid-January?

————

Forty minutes later, Torzi abandons us more out of boredom than fear, as we've hardly made a sound during this game. Occasionally, Jet has grumbled something about "predictable" play calling, but the more he's had to drink, the less interested he's appeared to be in the action on the screen. This game has gone exactly as we've expected, with Denver leading the whole time. The Raiders have kept it close enough to make their fans proud, but pride is the only thing the team is playing for, at this point. If they win, they'll be doing us a huge favor, but their season will still be over.

After supplying Jet with a watered-down version of his drink of choice and switching out his ice packs, I perch on the arm of the easy chair and lean back. He strokes my upper arm and stares blankly at the TV while sipping his refill. Following his first swallow, he holds his glass up to eye level, as if examining it for alcohol content. If he finds it lacking in punch, he's too polite to call me on it. Instead, he sets the glass down and says, "Y'know, babe, maybe this is for the best."

"I'm sure it is." *Whatever we're talking about.*

"Me and you, we have shit to *do* this off-season. We're gettin' married!"

"That we are."

"Are you 'cited? I'm 'cited."

"I'm extremely excited."

It's only a tiny exaggeration. And I *am* excited to be married to him. I'm not as thrilled, however, about our upcoming wedding.

What's not going to happen right now, though, is any attempt on my part to seriously discuss with Drunk Jet my misgivings about the big—and getting bigger by the day— ceremony his mother is practically forcing on us. Jet's paying for everything, including a full-time wedding planner named Mags, who occasionally runs things by us to make sure I get my weekly panic attack, but his mom is the one in charge. And if I have a problem with that, I have only myself to blame, because I couldn't care less about any of the details.

At least, that's what I told myself until I heard some of the details. Now it's too late to go all Bridezilla on everyone, so I'm determined to show up when and where they tell me to, wear the dress Gloria and Mags have determined is perfect for my "shape," which they always manage to say in a way that makes it sound like a cross I must bear, and say what I'm supposed to say, when I'm supposed to say it. The result is all I care about.

On April fifth, Jet and I will be husband and wife, and whether we had butter cream or whipped frosting on our sure-to-be-obscene wedding cake won't matter at all.

"Mags told Mom you di'n't seem all that 'cited. Said she's never worked with a bride who's so… so… I can't think of the word she used. But it means, 'not 'cited.'"

I swallow my irritation at the two other women talking about me behind my back, plus Gloria tattling on me to Jet. "Wedding planning isn't my thing. I'm leaving it to the professional."

"Cuz you're smart." He nuzzles my shoulder. "You're so smart, Maura."

"I don't know about that. But I'm not paying for it, either."

"Yes, you are! My money is your money now, babe. How many times do I have to tell you that?"

"Repeating something that's not true doesn't make it true."

"It *is* true, though! See, this is why I tol' my mom that I didn't want to do it like this. I tol' her you wouldn't be comfterbull making decisions or choices if we did it this way. But she wou'n't listen. She never listens to me. Treats me like a baby."

"You let her treat you like a baby."

"'Seasier that way. Jus' like you let her and Mags make all the decisions about the wedding."

Truth.

I rest my cheek on his shoulder and nestle the top of my head in the crook of his neck. "Well, it'll all be over in three months." I gulp at that all-too-real math.

"Le's jus' elope in Hawaii, at the Pro Bowl."

"That would work for me," I say lightly, knowing better than to get my hopes up. Gloria would absolutely crap a sand castle if we came back from the Pro Bowl hitched.

He shifts next to me and angles his upper body so he can look—albeit unfocused—into my eyes. "I'm serious, Maura."

The sudden lack of slur in those three words grabs my attention, but I merely chuckle into his face while caressing his cheek. "Aw. You're so drunk right now."

"I'm not. Well, a little. No, not drunk. Tipsy."

Hearing a six-foot-four, two-hundred-fifty-pound guy describe himself as "tipsy" is too funny. My chuckles turn into full-blown laughs.

"Hey," he says. "I may have had some stuff to drink, but I know what I'm saying, and I mean it. You don't want some big, fancy-schmancy wedding, do you?"

My laughter dies, and since I can't lie into those eyes, I smile sadly and shake my head. "No. I've never wanted that. I only want you."

"Same. 'Cept I want you, not me."

"Yeah, I got that."

"You know what? I say, 'screw 'em!'"

"Jet, you—"

"For real!"

"Don't tease me. When you sober up tomorrow, you're going to realize what a scary proposition going against your mom is."

"My mom's nice!"

If he thinks I'm going to refute that statement out loud, he's crazy. But I'm not so sure she *is* nice. The only reason I don't know for sure, though, is that I've never tested her. And I'm not in a hurry to do so.

Before I can half-heartedly agree with him, he continues, "She jus' wants us to be happy. Maybe she'll be disappointed at first, when we tell her, but she'll get over—"

*"Pete Jay is down! And he's not moving, folks. Trainers and players are running onto the field. Both benches have cleared, as a matter of fact. Oh, no. This is something you hate to see. He's still not moving."*

*"Charlie, that was a wicked hit he took, right to the head."*

*"Flags are down, most definitely for roughing the passer, although the penalty is beside the point right now, Dan. Oh, my. This is bad news."*

*"Our thoughts and prayers go out to him and his family right now, although we're not going to jump to any conclusions. Standard procedure is to keep a player immobile in situations such as these."*

Jet lowers the footrest on his chair and tosses the peas onto the floor at his feet. "Holy shit." Standing, he limps closer to the TV and stares at the screen, his palm rubbing against his chin. "C'mon, Jay."

I step up next to him and grab his free hand.

He glances down at our linked fingers, then over at me. Suddenly, he's more sober than a church basement full of people with first names only. "He'll be okay," he says less-than-convincingly. "They're telling him to be still until they can get him fully awake and talking. Then he can tell them what he's feeling and that he's okay. Concussion protocol."

My phone chimes on the coffee table, but a cursory glance tells me it's Rae, no doubt watching what we are and offering her professional opinion and commentary. Ignoring her, I say, "Oh, Jet. This is bad."

He starts to nod his agreement but perks up before he can complete the gesture and points to the TV. "I saw his hand move!"

Meanwhile, the announcers parrot everything we've said. It would be funny if it weren't so tense.

"Pete's a good guy. I hate to see this," Jet says with a shake of his head. "He'll have to come out of the game, for sure. He's going to be pissed."

"Coming out of a game is better than dying!"

"Depends on who you ask."

"That's not funny."

He widens his eyes at me. "I'm not joking! In a game like this? If it were up to him, he'd sit out a few series and be back out there after halftime."

"Thank God it's not up to him."

While the trainers continue to assess the situation and the announcers struggle to fill the dead air, I recall last year's Pro

Bowl, which I attended as Jet's guest. I barely knew my host, much less anyone else there. Unsure how to act or what to say around all these giants of men, guys I'd watched week in and week out, season after season, never thinking much about them as real people, I felt like the biggest outsider.

Pete Jay, one of the best to ever play the game, made a point to talk directly to me during the first dinner. He and his wife at the time, Monica, were seated at the same table as Jet and me, and he recognized right away how out of my element I was.

"Insane, isn't it?" he asked in his lazy Southern drawl. "All us big idiots take over this island like walking, breathing Tiki idols, in our flowered shirts, and people flock around us like we're a buncha gods, askin' for our autographs, and posin' for selfies with us, and it's like, 'What the actual hell?' Excuse my French."

"Don't worry about it."

"The thing is, in my head, I'm still a dumb jock high schooler with body parts too proportionally large to do anything well except play football. And my brain... I can't balance an equation or talk in complete sentences half the time, much less diagram one, but people think I'm all that, because I can throw a ball. Big freakin' whoopdee doo."

While I laughed, he swigged his water. Spearing a piece of pineapple on the end of his fork, he pointed it at Jet, who was deep in conversation with Pittsburgh's QB about the pros and cons of the no-huddle offense. "Anyway, tell me how that lucky sumbitch—pardon my French—Knox managed to convince someone like you to come with him to this here boondoggle?"

I blushed and admitted it took embarrassingly little convincing.

"It's that chiseled jaw, isn't it? See, some guys are blessed, aren't they? They hog all the good parts. Then there's guys like me. We get stuck with the leftovers. I got enough forehead that it should be called a 'fivehead.'"

As we laughed at that, Monica leaned over and snapped, "Pete, for the love of God, quit tellin' that joke. Everyone's heard it a million times."

But I hadn't. And I appreciated him making the effort to bring me up to speed with the rest of the table.

On the screen now, the cart comes out, and we watch, helpless and horrified, while the EMTs stabilize the veteran QB and load him face-up into the back, strapped down tightly, his head wedged between two pieces of foam.

I wipe my eyes. "I hope Pete and his fivehead are okay," I say quietly, wrapping my arms around Jet and receiving a side-hug in return. As the cart trundles toward the tunnel, Pete raises one arm and gives the cheering crowd a thumbs-up. "That's a good sign, right?"

Jet turns more fully toward me and squeezes me against his chest. I close my eyes and savor the firm embrace that borders on suffocating but remains on this side of comforting. "Yes. Awake and able to move some parts of his body. Definitely good. We'll have to wait and see on the rest. He's a fighter, though. Came back from neck *and* knee surgery one off-season, so we know he's tough." He lets up a little on the hug so I can breathe but keeps me close. "This sucks, though."

Our rivalry with the Broncos is fierce and nasty. We trade barbs with their fans year-round—they call us the Chefs; we call them the Donkeys, among other, not-as-clean things. But no decent person, no matter how big a fan they are, delights in serious injuries to players. I might joke when two of our rivals are playing each other and say I'm "rooting for injuries," but it's all silliness. Every football fan knows too well what it feels like to see one of our heroes hobbling toward the locker room or carted off on a stretcher. It's heartbreaking, and I wouldn't wish it on my worst enemy, no matter how many years they've bested us in our division.

In the case of our particular rivalry, the story seems to be changing since Jet's taken over as Chiefs quarterback. The teams have been neck-and-neck at the top of the division, trading off every other year with Playoff bids. Last year, we triumphed—and ultimately got clobbered by the Patriots in the Conference Championship. This year, it appeared to be Denver's turn to represent the AFC West. But now, without Jay leading the team and calling the plays, that's not as sure an outcome.

After another commercial break, the game resumes, with Jay's backup finishing the series. Not surprisingly, no points result from the interrupted drive. The fans are subdued, the stadium eerily quiet.

Jet says, "Now, it's up to the defense to hold. If they can't…"

My tummy twitches, and I immediately flood with horrified guilt at my hope, considering what's going on in the Denver locker room (or worse, an ambulance) right now. Our season isn't as dead as we thought it was.

I sincerely hope the same can be said for Pete Jay's career.

———

What a difference a couple of hours make. Jet and I grin at each other on the couch but catch ourselves at the same time.

Forehead crinkled, he speaks first. "Okay, before I say

anything else, it goes without saying that I hope Pete's gonna be okay, and— and this is not the way I'd have wanted to keep our season alive, but..." His earnestness slips as his lips twitch upward again. "We're in, baby!"

He vaults from the couch and, back arched, shakes his fists at the ceiling. I enjoy the view from behind and laugh at his celebration, which he punctuates with a booming, "GO CHIEFS!"

The windows practically rattle, and I get a clear idea of how he sounds on the line of scrimmage, when he's calling out plays, bellowing to be heard over the crowd. I clamp my hands over my ears, in case he's not finished.

Torzi, who rejoined us midway through the final quarter, when the Raiders took the lead for good, skitters to the back door and whines. I cross the room and let him out and remain where I have a full frontal view of Jet dancing like someone who's never had a muscle ache or joint pain in his life.

Hips thrusting and swiveling and hands twirling, he closes his eyes and does the whitest samba I've ever witnessed. He switches to a solitary conga, chanting around the perimeter of the room, "Going to the Wild Card! Going to the Wild Card!" He points his toe on the last word of each sentence, his calf muscles popping impressively.

My giggles grab his attention, so on his way past me, he snags me around the waist and pulls me into his dance. I gladly play along, having perfected my conga at numerous wedding receptions, although never while quite this sober. Or this happy.

Without warning, when we arrive in front of the couch, where all of this started, he transfers his hands from my waist to his own and jerks his pelvis forward and backward in rapid succession.

"Be careful!" I implore.

Breathless, he lurches forward, laughing. "You're right. I have a game to play in a few days."

"Yes, you do. Time to buckle down. Back on your diet, no booze. No twerking. And no sex, I suppose." I punctuate that last part with an exaggerated sigh. Not that he'd have been much in the mood if the team's season was a goner.

He pulls me close to him with his hands on my butt. Looking toward his forehead and closing one eye, he murmurs, "I'd agree with most of that." A twitching against my crotch lets me know exactly what's still a go.

"I don't know if it's worth the risk," I say, hoping the twinkle in my eye lets him know I'm totally kidding and want him continue.

He lowers me to the couch and rests most of his weight on top of me while lifting my t-shirt to expose my belly. "The only risk right now is me blowing my load too soon."

"Romantic!"

He laughs at himself. "It's been a while."

It's true that although he's greatly relaxed his regular-season abstinence rule for me, he still abstains before big games. "Old habits and superstitions die hard," he said after gently rebuffing my efforts at seduction the week before a division matchup. And going into the final stretch of the season, while we've been trying so hard to keep pace with Denver, there's been no intimacy at all. Six weeks, three days, to be exact. Not that I'm counting.

My body responds immediately to his attention. There'll be no second-guessing this decision. I don't give any credence to the silly practice, anyway, considering it's been scientifically disproved again and again. I no longer pressure him to abandon the practice he's followed his entire career, but I don't discourage him when he gives me an opening. Like now.

To the soundtrack of our phones pinging and vibrating on the table next to our heads, we quickly discard every stitch of our clothing and make slow, deliberate love, reacquainting ourselves with each other after what feels like much longer than a month and a half.

Several minutes later, he collapses onto my chest with self-deprecating chuckles. All I can see is the top of his head and his thick, dark hair when he says, sounding almost surprised, "Gosh, I love you more than football."

It's the sweetest thing I've ever heard.

## FOUR

## CROWDED HOUSE

It's odd to have paid friends. Not that Jet's housekeeper, dog-sitter, and dietitian/chef consider me a friend, but I can't think of any better way to describe Helen, Jacob, and Beau. I can't bring myself to view them as "employees" or "staff." Then again, I also can't forget they wouldn't be here if Jet wasn't regularly cutting them a paycheck.

"Acquaintances" is more accurate a term, but that sounds pretty cold, considering how warmly they've welcomed me into the household. Since I've become a more permanent fixture in Jet's life, they've included me in conversations, and they treat me like I've always been around. But as an introvert with an extremely small circle of close friends, I'm still not comfortable confiding anything more personal to them than, "I hate lima beans," or "I can do my own laundry," or "I don't think Torzi likes me." Coming downstairs for breakfast and socializing with people I don't know very well before I've had my first cup of coffee is going to take some getting used to.

This morning's crowded kitchen is a perfect example. Beau mans the stove, where he sautes vegetables with one hand and jiggles an omelet pan with the other, waiting for the perfect time to flip the pale disk of egg whites. Jet, Jacob, and Helen, sipping coffee, sit at the island, where they appear to be overseeing the chef. They're also engaged in an animated conversation—too animated for this early hour.

Until I walk into the room, that is. It becomes so quiet that I feel like the stick-in-the-mud boss who happens upon a comical story about herself in the break room.

"Hey, everyone," I say, my voice still tired from last night and croaky in its first appearance of the day.

Jet slides down from his stool and pulls out the one next to him before limping to the coffee machine.

Wincing, I pause between the island and him. "Oh, don't get up. Your poor knees!"

He smiles over his shoulder. "I'm fine. Feeling awesome this morning, in fact." He carries my black beverage to the island and sets it down, then pats the stool. "C'mon. We were talking about last night."

Helen pipes up, "I'll bet you slept well."

"Yeah," Jacob says. "I stayed out of your way in the guest house, but I'd imagine it was a lot more fun over here than any of us expected. When Torzi scratched at my door, I figured the celebrations had gotten too wild for his taste."

Is it me, or does everything sound like sexual innuendo?

Certain they're not talking about *that*, I sip my coffee, clear my throat, and smile, willing the blood to redirect away from my cheeks. "Yeah, it was a great surprise. Wild Card-bound, baby!" I turn to Jet. "Have you heard anything new about Pete?"

He winces. "Ligament damage in his neck. They're going to operate, maybe as early as today."

"Oh, my gosh."

"Yeah. That's probably it for his career. He'd already talked about retiring after this season. But he wanted to try for one more Super Bowl ring."

I stare down into my coffee. "Wow. That sucks for him. To go out like that."

Beau slides an omelet in front of Jet. "Eat up, Buddy." To me, he directs, "Your usual, full-fat cheese version?" with a gleam in his eyes.

I glance nervously at Jet, who digs more cheerfully into his breakfast than I've seen in weeks. Transferring his first bite to his cheek, he says, "I never thought I'd be so happy to eat another egg white veggie omelet. Go ahead. Eat whatever. You must be starving." He wiggles his eyebrows and nudges me.

His obvious reference to our post-game couchcapade reactivates the heat lamps in my face. I nod to Beau and mumble that whatever he makes will be fine.

Helen finishes her coffee and places her mug in the dishwasher. "I better get to it. Beds to strip, linens to wash, dusting to do. Everyone have a great day," she says as she exits the kitchen.

Jacob, whistling for the dog, smacks his palm against his thigh. "Gotta get Torzi to the groomer this morning. Mangy cur is way overdue for a haircut."

Jet wipes his lips, tucking his current bite of food into one cheek. "Mmm! Make sure they don't use whatever shampoo they used last time. That stuff reeked." He swallows.

Jacob flicks a sloppy salute. "Got it." Cooing, he leads the dog toward the mudroom, where his leash awaits. "You ready, boy? Gonna be so pretty! Yes, you are!"

Beau turns his back, busying himself with my breakfast. I trace the subtle herringbone pattern in my pants with my fingertip and sip my coffee while Jet continues to shovel food into his mouth like he hasn't eaten in days.

After washing down eggs with most of his huge glass of orange juice, he says, "Oh, man. Catching up with all of the calls and texts we ignored last night took me forever. Have you had a chance to go through your phone yet?"

I shoot another sideways glance at Beau. "No."

"Some people—like my brothers and sisters and some of the guys on the team—tried to get in touch a bunch of times. Couldn't take the hint that I was busier with more important things." He nuzzles my neck.

I stiffen. "Jet."

"Mmm?"

Gently, I push his face away from my throat. He straightens. "What?" Cupping his hand over his mouth and nose, he huffs and sniffs. "Do I have onion breath?"

"It's not your breath." I bury my nose in my coffee mug. "It's—" I sip. "We're not alone." *Who let the prude in the house?* I don't know, but she's here, and she's decidedly embarrassed.

He looks over at the chef as if noticing his presence for the first time. Then he laughs. "You mean Beau?"

"Uh, yes."

"He doesn't care."

"I do."

"You do? Since when?"

"Since... I don't know." I set down my mug but continue to stare at it. For the first time, I realize it's the cup "Torzi" gave me for Christmas, the one that says "World's Best Mom."

"For real?"

"PDA is gross."

"This isn't PDA! We're in my house. A private place. "

"Not *totally* private."

He sighs. "It's not like I'm over here being graphic or talking dirty."

"Still..."

Beau sets my perfect omelet in front of me, an omelet I no longer have any appetite for, and smiles warmly.

"Can we talk about this some other time?" I mutter through tight lips to Jet.

Before he can answer, Beau says, "I'll leave you guys alone. I can clean up later, after my workout." He pats my arm.

"Thanks for breakfast."

Tossing a wave and an "Anytime" behind him, he heads downstairs to the fitness room.

I prod my food around my plate, trying to ignore Jet openly staring at me. Finally, he laughs, shaking his head as he rises to take his dishes to the sink.

"It's not funny."

Over the running water while he rinses his plate, he says, "Yeah. It is. You're something else."

"What I am is uncomfortable."

"You're the who made it uncomfortable. Everyone else was just being... everyone."

"Yeah, and *everyone* is gathered around to see my morning walk of shame."

"Shame? What's there to be ashamed of?"

"Nothing! That wasn't the right word."

"Because I'm not ashamed. Of anything."

"I told you, I misspoke." I push away my plate. "What I meant was—"

"I love you, Maura. And I'm damn proud of that. Of you. You walk in here in the morning, and I wish there were more people to witness it."

"Oh, geez."

He drops his dripping plate into the dishwasher, slams it, and wipes his hands on a towel that he then flings onto the counter. "Yeah, I'm sure that makes me a caveman. I'm sure that breaks every feminist rule in the book, and you think it means I view you as property. Or something stupid like that."

"I—"

"But I don't. And you know I don't. I'm humbled every day that someone as smart and amazing and—yeah!—*beautiful* as you wants anything to do with an idiot like me. An idiot you'll probably be pushing in a wheelchair when we're old, because of what I do now."

"Jet!"

"So excuse me if I get carried away sometimes and don't give a damn who sees me or hears me when I want to tell you a tenth of what I'm feeling. And I'm sorry if it's not poetry. I'll try to embarrass you less from now on."

He storms from the kitchen, leaving me with my coffee dregs and cooling eggs. While I'm still recovering from the argument and his departure, he pokes his head through the doorway and says, "Don't forget; we have a cake tasting tonight," then disappears again.

This day keeps getting better and better. And it's not even eight o'clock.

## FIVE

## SUFFOCATION

If I imagine Jet's going to be the one to initiate our reconciliation, I'm sorely mistaken. Legitimate gripe about privacy—or
lack thereof—and boundaries notwithstanding, I'm the one
who's required to apologize in this instance, because I hurt his
feelings. But he's busy, and I'm busy, and I'm hardly going to
attempt making amends via text message or email, so by the
time we meet up with our wedding planner, Mags, at the
baker's, nothing has been resolved.

And talk about rumor mill grist: we're the coldest, least
enthusiastic couple outside of an arranged marriage to ever
taste wedding cakes. Jet can't (or won't) eat more than a
crumb of each sample, due to his strict diet, and after a while,
they all start to taste the same to me, so my apathy increases a
thousandfold with each bite.

Finally, I push away from the tasting table and say, "That's
the one," to the most recent sample.

Mags scrawls a note on her tasting scorecard. "Interesting.
That's… surprising."

I nod authoritatively. "Yep. Definitely." Truth is, it's pretty bland, but I'm nauseated from eating so much sugar on an empty stomach, and I don't care anymore.

"You don't strike me as the gluten-, lactose-, and casein-free type."

Oh. Shit.

I lift my chin. "Well, I'm not. But I'm sure there will be plenty of guests who are, so it'll be nice that they can eat the cake."

Jet smiles shakily and gulps some water. When Mags turns to him and asks his opinion, he says, "Whatever she wants. I don't have an opinion on cake. I like the look of that third one —I'm kinda traditional like that—but..."

"Then that's what we'll get." I seize my escape from the cardboard cake. "That was my second favorite."

Mags scratches more notes on her card. "O...kay. Well, maybe we can requisition a small version of your first choice, Maura, as an option for those with special dietary needs."

"Perfect." Grabbing my purse from the floor next to my feet, I dig through it for my car keys. "Sounds like a great idea."

"Now for the groom's cake..."

So much for that beach wedding fantasy. Not that I ever allowed myself to believe it was anything more than the ramblings of a "tipsy" guy trying to distract himself from his current disappointments—and joint pain. But it was a nice concept. And it's been disheartening how quickly our trip to Hawaii has disintegrated with the prospect of a Super Bowl now back in the picture.

After all, the Pro Bowl is for all-star players who don't make it to the big show. It's their consolation prize. Only two teams can compete for the ultimate title, and nobody on those two teams risks injury or so much as jet lag by attending the Pro Bowl the week before the Super Bowl. The guys playing for the Lombardi trophy stay home and focused and leave the fun and relaxation to the poor chumps who have nothing left to lose.

Considering how the Chiefs squeaked into the bracket through an act of God, it's hardly automatic they'll be one of the two teams in the championship game, but it's not unprecedented, either. And winners don't consider the prospect of losing at this stage. In their minds, they *will* be in the Super Bowl… until they lose. Therefore, we have to plan our lives between now and then like winning is a sure thing. And that means to even think about Hawaii is blasphemy.

So no Hawaii.

And no elopement.

Therefore… groom's cake.

I deflate into my seat, but I keep my purse in my lap. Maybe I can play up my nausea and add a phantom headache to it and skip out early. Nah. Then the pregnancy rumors will fly.

Jet grabs my hand and squeezes it. "I'm not sure about the flavor, but it definitely has to be football-themed, don't you think?" he asks both Mags and me.

The two of them discuss how peanut butter and chocolate not only make for a pleasing flavor combination but the colors are perfect for a football-shaped cake. "Of course," she says, "given the number of men in your party, it'll have to be a pretty big football. We might make the ball the topper, and surround it with a gridiron sheet cake underneath. That would serve considerably more."

The baker takes notes and adds his professional input regarding serving sizes and design, but I tune out at the word "fondant." I stare into space and fantasize about going home, taking off my bra, changing into sweats, and watching a movie. If my appetite has returned by then, I'll dig something from my freezer that hasn't been in there too long. And wine. I'll definitely have a glass of wine. Rich, red, and dry. I'm pretty sure I have an unopened bottle. Or I could swing by the liquor store on my way home, to be safe…

"Speaking of groomsmen, Maura, have you given more thought to bridesmaids, to even out the party?" Mags taps her pen on her overflowing legal pad.

I snap to attention and blink at the expectant faces still with me. At some point, the baker has departed, possibly while I was fantasizing about bra removal.

Bridesmaids. Bridesmaids.

"Bridesmaids?"

"Bridesmaids. Last we talked, you were still short a few." She flips through her notebook, as if trying to find the specific note that says *Maura has no friends.* Her cake card is no longer in sight, so official decisions have obviously been handed down. And now we're talking bridesmaids. I'm so sick of talking about bridesmaids.

I clear my throat. "Uh… Well… The thing is, Jet has a sister for each of his brothers. And Rae is my maid of honor. And my sister-in-law, Deirdre, will match up with her husband, my brother."

"Yes, yes. This is all familiar."

"But that's it. I don't— I have a fairly small circle of friends and family, so…"

Jet pats my knee. "You know, I can cut my list down. I haven't asked anyone specific to be in the wedding. Well, other than Jackson, my best man. But none of the other guys have gotten the official nod."

"What about your brothers?" Mags asks.

He winces. "Oh. Well. Yeah. I told them, obviously. I meant the other guys on the team I'd like to have up there with me. I guess they don't have to be. I just don't want there to be hard feelings."

"It's sweet that you care," I acknowledge, treading carefully. "But maybe they can be ushers. Or something. Or maybe they'd have a better time if they attended as guests."

Mags bites her lip. "If the party is too small, though, we run the risk of it looking like some simple civil ceremony at City Hall. The venue we've chosen practically demands at least seven people on each side of you. Otherwise, you'll look lost up there."

"Tell that to the royal family."

"But you're not the royal family. It won't look exclusive; it'll look pathetic."

I grit my teeth. "Short of renting friends, I don't know how to solve the problem."

"The guys on the team could be paired up with their significant others."

I look to Jet for support, but he seems to be considering Mags's suggestion. "They will be bringing dates."

"I don't know any of them!" I remind him.

He rubs his chin.

I pop to my feet. "This is getting out of hand. I have Rae and Deirdre. You go with Jackson and another of your buddies. And let's call it good. As it is, since we can't bear to exclude any of your nieces and nephews, we have a pee-wee football team of flower girls and ring bearers. It'll be plenty crowded up there."

Jet rises and wraps his hands around my upper arms, rubbing them. With a placating kiss to my forehead, he says, "Fine. That's fine. I want you to have whatever you want."

Whatever I want. Ha.

Mags sighs audibly behind us before standing as well. She clips her pen to the first couple of sheets in her notepad and says almost like a threat, "Gloria will be disappointed, but I'll explain we're at an impasse. She'll be glad we got the cakes sorted, at least. Oh, and Maura, has your friend, Colin, narrowed down his reading selections? We had a wonderful idea to have short quotes etched on the champagne flutes so each attendee would have a memento of your beautiful day." Her rapturous smile fades when I merely stare blankly back at her. "In any case, I can get those texts from you some other time. Or Colin can email them straight to me. That might be more efficient. He has my details, right? If not, send them along."

"Will do."

She gathers her jam-packed plastic box file labeled, "Richards-Knox" and heads for the door, but before we're completely free of her, she turns. "Oh! I almost forgot! The save-the-date cards have been ordered."

Since this is the first I've heard about such cards or any invitations at all, I flinch at their existence. Then I realize I don't care, considering they'll contain information I already know: our names and the date of the wedding. How they look makes no difference to me.

"Great," I manage.

Jet grins. "Make sure you send one to each of us, so we can pencil it in." This sends Mags into hysterics as she pushes through the door to the parking lot.

———

I'm home alone, but it was touch-and-go for a minute there in the cold parking lot. When Jet, hunched and squinting into the bitter wind, asked, "What's the plan for tonight?" I had to think fast. I painted my solitary agenda as a result of assuming he'd be busy with team "stuff," but when he said, "Nah. We've been cut loose for the day and told not to do anything crazy," I nearly panicked. Then he started throwing out names of restaurants we could potentially patronize without too much harassment, and I *did* panic. It's not that the rock-hard, pre-packaged meal waiting for me in my freezer sounded so appetizing, either, but quiet, alone time sure did.

Without thinking, I blurted, "This introvert needs some space."

And immediately regretted it.

Now I can't enjoy my wine, freezer-burnt TV dinner, or movie, because I can't stop seeing the quickly concealed hurt in his eyes and hearing his nervous chuckle as he opened his car door and said, "Gotcha. I guess I'll go home and memorize the playbook. Or something."

Was that a euphemism? Because we both know he already has the real one memorized.

Before I could backtrack and modify my plans to include him, he slid into his low sports car, flashed me a brave smile and wave, and drove off.

Now I have two things to apologize for. Not because what I've felt has been so horrible, but because of how I've conveyed my feelings. I glance up at my newest poster acquisition, a haughty Colin Firth as Mr. Darcy, and say, "Yeah, yeah. You'd be all over my ass with an epic letter-writing campaign."

But Jet's likely sitting at home with Torzi, wondering

what he did wrong. Or worse, he's lifting machine weights alone. Or worse yet, watching game video at the training complex.

Meanwhile Meanie Maura gets to stew in her own cruel juices.

When I can't concentrate on Arnold Schwarzenegger as an undercover operative posing as a suburban dad and husband, and Tom Arnold's usually charming and hilarious schtick grates on my nerves with every line I can practically recite with him, I turn off the television with a sigh. After staring at my phone for a while, contemplating calling Jet, I decide against that. I need advice before my insensitive mouth gets me into more trouble.

Since Colin was one of the people whose calls went to voicemail after the game that sealed Jet's postseason fate last night, I texted him back earlier today to tell him we'd talk more later. I guess "later" could be now.

"Lady Maura!" he greets me after a couple of rings.

"Lord Colin. You have a minute to talk?"

"For you, I have two minutes." He giggles. "Only joking. I have four minutes."

"Seriously. Are you busy?"

"Mmmm, no. This is me we're talking about. Having finished some beans and toast, I was contemplating how to fill the next few hours before it was acceptable for someone of my age to go to bed."

"And...?"

"I was leaning toward a YouTube marathon. There's a woman I heard on NPR this morning on my way to work, and her voice... Remember Charlotte Church?"

"Vaguely."

"Oh, you young thing! Anyway, she reminded me of her.

Only not as operatic. I was going to see if I could find some clips."

"Sounds relaxing."

"You mean, mind-numbingly boring?"

"No. Not necessarily. Soothing is good."

"But you've called and saved me from my middle-aged video surfing. What's up, Ducky?"

"I'm making good on my promise and returning your call."

"Mm-hm."

I pick at some pilling on my threadbare palazzo pants. "And, you know, catching up. Tell me more about this singer."

He pauses. "There's not much more to tell, really. Is everything okay?"

It's all the opening I need, so I blurt, "I don't care about wedding cakes or balanced parties, and I'm terrified of getting up in front of all those people, which—if I told Jet—would probably make him think I'm embarrassed or ashamed of him, since I made such a big, hairy deal about lack of privacy in his house this morning. But— Everything about his life is so big, so public, so... so... *out there!*" My voice cracks, but I clear my throat and pretend it was the result of a rogue cough.

"Oh, dear. That's loads of things."

"Right? It's bad, isn't it?"

"Typical, I'd say, of new couples trying to figure things out. And you two have a few unconventional issues, by nature of who he is."

I blow air through my lips. "It's all petty stuff, though."

"Little things lead to big things."

"So what do I do? I have no clue what my first move is. Any time I try to discuss this stuff with him, I hurt his feelings. Or he's too drunk to seriously talk about it."

"Jet Knox? Drunk?"

"It was only one time," I hasten to explain. "Last night before the game started. He had a few to take the edge off, so he was, um, silly."

"Ah. Well, seems to me like the most pressing issue is the wedding, considering it's three months away."

I squeak.

"You have to tell him you don't want it."

"I *have*. Sort of."

"Not 'sort of.' Definitely. As in, 'I won't be there.'"

I groan. "I can't make that threat."

"Then make sure it's not a threat. Or a bluff. Be firm. You're setting the tone for a life together. If you constantly ignore your own wants and feelings, you'll become resentful."

"The cake has been ordered; the save-the-date cards have gone out."

"Who gives a toss? It can all be canceled as easily as it was ordered."

"Gloria will kill me."

When I expect him to readily step in with another delightfully English version of "Who cares?", he surprises me by hesitating.

"What?" I prod.

He sighs. "Nothing. It's— Well— Here's the thing. And I speak from experience. It's difficult for a man to be caught in the middle of his mother and the woman he loves. A good mum tries her hardest not to put him there. But it still happens, even in the most normal of mother-son relationships. And Jet's relationship with Gloria sounds, admittedly, a bit abnormal. Not, like Oedipus Complex, or anything," he rushes to clarify. "But co-dependent. Mostly on Mummy's side of things. Which is good news for you."

"How is any of this good news? It's hopeless."

"On the contrary. This can be remedied. Or at least improved."

"You don't understand. It's— He can't tell her no. And I get it! Because I'm falling into the same pattern. She's scary!"

He laughs.

"And *I* don't want to put him between the two of us. I don't want there to be a 'between the two of us' at all."

"Well, that might be out of your control."

"It is. Definitely."

"Listen. Standing up to his mother is obviously something that distresses Jet. Therefore, if you were to stand up for him, and yourself, you'd be doing him a huge favor."

I scratch at a stress pimple on my jawline. "Let me get this straight. You're suggesting I go over Jet's head and talk to his mother about all of this wedding stuff without involving him?"

"No!" He wheezes and coughs. "No, no, no. That would be disastrous. You talk to him first, tell him how you feel about skipping the Kansas City social event of the year. Then you offer to be the one to break the news to his mother, so he doesn't have to. And so you can make sure it gets done."

"Oh, gosh. I don't know. That conversation…"

"Time to put on the big-girl knickers."

"But—"

"Stand firm. Set the precedent."

"The precedent for being the difficult marry-in who everyone hates?"

"The precedent for being a happy wife."

I say nothing while I contemplate all that would entail and how much would need to change for that to be possible.

"Presumably, the rest of your life will be with Jet. If you want that to have a chance of succeeding, you have to lay the groundwork. State your terms. He'll do anything for you. Anything. Trust me. But he's not a mind-reader. You have to tell him what you need."

"Since I've told you, can you find a much nicer, more diplomatic way of saying it and deliver the message for me? Because everything sounds better in an English accent."

His earnest reply, "It has to come from you," flattens my lame attempt at levity.

"Fine."

It's not fine, though. I'm not sure this is a hill to die on, especially not now, with postseason pressures pending. But what if the team makes it all the way to the Super Bowl? If I wait until after that, it'll be February, closer to the point of no return on this stupid wedding.

A tightness builds in my chest, and my vision narrows, as do my air passages. I try to conceal my labored breathing from Colin, but that only makes things worse; I don't want to pass out.

After a few seconds of listening to my gasping, he clicks his tongue. "Oh, Lady Maura."

"It's so stupid." Now, in addition to riding out the panic attack, I stave off humiliated tears.

"It's not stupid. Not at all."

"Such... first world... problems."

"But that's where you live now. It's extremely first world. And it comes with its own problems, which maybe aren't life and death but can lead to a quite miserable life if you don't deal with them."

"You know... how great... I am... at dealing..."

"Focus on breathing, for now. Have you got a paper bag? You should put your head between your legs."

His helpless advice almost makes me laugh. "I'm fine. I'm fine. It'll all be fine."

I simply have to figure out how to have this conversation about things that, in the grand scheme of things, don't matter. And I have to do it in a way that doesn't lead to me losing everything that actually does matter.

## SIX

## TOGETHER AGAIN

The Chiefs are one of eight on-the-bubble teams duking it out in Wild Card weekend for a piece of next week's Playoff action. If we win Sunday's game, we'll play the dreaded Patriots in the AFC divisional round next weekend, a rematch of last year's conference championship. That means they could knock us out a round earlier than they did last season. Nobody on or close to the team is saying that, but the fans and local media have repeated it enough for all of us, so it's definitely on the minds of all the players.

First, though, we have to defeat the Texans in three days, with some players—my boyfriend being one of them—still recovering from injuries sustained in that brutal loss to the Chargers.

Jet can now walk without wincing or limping too much, but that's only because he's never without ice packs, and he's spent a fair amount of time sitting in the ice tub at the training facility. I've made zero jokes about shrinkage, and I'd like credit for that rare show of maturity. Of course, I haven't been in much of a joking mood this week, so maybe it's not been such an astounding feat of self-control.

I haven't had much opportunity to tease, anyway. Since dismissing him Tuesday night, I haven't seen my fiancé, and we've barely communicated beyond one-line text messages, as he's been at the training facility before dawn each day and doesn't return home until nearly ten at night. I've had plenty of my precious alone time—and then some—at my own house, in my own bed, with my own thoughts. If only I'd waited one more day, I wouldn't have had to crush the guy!

I figured tonight would be another one of those solitary nights, so I'm surprised when I hear a key in my front door as I'm shoving a ten-foot-long strand of Ramen into my mouth in front of the television. Chewing furiously to cut the noodles down to size, I jump from the sofa and rush to meet Jet at the front door.

"Hey!" I say, throwing myself at him.

I'm doubly pleased when Torzi trots into the house and hops onto the sofa. I didn't realize how much I missed the little puffball.

Jet holds me tentatively at first, then more tightly. He pulls back his head and kisses me on the cheek before going for my lips.

"Mmm. Why do I suddenly feel like a college kid again?" At my sheepish smile, he laughs. "I like it. College was fun."

"Like you ever ate Ramen noodles in college, Mr. Football All-American." His thumbs rub my shoulder blades, and I shiver. I touch my nose to his. "I missed you."

"You mean, you've missed Beau's cooking? Because I had the distinct feeling you couldn't get rid of me fast enough the other night."

I stare at his teasing smile. "No, I've missed *you*. Tuesday night, I… Well, I panick—"

He captures my mouth in a toe-tingling kiss that somehow erases everything else from my thoughts. I can even block out Torzi perched on the back of the couch, panting as he watches us. The little perv.

As hands come into play, I pull back. "Whoa, whoa, Big Guy."

He pursues me into the living room like a dogged defensive end, but as he snatches me around the waist and pulls my back into his chest, I get my first good look at the dog and say, "What the— What happened to Quatorze?" The dog's usually round haircut has been squared off, giving him a decidedly block-headed appearance.

Jet sighs into my hair. "Oh. That. Yeah. The groomer tried something new." I jam my hand against the giggles that bubble from my mouth. "It's called a square cut. I guess it's trendy in Paris, or something. The groomer wanted to try it out, and Jacob thought I'd be cool with it, so…"

"Are you? Cool with it?"

"No! He looks like an idiot. More of an idiot than usual."

"Jet!" I turn and slap his chest.

He blinks. "Oh, come on. He's a designer dog. He's never looked that bright. Not that I have any room to judge. Just sayin'."

Glancing over my shoulder, I watch as the fuzzy white cube circles three times on a couch cushion and lies down, resting his chin on his paws and harumphing.

"You've hurt his feelings."

Jet rolls his eyes. "He thinks he's the shit. He's been prancing around the house like *Louis* Quatorze."

"Are you jealous there's a prettier Number Fourteen in residence?"

"You think that's pretty?"

"Did you tell Jacob to get it fixed as soon as possible?"

"Yeah. It's gotta grow out a little first, though, or the poor dog'll be shaved to the skin. It's too cold for him to have a buzz cut."

"You're such a good daddy," I say before thinking of the mine I'm stepping on.

"A good dad would take his own kid for a haircut and not leave it up to a gay manny who's game for fugly trends."

I laugh.

Suddenly serious, his green eyes search mine when he says, "I promise, I won't delegate stuff like that with *our* kids."

Swallowing hard, I look away. "Oh. Right. Well, that's…"

"…*a really long time from now, I hope.*"

"…*something I'd rather not think about right now.*"

"…*unavoidable, given who you are and what you do for a living.*"

"…okay," I finish lamely. I still can't help it that I pass the empty rooms in his house on my way down the hallway to his bedroom and imagine them filled with Little Jets and Mauras, which leads me to think of where those Little Jets and Mauras would originate, and my cervix sobs. Deep breath.

With a quick peck to his chin, I step away before panic grips me and pick up my half-eaten, now cold and mushy bowl of noodles. Carrying them into the kitchen, I say over my shoulder, "I'm surprised to see you here tonight. Figured you'd be hitting the sheets early."

He follows, leaning against the fridge while I clean up the few things that were required for me to make my collegiate dinner. "Coach let us go. Told us to go home and relax, prepare for travel day tomorrow."

"That was nice." I set my bowl and spoon in their designated dishwasher spots but decide to clean the large stainless steel stock pot by hand. Squirting liquid dish soap into it, I turn on the water and watch the bubbles rise. "I'm glad you're not playing one of the Saturday games. Give your knees one more day to recover."

"Exactly."

His body heat clues me into his proximity before I hear him, so I'm not startled when he places his hands on my hips and his lips on the side of my neck. Not startled but far from unaffected, either. I close my eyes.

"Come with me to Houston?" he says against my skin.

My eyes fly open. To buy time—and resist blurting a loud "YES!"—I turn off the water and reach for the dish scrubber. Swirling it into the apple-scented foam, I moderate my response while scrubbing pasta and broth residue from the sides of the pot. "Ummm... Well..."

"Please, Maura?"

"I don't know. I—"

"You don't want to?"

I chuckle. "Oh, I want to!"

"Then c'mon. I'll help you pack. You can stay at my place tonight. We have to head out early in the morning."

With a sigh, I dump the contents of the now-clean cookery. Jet steps back and gives me some space as I rinse it, but he snatches the towel from my reach on the counter and takes over drying as soon as the soap has been cleared. In his massive hands, the heavy metal pot looks light as a feather and not much bigger than a cereal bowl.

I blot my hands on the trailing tail of the towel that he works over the shiny surface. "I want to go," I repeat, in case he's forgotten that part, "but I don't want to be a distraction."

"You're not! I've told you a billion times, it doesn't work that way. I play harder for you."

"I don't want you thinking about me at all, though!"

"I'll be thinking about you, wherever you are." He raps his knuckle against the pot. "Where's this thing go?"

I gesture vaguely to the cabinet under the counter top range. While he nests the smaller pots and pans already there inside the larger one, I nibble my thumbnail. "I have work tomorrow. And a full schedule. And I need to get crackin' on the spring job fair plan. Executing it, anyway."

He straightens and pulls his phone from his pocket. "I'll get you on a later flight than the ones the other WAGs will be on."

Which leads me to the next thing: the other wives and girl-friends. "Jet, I'm not—" He pauses and looks up from his tapping when I stop. His crinkled forehead and expectant expression, mixed with hope, break my heart, and I can't finish what I was going to say.

Instead, I smile and pretend I'm teasing when I say, "You're such a bully."

He laughs and goes back to his reservation-making. "I am not! I want you there."

"It's not the Super Bowl!"

"It's more important than the Super Bowl."

"Bite your tongue!"

"It is, though. Because we'll never get to the Super Bowl if we don't win this week. And the next week. And the week after. I need you there."

"At *all* of those games?" The strange mix of stress and excitement weakens my knees and pops sweat from my pores. This must be what it feels like in the locker room before a big game, listening to a pep talk.

"Yeah."

"I— I can't do that, though, right?"

"Sure, you can! Why not?"

Knowing he'll wave away my first answer (*"Money, money, money"*) like an annoying mosquito, I don't bother saying it. Cost is never a factor when an all-pro, franchise quarterback wants something. And admitting it's a factor for me only leads to uncomfortable discussions.

"I have a life, you know."

"You won't miss any work. Not a single hour."

"All that traveling alone, though…"

"You wanna bring someone with you?"

"What? No."

"Yeah! That's a great idea, because I won't be available, so—"

"That's another thing. All this effort and expense." There. I said it. "But it won't be any different for you than if I was watching it at home. We won't be able to see each other."

"It does make a difference to me, though. C'mon."

How can I say "no"? All I ever do lately is reject and disappoint him. And I *do* want to support him. Experiencing the postseason live would be amazing, too. I weaken. "I guess if it means that much to you…"

"It does."

"And I don't have to miss any work…"

"You don't!"

"Okay."

"Yes!" He pumps his fist. "Now, who do you want to take with you? Greg? Oh, man. I'd be the best brother-in-law ever." He grins.

The thought of watching such an important game (or

games) live with my brother produces hives. "Uh, no! Not Greg!"

"Colin then? Yeah! Colin! He'd be fun."

"Colin has a life, too."

But Jet and I both know our friend would drop everything in an instant to go on a football tour. And it's true if there's anyone I'd be willing to spend all that time with, other than Jet, it would be him.

*Weakening...*

"Maybe the first game. I don't need a handler."

"Who knows? There might only be a first game. I'll text Colin now and ask if he can meet you at the airport tomorrow night at seven. That's the second-to-last flight to Houston. You don't want the last flight, because if it's canceled, you're screwed." Thumbs a blur as he pulls up a travel site on his phone, he glances up at me and beams. "This is going to be awesome."

*What is happening?*

———

It's crazy how commonplace this has become. And by "this," I mean me, sitting on a plane, flying back to Kansas City after watching the team beat their opponents in a game where not only were they the underdog, but they were playing on the other team's turf. If it weren't so thrilling, it would be disturbing how "Meh" the experience has become after the two most whirlwind weeks of my life.

I blame the other WAGs. The detachment they display is contagious. It's almost as if *they don't even like football!*

But that can't be true, right?

Because how do you survive this life without having a

passion for the game? If nothing else, you love it because your spouse or significant other does. Or less romantically, because it pays the bills. Right?

I'd ask Colin his opinion, but he's in the bathroom. And the woman we're sitting next to on this flight isn't one of the nicer WAGs. In fact, she didn't bother to stifle her sigh when she saw we were her neighbors for the trip home.

Which is fine. She's in the minority. Most of Jet's team-mates' partners have been extremely nice, if not a bit conde-scending with their "Aren't you cute that you still get excited and nervous about games?"

But this one, Kent "Tiff" Tiffenauer's girlfriend, Tiffani, is a real piece of work. She's newer to the "team" than I am, yet she flounces around like she owns the WAG suite. She parks herself in the front row of seats and has her nose on her phone the entire time. Well, when she's not taking pouty selfies and sharing them with her 3,587 Instagram followers. (She told me the number before she decided I wasn't worth bragging to.) I shamelessly looked over her shoulder this week to see how she captioned a particularly disinterested pose, and it said, *Another boring game. Supportin' my man.*

The funniest thing is, if anyone wanted to be snooty about it, they'd point out to her that her boyfriend is a scab. He wouldn't have ever been a starter if Keaton Busch hadn't been caught in that sex-for-points game, dubbed the "Bedroom Bowl," by the media, at the beginning of the season. In fact, Tiff likely would have been released to free up salary cap space. And he's not all that great now. He fumbles. A lot. Did so again today, in fact, and was lucky that another teammate was right there to fall on it. But she acts like his performance is completely irrelevant.

Colin returns from the bathroom and edges his way past

us to his window seat with several "Pardon"s and "Excuse me"s, but his manners have no effect on Tiffani's disgust. She sighs and rolls her eyes while making zero effort to give him more space to get through.

I ignore her, but when he's settled once more, Colin can't help himself from saying—again—"Sorry about that. Last time, I promise. Bladder the size of a chickpea."

While I snicker at his profuse apologizing and explaining, Tiffani flips through her fashion magazine and yawns. "TMI."

"Right. Sorry."

"Stop apologizing to her," I hiss under my breath.

"It's only polite," he whispers back.

"She wouldn't know 'polite' if it smacked her upside her ombre'd head. Let it go."

Tiffani slams her magazine shut and emits a frustrated noise, something between a groan and a sigh. "So bored!"

I keep my shoulder turned toward her, pretending to look out the tiny window past Colin's chest.

"What's the deal with you two, anyway? Are you, like, a thing?"

I'd laugh, but I don't want to entertain for a minute some crazy rumor that Jet's into threesomes.

Colin raises one eyebrow and points back and forth between himself and me. "Me? And Lady Maura?"

"Lady Maura? Who's that? Oh. You mean, Jet's girl?" She taps me on my upper arm. "What are you, like, her butler?" She snorts. "You travel with a butler?"

I'm too busy glaring at Colin for sounding so disgusted at the idea that we could be a "thing" to correct Tiff's misconceptions, most of all that I'm nobody's "girl." Before I can recover, Colin says, "Oh, let's not be coy, Maura. Tiffani here seems trustworthy enough to know the truth." To "trustworthy Tiffani," he says in a near-whisper, "I'm not her butler. I'm her bodyguard. A copper."

She pulls a face. "For realsies?"

He nods earnestly and pretends to look around us for suspicious activity. "Absolutely. But don't tell anyone. She's received some threats. You know, being connected with the team's capt— er, quarterback comes with a price."

Again, the wrinkled nose. Then she inspects her nails. "Not *that* one. He's too boring to attract threats."

"Boring?" I can't help but ask. I want to not care what this groupie thinks, but for some reason it's important for me to know if she's talking about his playing or his personality.

"He's such a Boy Scout."

I grin proudly.

"And a ball hog. Half the time, Kent is wide open down the field, but Jet keeps the ball and runs with it! It's like he can't throw more than ten yards."

My smile fades. I clench my jaw.

This season, I've made it a rule not to engage in football-related arguments. Not with Greg, not with my parents, not with co-workers or clients, not with other fans, and not with Jet. Although sometimes they're unavoidable with him. But this woman? I suddenly get a clear vision of police meeting us on the tarmac upon making an emergency landing at some airport between Boston and home, because I've ripped out her extensions and flossed my teeth with them.

But that's gross.

Therefore, I merely say, "Actually, Tiffani, when Busch was the tight end, the playbook was a bit wider open than it is now. Because Busch had great hands." I clear my throat and nudge her. "Got him in a bit of trouble off the field, too, am I right?"

She snarls at me and edges farther away, practically hanging over her other armrest, into the aisle.

"But now, you're right; Jet's much more conservative. *Your* man has a bit of a fumbling problem. It happens to everyone. Some more than others. And it definitely affects the play calling. In clutch situations, you don't want to give it to someone who might lose the ball, no matter how wide open he is."

"Knox has fumbled it, too, this season, and you don't see everyone up his ass about it."

I sniff and return my attention to the head of the person in front of me. "Because they're too busy being 'up his ass' about everything else. Like being 'boring.' Or running for first downs too often. Or refusing to throw it to Fumbelina."

Tiffani harrumphs at the nickname, and I realize I've gone too far. Plus, now I feel horrible. Despite his shortcomings on the field—and his loathsome girlfriend—I like Kent Tiffenauer. He's a nice guy. Jet and I have talked more than once after tough games about how Tiff's confidence has been badly shaken by his recent challenges with holding onto the ball. I've suggested Jet give the tight end the ball *more* often, to up his success rate and rebuild his confidence, and Jet's agreed… in theory. But on the field, in win-or-lose situations, it's harder to take that risk.

I sigh. "Listen. I'm sorry. That was— That was uncalled for."

She glowers at me. "Is that what you and your stuck-up boyfriend call my man? Fumbelina?"

"No! Of course not!"

"You think it's fun to mock people? Make them look like idiots and make yourself seem more important by calling them names and laughing at them behind their backs?"

"No!"

"I'm sure you and Boy Scout have had a field day with 'Tiffani Tiffenauer.' For your information, I'll be keeping my maiden name after we get married. Not that it's any of your business or that I care what you think."

*Busted.* "I— It's—"

"And you!" She leans forward to look around me at Colin. "You're not a bodyguard. Too puny."

He smiles sheepishly. "Uh, well spotted, you! Although I would protect her in times of trouble. Like now, perhaps, if you were—let's say—determined to do her bodily harm."

Following a few bubbles of turbulence, the "fasten seatbelt" light comes on with a ding. Tiffani cinches her belt. "I wouldn't waste my energy. I might break a nail."

Relieved, I chuckle. "Okay, then. So, uh, you've gone to all the games this season?"

"I'm done talking to you, bitch."

"Fair enough."

I exchange glances with Colin but quickly look away, for fear I'll start laughing. If I do that, I worry not even protecting her precious manicure would prevent her from peeling my face.

## STILL LEARNING

We manage to land without any violence, and I walk with Colin to short-term parking, where we find Jet waiting for us, trying to keep a low profile. He's been back for hours, having flown on the team charter, not commercial, like us plebs. In fact, he's been home long enough to go back to his house, change into more comfortable clothes, and switch out cars.

While Colin places our small suitcases in the trunk, I open the front passenger door, noticing the piece of mail on the seat.

"What have we here?" I ask. In fact, I immediately recognize the "Save the Date" card, considering there's an identical one in the mountain of unopened mail, including bills, at my house. I pluck the silver envelope from its leather perch and lower myself into the car. "You carry this around with you, like some lovesick teenager?"

Jet leans across the center console and kisses me quickly, laughing while I lift the already opened flap on the card. The trunk slams shut, and Colin slides in behind us.

"I say! Cracking match, sir." He claps Jet on the shoulder. "You were brilliant!"

"You ran too much," I say with a cheeky wink. "But way to get your revenge on those jerks, finally." I pull the postcard from its envelope and cringe at the bright red foil hearts and flowers on the white background. "Oh, geez," I can't help but mutter out loud.

"Whatcher got there?" Colin asks as Jet reverses from the parking space. He peers over my shoulder. "Oooh, yes! Mine is on the refrigerator at home. I've saved the date, as it were."

I stare a while longer at the graphics, almost not caring enough to read the script on the right side but wanting to make sure they got the date right, at least.

"By the by," Colin continues, sitting back, "I had no idea your Christian name isn't Jet."

"Ah, yeah. That."

"What?" Now my eyes can't zoom sideways and skim down fast enough. "What do you mean, your name's not— Ohmygosh."

*Save the Date for the wedding of*
*Micah Edward Knox & Maura Vivienne Richards*
*Saturday, 5th April*
*Ridgeway Presbyterian Church*
*Mission Hills, Kansas*
*Formal invitation to follow.*

Micah and Maura. This is payback for laughing at "Tiffani Tiffenauer," isn't it? *Oh, karma, you righteous—*

Colin slaps the leather next to his thigh. "Oh, come off it. Like you didn't know."

"I… I… didn't!"

He giggles. "Bloody hell. This oughta be good."

I gawk at Jet's pink profile. "Explain."

Shrugging, he makes a big show of navigating the concentric roads leading from the parking lot to the line of guard shacks full of attendants. He flashes his special pass to the old guy, who gives a thumbs up and lifts the gate for us to drive through. I wait.

And wait.

Finally, as we merge onto the interstate, he says, "Nobody calls me that. Ever. Not even my mom when she's mad at me. Until I have to sign a legal document or… or… send in my taxes, I forget that's my real name."

"You forget. You just *forget* you have a different name?"

His ears redden more deeply. "When you say it like that, it sounds stupid. But yeah."

"And that's why you 'forgot' to tell me that I'm marrying"—I read it from the card, as if I don't already have it emblazoned on my brain—"*Micah* Knox on April fifth?"

Colin snorts, reminding me of his presence.

I whirl on him. "You're in trouble too, mister!"

"Me? Whatever for?"

"You knew about this? And didn't tell me?"

"Silly me, I assumed you were aware of the legal name of your betrothed."

"But— But— I can't believe you haven't teased me about it. Or— Or—"

"It's not nice to tease. And anyway, it's not *that* bad a name."

"I hate it," Jet says.

*Oh, thank God.*

Instead of saying *Me too,* I manage to sputter, "It d-doesn't fit you, that's all."

He smiles over at me. "You really thought my given name was Jet all this time?"

Now it's my turn to blush. "Yes!"

"Who names their kid Jet?"

"Californians," my Midwestern brain supplies before I can filter.

He rolls his eyes at my shameless stereotyping and sighs. "It's my nickname. Has been since I was a baby. Mom almost didn't make it to the hospital before I was born."

"I can't believe I didn't know that," I mumble.

"I can't, either. My mom tells that story constantly."

"Not about your birth! Your name! I can't believe you haven't told me your real name!"

"It never came up. And I guess I assumed you'd heard it or read it somewhere."

"Ego," I grumble. "Like I spend all of my free time clipping articles about you or editing your Wikipedia page for accuracy."

He laughs nervously but doesn't admit or deny he's considered the possibility.

For the rest of the drive to Colin's place, I remain silent, recalling all the times I've heard commentators say Jet's name and trying to remember if they've ever dropped his real one in any of those air-filling tidbits they're so fond of tossing out. Nope.

And I definitely can't imagine them saying, *"Knox drops back and scrambles… He's in trouble now, but he's deceptively fast, and he's found a hole… Dodges that tackle and… he's going for it! Touchdown! Kansas! City! That Micah Knox, he'll make you pay for silly defensive mistakes."*

Nope. A guy named Micah doesn't make anyone pay for

anything but the coffee he prepares and rings up at the nearest Starbucks.

Next, I think of all the times I've cried out "Jet!" and try to substitute it in my mind with "Micah!" No way. Micah is the name of a barista, not a rockin' hot guy who licks you from lip to tip.

An involuntary shiver shakes me.

Jet/Micah asks, "Are you cold?"

Am I? I must be, to put so much stock in a name. Maybe not cold, but shallow, for sure.

I smile wanly at him. "No. I'm fine. Tired."

He parks in Colin's short driveway and turns in his seat to face our friend. "Your stop, man. Hey, thanks again for making the trip."

"Thank *you*. Boston reminds me a bit of home. It was a lark."

They go back and forth for a while, playing their Yankee Doodle and Redcoat roles while I pretend to listen, smiling affectionately, but I've tuned out. I'm too busy adjusting to the idea of being one of two M's in our M&M duo and wondering what it says about me that I care. (Hint: it doesn't reflect well.)

After all, it's hardly a deal-breaker. I'm sure at some point, I'll be like Jet, able to forget that's his name. I hope. Until then, I need to get a grip. I need to stop using my embarrassment at not knowing such a basic fact about the man I'm going to marry—and being exposed as clueless in front of someone else—as a distraction from the other, real anxieties in my life.

———

What are my biggest problems right now? A dearth of vacation days to take so I can follow my boyfriend around the country playing for a title, ring, and trophy? An overbearing future mother-in-law and annoying wedding planner? A dreaded wedding day—*one day*—resulting from that nightmare team-up? A lack of privacy in a house that doesn't feel like home and probably never will? It's downright shameful how entitled I am.

Have I succumbed to this absurd life already, where the inane and insignificant take center stage in the absence of legitimate worries? Am I becoming accustomed to the epitome of a bad day involving an ugly dog haircut or finding out my fiancé's unfortunate legal name?

Recognizing this and writing it all off are two different things, though. The issues at the root of the discontent may be more valid than I'd like to admit. As Colin pointed out, repeatedly dismissing my worries as insignificant will lead to resentment, not contentment. I can't say, "Well, I shouldn't be bothered by that; therefore, I'm not." Feelings don't work that way. Unfortunately. Oh, that they did! What an effortlessly happy existence so many of us would lead!

I must address, not suppress, these niggling annoyances, before they become something bigger, less manageable, and more destructive.

Again, easier said than done. Opportunity is scarce. And when it does present itself, I hesitate to spend what little time Jet and I have together discussing anything that might lead to unpleasantness or disagreement. He's so... focused. And not on me, for once. Which is absolutely expected and understandable and not at all a problem. A bit of a relief, to be honest. I have plenty to keep me busy while he prepares for the conference championship.

For the spring job fair, I've selected an Academy Award theme, complete with red carpet, which is harder to find for a reasonable rental price in the middle of the country than you'd think. I'm about to give up altogether, buy a bolt of red material at the closest craft store, and call it good. Instead, I'll focus on my papier-mâché Oscar statuettes. I have to make one for each of the forty-one employer booths.

So far, I've completed three.

As usual, I've seriously underestimated the level of work involved to make my vision a reality.

No matter. Simple math tells me I only need to make four of these per week—in between seeing clients, attending nerve-wracking football games, and sort-of planning a wedding—if I want them finished before we leave for our honeymoon. And I do. Because although I'll have almost exactly a month between returning from St. Bart's and the spring fair, I don't want this arts and crafts project—or anything—hanging over my head while I'm honeymooning. Everything needs to be resolved and perfect by then, so I can relax.

Everything.

That gives me nine weeks between the absolute end of the football season and the wedding to fix everything else.

More "simple math" tells me I'm screwed.

Screw math.

I'm going to take this one problem at a time, and right now, the most pressing problem is the sticky, gluey mess on my dining table.

Rubbing my itchy nose with the mostly clean back of my hand, I admire my latest statuette. Well, I wish I could admire it. There's not much to admire at this point. But it'll look better once it's covered with the gold foil and has dried. Experience has taught me this.

The first one was a different story. When I got it to this point—about halfway through the process—I nearly collapsed with frustration and panic, because my creation was so ugly. But I persevered through the rest of the project, if only to prove to myself that it was a failure, and I needed to choose a different art medium. Foam, perhaps? Cash? As in, paying someone else to make these for me?

Since that last one wasn't an option, I soldiered on. And he turned out okay. I don't want these to look too authentic. That's what I've been telling myself, anyway. And it's worked.

I was gratified when Rae seemed impressed by the one I brought to work to put on my desk as a reminder (as if I needed one) to keep pressing on. Then she had to go and ruin it by being all practical.

"How long did that take you?"

"From start to finish? About three hours. Then overnight drying."

She snorted. "Three hours. Per figure."

"I'll get faster. Maybe."

"Still. You said you're making about forty of these?"

"Forty-one."

"Uh…"

"Yeah, I realize how long it's going to take," I snapped. "I have to do one every other weeknight. Maybe a couple on the weekends. I have plenty of time."

"Why didn't you do small cardboard standies?"

"I wanted them to be three-dimensional. Plus, I did cardboard standies in the fall, remember? And it rained. And it was almost a disaster."

"But those were life-sized."

"I didn't want to do that again, okay?"

"Okay! What about dollar-store Ken dolls? You know, the

old-fashioned ones with the plastic hair? You could spray paint them gold."

Shit. I wished I had thought of that. But I hadn't. And her suggesting it after I'd already bought all of the supplies and committed to the papier-mâché plan pissed me off. I pointed to the sculpture. "Does it look okay, or not?"

"It looks great!"

"Excellent. Then this is what I'm doing."

"I'm only trying to save you tons of time and trouble. Sheesh. C'mon. You need a drink—or thirty—more than I realized."

That's the last time we hung out. Granted, as one of the Chiefs' trainers, she's been as busy as Jet, only focusing on a different aspect of the game plan: keeping the guys healthy; managing the pain from their minor to moderate injuries, so they can keep playing; and being one of the bad guys, telling them when they *can't* play, due to concussions or more serious injuries that could be made worse by trying to tough it out. Nobody wants to miss out on postseason action, especially not the starters who got the team this far. I don't envy her at all.

Nor do I want to put myself in her path during all of this. I send her a text every other day or so to let her know I'm thinking of her and to make sure she's still alive, but I'm finished being her whipping girl. Something tells me she's not all that eager to hang around stressed-out me, either.

It's just as well. Oscar's a pretty high-maintenance friend. One of those at a time is plenty.

## EIGHT

## SUITE VICTORIES

Those two wins on the road have earned us a much-appreciated (by all) home game. The team is glad to be back on familiar turf, and I'm glad my weekend won't involve roaming any of this country's finest airports. Colin was the only one in the entire city disappointed we didn't have to go on the road this week. "I'd forgotten how much I enjoy travel."

Yeah, well, it's not my favorite thing, unless there's a beach and several pastel-colored drinks waiting for me at the end of the trip. A couple of years ago, traveling to watch postseason NFL games live would have been a dream come true, and I'd like to enjoy it now, but when you're worried for your boyfriend's life every five minutes, it's not as fun. Funny how that works.

Greg begged me to let him be my plus-one to the conference championship against the Cincinnati Bengals, which was fine by Colin, who welcomed a "pipe and slippers" Sunday at home. And I had to admit, it would be cruel to deny my brother, the ultimate Chiefs fan, this opportunity.

If only I'd thought to bring duct tape.

"…And we're gettin' down to crunch time, you know?" As if demonstrating, he shoves a cheese-drenched tortilla chip into his mouth and clamps down on it. Too soon, he continues around the food, "I have one green wall, one pink wall, one brown wall, and one turquoise wall, and Deirdre can't make a decision. But you know as soon as I make an executive decision and pick a color myself, she'll be adamant that it has to be one of the other three. Nightmare." He licks cheese sauce from his fingers.

"Sounds to me like you guys need to sit down and make one of those pros and cons lists you both love so much," I say distractedly, keeping my eye on the action below the luxury suite. Meanwhile he rambles on and on about how emotional Deirdre is, turning the most routine, innocuous conversations into major dramas that almost always end in tears. Deirdre? Crying all the time? I was always under the impression she had no tear ducts.

Post another one in the "win" column for effective, reliable methods of birth control.

Our defense is out there now, so I don't have to be on high alert for disaster, but I don't want to miss anything exciting, like a turnover. I'm busy up here, praying for repeated interceptions or fumbles returned for touchdowns. That means our defense scores the points *and* stays out there to defend again, keeping Jet safe and on the bench.

I wonder if any team has made it to the Super Bowl on all defensive points.

"How's the wedding planning going?" Greg suddenly asks on a suppressed burp after gulping down another complimentary beer.

With a glance around the suite to make sure nobody's

listening to us, I wave his pesky question away. "I don't want to talk about it."

"That good, huh?" He chuckles. "It's like you and Knox have switched traditional roles, which shouldn't surprise me, come to think of it. You're such an oddball."

"Apathy about cotton bond paper and silver versus gold foil on invitations doesn't make me an oddball. There are more important things in life." My own mention of gold foil reminds me I haven't produced an Oscar statuette in days, which means I'm falling behind on my quota. I push away that annoying thought, too, though, while I watch Jet don his helmet and take the field after our defense forces a punt. "Can we watch the game?"

My brother shrugs. "Of course. I was only making conversation."

"It's impossible to pray and talk to you at the same time." I bite my already-minuscule fingernails and move on to my ragged cuticles.

Greg slaps my hand away from my mouth. "Stop that. It's so gross."

"You're so gross!"

"You are! And you're bleeding." He hands me a napkin, which I wrap around my oozing middle finger.

The instability of my mental state is confirmed when I have to blink away my emotions after he rests his arm around the back of my shoulders and pulls me to him in a rare hug. "Hey. We've got this. These guys are no match for us."

I sniffle. "I don't give a shit about the score."

"Shhh!" Now it's his turn to look nervously around the suite at the WAGs and other team guests. "You don't mean that."

Although I'm pretty sure nobody heard me—Tiffani's in

front of us with her nose on her phone, as usual, and everyone else is riveted to the game, both on the other side of the glass and on the big screens scattered throughout the room—I lower my voice. "I do mean it. Do I want to win? Yes. But only because that's what will make Jet happy. I wish he'd be happy no matter what. That way, we could lose this game and go home, and I wouldn't have to worry anymore this season."

"You'd have other worries. Like a completely miserable fan base hating your man throughout the entire off-season."

"Not necessarily."

"You know that's how it works, fair or not. Plus, you want the team to show the big guy the money in a couple of years when his contract is up, right?"

"I don't care about that, either."

"You should. It'll be all yours, too, by then."

Focusing once more on the field, I scoot toward the front of my chair and press my bloody napkin to my lips to suppress the squeal I would definitely be emitting if I were somewhere private, as Jet scrambles out of the pocket and searches down-field for a receiver. Finally, Tiff evades his defender and stays open long enough for Jet to rifle a bullet into the tight end's waiting arms, only to be dropped at the goal line.

Jet claps his hands together once and drops his head back as if asking God for patience not to kill his teammate when Tiff arrives in the huddle for the third down play call. I burn a hole through the back of Tiffani's head, like the entire thing is her fault. She doesn't react at all, though. She's either missed the action or doesn't care that half the people in the suite, including my boisterous brother, are cursing her boyfriend right now.

Still staring at Tiffani's lacquered hair, I murmur at Greg,

"Can someone please sedate me until mid-February? I'm not going to make it if I have to witness every play."

"You mean every drop by that clown?"

I'd implore him to be quiet to spare Tiffani's feelings, if she weren't such a brat. Or if she, herself, showed any sign of caring.

"You or I could suit up and do a better job," Greg says, slumping in his seat. "God bless."

"An incomplete pass is better than a fumble," I point out.

"Result is the same: no points."

"But we still have the ball." As if to prove me wrong, the team fails to secure the first down and keep the drive going, so we have to punt it away.

Greg raises his eyebrows at me. "You were saying?"

I scowl at him. "Shut up."

He pushes my shoulder. "You shut up."

"No, *you* shut up."

———

About halfway through the second quarter, I leave the suite to go outside and take in some fresh, freezing air. Outdoor heaters hanging from the eaves radiate warmth, and the concrete walls that separate our suite's balcony from our neighbors' block the wind, making it surprisingly cozy for an outdoor setting in late January.

The fans in the stands don't look nearly this comfortable, huddled together under blankets in their puffy coats, tightly wound scarves, knit hats, and heated gloves and socks. Then there are the shirtless crazies in their red, white, and yellow body paint. Something tells me the nearest hospital is going to have a few cases of hypothermia before the end of the day.

Coach Bauer's wife, who's been sitting out here alone for most of the game, promptly moves from the row behind me to the seat right next to me. She offers her gloved hand. "Hi, there. I don't think we've ever been formally introduced, if you can believe that. I'm Sandy."

"Maura," I reply, grasping firmly.

Scrunching her shoulders up near her ears, she grins and looks out over the sunny field. "Don't you just love this game?"

"I do." I cringe as I watch a linebacker hit Jet, who tumbles to the ground after getting rid of the ball in the nick of time. He immediately hops up and pats the opposing player on the back as they move down the field together to regroup with their own teams on the line of scrimmage.

Sandy opens her mouth to speak, seems to think better of it, then squints knowingly at me and says, "Pardon my saying so, but you don't look like you're enjoying yourself."

I groan. "I want to be. It would be more fun if we were winning."

She laughs. "Ah, yes. Winning is a prerequisite for happiness in our house, too. But the score's close. And there's still a whole other half to play."

I nod. "Yeah. True, I guess."

Sandy follows my eye line, which has strayed once again to the field. "Mm-hm. It's different now, isn't it? Especially after you watch them recover from an injury, no matter how minor it may seem to the people at home. You see them in pain. You see them frustrated and worried. It's hard."

She nudges her nose toward the Chiefs' sideline below us, where Jet sits on the bench after another frustrating series resulting in no points. Coach stands in front of him, gesturing and obviously trying to explain something. Jet nods and opens his mouth to squeeze a stream of water into it from the bottle in his hand.

It's odd to think those two guys belong to the two of us, sitting up here, chatting. I guess "belong" isn't the right word. Then again, yes, it is, if I can presume some things about the Bauers' relationship. We belong to each other, as in, we're a match, a pair. Like cleats. Or something less stinky. Mittens, perhaps.

I pull from my coat pockets the Arrowhead-emblazoned red ones my mom got me for Christmas and slide them onto my hands.

Sandy adjusts the scarf that would perfectly complete my winter ensemble. "Dick has worked with scores of injured athletes, most of whom think the team can't survive without them. They pester him and the doctors to release them earlier than they should, before they're fully healed and ready to play again. Not the case with Jet. Dick said Number Fourteen did what the doctors told him to do to get that hand back in good shape, and he was patient and kept calm, which was a huge help with the backup situation."

My chest feels like it's about to burst, but I manage to keep my pride in check when I say, "He's a good guy."

Both of us tune into the game when our defense holds the Bengals to a quick three-and-out series, and Jet and the boys take to the turf again. After a moderately long drive down the field that brings us into the red zone, Jet has to call a time-out when he can't get a decision from the sideline before the play clock runs out. He slaps his helmet, as if to signal the communications device inside isn't working, and jogs to the sideline to get clearer instructions.

While we wait for the action to resume, Sandy says, "Jet hasn't given Dick a minute of trouble. Well, there *was* that whole locker room interview brouhaha." She nudges me with her shoulder. "But even then, Dick was like, 'The guy said what most of us have been thinking.'"

"Jet felt terrible for losing his temper."

"Better to do it in that way than in a way that gets you in trouble with the law. Or worse, the Commissioner." She winks.

I smile faintly. "Right? I told him it wasn't the end of the world, but he was freaking out. Turns out, he didn't say half the horrible things he thought he did."

Sandy raises an eyebrow at that tidbit.

I shrug. "He'd say, 'too many knocks to the head.'"

She cracks up at that. "Oh, goodness! He's a card, isn't he?"

"Yeah, he is."

Two plays later, I slump in my seat as the field goal unit trots on to make yet another three-point attempt after the defense thwarts our efforts to penetrate the end zone.

"Well, Dick sure likes him. I probably shouldn't say that. There's more than likely some silly rule against players knowing their coaches like them."

"I won't tell."

She waves off my promise. "Phooey. Maybe fewer players would find themselves in trouble if they liked their coaching staff enough to care what they thought about them. Might make them think twice before doing something dumb."

"Maybe."

Finally, the clock winds down on the first half, with our team trailing by ten, and Sandy stands. "Well, it was great talking to you, Maura. I suppose I should mingle inside during halftime."

"I should make sure my brother hasn't fallen into a food

coma. Or passed out drunk in there," I say before thinking better of it, but I don't get up.

She rests her hand on my shoulder while laughing at my too-honest statement. "You know what? You're going to be just fine in the NFL."

Before I can voice my chagrin at how obvious my self-doubt is, she says, "We all worry about it, especially at first. Trust me." She edges down the row of seats to get to the aisle leading back up to the suite. "You have a great sense of humor, and you care about the team. Teams change, though. You seem to know that it's important to be loyal and supportive of the one *person* on the team you care about most."

When I don't reply right away, she opens the door to the suite. "Try to enjoy the rest of the game, no matter the outcome. Our job is more important when they *don't* win." She winks. "But I think you've already realized that, too."

## NINE

## CONTAGION

Proving Sandy Bauer's theory will have to wait, though. By some miracle (a lunging quarterback sneak across the goal-line that will go down as one of the gutsiest last-second plays of all time), we won. Which means, we're Super Bowl bound. The entire city is in a frenzy.

When Jet and I were finally alone at his place after the conference championship victory, followed by celebrations at the stadium, he said with a grin, "I'm sorry-not-sorry about Hawaii."

I smiled back as convincingly and unselfishly as possible, unable to believe how torn I was about such a phenomenal opportunity—for both him *and* my favorite football team. After all, as a fan, this has been a dream of mine for my whole life. Only... Sandy is right. It's different now. Worrying for your fiancé's life during the biggest game of his career is a stress nobody should have to experience, though.

But since it wasn't—and isn't—about me, I dismissed his half-apology. "I've heard Dallas is a cool town. Anyway. Dude. You're going to the Super Bowl!"

Our arms wrapped around each other, we hopped up and down in one spot in his living room, laughing hysterically at ourselves.

"I know! I mean, I can't believe it!"

"Believe it!"

"I do. And I have the confetti in my underwear to prove it."

"Oooh... show me."

Sure enough, he did.

Out of breath, I placed my hands on my hips and beamed up at him. "I'm so proud of you."

There. That was true.

"Yeah?"

"Absolutely."

He grabbed me again and squeezed, lifting me off the floor and mashing his lips against mine in a kiss that started out silly but got serious in a hurry. Seriously serious.

"I love you so much," he gasped against my mouth a few minutes later.

"I love you, too."

"Oh, Maura. This... This is the best day of my life so far. But the best part is, it won't come close to some of the others I'll have with you someday."

"Jet—"

"I'm not talking about winning the Super Bowl. Hell, I don't want to jinx that. But our wedding day is less than three months from now! And when our babies are born..." He pulled back so I could see the tears in his eyes.

Oh. My. Gosh.

I sighed, hoping it conveyed contentment, not despair. There was no way, at that point, I was going to take a big ol' whiz on his festivities. He was in a well-deserved great mood, high on life, and I truly was happy for him. And happy for the fan in me, wherever the hell she went. And happy for me, in general. Winning beats losing, any day.

But that small, scared introvert who lives not-so-deep down inside of me and still balks at public appearances and social gatherings loves Jet, too. She loves him all to herself, in private, which is such a rarity in our lives.

It's especially rare now, a few days later, with a Mama Knox invasion on my hands. In fact, that silly-turned-serious moment in his living room was one of the last times I had a one-on-one conversation with the man, the myth, the legend, Micah "Jet" Knox.

His parents arrived on Tuesday, when I would have been gleefully planning and preparing and packing for the Pro Bowl, if things had turned out differently. Instead, I was blocking out memories of palm trees, warm breezes, and salty air—things I'd seen, felt, smelled, and experienced for myself a year ago—and trying to stay focused on the other tremendous opportunities facing Jet in the next couple of weeks.

Gloria and Ned's arrival was a decent distraction. That is, until I realized that, in person, Gloria was going to have two modes: "NFL Mom" mode and "Wedding Planner" mode. I would have watched a thousand hours of someone else's tropical vacation videos with toothpicks holding open my eyes, if necessary, to avoid either topic.

Mom and Dad have tried to take the heat off tonight, the Knoxes' second night here, by going out with us for dinner. I figure, with Jet stuck at the training complex and unable to accompany us, Gloria will feel free to talk about other things, especially with my mom.

And it's worked. Sort of. My parents' travels took up a lot of conversational space. But unfortunately, it's led them to a discussion (criticism) about Jet's and my upcoming honeymoon.

"The beach," Mom says with a shake of her head. "There are so many more exotic, lovely, romantic destinations. I tried to talk them into Venice or even something as clichéd as Paris, but no. Mo wants a beach. And Jet wants what Mo wants, so…"

Gloria smiles indulgently at me. She pats my mother's hand. "There's always the babymoon. They can use your suggestions then."

Dear. God.

I excuse myself to go to the bathroom and hyperventilate in a stall for a while. Then I splash water on my face, reapply my makeup, and return to the table with a bright smile and a sunny joke about all the excitement catching up to me.

Mom and Gloria exchange knowing glances I want nothing to do with, so I quickly introduce the next safe topic—one of several I brainstormed when I set up this little date: familiarizing my parents with the Knox clan. Gloria can hold court for at least an hour bragging on her children and grandchildren, and Mom and Dad will need to take careful notes—possibly including a flowchart—to keep it all straight for the Super Bowl and wedding.

Make no mistake, the biggest event in Gloria's life has now most definitely shifted from our wedding to the Super Bowl, which is fine by me. While my future mother-in-law explains the logistics of getting all of Jet's siblings and their spouses and kids to the big event next Sunday, I sit back and smugly tuck into my dessert.

I've earned this chocolate mousse. I've been dreaming about it since making this reservation. Sure, it's not as good as it was when I ate it off Jet's abs that one time, but if I close my eyes, I can pretend… No. Not a good idea, I decide when a moan bubbles around the spoon in my mouth. The rest of the table silences.

I open my eyes to find my companions' attentions glued to me.

Smiling sheepishly, I ask, "What?"

"Is that good, dear?" Mom asks, channeling the 1950s housewife she reserves for times of particular embarrassment.

Hoping I didn't make the noises I was making in my imagination, I blush. "Uh, yes. Would you like to try a bite?"

She shakes her head and dabs at the corners of her mouth. "No. And maybe you'd like us to leave the two of you alone?"

I push away the small ramekin, which still holds at least one or two orgasmic bites, in an effort to prove there's nothing inappropriate going on between the dessert and me. Clearing my throat, I begin to recite what I assume the older women were discussing while I was in my happy, happy place. "We're all meeting up in Big D a week from today, on Wednesday, with the exception of Cyndi, who's flying in from Germany with her husband and son on Saturday, right?"

"Only her and Mikey, I'm afraid," Gloria says while fiddling with her unused dessert fork. "Justin already has leave time scheduled for the wedding in April, but he couldn't get away now on such short notice."

Ah, yes. The Air Force doesn't give a rat's patoot about one's brother-in-law's once-in-a-lifetime opportunity, not even something as all-American as the Super Bowl. Something about protecting and serving, or some such thing.

"Oh. Well, it'll be nice to meet Cyndi."

"And Jet's namesake."

For about the millionth time since learning about "Micah," I experience one of those lightbulb-in-a-dark-room-that-turns-out-to-be-a-scary-closet-that-should-have-remained-dark moments. But instead of revealing how stupid I feel, I simply turn off the switch with a curt, "Of course. Mikey. Micah."

Gloria flips the switch back on. "Jet was so touched when Cyndi and Justin named him that." She laughs. "Then we all promptly called him 'Mikey.'" With a head tilt, she ponders in my direction, "Maybe you and Jet can finally have a Micah we all call Micah. That would be nice."

It would look weird if I left the table again, wouldn't it? But that mousse… It seems to be planning a coup.

Dad sets his hand on the back of my neck. "You okay, Mo?"

I bob my head robotically. "Fine."

"Have you been getting enough sleep?" Gloria asks. "I've been lecturing Jet about that all month, it seems. This post-season schedule is brutal, and what they don't take into account is that the human body needs rest as much as anything else, if it's going to operate at peak condition."

Ned nods, something he does often while his wife pontificates.

"Maybe we should get you back home," Gloria says, signaling for the check, although I'll be the one paying it, albeit with Jet's credit card.

My view of the room narrows, which is a blessing, in a way, since the other tables and diners have started to spin like we're all on a giant version of that whirling teacups ride at Disney.

The thing is, "back home," is *not* home. It's Jet's house, where I'll be staying all week, playing host to his parents while trying to also maintain some semblance of normality at my job, where nobody wants to talk about anything but the one topic I go there to avoid right now: football. And feeling like I do at the moment, all I want is my own bed. In my own house. With my own smells. And no roommates.

Since that would create drama I'm not willing to endure, I merely smile at Gloria through gummy lips and say, "A good night's sleep is all I need," while I hand the credit card to the waiter over my shoulder.

She and Mom share one of *those* looks again. Then they perform a whispered exchange while I give our server a one-hundred-percent tip to avoid having to do any math. Hey, it's not my money.

In a montage-like dream state, I say goodbye to my parents in the parking lot, and Ned drives us "home" using the on-board GPS in the Mercedes he and Gloria have commandeered this week. Gloria tucks me into Jet's bed, the inappropriateness of which escapes me in my stupor. I wake up hours later and climb over a passed-out fiancé to scramble to the bathroom, where my entire five-star meal goes down the toilet.

———

Mama Knox has jettisoned a bewildered Jet from his own bedroom in a display seemingly designed to show me how inadequate my understanding of "helicopter mom" has been up to now. He stands outside the closed, *locked* door for several minutes, knocking and trying to wheedle his way back in.

"Mom, c'mon!"

"No. You can't afford to get sick right now."

"I'm not going to get sick. I'm taking more vitamins than a racehorse."

"Not safe."

"They're perfectly safe!"

"No, it's not safe in *here*. You've already been exposed."

Almost too weak to speak, I still manage to rasp, "Do you two mind talking somewhere else? In the same room? But a different room than this one?"

She pushes me into the pillows with a hand to my forehead. "You're burning up. Which is good." Before I can question her logic, she says, "Last night at the restaurant, I thought you were pregnant. The alternating paleness and flushed cheeks, that chocolate mousse…"

I groan at the mention of any food, much less that.

Oblivious to—or uncaring about—my discomfort, she pulls the covers up to my neck and folds them down exactly so. "I thought if you were pregnant, I'd give you a pass on the mousse, because—let's face it—we'd have to let that dress out anyway. Otherwise, you have no excuse. You need to lay off the sugar. It's only two more months of watching what you eat. Then you can stuff your face all you want."

Right now, I can't imagine wanting to eat again. Ever.

"I had to have this same talk with Gidget. The girl's automatic response to any stress is to eat. The months before her wedding, I could have hired someone to follow her around and slap food from her hands."

"No more talk about food."

"Oh. Right. Sorry. But you know what I'm saying."

Jet pounds on the door. "Can I at least get some clothes?"

Gloria sighs and rises from the bed, enabling me to breathe fully for the first time in several minutes. With a disturbing familiarity, she pulls a long-sleeved t-shirt and pajama pants from Jet's dresser and takes them to the door. Unlocking it, she passes the articles through the smallest crack possible. "Now, go. And how many times have I told you to wear pajamas? What if there was a fire?"

Reminiscent of his game-winning move last weekend, he wedges his shoulder against the wood and dives into the gap between the door and the frame. Poking his head into the room, he takes one look at me and frowns. "Geez, Maura. Are you okay?"

I want to cry and tell him the truth. No. I'm not okay. I haven't been okay in weeks. This is merely a physical manifestation of what's been happening inside of me for a long, long time.

Instead, I close my eyes and turn onto my side—with some difficulty under the tightly tucked covers. "I'll be fine. You stay away and stay healthy."

"But what about—" He stops, and I hear him swallow. "Never mind. You get better. Mom will fix you right up. She's the best nurse ever."

"She needs to sleep, son. And you do, too. Go find another room and take a shower. Then get back to bed. I'll have Helen disinfect *everything* tomorrow. Go!"

If I open my eyes to watch him, conflicted between staying healthy and staying with me, I'll lose it. In more than one way. I squeeze my eyes shut more tightly and focus on breathing to keep the nausea at bearable levels.

"I love you," he says.

"Love you, too," I mumble back, hearing Gloria say the same thing.

She laughs. "Oops. I thought you were talking to me."

"I love you, too, Mom," he says, a rueful smile in his voice. "Even if you *are* kicking me out of my own bedroom."

"It's for your own good. Now, go! And don't you worry; I'll have her good to go in time for Dallas."

TEN

## THE COVER-UP

I'm ready, all right. Ready to be anywhere other than that damn bed, with Gloria nagging me to, "Drink this water," "Try some toast," "Stretch your legs," "Take some ibuprofen," and —my favorite—"Pee on this."

Yes, when I rallied for two days in a row but had relapses at the same time both evenings, she brought a pregnancy test into the room as if she were sneaking contraband to a prisoner and demanded I go into the bathroom and submit to the test. I did, but only to put *her* mind at ease. I was already perfectly confident that pregnancy is about the only complication I'm not currently experiencing.

When the test came back negative, as expected, I showed it to her, threw up, and shuffled back to bed.

If she's had any lingering concerns about false negatives during the longest week of my life, they're well and truly put to rest this morning at the first sight of her son.

"Oh, Jet, you look terrible!"

My eyes snap up from the bowl of plain oatmeal and dry toast triangles I've been attempting to eat as my proof I'm well enough to be back among the living and, further, to go to work later today. Sure enough, Jet's sporting the greenish-gray pallor I've seen in the mirror this week, plus a pair of purplish under-eye circles.

*Noooooooooo!*

He waves off his mom's concern and the plate stacked high with pancakes hot off the griddle. "I'm fine. Nerves. Didn't sleep well last night." When Gloria tries once again to slide the plate of hotcakes in front of him as he sits at the breakfast bar, he pushes them away. "No thanks."

"But they're buckwheat! Beau said that's what you always eat on travel days."

"Not this one."

"You have to keep your strength up."

"The game's six days from now. I'll be okay."

"But how are you going to travel like that? Or practice? Or sit through press conferences? Media day is tomorrow!"

Ned sets down his tablet and lifts his coffee mug to his mouth but says before drinking, "Gloria. Give the guy a break."

It's the first time I've ever heard him tell her to do anything, and if I weren't so weak, I'd react more strongly, but all I can do is mumble toward my bowl, "I'm so sorry."

"Why?" Jet asks.

"I got you sick!"

"I'm not sick."

"Yes, you are. You look... I've never seen you look like that."

"Like I said, I'm nervous, that's all. See? I'm fine." He pulls his plate of pancakes closer and cuts a bite with the side of his fork. But it barely clears his lips before he has to set the utensil down again. He swallows three times in rapid succession, then vaults from his bar stool and rushes from the kitchen toward the nearest bathroom. Through the walls, we hear the evidence that contradicts his claims of being "fine."

"This is a nightmare," Gloria says, wringing her hands.

I fold my arms on the surface in front of me and rest my forehead on them.

"Now, now," Ned consoles the two of us. "It'll be okay. He's a strong, healthy guy. He won't be down long."

Gloria moans. "He can't be down at all! He has to travel today. With the rest of the team! What if he gets *them* sick? Everyone will blame him if they lose."

"If they lose, everyone's going to blame him, anyway."

"Not necessarily! Kickers screw up. Coaches call bad plays. Receivers and runners fumble. Refs blow calls."

While my in-laws argue the myriad ways the team could implode next Sunday, I slink from the room to check on the guy currently blowing his stomach contents into a toilet. I knock but don't wait for an acknowledgment before nudging the unlatched door wider so I can enter.

"Are you okay?"

He quickly pushes himself to his feet, flushes the toilet, and smiles weakly at me on his way to the sink, where he rinses his mouth and splashes water on his face. Through the mirror, he says to me, "I'm much better now."

"I knew I should have gone home and stayed away from you, but it was probably too late, anyway, and your mom... She was holding me hostage up there! Now you're sick. And the Super Bowl is—"

"I'm the one who kept sneaking in to check on you." Head hanging, he grips the sides of the vanity. "It's— It's going to be okay. I'm hardly ever sick. And when I am, it's not for long. It's good I threw up. I won't do it again."

Recalling my own experience from the past couple of days, which would contradict his prediction, I rest my hand in the middle of his back but choose to say nothing to that. Heat soaks through his shirt to my palm. "You're burning up."

"I am? I'm freezing." His arms tremble, but he squeezes the counter more tightly, and they still. "Here's what we're going to do."

Hope lightens my chest. Normally, I hate plans, but even I have to admit we're desperate for one here. *Okay. Yes. A plan!*

"You're going to call Rae. And tell her what's happening. And she's going to meet us at the training complex before we have to leave for the airport. She's going to give me an IV of magic stuff to make me feel better. I'm going to fly to Dallas with the team. Nobody's going to know any of this is happening."

"Until *they* get sick. You can't be around the other guys."

He sighs. "Okay. Right. I guess Coach needs to know what's going on. And the Wises. I'll fly with them."

"How are you going to explain to the team and to the media that you're hitching a ride on the owners' private jet?"

"Coach will figure it out."

"Jet, people are going to have to know."

His eyes bulge. "No. They can't. Nobody can find out. Because then the Panthers will know I'm weak. And they'll target me. And I'll ruin everything."

I rub his gooseflesh-covered arms. "All right. All right. Shhh. I'll call Rae; you call Coach Bauer. We'll start there."

———

That's how I ended up on a private jet, rather than behind my desk, on this Monday morning, days before my originally planned departure for Dallas.

Rae, Jet, and I stole onto team owners Lyle and Brendan Wise's plane with a small army of other people, including Rae's boss, an older guy I only know as "Doc." Coach Bauer accompanied the rest of the team on the bus to the airport and described the situation to them before boarding the charter, while they still had some privacy. Until Jet is no longer contagious, he's going to be kept separate from the others. To justify his separation from the team, the media has been told he's had a family emergency that will limit his availability, but he'll be joining the team and participating in pre-game events whenever possible.

In the meantime, Rae and a handful of the team's other medical professionals are working furiously to manage his symptoms.

"You can't rush a virus," she says, something I wish she'd been around to tell Gloria last week.

Doc tapes down Jet's IV, reclines the patient's seat, covers him with two blankets, and adds, "But we're gonna do our damnedest to trick his body into thinking everything's fine."

Jet closes his eyes and licks his chapped lips. "I already feel a lot better."

"You're going to feel like Superman by the time we're done with you," Rae says, uncharacteristically sunny.

I drag her aside and whisper, "What's in that IV, anyway?"

"Nothing illegal!"

I pull my head back at her preemptive defensiveness. "Okay..."

She checks her tone. "It's all perfectly above-board. Nothing that would get anyone in trouble. Plus, it will have cleared his system before the game. Electrolytes for rehydration and anti-emetics for his nausea. And Valium."

"Valium?"

"His body's going to take that much longer to fight this bug if he's uptight. Do I need to have Doc prescribe some for you, too?"

"No. I'm fine. I'm—" I lean closer to her and whisper, "I'm freaking out that I got him sick before Super Bowl week, of all times."

"Yeah. Way to go, dillhole," she says at normal volume.

"I didn't mean to!"

But I also didn't make him leave when he'd come up to visit me, under the guise of "taking a shower" or "resting" or "making some calls." They were never long trysts, usually stolen moments here and there after his mom went to bed or while she was eating or showering, but he sat on the side of the mattress and commiserated about his smothering mom and kissed my hand and forehead. I was so starved for contact with him—with anyone other than Gloria, in fact—that I selfishly allowed him to expose himself to my illness, like the teenager who foolishly believes the stupid things she does will never have consequences.

These are huge consequences.

And the one time Gloria came to check on me while he was still with me, he stole into the closet and waited her out for more than thirty minutes while she fussed around me and tried to force a decision from me about centerpieces for the wedding reception. I faked dozing off in the middle of our conversation to get her to leave.

Jet emerged, sweaty and pale, from the closet. "I don't like tight spaces," he said, wiping his brow. (Yet another thing I didn't know about him.)

Now, I buckle into the seat next to him while the pilot does his pre-flight checks, and everyone else settles into their spots, as far away from us as possible, looking more tense than they would if the plane didn't hold such an important patient. And so many germs.

He grabs my hand and pulls it under the blanket, resting it on his leg. "This was my plan all along, so we could spend more time together this week," he says, eyes still closed but lips twitching upward.

"Yeah, well, your plan sucks."

"It'll be okay, babe."

"It's not okay. This is horrible."

In an attempt to get more comfortable, he rubs the back of his head against his seat. "Remember last time we were on this plane? For the Pro Bowl?"

"Of course." It was the most surreal experience of my life, to date. So much has happened since then, but I'll never forget that first trip to Hawaii with him.

He sighs. "I already loved you so much."

"No, you didn't! We hardly knew each other."

"Didn't matter. I told my mom, 'I'm gonna marry Maura Richards.'"

Patting his leg, I try not to snort-laugh, but I do roll my suddenly much-moister eyes. "Yeah, right."

"It sounds cheesy, like something from a dumb movie, but you can ask her. I said it."

"I'm sure she was thrilled, too."

He opens his eyes, suddenly clear and bright. The drugs must be kicking in. "For the first time in my life, I didn't care how she felt about something. It wasn't about her. It was about you. And me."

"In other words, she told you you were crazy."

He grins. "Maybe." His smile abruptly fades.

"You need the barf bucket?" I ask, reaching across him for it before he can answer.

He holds me in place and shakes his head. "No. I'm fine. I've never been better."

"Somehow, I doubt that."

"I want you to know that if I had to choose between winning the Super Bowl and being there for you, in sickness and in health, I choose you every time."

"That's the Valium talking, sweetie," I say through a tight throat.

"No, it's not. Because you'd sacrifice just as much for me. And whatever happens on Sunday, it's only a game. Compared to everything else that's ahead of you and me, it's— It's nothing."

I blink and try to compose myself enough to respond, but he's oblivious to the effect his words have had on me. Squeezing my fingers, he closes his eyes. "Sleepy. So, so sleepy..."

## ELEVEN

## NURSE MAURA

Yet again, I'm confined to a relatively small room with a bed as its main feature. Two beds, in fact. One for Rae—as it's her room—and one for me. Families aren't supposed to arrive until Wednesday evening, so I have to keep a low profile to avoid becoming a bigger distraction than my germs have already caused. In other words, I'm in quasi-hiding.

The other person Rae was supposed to be rooming with, her girlfriend, Ana Paula, has graciously offered to stay on the couch in a room with two other trainers. We'll redistribute as soon as my suite is available with the rest of Jet's guest reservation block tomorrow night.

For someone as content with solitude as I am, this is still a stir-crazy situation. I've read eleventy billion books, reached the end of the Internet, and racked up some major expenses with pay-per-view and room service. It's Day Two.

I wish Colin were here. I text him periodically throughout the day, but he's at work, so he can't always get back to me or engage in long conversations. He won't be arriving with everyone else, either, because when he found out how much the players were paying for each of their guests' tickets, he refused to attend, on principle.

"That's vulgar. I'll simply watch and support via telly, thank you. Perhaps I'll go to a pub, so I can feel part of a community—and have someone nearby to enlighten me when I don't understand what's happening. But no, I can't afford those tickets, and Jet's already shelled out enough dosh for me to accompany you to all those postseason matches. I'll be there with you in spirit, Lady Maura."

His spirit's not doing me much good in this boring hotel room. But I respect his point. All of this *is* a bit over-the-top and not at all something he'd enjoy.

Finally, Rae finishes with work for the day and returns to our room, where we play cards while I talk her ear off until Jet arrives, chalk-white, shaky, and solemn.

He collapses face-down on the bed. Rae observes his theatrics with nary a twitch or move to do anything about it, but I rush to his side, raking my fingers through his hair with one hand and rubbing his back with the other. "What can I do?"

After a long pause, he says, "Go back in time and get rid of Media Day as a thing."

From her position across the room at the table, Rae laughs. "I heard it was ridiculous."

"I had a Chinese entertainment reporter ask me who I thought would win in a fight between Kim Kardashian and Beyoncé. I thought the translator got the question wrong. But no. That was really what they wanted me to weigh in on."

I wait for him to continue, but when he doesn't, I ask, "Well? What did you say? I'd pick Queen Bey. Although, I can see Kim K. fighting dirty."

"I dodged the question, I think."

"You think?" Rae asks.

"I was trying pretty hard not to puke by then. My anti-barf drugs were wearing off. I said something about boxing not being my sport."

I squeeze the back of his clammy neck. "Good call. Way to think on your feet."

"This is so miserable," he whines. "It's supposed to be fun. I'm supposed to be recording this on my phone like all the other guys and goofing off and giving witty answers to all these questions, especially the stupid ones from people who make no sense being here. But all I can think is, 'How many people are getting sick because of me?' and 'How the hell am I going to play football when I can't even put a sentence together?' and 'How obvious is it that I'm half-stoned out of my mind to get through all this?'"

Rae stands. "Uh, you're not 'stoned.'"

"Whatever."

"No. We have to be clear and consistent on that. You're under legitimate medical treatment for an illness."

"Except nobody knows that. So I seem stoned. Or mysteriously absent. Like now. All the other guys are together, laughing about the dumb questions they had to answer and comparing notes. And I'm face down on this bed."

Sliding the legs of his track pants up, I massage his calves. "It's only Tuesday. You'll be better in a couple of days. I promise. It's amazing how fast your body can recover. And yours will recover faster than mine, because you're in much better shape, and you're getting IVs to keep your electrolytes up." *And your mom's not in your face, harassing you about wedding plans and force-feeding you salty soup.*

"Speaking of..." Rae steps into the hallway. "I'll be right

back. You kids keep it clean in here." She closes the door, which latches and locks, leaving Jet and me in stifling silence.

I don't know what else to say. Or if I should say anything. The last thing I want is to be like Gloria, cloying and annoying and convinced I can chat the illness away, so I say nothing.

He doesn't seem able to process a pep talk or do much more than breathe and exist, anyway. And I get it. The muscle cramps, chills, and nausea are fresh in my memory. All I wanted was to sleep until my body decided to stop hating me.

Within seconds, he *is* asleep, so the pressure's off. I grab the extra thermal blanket from the shelf in the wardrobe and drape it over him. He curls into a ball and scoots higher onto the pillows so his feet no longer hang off the corner of the mattress.

Rae returns with Doc. While the two professionals rouse Jet and insert the IV, I wet a washcloth in the bathroom and retrieve a bottle of water from the mini fridge. As soon as I'm sure the fluids are flowing and the injection site covered from view, I return to the bed. Doc and Rae excuse themselves, promising to be back when they estimate the IV will be finished.

With a weak smile, Jet takes the bottle of water I offer to him. "Thanks." The color returns to his cheeks as the cocktail in the bag next to us drains into his veins.

I place the washcloth on his forehead. "You gonna be okay?"

"Of course. This is a dream come true, right?" The folded wet fabric slips lower, toward his eyes, so he props his water bottle in his lap to free up a hand and hold the cloth in place. "I'm sorry I keep falling asleep in the middle of conversations. Did I say anything sappy this time?"

I laugh. "No. And what you said on the plane wasn't sappy. It was touching."

His color deepens further. "I guess."

"What are you saying? You didn't mean it?"

He tilts his head back, takes another swig of water, and keeps his face pointed toward the ceiling for a hands-free washcloth experience. "Oh, I meant every word. But it's not very manly to blurt your deepest feelings."

"Screw manly. Manly is overrated."

"Then right about now I'm seriously… rated." He chuckles at his inarticulate statement. "Oh, gosh. I hope I didn't say anything that stupid on-the-record today."

"I'm sure you were great. What's up tomorrow?"

He sighs. "Practice. Running through the stuff we planned last week."

"Oh."

"Yep. I'm sure I'll feel better in the morning. Right?" He cracks an eyelid to catch my reaction to his prediction.

"Yes. Absolutely. You'll feel better every day. The nausea was almost gone by the third day, and I was mostly tired. Still no appetite, but…"

"Is that the day my mom made you take the pregnancy test?"

His twitching mouth is somewhat of an indicator of his feelings on the matter, but his eyes are closed again, so I can't tell for sure what he's thinking.

"How did you know about that?" I ask, rather than directly answering.

"She told me." He licks his lips. "Said something like, 'At least things aren't *that* bad,' and I about came unglued. Told her it was none of her business, anyway, but if we *were* going to have a baby, I'd be thrilled."

*I'm sure.*

"That's not part of your plan right now," I say, making sure to inject plenty of teasing into my tone. "You have a Super Bowl to win and a few more seasons to play before that, right?"

He pauses, then opens his eyes and lowers his head. The washcloth plops into his lap. "In theory? Yeah. I guess. But after I was finished being mad at my mom for what she did and what she said, I realized I was mostly disappointed. Because having a baby with you would be awesome."

"But not right now." That nausea I claimed was gone returns with a vengeance.

"Whenever."

"But not now."

He holds my eye contact. "No. I guess not."

I pluck the washcloth from his lap and try to put it on his head again, but he waves it off, so I use it as an excuse to put some distance between us and take it into the bathroom.

"Anyway!" he says. "Everyone will be here tomorrow, and you'll be able to check into your own room, so that'll be good."

I clear my throat so I can match his brightness. "Yeah! It'll be nice to move freely throughout the hotel and the city. And I never thought I'd say this, but it'll be good to see my brother."

"I still can't believe he's coming here without Deirdre."

"She doesn't want to travel this close to her due date."

"Yeah, I get that. I can't believe *he's* coming, anyway."

"Like he told me, 'There'll be other kids.'"

Jet's laugh holds plenty of wince. "Ouch. On more than one level. I guess he thinks this is the one and only time the team is ever getting to the big show."

"He realizes how incredible this is, and he's not taking it

for granted. Plus, they're still three weeks from their due date. It's not that big of a risk."

"I would never do that."

Since I'm still in the bathroom, folding and refolding the washcloth I'll eventually throw in the heap of soiled towels on the floor, it's safe to roll my eyes, as long as I keep my voice steady when I say, "Noted."

And disregarded, because he most likely won't have a bit of control over that. He knows it, too. Returning to that topic is definitely something I want to avoid, though, so I toss the wet fabric square over my shoulder, turn off the light, and return to the room. The IV bag is more than half-empty (or is it half-full?), and Jet's complexion is almost back to normal.

"You look much better."

"I feel much better."

"Excellent. You'll get a good night's sleep, and there's no substitute for that."

He wiggles his eyebrows at me. "There's something else that would help me sleep."

Now I do roll my eyes so he can see, and he laughs. Truth is, I'd be all about it, but that tube running from his arm to that bag is kind of ruining it for me. I crawl up the bed, kiss his chin, and stretch out along his right side, using his chest as a pillow. "Don't be a tease. Now, tell me about the itinerary for the rest of the week. How much quality together time will your mother and I have?"

———

The answer is, "A lot." So much quality time that by Saturday, when the team departs our current hotel to move to their pre-game lodgings, away from all distractions, including family and friends as much as the media, I'm not above begging them to take me with them. But I resist the selfish urge and join the throng of well-wishers in the lobby for our final goodbyes.

It's not the time to make it about me. Cyndi arrived at the hotel barely in time to give her brother a good-luck hug, and since nobody in the family has seen her or Mikey in nearly two years, she's the deserved star of the moment—after Jet, of course.

It's actually a relief. With all of the sickness drama (which is finally over, thank goodness), I'd forgotten I'd be the subject of media scrutiny, myself, this week, as Jet's soon-to-be-wife. Gotta keep people not that interested in sports riveted to the human interest stories, like they do during the Olympics. Duty dictated I submit to more than one interview, which— under normal circumstances—would have been a nightmare. However, sitting down with that *People* reporter released me from yet another hectic family excursion. Then I skipped one more when *TMZ* and *Entertainment Tonight* wanted to do a joint interview. Friday, I was practically seeking out the media to solicit more opportunities for escape. An agent would have come in handy.

Now, while I'm giving Jet and his baby sister as much privacy as they can get in a lobby jammed with a few hundred people and saying, "So long," to Rae and Ana Paula, who are passing through on their way to the charter bus outside, a pair of large hands encircles my waist from behind.

Near my ear, Jet whispers, "Hey, Beautiful. Got a minute to wish me luck?"

Rae smiles and waves one last time. "See you on the bus, Knox. Don't keep us all waiting, like some big shot."

I turn to face him, relieved to see his characteristic twinkling eyes and playful grin. The rest of the room fades into a blurry murmur around us. For the first time all week, I'm not worried about anyone else. I'm not worried about any*thing*. It finally hits me why we're here. This isn't a crazy family vacation, or even a weird away game experience. This is The Big Show. My stomach clenches, and my heart races. I lick my lips and try to focus on the person holding me, not the enormity of what he's going to have to do tomorrow in front of millions of viewers. Swallowing is suddenly a tall order.

"Look at you," I manage to choke out. "This is it, huh?"

He looks toward his forehead and closes one eye. "It will be, yes. After the longest night of my life, followed by the longest day of my life."

"They'll keep you busy. You look ready."

"I am. I wish we could play tonight."

"Sorry. The stadium's not reserved until tomorrow."

He chuckles. "Darn." Sobering, he tucks a piece of hair behind my ear. "Hey, uh, I know it's going to be a long twenty-four hours for you, too."

I flap my hand at him. "Bah. Don't worry about all of us. We'll be fine. It's time for you to focus on the team and the mission."

"Sounds like we're talking about something much more important than a football game." He takes a deep breath. "But we're not. So. Whatever. Win or lose, this has been an unbelievable experience."

"That's a great attitude."

"Isn't it?"

"But you need to win tomorrow."

"Got it."

"Good." I study his face one more time, trying to memorize how he looks, how this feels, before everything changes. Because no matter the outcome tomorrow, going through it will alter us, as individuals. Maybe not as much as we hope (or fear), but slight change is still change. And I like the way we are now.

Therefore, I'm using this as a save point. If the changes that result from this weekend aren't for the better, I want to remember this moment, this feeling, this *version* of us, so well that I can get us back to here, if need be. System restore.

Cool air hits me as the crowd shifts and thins around us. I spy several players pushing their way through the doors to head outside.

"Well, Number Fourteen, you're about to miss the bus."

He looks around. "They *will* leave without me, too. They're about done with my high-maintenance bullshit this week. Who do I think I am, anyway? Drew McKnight?"

We share a laugh at the expense of one of the league's most notorious prima donna QBs, and before things can get serious again, I throw my arms around his neck and say, "Do *not* break a leg tomorrow. Or anything, for that matter."

"Hey, no promises," he murmurs next to my head, squeezing me tightly. "I'm leaving it all out there."

"I would expect nothing less. It's one of the million things I love about you." I close my eyes for two beats before pushing away and waving him off. "Now, get out of here. Everyone's staring at us."

With a final wave to the cheering crowd, he and a few other stragglers exit the lobby and climb the bus steps without a glance back.

## TWELVE

## LITTLE SISTER

A knock on my door interrupts my preparation for another—hopefully the last in a while—insane dinner experience, courtesy of the Knox Family Circus. I expect to find Gloria in the hallway, so I'm pleasantly surprised to see Cyndi, with Mikey on her hip.

My relief dies a quick death when she pushes past me and sets her son on my bed, saying, "I can't go to this dinner."

I close the door. "What's the matter?"

She paces at the foot of the bed. While I wait for her to answer, I note for the umpteenth time since meeting her that it seems they ran out of material by the time the baby of the Knox family was born. She's tiny by any standard, much less theirs. But somehow she still looks like the rest of them, only in miniature. She's the Tinkerbell of the clan, with her pixie-cut hair, button nose, and those green eyes. She's adorable. And obviously distressed at the moment.

Finally, she stops and says, "I need a break. I mean, I haven't been around them in so long. I forgot. I forgot how overwhelming and... and... obnoxious— No. That's a bad word."

"Bad word!" Mikey parrots.

She smiles down at him and smooths his hair away from his forehead but quickly returns her attention to me. "You know what I mean? Or no? You're used to it already? Dear Lord. I'm sorry. It's just... I-I'm half a world away from them. All the time. And... and I like it that way. That makes me a bad person, probably, but—"

"It doesn't make you a bad person."

"And now we're here, and... it's this crazy experience, even crazier than it would normally be when we're all together, and this is about Jet. I get that." She presses her hand to her forehead and takes a deep breath. "But we're supposed to go out to dinner as a group? Where? Where the heck are we all going to fit? I'm not hungry, anyway." Her hand falls to her stomach. "I'm so nervous for my brother and wondering what he's going through right now. I don't want to sit next to Keith, who's playing the big man, because he lives in this obscene state. I don't want to hear David recite the plays he thinks the team should use tomorrow. Even Gidget's getting on my nerves. All she does is complain about her kids. Constantly. And the kids... Oh, my gosh." She rubs her temples. "They're so loud. All the time. I'm not loud. Justin's not loud. Mikey's not loud... most of the time. We're quiet people. Was I hatched?"

"Uh, maybe?"

Hand still on her stomach, she paces. Mikey watches her and giggles at what he perceives to be silliness. "And Mom. Poor Mom. As nervous as I am, she must be coming apart inside. That's her baby boy who's going to be out there. All those years of practices and injuries and watching awful games in the rain are about to pay off—or not—so I under-stand she has to focus on something else, but can that some-thing else not be me? Or your wedding? I can't hear about centerpieces anymore. And I've only been here a few hours."

"You'll get used to it."

"Yeah. Okay. But not tonight. Tomorrow. We have all day tomorrow with them, remember?"

I could never forget.

"Tonight I need to not be with them."

"Okay. You want me to tell them you're sick? Jet-lagged?"

She plops onto the end of the bed. Distracted, she puts her arms around Mikey and kisses his head when he scrambles into her lap. "No. Please. Please, don't leave me alone. I realize you just met me, and this probably seems so weird, but—"

"I get it more than you might realize." Tapping my lips, I come up with a plan. "Okay, how's this? I'll tell your mom that your body clock is saying it's one in the morning, which is true. That's late, especially for that little guy!" I nod toward Mikey.

"He slept all the way here on the plane, so he's doing better than I am."

"She doesn't have to know that. I'll also tell her that you and I want to get to know each other better. She'll eat that up. You're going to California with your parents to visit for a few days after this, right?"

She looks down at the carpet and mumbles, "Yeah. Some-thing like that."

"Then it won't be that big of a deal if you skip one dinner. Hang on. I'll be right back."

When I return from Gloria and Ned's room, Cyndi's already flipping through the channels on the TV, trying to find something for Mikey to watch. She looks expectantly at me as I close the door.

"We're all set," I say, deciding it's not important for her to know it wasn't as straightforward convincing Gloria of our modified plan as I thought it would be. Instead, moving on with the evening, I pick up the phone on the bedside table. "Room service?"

"I think I'm going to love you," she says to me, her green eyes brimming.

———

A couple of hours later, Cyndi gets her second wind, but Mikey's down for the count. I help her tuck him under the blankets after she asks me about thirty times if I'm sure it's okay for the toddler to sleep in my bed. With the soft lamp-light and at this angle, the two-year-old looks remarkably like his namesake.

Cyndi catches me staring and says, "It's creepy, isn't it? We all look the same. -Ish."

"Uh-huh." I tilt my head, and the resemblance isn't as strong. But straight on again, and there it is. Mini-Micah.

As I repeatedly tilt and straighten my head, I giggle at the phenomenon. Cyndi makes a noise I initially mistake for a mirthful snort, but when I look more closely at her, I see her face has crumpled.

"Oh, no," I say, rushing around to her side of the bed. But when I arrive there, I'm not sure what to do. My instinct tells me to comfort her. But how? Is she a hugger, or will that make it worse? Thinking fast, I wrap one arm around her, drawing her to my side. "Hey. Are you okay?"

"No!" she wails. "I'm not okay!"

Mikey stirs, so she covers her mouth to stifle her sobs and turns into me, pressing her face against my chest.

Okay. Well, this is… intimate.

I pat her back. Since I barely know this person, I can't begin to guess what's wrong, much less offer any words of meaningful encouragement, so I keep rubbing her back until she muffles against my shirt, "I'm not going back to Germany. Ever."

I freeze.

She pushes away from me and flicks tears from her face before turning and grabbing a tissue from the box on the nightstand. Following a dainty snot-clearing, she says to the ceiling, "I was going to wait until after your wedding, because I didn't want to put a damper on your and Jet's happy day."

"You shouldn't worry about that."

"But then this opportunity came along, and I grabbed it."

So many questions. Yet I don't even know where to start.

Fortunately, Cyndi does. I follow her to the pair of chairs by the window and listen for the next hour as she describes her failing marriage, being so far away from everything and everyone she's ever known, and—the complication to complicate all others—expecting her second child. Unexpectedly, of course.

"Then I get here, and I— I realize I don't know how to be around my own family anymore. I can't live over there"—she gestures in the vicinity of Canada, maybe, but my sense of direction isn't all that great, so she could be pointing straight to Europe, for all I know—"and I'm having panic attacks here." Her voice chokes off. "What am I going to do?"

She's asking me? The Queen of Inconclusiveness? I can't make adult decisions to save my life, much less someone else's. And when that life involves one—two!—children? No way. No how. No—

"First, you're going to cut yourself some slack and remember you just landed here. Like, hours ago. You're exhausted, you're stressed out, and you're overwhelmed."

She sniffs and dabs at her eyes with a balled-up tissue. "Don't forget hormonal."

"Oh, I haven't." I laugh sadly. "But good point."

"I thought this would be perfect, because the excitement would distract me from my problems, but..." She stares at her hand dangling from the arm of the chair for several seconds, studying the light as it glints off the diamond in her engagement ring. Then she looks up at me and smiles. "Never mind. It's not turning out the way I planned. But it would have been a thousand times worse if all this was fresh at your wedding."

Ah, yes. That thing.

"Listen, if you can't or don't want to—"

"No! I do want to. Are you kidding? We've been trying to marry off Jet forever."

When I pull a face, she explains, "All of my friends had crushes on him. It was so annoying. I swear, most of them didn't like *me* that much; they only wanted to hang out at our house for the chance to see *him*. Ugh. I tried to tell them he was gross and walked around in his underwear all the time, but that only made them more eager for sleepovers."

I laugh, which prompts a mischievous smile from Cyndi.

Really getting into her story now, her eyes glimmering, she continues her affectionate tale-telling about her big brother. "I'd beg Gidget, Keith, and David to set him up with girls from their classes; that way, I could tell my friends, 'He has a girlfriend.' It didn't work half the time, though. He was so focused on football. The coaches beat it into the players that they didn't have time for girls. Anyway, when he did have someone he liked enough to date or ask to dances, that made him more unattainable and attractive to my friends. Teenage girls are so stupid." She blinks down at her fidgeting hands. "I feel like one right now, though."

"You're not stupid."

"Yeah, I am. I want what I can't have: an uncomplicated life, back here in the States, with a husband who's not married to the military and still makes me feel like we did when we were first together." She stares into space. "Nobody has that last thing. That excitement fades with familiarity. It's unavoidable. Then you're stuck with someone who eats food straight from the can, pees in the shower, grunts responses to questions, and never says, 'I love you.' Except during sex. Which doesn't count."

"I'm pretty sure that counts."

My interjection startles her from her trance. "What? Oh. Yeah, I guess. But not if it's the *only* time he says it. It's like saying 'Bless you' after someone sneezes. It's a reflex."

I wrinkle my nose at that somewhat unappealing comparison when my brain takes it all the way to its snotty conclusion.

Cyndi seems oblivious to my disgust. "Anyway! I'm sorry I'm such a downer. I can tell you and Jet are still in that great first phase of your relationship, where you can ignore each other's faults or still see them as cute quirks, and that's the way it should be. I'm not trying to play the part of the cynical marriage veteran. That's more annoying than high-school Jet walking around in his underwear, scratching his crotch in front of my friends."

I laugh at the thought of it. "He outgrew that, by the way."

She smiles, too, and sighs. "And not all familiarity breeds

contempt. My parents are still in love—or at least they can still tolerate each other. Your parents seem happy. My siblings seem relatively content with their spouses, after several years together. Maybe it's me. Maybe I'm expecting too much. Maybe there was no way my life could match my expectations." Smiling dreamily, she recalls, "It seemed so romantic, marrying my man in uniform and being whisked away to a different country. None of my brothers or sisters or friends had that. They were stuck here, in the boring U.S.A." She blinks her eyes back into focus. "Except Jet. His life was always going to be exciting and glamorous. But I didn't want what Gidget or my brothers' wives had: an upper-middle-class existence marked by a new minivan every four years or kitchen and bathroom renovations. I wanted something more exotic than that. Life on a military post isn't anything close to 'exotic,' though."

"I wouldn't think so."

"Well, I was young and stupid and didn't know any better. I thought, different country, different world. But it's not. It's America—with lame substitutions for everything we have here—plunked down in the middle of Europe."

"You're still young, you know."

"I don't feel it. I feel old. And beaten down. And discouraged. And that's not the jet lag talking. I've felt that way since it became obvious that having kids hasn't changed things for Justin and me. If anything, it's made things worse." She slaps the top of her thighs and stands. "There I go again." On her way to the bathroom, she says, "When I'm finished in here, how about we talk about something else?"

"Not weddings."

"No."

"Or football."

"Definitely not. It hurts my stomach thinking about tomorrow. How about we watch a movie?"

"Okay." I reach for the remote.

"No rom coms, though," she qualifies. "Or weepies."

This sounds like a job for Jason Bourne.

## THIRTEEN

## SUPER BOWL SUNDAY

*This* is how a bride feels, I bet, as she waits in her uncomfortable dress with her hair shellacked and her makeup too perfect for her to attempt anything more than breathing. Except I'm not at a church in a dress, all dolled up. I'm in a temple built for the football gods, the largest stadium in the NFL, dressed in my lucky Knox jersey, and it's a miracle I have any hair left. Or makeup. I'm an emotional mess.

Trust me, that's earned me several scrutinizing glares from my future mother-in-law, but I'm not peeing on anything in her presence on Super Bowl Sunday. Or ever again, for that matter. In due time, she'll know everything her youngest daughter is going through, and her focus will most definitely shift to her. Thank God.

Okay, that sounds cold. I'm sorry Cyndi's having a rough time, and I'll be here for her, whatever she needs, but I'd be lying if I said I hadn't thought of how it would affect the level of attention I'm currently suffering... er, receiving from Gloria.

Cyndi and I both fell asleep fully clothed during the second

*Bourne* movie last night and this morning tiptoed around each other like two people recovering from a one-night-stand.

Finally, Cyndi said, "Is this the part where we exchange numbers we never plan to call?"

Relieved she was getting the same vibe, I laughed. "I don't know. As commitment phobic as I was in my early twenties, I still don't have much experience with that. What's the protocol?"

"Like I'd know! I was practically a child bride."

Unlike two typical lovers of convenience, however, we've remained inseparable all day, keeping each other moderately sane. When I've recognized the wild-eyed look, similar to the one she was sporting when she arrived at my room last night, I've pulled her away from her family for a few minutes. And I must exhibit my own nonverbal cues when I'm imagining everything that could go wrong during tonight's game, because I never wander too far into my scary daydreams before she tells Mikey to show me one of his tricks or sing one of his songs. Or she'll ask me to keep an eye on him during her frequent trips to the bathroom. I take my responsibility seriously—and literally—not taking my eyes off the kid the whole time she's gone. Since the kid's had a full night's sleep, he's unstoppable. Keeping him alive while in my temporary care has required every ounce of my concentration today.

But there's no distracting me now that it's game-time and all twenty of us are here, in the stands. The kids have their hearing protection—that's a thing now—which I'm pretty jealous of, to be honest. If only I could put on a set of noise-canceling headphones and block out everything for the next three hours. A blindfold wouldn't be unwelcome, either. Those things might be construed as "weird," but if my brother keeps tapping my shoulder every three minutes, I might go back to the hotel and watch from my room. Alone. Yes. That sounds lovely.

At one point, I half-rise to do exactly that before I realize what I'm doing and that I can't. From her seat directly behind me, Mom rests her hand on my shoulder and shouts near my ear, "Are you okay, dear? Isn't this exciting?"

That's one word for it. Like a ride in a barrel down Niagara Falls.

I merely nod.

"You might want to touch up your lipstick. You look pale, and I'm sure they'll be getting shots of you on camera during the game."

Great. Another thing to worry about. Do I look pretty enough to hold up to scrutiny on the big screen as I sit through this torture? No way.

Cyndi, sitting right next to me, grabs my hand and squeezes. "You look fine. Hey, some lady's waving at you, trying to get your attention." She points down our row, past her parents, who are both sitting ramrod straight in their seats, like the Queen of England is about to enter the stadium. At least their nerves are keeping them silent.

As I follow Cyndi's gesture, I see Sandy Bauer, Coach's wife, and give her a stiff smile and wave. She mouths, *"It'll be fine!"* and I laugh at how it seems like she's telling herself that as much as me.

I blow my bangs off my forehead and make a shooting motion toward my temple. My pantomime makes her giggle, and her cheeks flush. Maybe we can do this the entire game and keep each other entertained and distracted. But after that, she turns her attention to the field as the teams arrive amid an epileptic's nightmare of strobe lights and indoor pyrotechnics.

For the millionth time, I wish I was watching this on TV,

away from here, in private. A private suite at the stadium would have worked, too, but Jet and I agreed it wasn't fair how many other players' families didn't get that choice, so we opted for seats in the stands, among the general population. Seemed like a good, noble idea at the time. Now, I'm regretting that impulse. Screw "noble." Just kidding. Sort of. Not really.

I stand with everyone else and crane my neck to get my first glimpse of Jet. Our seats are excellent, but it's still hard to see his face. The cameras are getting some extreme close-ups, I can tell, and I'm jealous. Then I remember the enormous screen above us, and I zoom in on that.

Sure enough, there he is, bigger than life, looking exactly as he ought to look: focused, strong, and confident. Only his swaying from foot-to-foot belies his nerves. The shot switches to the other team's quarterback, so I have to rely on my far sight once more. Can he sense me staring at him? Can he hear me silently willing him not to run with the ball so much tonight? Would he heed my advice, if he could hear me? I'd probably be better off sending a message he'd be happy to receive, so I close my eyes.

*I love you. I'm proud of you. I've missed you every minute we've been apart this season and this week. Okay, that's a tiny exaggeration, but whatever. I can't wait to spend the rest of my life with you. So, let's do whatever we can to ensure we have a future. In other words, get rid of the ball and don't run with it so much. Don't get yourself killed out there.*

He tilts his head back, closes his eyes, and laughs. My heartbeat stutters so hard, it moves my hair. Then he half-turns and punches Jackson in the shoulder, and I realize he must have been reacting to something his buddy said, not anything I was thinking.

Of course.

Duh.

I've officially lost it.

The announcer tells us to rise for the National Anthem.

Here we go!

————

My first mistake is to relax in the fourth quarter, when we're ahead by fourteen points. A comeback of this magnitude, this late in the game, on such a big stage, is rare, if not impossible. Therefore, I allow myself to feel giddy, to believe Jet's dream and the dreams of thousands of Kansas City fans, including me, is about to come true. They're going to be champions, and the Lombardi trophy is coming back to KC after decades away.

One glance at the sidelines, and there's no need for a scoreboard to tell which team is winning and which is not. Between series, the Chiefs players slap each other on their backs, laughing and reliving their favorite moments. On the field, the defense remains all-business, not wanting to give a single inch of this victory. When the offense gets their turn, they're a bit looser. Jet and the guys try to burn off as much clock as possible, meaning there's plenty of time between plays for the guys to jaw and trash-talk (all in good fun, of course).

The losing team is becoming understandably chippy. Multiple whistles sound as players push and shove each other after each snap.

"Settle down, babies!" my brother catcalls behind me.

I turn to laugh at his ironically juvenile behavior.

Taking my eyes off the field is my second mistake. I'm

faintly aware of hearing Jet call for the ball to be hiked, but I'm still facing backward, making faces at Greg, when I hear the collective intake of breath, the gasp that I'll likely hear in my sleep for years to come.

My brother's eyes widen, and he yells, "Hey!"

I spin in time to get a view of multiple medical personnel running onto the field toward a pair of cleats sticking out from the center of a crush of huge bodies. Helmets fly, as do fists. Stupidly, I search the brawling players for Jet, hoping, praying he's inserted himself between two guys so mammoth they're hiding him. But his familiar figure isn't one of the upright people. In fact, the more I look at those feet, I know they belong to him. Obviously, I can't identify him based on his size thirteen cleats, but my gut knows they're his.

I glance down the row at Gloria, who looks like she's about to vault the few rows in front of us to get to the field. I can totally relate. It takes all of my control to stay where I am, to not run out there and start throwing punches of my own. Deep-seated, paralytic fear helps.

Whistles pierce the quickly quieting stadium, and yellow flags litter the field.

The feet move.

Gloria and I make a similar noise, something between a squeak and a sob. Cyndi shifts Mikey to her other hip and grabs my hand.

Then they show the replay on the twenty-five-thousand-square-foot video board. Those nachos I stole from Mikey threaten to reappear as I watch the linebacker plow into Jet well after he releases the ball, and the back of Jet's head slams against the turf, bouncing in a way a head's not supposed to do. They show it again. And again. I close my eyes, open them, and refocus on the feet.

The officiating team sorts out the fouls, but I don't process a single word the ref says after "Roughing the passer," followed by Greg's furious, "Ya think?"

A few seconds later, I vaguely register the boos from Chiefs fans, so I assume thrown punches have garnered a few of our players some penalties of their own. But I don't care about lost yardage or loss of down. I continue to stare at those twitching feet.

A roar goes up when Jet sits with the help of Rae and Doc, but my throat has clamped shut. There will be no more noise from me. Maybe ever. This experience may strike me mute.

Doc gently removes Jet's helmet. Rae shakes her head and responds to something Jet has said. Another person, one I don't recognize, kneels in front of Jet and shines a light in his eyes. More conversation between the four of them ensues. Jet tries to stand up by himself, but the medical staff is having none of it. They grab arms, elbows, and hands—anything they can grasp as he tries to shrug them off—and steer him toward the sideline.

The crowd cheers his toughness, relieved he doesn't have to be carted off, that this isn't one of those victories tempered by tragedy. But he's obviously dazed. He couldn't pass a road-side sobriety test right now if his life depended on it, but he's aware enough to know exactly who's responsible for his ringing ears and double vision. As he passes one Carolina line-backer in particular, he shouts something we can't hear in the stands. Something tells me he's not urging the guy to have a lovely off-season. That suspicion is confirmed when Jet tries to take a step or two toward the guy who outweighs him by at least a hundred pounds—yet another sign he's not in his right mind. His escorts pull him away, but he continues to jaw at the unimpressed giant.

Greg whistles and yells, "Yeah! Tell 'im, buddy!"

Keith and David shout words of encouragement toward their baby brother. Gloria murmurs something to Gidget. Cyndi and I squeeze each other's hands like we're trying to fuse palms. Mom leans down and kisses my hair, then says, "He's okay."

I merely nod, because what's the point in arguing? I don't have the wherewithal to get all technical with her anyway. I can barely sort out the jumble of words in my own mind; verbalizing them would be impossible. They're too scary to say out loud. Things like "brain trauma," "concussion proto-col," "dementia," and—the scariest of scary—"chronic trau-matic encephalopathy" have no place in this setting, but they're having a grand old time in my head.

It seems like hours have passed, but it's only been minutes. The game continues with Jet's backup, Michael Wilcox, taking the next few snaps to get us into field goal range, where Schoengert easily knocks one through and increases our lead by another three points.

I keep my eyes on the bench while the trainers continue to examine Jet. He seems irritated, like this is all a huge inconve-nience. Bodies occasionally block my view of him, but that doesn't stop my staring. If I try hard enough, maybe I'll develop X-ray vision. Then I'll be able to see through his skull, too, and figure out what's going on in there. (He'd gamely say, "Nothing.")

Eventually, and to his obvious disgust, Rae, Doc, and some other trainers lead Jet into the locker room. He tosses some limp waves and high fives at a few fans hanging from the stands as he passes them on his way through the tunnel.

I want a high five.

No, I want a hug. I want a hug and a kiss. And more. I

want him to say my name, so I can be certain he remembers who I am. I want him to get annoyed at *me* for being worried. I want him to hold me and tell me he's okay, that he'll always be okay, that he's not going to end up like some of those Hall of Famers they cart out for special occasions, guys who have vegetable soup for brains and maintain a full-time drool-wiper on their payrolls. Not that it would change anything if he can't promise that. I'm in it for the long haul. I'll wipe his drool, myself, if it comes to that. I'll push his wheelchair and help him to the bathroom, too. But if he can't remember any of this, if he can't remember *me* or the best parts of our life together, what is the point? Is this worth it?

I can tell by the shifting and murmuring around me that I'm on the big screen again. This little drama is a gift from God for the network, keeping people who would have otherwise switched off the game glued to their TVs, despite the disparity in the score. Plot twist!

Well, screw them. This is our life, not an NFL telenovela. In fact...

I raise both middle fingers in the general direction of the Carolina bench. "Screw you, Panthers!" There. That'll get the camera off me. Have fun with that FCC fine, TV peeps.

"Mo!" Mom gasps behind me. "Be classy!"

"Eff classy!"

Cyndi giggles.

Mikey yells, "Classy!"

Gloria burns a hole in my cheek with her laser glare, but I don't give a shit. I don't care about anything right now but that guy in the locker room, and if everyone could stop staring at me, that would be great.

Time winds down, and when the Panthers' last-ditch effort at an onside kick fails, the Chiefs bench and fans erupt.

The game is over. We won.

But did we?

———

When Rae emerges from the locker room and wends her way through the stands to personally give us an update, the confetti shower is still in full force, and the stadium crew is working furiously to set up the stage for the presentation of the Lombardi trophy. But those of us only here because of Jet may as well be fans of the losing team, to look at us.

"He's fine, everyone!" Rae yells over the booming music. "Or, he will be. But he definitely has a concussion, so under protocol, we have to keep him isolated. That means limited stimulation. No talking to the media and no wandering around out here, with all these lights and sounds. We're going to have to take him back to the hotel soon, before it gets crazy in the locker room. But if you'll follow me, I'll take you to see him."

Gloria pushes past the rest of us like someone trying to get to the last big-screen TV on Black Friday, but Rae freezes her with one stern glance and a firm, "Let's go, Maura," as she holds out her hand for me to lead the line with her.

Outside the locker room, though, I allow the others to go first. I don't want my visit to be rushed while they wait to check on the patient and congratulate the victor.

While I pace in the hallway, my parents and Greg observe helplessly, knowing better than to try to make it better with words. Finally, Jet's siblings and their kids return, looking much happier than when they went in.

Cyndi grins at me. "Someone won't stop asking for you."

I don't need any other invitation. Despite not knowing

exactly where I'm going, I rush through the door, following the voices until I round a corner and enter a plastic-sheeted room, all ready for spraying champagne. Jet, still talking to Ned and Gloria, with Doc observing close by, straddles a bench. He's out of his pads and shoes but still in his uniform pants and socks and wearing a "Super Bowl Champions" t-shirt and ball cap.

All four of them turn when I arrive. With Jet's grin, I take my first full breath since watching that replay.

"Hey," I say, trying to play it cool but still hardly able to speak.

He starts to stand, but Doc keeps him down with a gentle hand to his shoulder. "Let her come to you." He waves me forward. "It's okay."

I nod and blink, then step up to the bench, where I perch on its end and slide down the smooth, shiny wood until I'm pressed against Jet's still-sweaty flank. He pulls me in for a crushing hug that I return, clutching my emotions with equal ferocity, considering our audience.

Over my head, he says to his parents, "I'll see you guys later, huh?"

*In other words, scram!*

Gloria starts to protest, but Ned talks over her. "Sure thing, son. See you back in Kansas City. Don't party too hard."

"They won't let me," he says with a laugh.

As soon as they're gone, I kiss him with an intensity that skews his ball cap and eventually knocks it backward to the floor. He laughs against my lips and glances nervously at Doc, who's backed off but remains focused on his patient. The guy may as well be a mannequin to me. If he has to be here at all times, and it gets him off to watch this, fine. But I'm not holding back anymore.

It does occur to me, though, that I should be gentler with the injured player, so I pull back and ask, "Are you okay?"

"I'm fine! I want to go out there with the rest of the team, but..."

"You can't."

"Trust me; I've been told a thousand times."

"Good."

I search his eyes, which look normal to my untrained eye. No wonky pupils or glazed whites. And he seems to know what's going on. He's speaking coherently, anyway. And unless he's okay with making out with any random person who walks in here, he seems to recognize me. But who knows? Maybe this whole time, he's been sitting here, thinking I'm some stray groupie sent in to cheer him up and make him feel better.

The possibility, however unlikely, of that being the case releases emotions too powerful to hold back.

"Aw, Beautiful, don't cry."

His use of my nickname makes me cry harder, only this time from relief.

He rubs my back. "It's okay. I'm okay. We won! We're Super Bowl Champs!"

"I hate caring!" I wail. "I hate it so much!"

"Caring is good, though."

"No, it's not. It makes me want to throw up. All the time. It ruins everything, even the Super Bowl! I saw you hit your head, and— Your feet. They weren't moving! Were you knocked out?"

"Only for a second."

"Your brain! Your poor brain!"

"Right? Like Rae said, I can't afford to lose any more brain cells..."

"It's not funny!"

"Oh, c'mon. Now, you sound like my mom."

That shuts me up in a hurry. I painfully swallow a sob and wipe the tears from my face with the heels of my hands.

"I'm kidding," he quickly says, hugging me again. "But I don't want you to be upset. I don't want anyone to be upset."

"Too late."

"Aw, shit. I'm ruining this for everyone. But I threw the ball, like you're always telling me. I got rid of it. That jerk, Baker, is dirty. He better get fined for that."

"Unless his money can buy you a new brain, a fine means nothing to me. You were seriously knocked out?"

"Yeah, but—"

I grind my back molars.

"Oh, man. Don't do that to your teeth."

"Do you want me to cry or grind my teeth? Pick one."

"Teeth, I guess."

"And how do you feel now?"

He hesitates. "Weird. Like, fuzzy. Like my tongue's too big for my mouth. And I get randomly dizzy."

Deciding to acknowledge Doc's presence again, I say to him, "Are you hearing this?"

Before the guy can speak for himself, Jet cuts in, "I already told him. They know everything. And they'll be checking me all night. Plus, I'll have to report to them once a day for the next week, or until I'm back to my baseline neuro. I'm not messin' around with this or downplaying it."

"But it's part of the game, so get over it?"

He shrugs. "Kinda."

Grind, grind, grind.

He tousles my hair. "You're a rookie, but you'll see. Next season, you won't worry so much, because you'll have been through all this, *and* we'll be defending champs. I'd yell, 'Go Chiefs!' but my head hurts too much."

"Hilarious, Mr. MVP."

"Did I seriously get MVP?"

"Probably. The quarterback always does. It's borderline unfair."

"Hey! I sacrificed precious gray matter out there. I'm pretty sure my entire sixth grade year was wiped clean. Goodbye, scientific method. See ya, fractions and ratios."

"Keep joking."

"I will. Laughter has healing powers." Suddenly, he sobers, chewing the inside of his cheek and looking down at his sock-clad feet. "But man. This sucks. I won't get to accept my award. Or lift the Lombardi Trophy. Or dance in the confetti. Or party with the guys. Or get drunk and pass out on the plane."

I grab his hands. "I'm sorry."

He quickly looks up and smiles. "It's not your fault."

A breathless Rae runs into the locker room. "Yo. Knox. They're about to do a bunch of mushy man stuff up on stage, and everyone's wondering where you are."

"Ha. Did you tell them I'm on the way to Disney World?"

She rolls her eyes. "No. I generally don't make wise-ass remarks to the NFL Commissioner, especially when he's ordering me to drag your butt out there, in a wheelchair, if necessary."

Doc raises his eyebrows. "Protocol states—"

She shrugs. "I guess they make an exception when there are trophies and television ratings involved. Now, is he walking or riding?"

"I can walk." Jet scrambles under the bench for his shoes, jamming his feet into them in double-time. I retrieve his cap from the floor and gently slide it onto his head. He adjusts it to fit more securely.

"Award, trophy, back in here," the doctor says sternly. "I'll pull you off the stage myself, if I have to. No speeches. No interviews." He points at Rae. "You. Over here."

She obeys him without any of her usual sarcastic retorts and sits on the bench, on the other side of Jet. Crossing the room, the doctor lifts aside some plastic and opens a cabinet, coming out with a vial he pops open with his thumb. Into his hand, he shakes two foam nubs and extends them to Jet. "You'll want to wear these to block out some of the noise. It's going to be loud, and that's not going to feel good on your head. The bright lights are going to be bad enough."

"He could wear sunglasses," Rae suggests, which earns her a killer glare from her boss.

He grumbles, "Make sure you're supporting him fully all the way to the stage and the whole time he's standing up there. I'm going to run ahead and make sure everyone knows the ground rules."

After he leaves, Rae tells Jet to stand, and we wait with our arms woven through each of his while his initial vertigo passes.

"You okay?" she checks. "If not, there's no shame in using the wheelchair."

He snorts. "I'm fine. No need to put me in one of those just yet. Let's go."

At the mouth of the tunnel, we pause to let his eyes adjust to the light. Squinting, he looks down at me and asks, "How do I look?"

"Like a champ, Champ."

## FOURTEEN

## BAD DAY

Having a Super Bowl MVP boyfriend who's a hero in this town holds little sway with my boss, Cynthia, when she pulls me into her office this morning, closes the door, and says, "I was hoping we wouldn't have to have this conversation, but here we are." She coughs that nervous laugh of hers that has always made it difficult for me to tell if she's joking, sincere, or just plain weird. It's also earned her my private nickname for her, "The Giggler."

"Okay. That sounds ominous." I emit a nervous chuckle of my own, which is appropriate, given the circumstances.

She sits behind her desk but doesn't invite me to take the other chair in the room, so I remain standing. With any luck, this conversation that neither one of us wants to have will be a short one.

"Your recent poor attendance is a problem. I need you to step it up, Maura. Or at least, show up."

"Right. I... I'm sorry about that. I—"

"It's not fair to your fellow counselors, who are often

double-booked when you call in at the last second, and we still have to somehow accommodate your appointments."

"There's been a lot—"

"Yeah. We know. We all know. And I've tried to be understanding, because these are some extraordinary circumstances. But The Career Center deserves your full attention when you're supposed to be here." Giggle, giggle, giggle.

My cheeks flush, and I'm pretty sure passersby on the street can hear my heartbeat.

Oh, geez. That sudden rush of adrenaline means I care about my job now, too. See? This is what happens. It's a slippery slope. Start caring about one little thing, and it leads to caring about *everything*. Suddenly, I'm this overachiever, addicted to approval and seeking it everywhere.

Channeling the old Maura, trying to remember what she would say or do in this situation, I bite back my instinct to explain or excuse. I can't use anything related to Jet as leverage, because nobody likes a name-dropper. Plus, I spend most of my time around here trying to make people forget he's my fiancé—or at least not talk about it incessantly. And being sick, while legitimate, only cost me two days away, as opposed to the entire week I called in so I could accompany sick Jet to the Super Bowl. Then there were the two days this week when I took off to escort him to his neurology appointments.

After considering and discarding several responses, I merely say, "You're right."

She opens a folder on my desk, which I notice for the first time. The dreaded personnel file. Mine is relatively thin and clean. No disciplinary forms… yet; merely the usual copies of my driver's license and tax forms, from what I can see upside down.

Her fingers rest on one form in particular, a print-out of

what appears to be a balance spreadsheet. "Which brings me to my next point, one of a more administrative nature: I'm assuming you'll be taking less vacation in April, to try to recoup some of this recent extra time off?"

I hold my breath while I wait for her barking laugh to stop. "Less vacation in April?" I parrot on a squeak.

"You originally scheduled two weeks off, but you don't have enough remaining days to take that." She pulls the spreadsheet to the top and looks down it. "Says here you have… five vacation days and one personal day left for the rest of the year. And it's"—she glances up at her computer monitor—"February. Ha ha ha."

"Yeah. Wow. That's bleak."

"Which is why I thought we should touch base. Seems like things are, maybe, happening faster than you realize."

*Oh, I realize it, lady.*

Despite her lack of invitation, I slump into the chair in front of her desk. "I'm sorry."

"No need to apologize. Be aware. And let's get it back on the rails." Based on her bright tone and continued chuckles, we could be talking about something as cheerful and unimportant as our Oscar predictions.

"Yeah, okay."

"So?"

My head snaps up. "Yes?"

"I can officially strike that second week off in April?"

My honeymoon! The only thing that's been getting me through all of this other nonsense.

Despite my panicky, racing thoughts, I remain outwardly calm and sigh. "I guess so. I have no choice, do I?"

Saying that out loud did *not* help matters. At all.

She laughs more sincerely now. "You always have a choice.

In fact, you, of all people, have plenty of choices right now. You could take that second week unpaid, if you wanted. That's always an option."

"Not likely. I need every one of my paychecks."

"Do you? I suspect by then you'll no longer require the income from this job." She steeples her fingers under her chin, digging her blunt, unpainted nails into the sagging skin there. Obviously uncomfortable with my disapproving silence, she titters.

I say as evenly as possible, "This is how I make a living."

"Is it?"

"Yes. It is."

She closes the folder with a slap. "I hardly think you'd be left on the streets if you didn't work here anymore. Especially now. Well, anyway, that's none of my business."

"No, it's not."

"What *is* my business is how this place is run." She wags a finger at me and stifles more nervous laughter around what she tries to portray as a tough act, complete with exaggerated frown. "I've been a bit lax in regard to you lately, trying to cut you some slack, because we all like you. And we like Jet. And we LOVE the Chiefs. By helping you out, we've all felt like we're part of the team. It's time to get back to business, though. Which reminds me, I haven't seen a thing from you about spring job fair plans. That'll be here before we know it."

As if I need a reminder. I have a dining room full of art supplies and creepy "gold" statuettes—although not nearly as many as I need—as proof.

"I want a detailed report on your progress, including budget update, by the end of the week, please." Following yet another uncomfortable cough-laugh, she looks across the desk at me and raises her eyebrows expectantly, which is obviously my cue to go.

I stand. "Will do. And, uh, yeah. You can scratch that second week off in April. You're right; I've been away enough, and I'll need to catch up on stuff, especially that close to the job fair."

She jots something on a sticky note and presses it, perfectly centered, on my folder, which she slides into a desk drawer. "Excellent. I'm glad you're choosing to stay with us and recommit to your career, as well as the careers of your clients."

With as much dignity as I can muster, I nod and open her door, exiting her office and walking across the reception area with my head down, ultra-aware of my co-workers' stares.

A few weeks ago, I'd say they were staring because they saw an unflattering photo of a dirty-haired, palazzo-pants-and-baggy-t-shirt-wearing me buying tampons late at night. Or a picture of me volunteering at the pediatric ward of the hospital with Jet. Now, I'm not sure if their stares have more to do with watching me on national television when I accompanied Jet on stage to accept his MVP award or knowing I got chortled off by our boss.

Hell, maybe it's both.

———

*How's the first day back?*

Colin's text pings while I'm staring into space and drinking what Beau calls poison, and the rest of us know as "diet soda." My lunch break hasn't included any lunching so far.

I sit straighter on the bench in the indoor botanical garden

and bend down to set the aluminum can on the ground next
to my feet. Upright once more, I tap back:

*Not the best, honestly*

*Hard to get back to reality? Everyone swarming you with
questions?*

*More like everyone hates me for being a slacker.*

*What??*

*I got pulled into The Giggler's office and told I'm letting down
the team here*

*Jealous twits*

Before I can confirm or refute that theory, another text
from him pops up.

*Bloody autocorrect. That word was supposed to have an a in it,
not an i*

I laugh despite my blue mood.

*They may have a point. I've been gone a lot*

*You were sick!*

*Two days*

*If you'd been sick the whole time, they wouldn't complain. They'd sympathize*

*I wasn't sick, though. I was partying down in Dallas*

*I'd hardly call your week in Dallas a party*

*They don't—and can't—know that, though*

*Why ever not? Now that it's all over, you can tell all*

*It would sound like I was complaining about an experience they'd kill to have*

*True. Well, sorry you had a rough go today. Tomorrow will be better*

*I'm counting on it!*

*Would you like me to come over tonight and bring dinner?*

*I would! BUT I'm staying at Jet's. He still has \*guests\**

*Oh, dear*

*Yep*

*When do they leave?*

*Saturday morning*

*Crikey*

*And Cyndi may or may not be going with them. Things are
tense since she told them everything*

*Blimey*

*So… see you in April at the wedding*

*Ha ha*

We leave it at that, pretending I'm joking, when it could be
the depressing reality.

I retrieve my beverage from the ground, drain the rest of
the liquid from it, and drop it into the nearest recycling bin,
hoofing it in double-time to ensure I return to my desk with
time to spare. Can't be a minute late.

———

If I'm being more diplomatic than I usually allow myself to be
(a.k.a., "less entitled" and "less selfish"), I have to admit that
having three adult family members with Jet this week has had
its distinct advantages. It's allowed me to go back to work,
knowing he has someone with him at all times who can take
him to his follow-up neuro appointments. But then the true
me resurfaces and wishes they'd all fade into the background
when I arrive at the house in the evening. It's ungrateful, I
admit, but there it is.

In fact, two days after my dress-down and loss of honeymoon time (which I haven't had the guts to reveal to the
person who's supposed to be accompanying me on that trip), I
pull my car into Jet's driveway and have to sit in it for a while
to steel myself for the activity inside.

*One more night. They're leaving tomorrow. Maybe. Gloria and Ned are, anyway. And Cyndi's great. And Mikey's sweet. Don't be a selfish a-hole.*

By the time I'm mentally ready to face another family-filled evening, several minutes have elapsed, and when I come through the front door, I nearly trip over Mikey.

He raises his hands and shouts, "Mo-Mo! Boo!"

I don't have to pretend too hard to be startled, since I wasn't expecting him to be there, and it's a miracle I didn't knock him out with the heavy wooden door. Since I didn't, though, and everyone's all right, I laugh at the greeting and press my hand to my chest. "Oh, goodness! You scared me!"

"I know," he says on a bored sigh, as if that was exactly his intention but wasn't as entertaining as he'd hoped.

I crouch down to his level. "How's it goin', Bud?"

He throws himself at me and knocks me on my butt on the hard slate floor. "Oomph. Wow. This is quite the greeting."

Torzi, sensing someone receiving *his* attention, leaps into the entryway, inserting himself onto the heap. Mikey and I make a big deal about being licked, which only encourages the dog to lick more. The toddler's giggles, unlike my boss's, are infectious, and soon I'm laughing so hard at the situation that my abs and cheeks ache.

"Oh, my gosh. There you are!"

I open my eyes to see Jet. Or Jet's feet and legs. I look up his body and say sheepishly, "Hello."

He smiles at me and returns my greeting, but he immediately addresses his nephew with a fake scowl. "Dude. I've been looking all over for you. I told you not to wander off."

"Two-year-olds aren't that great at following directions. Even I know that."

Jet lifts the small bodies off me, and as I clamber to my

feet, I notice the silence for the first time since arriving. "Hey, where's everyone else?"

Clearing his throat, he shoots me a meaningful glance but keeps his tone light for Mikey's sake when he says, "Talking about boring stuff."

Oh, Lord. Is it too late to get back in my car and drive home?

"I'm so glad you're here. I'm in charge of Mikey, and—"

"I see that. Sort of."

"—when I used the bathroom, he ran away from me."

"You're supposed to take him in there with you."

"I did! But he kept trying to stick his hand in the stream, so I had to sit down to finish."

I cover my mouth to stifle my amusement.

He glares at me. "I sat down, and the little shi— goober opened the door and ran out. And hid from me. Like, in a cupboard, or something. I couldn't find him! I guess he came out when he heard your car door, but by then I was looking for him in the backyard. I honestly thought I was going to find him floating face down in the pool."

My laughter chokes off when I realize how serious Jet is. "Oh, geez. Well, he's fine. He wanted to greet me at the door. With a 'boo.'" I chuck the toddler under the chin. "Right, Mikey?"

He nods and struggles to be let down. As soon as Jet sets him on his feet, he runs away from us. We immediately pursue him, and the professional athlete catches up to him first, wrapping him in a bear hug and wrestling him to the floor, trying to tickle him into submission.

Torzi and I join the melee, and when we all have our breath back, lying on our backs and staring at the ceiling beams, I look over at grinning Mikey and say, "Hey. Stay with us, okay? Don't run away. We're fun."

He nods solemnly, looking so much like Jet, it makes me want to sob. "Okay."

Wondering how much longer we'll be in charge of this ball of energy, I quickly scramble to remember what kids do and need. There's playing (check), sleeping (not quite yet), pooping and peeing (I'm assuming he'll let us know when that's necessary, or happening, or has happened), and...

"Are you hungry?"

"Yes."

I laugh at his earnest, immediate answer. "Well, I bet your Gigi has stocked fifty years' worth of leftovers in the fridge to choose from."

"Hot dogs!"

"Or hot dogs."

Jet sits up. "You can't have hot dogs. You had them for lunch, and your mom said no more."

"Hot dogs!"

"How about spaghetti?"

"Hot dogs!"

"No."

The little guy's face crumples, and he opens his mouth. Several terrifying seconds elapse where nothing happens. Then an unholy noise spills from that hole, a noise so loud and horrible and seemingly infinite that after only a few seconds, I'll do anything to make it stop.

"Hot dogs, it is!" I say, grabbing his hand and pulling him up with me, dragging him toward the kitchen.

Jet scrambles to catch up to us. "What? No! Wait!"

I wheel on him and widen my eyes. Through clenched teeth, I say, "Go with it."

"But Cyndi said—"

"Cyndi's not here now, is she?"

"No, but I—"

"Shut it, Champ."

He snaps his mouth closed and pulls his chin back.

The tyrannical two-footer behind me proceeds to open every cabinet within his reach, which totals about fifty doors in this massive kitchen. I bob my head toward him. "The kid wants a hot dog. We're going to give him a hot dog. You know why?"

"Because it stopped him crying?"

"Bingo. And he's not our kid, so..."

"But that's exactly why we can't do it. Cyndi specifically told me not to give him a hot dog for dinner. If she hadn't said that, I could be all, like, 'Oops. I didn't know.'"

"Say you forgot. Play the concussion card."

He laughs. "That's not— Hang on. That might work. You're a genius." He pats my arm on his way past. "Okay, Mikey. Hot dog. Whatcha want on that bad boy? Ketchup, mustard, peanut butter, chocolate sauce?"

"Ketchup!"

———

A couple of hours later, after we've been abandoned by a red-eyed Cyndi, a sleepy Mikey, and a scarily silent pair of parents, I turn to Jet in the strangely silent living room and say, "Hey, speaking of concussions..."

"Were we?" Turning off the TV, he rubs the back of his neck and paces to the window, where he looks out at the steaming, illuminated pool in the backyard.

"A while ago, yeah. When we were devising that hot dog loophole."

He snorts. "Right. We'll see how well that works if Cyndi thinks to ask Mikey what we had for dinner."

"Something tells me she has more pressing things on her mind than her son's processed meat intake."

She barely said two words to us when she, Gloria, and Ned finally surfaced from the basement, where they were having what I assumed to be another serious talk about her future. She told Mikey it was bedtime, ignored his protests and pleas to finish the current episode of *Curious George*, and escaped upstairs with a choked, "Good night," to the rest of us.

Gloria sighed and muttered something about needing to pack for their departure tomorrow, and Ned dutifully followed.

It's nice to be alone with Jet, but I wish it wasn't under such tense circumstances. In an effort to distract us from the unhappy people in the bedrooms above, I ask, "What did you find out at your neurology appointment today?" I wave him over and pat the sofa cushion next to me.

He lowers himself to the couch. "Not much. More of the same. I'm almost back to baseline."

"Good. And that's a miracle, considering how much you've bent the rules this week."

"It's not my fault! I couldn't *not* ride in the parade. It's bad enough I can't talk to the media, so all the other guys have to pick up my slack."

"They're loving it."

"Not really. Especially because so many of the questions are about *me*. I don't blame them for being annoyed."

"They'll be fine once they have those fancy rings to show off."

"That's going to be a few weeks. In the meantime…"

"It'll settle down." I wrap my arms around his torso from the side and kiss his bicep. With my nose still pressed to his arm, I say, "With great wins come great responsibilities."

His faint smile at my modified movie quote is disappointing.

"C'mon. Cheer up! You won the Super Bowl! You're supposed to still be feeling invincible and euphoric and… and… all those things!"

He shrugs. "I'm worried about Cyndi. It's weird—wrong—being happy when she's going through such a hard time, with Mom and Dad on her case like she's some stupid teenager."

Irritation at all of the people putting a damper on this experience for him—including Cyndi—blooms in my chest and belly.

"Your sister is going to be okay. And she wouldn't want you to worry about her." When he says nothing to that but continues to space out, showing me his profile, I sigh and let go of him.

When I stand, he blinks at my withdrawal. "Where you goin'?" The anxiety in his tone breaks my heart.

"Nowhere," I answer softly on my way to the kitchen for a much-needed glass of wine. "I'm not going anywhere."

## FIFTEEN

# DELAYED CELEBRATIONS

This morning dawns with one thought in my mind: *After today, he's all mine.*

Well, almost. If you don't count public appearances and media interviews and endorsement meetings and team obligations and the seemingly endless ceremonies and parties and galas associated with the Super Bowl win. The one good thing about Jet's injury is that he's been excused from several events already, and this first week home has been relatively quiet, compared to what it would have been if he'd been one hundred percent healthy. Balance that with the worries associated with concussion and its long-term effects, plus the somewhat downer presence of his parents and younger sister, though, and I might prefer sharing him with the team and the media. We'll see.

Until he's cleared by Doc, though, things will remain low-key. Is it wrong for me to hope he heals slower than expected? Yes, it is. I'm not hoping that. (Not really.) Perhaps, though, it would be nice if the doctors were to err on the side of caution and hold off on clearing him for a while. If I had any influence—or money—I'd be all over making that happen.

As it is, I have neither. Selling every movie, poster, and screenplay in my precious collection would hardly amount to a decent bribe. If I thought it would, though, I'd do it in a heartbeat.

Oh, gosh. I've got it bad for the boy.

We still have a few minutes before it's time to get up and take our guests to the airport, so I snatch this rare opportunity to be a creeper and watch Jet sleep. After all, he's normally up well before me, working out in the basement or swimming laps or already on his way to the training facility for any number of obligations. This week, despite the absence of those things on his schedule, he's been awake and downstairs by the time my alarm has gone off for work. He's held court in the kitchen, making Mikey giggle at how he can shove an entire banana in his mouth at once while prancing around the room, scratching his armpits and hooting like a monkey. He's also made sure his parents and sister have everything they need to feel at home. I'm glad he's sleeping in today. And not only so I can stare at him.

But mostly because of that.

Unfortunately, he doesn't look as peaceful in repose as I'd hoped. Asleep on his back with one arm flung over his head, he looks worried, his eyes pinching and relaxing, his forehead wrinkled, his mouth clamped shut—until he mutters something I can't quite make out. I sit up and swivel on my butt, folding my legs and facing him, my knees against his ribs and hip. Again, he mumbles, and this time I make out the words, "...doesn't fit..."

Hm. Whatever *it* is, its lack of fit is vexing. The hand on his pillow clenches into a fist, then relaxes slowly open again.

A curse word slips out next, and despite my sympathy that he's obviously having a bad dream, I smile and stifle my laughter, because it's only a dream, after all. And he'll wake up soon. Plus, he looks so darn cute when he's earnest. I can't wait to hear what his subconscious has him worried about. Dreams, especially his, are absurd. We laugh about them all the time.

I rest a hand on his rising and falling chest and lean over to lightly kiss the skin next to my fingers.

He gasps, bringing his arm down on the back of my neck with such force, it smashes my face against his pec.

"Ow!" I muffle, my lips grazing his nipple.

"Maura! Oh, gosh." He lifts his guillotine appendage, so I can straighten and rub my assaulted neck. "I'm sorry! I... I thought you were a spider."

In spite of the pain, I laugh. "A spider?"

"Your eyelashes or hair or something. I don't know." He sits up and pulls me to him, palming the red skin where my neck meets the rest of my body. "Are you okay?"

"I'm fine. I didn't mean to scare you. I was trying to wake you up gently from your nightmare."

"I wasn't— Oh, yeah. I *was* having a bad dream. How'd you know?"

"You were talking. Mostly swearing. And saying something didn't fit." I wiggle my eyebrows. "Don't flatter yourself, Big Guy."

His chuckles end on a sigh as he falls back on his pillows, taking me down with him. I nestle against his chest and side, twining my legs with his. For a few seconds, while we get comfortable, he says nothing. I rub my foot up and down his hairy ankle, waiting.

Finally, he says, "My ring. My Super Bowl ring. It didn't fit.

And they were all like, 'If the ring doesn't fit, the win doesn't count.'"

I snicker. "Like the glass slipper? Or OJ's glove?"

"I guess. And everyone else's rings fit, but because mine didn't, the whole team had to forfeit the Super Bowl. I had to go into the locker room and tell every guy, one by one."

"That would suck."

"It was horrible."

With a fair bit of pain, I crane my sore neck so I can see his serious face. "It was only a dream."

"It felt real, though. Like everything else this week. Frustrating and disappointing."

"Are you going to be okay?"

He tilts his head down, frowns, and kisses my forehead. "Yeah. Of course. It's just, you know, everything."

I push up on my arms and roll more fully on top of him so I can look straight down into his face. "Enough."

"What?"

"After we drop off your family at the airport, we're going to do something fun. In public. That way, you'll be surrounded by people who adore you, who want your autograph, who can remind you of what you accomplished a few short days ago. All this family drama and concussion nonsense has ruined that for you, and it's pissing me off."

He laughs. "Okay. But I have to check in with Doc after the airport."

"Fine. But you're all mine after that."

He tightens his arms around my back. "I like the sound of that."

"Good. Because it's happening."

"Don't you have stuff you need to do? I've been hogging you. Rae and Colin and your family must miss you."

"My family is fine. Mom and Dad are planning their next trip, and Greg and Deirdre are nesting, putting the last touches on the nursery. Maybe we can meet up with Rae and Colin later, as part of our fun. Don't worry about it, though. No worrying today."

After all, four huge worries are going to be flying away in a few hours.

The grin I've missed so much and that was a permanent fixture in all of my post-Super-Bowl fantasies finally makes an appearance. "All right." His hands slide lower and rest, warm and heavy, on my butt. "I'm definitely asking Doc about sex today."

"You do that."

"Everyone else has gotten their championship lay but me."

"Even Schoengert?"

"Probably. That's how bad it is."

I place a peck on his neck and rest my head on his shoulder, letting my fingers wander in his chest hair. Under the covers, he grinds against my hip to let me know there's no boo-boo down there. "In due time," I reassure him. "And it'll be lovely."

He snorts. "'Lovely' ain't at all what I have in mind, Beautiful. We'll save 'lovely' for some other time."

On that note and to the soundtrack of much good-natured grousing, I take my leave of the bed and scurry to the shower. Make that a cold one.

———

Seeing those four backs disappear through security was one of the sweetest sights since watching Jet hoist the Lombardi trophy. In fact, it brought a tear to my eye. I let Jet believe I was emotional about having to say goodbye, because it earned me a hug. And it made me seem like a better person than I am.

Then, in the middle of his squeeze, he chuckled and said, "Aw, don't cry. Mom'll be back in a few weeks to help with final wedding preps," and I knew I wasn't fooling anyone. Oh, well.

It's not that I don't like Jet's family, but I like my quiet life more. And entertaining guests is tiring, under the best of circumstances—which these were not. It'll be nice to return to some semblance of normal, however temporarily. And however changed our "normal" is.

Case in point: it took us more than an hour to leave the airport after saying "Bon Voyage," to Ned, Gloria, Cyndi, and Mikey. Word traveled that a newly crowned Super Bowl MVP was present, one who'd been relatively elusive since his victory, and the other nearby occupants surrounded us. A few weeks ago, in a setting like this, a handful of people would have seen and recognized Jet and asked for autographs or wanted to talk football with him. Today, as soon as they saw he was finished with his personal business, everyone wanted a piece of him. It was nice of them to wait, though.

As we crept from the departures area to the door to get to the short-term parking lot, the mass of people edged with us. One person would get their autograph or high five and peel off, only to be replaced by someone else. A woman asked him to sign her abs, which she was all too happy to expose. Jet blushed and said, "It'll last longer on a piece of paper, you know," but he quickly scribbled on her tan, toned stomach while I looked on, trying not to laugh at the absurdity of it.

Finally, airport security had to get involved, ushering us to an area where we weren't creating a fire hazard or blocking the way for travelers in a hurry to get to their destinations. Jet kept apologizing, but the security guard dismissed it, saying his appearance was the most exciting thing that had happened since that entire boy band came through on their way to their next tour stop.

Eventually things settled down, and we were left with only the die-hards who would have gladly missed their flights in order to rehash the entire Super Bowl, especially the gory details of Jet's injury. ("Did your ears bleed? I heard that can happen if you hit your head too hard.")

We waved goodbye for good and escaped before more kids showed up, because "I can't say no to kids."

I smiled proudly at him. "I know. That's why they love you."

He grinned while stepping back and letting me go first through the narrow sliding door to the parking lot. "That was something else."

I let him bask. He deserves it. And who knew a simple trip to the airport would brighten his outlook so much? I can only imagine how great he's going to feel after a whole day of similar experiences.

Now, at the exclusive medical facility, he returns from his latest MRI and gives me a thumbs-up behind Doc's back. It would be funny no matter what, but it's even more hilarious with him in that surgical gown, wrapped and held tightly so as not to show the few people milling around here his—in my opinion—perfect bottom, while ironically displaying much more than that with the thin cotton pulled so tightly against his front.

Doc glances over his shoulder to see what's so funny, but Jet sobers and clears his throat as he takes a seat on the exam table in the middle of the room.

"It looks good," Doc says to me what he's obviously already told an ecstatic Jet. "He's back to baseline and can resume normal activity. That being said..." He raises his voice to be heard over Jet's slow clapping. "You'll still want to avoid some things for a while. No roller coasters or jarring rides. No loud concerts. Flashing lights are a no-no, too. Be mindful of what you're doing and how it might affect his brain." He levels a serious look directly at me. "I'm telling *you* this, because most players need someone else to remind them they're recovering."

"It's because we legitimately can't remember," Jet cracks, laughing at the glare he receives from the physician. "Aw, c'mon, Doc. That was funny."

"I don't find head trauma funny."

"Me neither." Nevertheless, I snicker at my scantily clad boyfriend. "But you're hilarious."

He bows the best he can from a sitting position with his feet dangling above the floor. "Thank you. I'll be here all day. And all night. Only one form of payment is acceptable, and it ain't cash."

I roll my eyes at his crude allusion, but Doc actually cracks a smile at that one. "You guys get out of here and enjoy the rest of your weekend."

"Oh, we will, Doc," Jet says, hopping down.

"If you experience a headache, nausea, dizziness, or any of those other warning signs we discussed, you call me right away, no matter what time it is. And a seizure is an automatic ambulance ride to the ER. You hear?"

Jet shoots off a sloppy salute. "Yes, sir."

With a final shake of his head, Doc takes his leave and mutters toward me, "Good luck with that."

As soon as he's gone, Jet grabs his clothes and shucks his

gown. I openly stare at him while he steps into his underwear, and I plot the moment when I can tug them off again.

Oblivious to my rampant fantasizing, he says about the departed doctor, "That guy loves me."

"Yeah, I could totally tell."

In an amazingly short amount of time, Jet's dressed and sliding his feet into his shoes. With a wiggle of his eyebrows, he asks, "Your place or mine?"

## SIXTEEN

## POWER STRUGGLE

His place was closer, but considering Helen and Beau are spending the day at Jet's, trying to return everything to normal after his guests' departure, mine was quieter. The longer commute was worth it. Our ragged breathing, thumping hearts, and beeping, buzzing phones—all the way down the hall in the living room—are the only sounds as we recover from a reunion that was "lovelier" than Mr. Big Talker predicted, despite taking place against the wall... then on the floor... and never quite making it to the bed.

I crawl toward softer sanctuary, but Jet grabs my ankle. "Where do you think you're going?"

Dragging myself to my knees with handfuls of bedspread and flinging the covers back, I break his hold and slink onto the mattress. "Somewhere comfy."

He follows me, placing kisses from my hip to my neck. Pressing his warm front against my back, he pulls the blankets over us and settles with his chin on my shoulder, his ear pressed to mine. I close my eyes and relish the shiver when he runs his hand up my side and cups my breast, and I rest my own hand over his, rubbing my thumb back and forth over his knuckles.

"MVP-caliber performance there, Champ."

"I don't know. We might have to share that trophy."

"I'm okay with that. It could spend one week here, one week at your place. We could make it work."

His smile fades against my cheek, and he stills.

My eyes open, but I don't otherwise move. "What's the matter?"

"Nothing." But the answer is too quick, and it doesn't fool me any more than my tears at the airport fooled him.

"Spill it, Knox."

"I already did."

I laugh-groan. "Ew."

Once again, his cheek pulls upward on mine. "Nothing's *wrong*."

I wait, blinking.

He takes a deep breath and turns his head slightly to kiss my face. "What if... What if the MVP trophy didn't have to live in two places?"

"You do know there's no MVP sex trophy, right?"

He tweaks my breast. "I'm being serious."

"No, you're speaking in riddles, because you're afraid to come out and say what you're thinking."

Frankly, I'm afraid, too. And I don't have an answer—at least, not one he's going to like—for the scenario I suspect he's proposing.

"Okay, fine." He pulls me onto my back and looks down into my face. "I think it's time you sell this place and move in with me."

I bite my lower lip.

"You don't want to?"

"That's not it."

"What is it, then?"

"It's…" I scramble for all the reasons I've given myself during the past few months of driving back and forth and living out of duffel bags.

Before I can land on the most persuasive argument, he says, "You're at my place most of the time, anyway."

"Lately, yes. But those have been some unusual circumstances."

"And in less than two months, you'll be moving in for good, so why not bump it up a little? Save yourself the hassle of maintaining this place, when you're hardly here."

Considering I own half a duplex in a neighborhood with an association that does all the mowing and upkeep, maintenance is the least of my worries, but we both know he's referring to the mortgage payment, and I appreciate him tiptoeing around the exact words. Money talks are always so uncomfortable.

While I formulate my response, he continues, "I want to wake up next to you every day."

"You will!"

"Now. And I want to know that when I get home at night, you'll be there. Or I'll be there when you get home. I-I want to get into a routine, a rhythm." He underscores that last word with a thrust of his hips against my pelvis. "I'm sick of 'sometimes you're here, sometimes you're there,' and never knowing which one it's going to be."

"We'll be more consistent. And you can stay here sometimes."

He wrinkles his nose.

"What's that for?"

He smiles sheepishly. "I don't know. This place is so tiny."

"How much room do we need?"

"This *bed* is tiny. I hang off the end of it."

I snort. "It's not my bed's fault you're a giant. It's a standard queen."

When he grouses "Too small," I sigh. "I'll get a bigger bed."

"For two months? That's almost as dumb as I am. It's not about the bed, Maura."

"Duh."

"Yeah, duh. It's about us. I wish we had set the wedding date for Valentine's Day. Or something closer to the end of the season. April seems forever away." He presses his forehead to mine.

"That would have been insane. Final planning on a wedding while you were playing in the postseason and preparing for the Super Bowl? It was bad enough, as it was. We would have gone crazy."

"I guess."

"We put a ton of thought into the 'when.' It's when it is for a reason."

"Okay, but that's all the more reason for you to move in with me. It'll be easier to get all this last-minute stuff done if we're in the same house."

I close my eyes. "Your house…"

"You don't like my house?"

*Gaaaaaaaaaaaaaa!*

"No! I mean, yes! I mean, that's not the point."

"But it's the truth."

"It's not that I don't like it." *Liar, liar, liar.* "It's just so… huge."

"It has to be. Where else am I going to put my family when they come to visit?"

I stare at his chest while I trace my finger along the edge

of his muscles and around his nipple, which twitches. "There are these buildings. And they're super-nice. For a nominal fee, everyone gets their own room, including their own bathroom. Some provide meals and laundry service. Kansas City has a bunch of them, fancy ones, even. They're called... 'hotels.'"

"I'm not going to make my family stay in a hotel!" He rolls onto his back and nearly falls off the edge of the bed. I scoot to give him more room but immediately snuggle against his side when he resettles.

"Why not?"

"Because I want to spend time with them."

"We will. But we'll cut out the annoying parts. You know, waiting for everyone to get ready in the morning and kids crying when it's time for bed and kids getting up at the butt-crack of dawn and running up and down the hall, knocking on your bedroom door."

"That's not annoying; it's cute."

"You were annoyed at Christmas."

"I had a game the next day. Anyway, one day, it'll be our kids, and we'll need that space all the time."

*Heaven help me.*

I grab the steering wheel of the conversation and yank it hard to the right before we veer off into a deep, dark, dank ditch. "We won't need all that space. Even after we have a kid. Or two." *It's time to quantify—and limit—this future goal.* With a placating hand under the covers, on his warm belly, I soften the intensity in my voice. "Listen. I want someplace that's ours. Together. Something that reflects both of our personalities."

"My house can be that. Moving is such a pain in the ass, Maura. I really don't want to do it."

"I don't want to, either, but I don't have a choice. I've resigned myself to that."

"Resigned yourself? Geez. Sorry marrying me is such a chore."

Eek! Would it be too transparent a diversionary tactic to move my hand lower under the covers? Probably. I settle for turning onto my side, propping my head in my hand, and attempting a smile. "That's not what I meant. I get that we can't live in my dinky duplex in Overland Park. What I'm not as sure about is why *you* get to keep everything the same while I'm uprooted."

"I don't know. I never thought about it."

"It's because you have more money; therefore, you have more power in this relationship."

"That's such a load of bullshit."

"It's not."

He rolls onto his side to face me, mirrors my pose, and pokes me between the breasts. "*You* have all the power. Because I'd do anything for you. I'll live in a damn teepee, if that's what you want."

Coming from a guy who plays for a team called the Chiefs, the borderline racist comment doesn't shock as much as it should. In the interest of moving the conversation along—and hopefully ending it soon—I let it slide this once.

"I want us both to have what we want."

"I thought we already had it," he mutters, picking at the sheet between us.

Oh, Lord.

"We do!" I grab his hand. "Jet. Honey. Sweetie."

He glances up from our locked grips.

Reaching the point of exasperation, I stifle a sigh. "I... I'm trying to come to grips with everything, and I'm sorry if it's taking me a while to get it all straight in my head, but—"

"There's nothing to keep straight." He pulls me against his chest. "What's mine is yours, and what's yours is mine."

"In Jet Knox Fantasy Land?"

"No, in real life. In marriage." He practically drops me as he flops to his back again and lifts his arms, propping his head on them while staring at the closet door a few feet from the foot of my bed. "If you married some—I don't know—dude you met at work, another job counselor, or something, you'd combine your accounts without thinking twice."

"Because it would be equal...ish. It would be relatively half and half." He'd likely make more than me, because he has a penis, but that's a rant for another day. I try to stay on topic. "With you and me, my income in a joint bank account would be like me pouring a shot glass of water into Lake Superior."

"It's not just about money, though. Personally, I'm psyched about my new movie and screenplay collection. I don't have anything half as cool as that to bring to the table."

"Don't forget my posters and my almost-classic car. Those are yours now, too, according to your weird logic."

"Now you're getting the hang of it. See? I don't know why it's so difficult for some people to understand." He sits up, swings his legs over the side of the bed, and walks toward the bathroom.

I sit and hug my knees as I watch his progress. Before he crosses the threshold, I say, "'Some people'?"

He pauses in the doorway, hugging the frame. "Huh?"

"You said you don't know why it's 'so difficult for *some people* to understand.'"

His eyes glaze as he stares into the middle distance, like

he's trying to rewind the conversation and listen to it again. "I did?"

"Yes."

He frowns. "Oh. Well. Whatever. I meant, you. Why is it so hard for *you* to understand?"

"But I'm only one person. 'Some people' implies multiple persons have questioned the redistribution of your wealth... to me."

Clearing his throat, he shrugs. "I didn't mean for it to come out that way."

"But it did."

He jabs a thumb over his shoulder. "I really gotta pee. And then we better get moving if we're going to catch up with Rae and Colin. Right?"

I turn my head sideways and hum, "Mm-hm."

"Good. I'm starving." He disappears into the bathroom and closes the door.

Emptying his bladder isn't the only thing bringing him relief right about now, I'm sure, having escaped that conversation. But if he thinks I'm going to forget his little slip, I want a second opinion on all of those MRIs.

## SEVENTEEN

# NIGHT OUT

I hate to be one of *those* people, but after some extensive facial contortions at the table, I manage to get Rae to understand that we *both* need to use the bathroom before we leave the restaurant for the movie theater. After I check under each stall door to ensure we're alone, I straighten and face my friend, who stands before me with her arms crossed over her chest.

"Care to explain why you're being so weird tonight?" she asks.

"I'm pretty sure Gloria is trying—or has tried—to get Jet to make me sign a prenup."

"He hasn't already made you sign one?"

"No!"

She chuckles. "Wow. Just when I think that guy can't get any dumber..."

"Rae!"

She raises her hands in front of herself. "Sorry, sorry. But seriously. His mom is right... if, in fact, she wants him to do that, which makes sense, because she seems like a smart lady.

Ned, on the other hand... Jet's apple may have fallen closer to that tree."

"Are you finished insulting my future husband's intelligence?"

"Are you finished being dramatic about something that's pretty standard in the world of celebrity?"

I consider that for a second but answer, "No. Although I get what you're saying." I nibble my thumbnail. "Aren't prenups an—I don't know—acknowledgment that a marriage isn't going to last, and when—not if—it does break up, a way for the person with all the money to leave the other person high and dry?"

"Maybe on the last gripping episode of your favorite soap opera, but not in real life. In real life, they're protection against those who may not have the purest motives for being with someone else. And given Jet's status, not to mention his personal history with the first future Mrs. Knox, do you blame Gloria for being paranoid?"

"Yes! Yes, I do! Because I'm not Ginny. And maybe if Gloria wasn't so— so scary and intimidating, Ginny would have stayed with Jet and not moved on to someone in the locker room with a less intense mother."

"Well, you'd be shit outta luck if that had happened, so I guess you should be glad Gloria's such a tiger mom and Jet's such a mama's boy."

"That's not—" I drop my head back and stare up into the fluorescent lights. "I don't know why I try to talk to you. Oh, that's right. Because Colin can't come into the ladies' room."

"Ouch."

I lower my chin. "Sorry. That was horrible and bitchy and not true."

"You're right; Colin could totally pass and come in here

without anyone batting an eyelash. Do you want me to go get him?"

I laugh. "No! I want you to help me to not take it personally if my future mother-in-law has such little faith in me that she'd give Jet that advice. That she'd think I'm a gold-digger or another glorified groupie… That hurts!"

"Does it hurt as much as a friend saying you're only her confidante because you have the right 'equipment' to accompany her to the restroom?"

"I don't know. How much did that hurt?"

"Not that much. I get it. Sort of." She shuffles her feet.

"I'm sorry. I really, really am. You would have been my first choice, vagina or no vagina."

"I prefer vagina. Now, before we go any further, I need to know why you're so sure Gloria gave him this advice."

As quickly as possible, keeping in mind that we've already been in here a while, I relay the basics of my earlier conversation with Jet, finishing with, "It sounded to me like he's talked about this with someone other than me, and that someone disagrees with his theory that his money is my money now. Who else would care but his mom?"

"His dad? His siblings? His financial advisers? His lawyers? His agent? Other guys who've been through this and whose asses were saved by a solid prenup? It could have been any number of people. Hell, knowing your brother, it was Greg."

I pull my chin back to refute that theory, then realize she's right. "I'll kill him," I say through clenched teeth.

"I'm not saying it *was* him. My point is, it could have been anyone. Or several people. Instead of getting all hurt about it, you should focus on the most important detail, which of course has escaped you. Because you're you."

"Enlighten."

"Jet hasn't made you sign one. He hasn't so much as mentioned it. And he argues with you when you try to reject his money. Speaks volumes, don't you think?"

"I guess. It still sucks to know that someone's in his ear, talking smack about me."

"They're not talking smack about *you*. They're reminding him that people, in general, are money-grubbing a-holes, and he has plenty of money to grub. He should probably do what he can to protect himself. He's going to need every dollar he has for a new brain someday, when that becomes a medical possibility."

I grab the door handle. "I take back my apology. I'd rather talk to Colin. You're so mean."

"Oh, whatever."

"And you love Jet, but it would kill you to show it in any of the normal ways."

She rolls her eyes. "Thanks, Dr. Philomena. Anyway, our playful banter keeps him grounded. It doesn't help that he's such an easy target. I try to be nice to him, but…"

"Try harder."

She sticks out her tongue at me and nods at my arm. "Are we going to—"

A timid knock comes from the other side of the door. "Everything okay in there?" Jet says through the wood and metal.

I swing open the door and smile at him. "Hey! Sorry it took so long. I had a, um, wardrobe issue."

He looks me up and down and tries to see behind me to spy the problem, but I wave him off. "We fixed it. Ready?"

"Yeah. I signed about a zillion napkins while you guys were

in there. We'd better get to the theater if we're going to catch the beginning of the movie."

As we join Colin on the sidewalk in front of the restaurant and begin the short walk to where we're parked, Rae says, "Hey, Knox. You may not want to linger outside women's restrooms, huh? People'll think MVP stands for something else, like Most Visible Peeper."

"Or Massive Voyeuristic Pervert," Colin adds with a snicker, holding out his hand for a fist bump that Rae stares down with a sneer.

Jet grazes knuckles with our English friend, instead. "Hey, I won't leave you hanging, even if you're totally making fun of me."

"I rest my case about that brain transplant," Rae mutters.

———

*He's a lowly office worker, slogging through each week, working for the weekend, doing the bare minimum to draw a paycheck to pay his bills. Then, during one of his daily marathon toilet sessions, he overhears something unethical—and downright illegal—is happening at the company. Discovered eavesdropping by the two other men, he's given the choice by the undercover white collar fraud investigators to either help them take down the company's CFO or be out of a job, one he needs to pay the child support for the son in the framed picture on his desk (yeah… you knew there had to be a cute kid in there somewhere to raise the stakes).*

That's what's happened so far in this mindless-but-enjoyable comedy that's gone a long way toward distracting me from my worries. Going the rest of the way is hearing Jet giggle and belly-laugh his way through the film, much of which involves physical humor, exactly how he likes it. The man can watch sports bloopers all day, so I knew by its description on the theater website this would be the perfect film for him.

Our intrepid, albeit lovable, awkward, and reluctant hero is about to kiss his office crush—and undoubtedly screw it up in the funniest but worst way possible—when a light to my right blinds me. I squint and shield my eyes from the glare.

"Hey," I hiss at Jet. "What are you doing? Turn that off before someone complains."

He slumps in his seat and says near my ear, "I missed a call from my mom during dinner, and now she's texting me like crazy."

I sigh. Seriously? The woman's been away from her precious baby boy for mere hours.

The crowd around us erupts as the inevitable happens on-screen, and our protagonist starts to feel the effects of the expired sandwich he purchased from the vending machine and scarfed a few scenes ago.

"I'm going out to the lobby to call her back, make sure everything's okay."

"I'm sure everything's fine. She probably wants to tell you they got home."

"If that was all, she'd text me once and leave it at that. She keeps texting, 'Call me.'"

"Maybe she saw someone wearing your jersey. You know how excited she gets, like every time is the first time."

Rae leans forward and shoots a dirty look down the row at our murmured conversation.

"I'll be right back," Jet whispers, standing and edging past my legs to get to the nearest aisle.

I tighten my jaw and try to return my attention to the

movie, but it's hard to seethe and laugh at the same time. In fact, it's impossible. And seething wins out.

This is the first relaxing evening Jet and I have had in weeks, and Gloria couldn't let us have it. Unbelievable.

Why didn't she stay, if she can't bear to be separated from her youngest son? In fact, I kept waiting for her to announce it would be easier for her to plan and finalize the wedding here, rather than flying home to California, only to return here in a few weeks. Now, my elation at seeing her go through security at the airport earlier this morning is nothing but a fuzzy memory.

Because she never did leave. Not really. I've been thinking about her most of the day, thanks to my suspicions about the prenup. Hell, maybe that's what she's calling about now. *"Did you pay for Maura's dinner tonight? Her movie ticket? The girl is bleeding you dry. Get those papers in front of her!"*

Okay, maybe not.

Still. She must have cringed every time I used Jet's credit card while they were visiting. But I wasn't going to gas up his cars on my dime to shuttle them around. And when we went out to dinner with my parents, *she* chose the restaurant, a place way out of my price range. Regardless, Jet wouldn't hear of me paying for that. Then the Super Bowl tickets for my family and me... She must think we're the biggest mooches.

Well, we're not. Jet insisted on treating us to our week in Dallas. He called it his early wedding gift to us, a "welcome to the family." "I want you all there with me." Who says no to that? Nobody.

Thirty minutes pass with me hardly registering anything happening on the screen in front of me or the auditorium around me. There's a supply closet and some rigged-up surveillance equipment (a cell phone and some binder clips) that capture the boss and his secretary doing some hilarious "erotic" role-playing, but while the rest of the audience roars at the actors' antics, I fume that the seat next to me is empty while my date deals with his mother's latest demands.

My purse lights up at my feet. I stare into the glowing bag, tempted to ignore it. But Jet's been gone so long that now I'm starting to worry there *is* something wrong. That would be unfortunate, considering I've been sitting here, stewing like a snotty kid. Cupping my hand around the device to minimize the light it emits, I slide it just far enough from my purse to read the screen.

*We have to go.*

Disappointment and worry grab and wring my stomach like two hands with a wet rag. Fortunately, we all met at the restaurant, so Colin and Rae aren't relying on us for transportation, but I still hate to have to whisper at them, "Something's up. Jet and I have to leave."

"Is it Jet? Is he ill?" Colin asks, his forehead wrinkled.

"No! He's fine. Probably Gloria being dramatic." In a swift reversal of sentiment, I feel horrible using her as a tool to downplay all of our fears. Deep down, I know it has to be something bad for Jet to prematurely end our date. Still, I don't want to ruin our friends' night, so I manage to smile shakily at them and rise. "Let me know how the movie ends."

"Read the synopsis online for yourself," Rae snarks back with a wink. "Seriously, though, if there's anything I can do, call. You know, two heads are better than one... and a half."

I stick out my tongue at her, gather my purse and trash, and scurry from the theater, hoping we haven't been too disruptive. I'm a pretty laid-back person—or used to be—but nothing gets me more uptight than rude moviegoers.

At least, that used to be the case. I long for the days when being annoyed by a texting person in front of me or a whispering couple behind me were my biggest complaints. What a charmed life I led, without realizing it! I can't even enjoy a night out at the movies anymore, and my ruined experience has nothing to do with rude people who treat the theater like an extension of their living room.

In the relatively bright lobby, I blink to get my bearings and search for Jet in the teeming mass of people milling around, waiting for auditoriums to be open for the next shows.

*Where the...?*

Oh, of course.

In addition to the lines at concessions, there's a line in front of a tall, dark-haired guy whose smile is tighter and laugh is more forced than it was at the airport earlier. He poses for selfies and group photos, signs popcorn tubs, napkins, and candy boxes (no body parts this time), but when his eyes meet mine over the line of heads, they scream, *"Get me out of here!"*

Time to play bouncer.

I gently push through the crowd, saying, "Excuse me," about a million times before I reach his side.

"Ready to go?" I ask loudly enough for most of the fans to hear.

He swallows and stares down the queue of folks clamoring for his attention. "Uhh, yeah. Just let me—"

I'm not about to deny anyone their autograph, but this isn't a meet-n-greet; it's a movie theater lobby. With each person who steps up, I explain as apologetically as possible, "Quickly, okay? We have somewhere else to be. Family emergency."

I have no idea if those last things are accurate, but they

work wonders. Nobody lingers. Everyone understands and walks away grateful to have received their scrawled memento and a smile from the Super Bowl MVP. In no time, the line is gone as everyone wanders off to get to their own movie. The only people left are a girl of about five and her dad.

The man nudges her forward. "Go ahead," he says with a proud smile.

While I expect her to ask Jet for his autograph or give him a hug (that's usually what the kids want to do), she steps up to me and wraps her arms around my legs.

Despite my surprise, I immediately return her unexpected embrace, laughing at her dad, who shrugs and explains, "She wanted to hug 'the nice lady with that big guy.'"

Given my thoughts for the past hour, I don't *feel* nice, so her compliment hits a raw heart string. I crouch down to her level. "Oh. Well, thanks! I appreciate that."

She smiles shyly and whispers, "You're welcome."

"You're nice, too. Do you want Jet to sign something for you?"

Marker poised, Jet stands by. She looks up at him but shakes her head. "Nope. I can write my own name. I'm in kindergarten."

She returns to her dad, who says, "If you don't mind doing one more autograph..." He holds out a candy box, full and ready to feed him during whichever feature he's here to see with his daughter. Jet signs his name, says, "Have a good night," and nervously eyes the next group of people entering the lobby, having recently purchased tickets at the box office.

"Let's go," I say, pulling him to the doors before any of the newcomers recognize him.

The whispers follow us to the sidewalk, but we keep moving, heads down, until we reach the car. There'll be plenty of time on the way home for him to fill me in on what's happening.

———

Up-to-speed by the time we get to Jet's, I'm not surprised when Cyndi greets us in the mudroom by flinging herself into her big brother's arms. He pets her hair and murmurs something against her head that makes her cry harder while I watch helplessly, feeling like an outsider but unable to look away. He silently holds onto her until she calms and releases him.

Wiping her tears from her puffy face, she emits a self-deprecating groan. "I'm sorry. Hormones."

"It's okay," Jet replies, hanging up his car keys and jamming his hands in his pockets.

"Yeah, it's okay," I echo, not sure what else to say. She doesn't need my approval, after all, to release the emotions she's been holding onto for who knows how long.

"Mikey's in bed," she says, leading us through to the kitchen, where it looks like a bomb went off. I freeze and hope I'm hiding my shock at the sight before me. In case I'm not, I cross to the fridge to hide my face in there, in the guise of searching for something to drink.

"Sorry about the mess. I bake when I'm upset. Everything's better with cookies, right?" She shakes her head when I offer her a bottle of water.

I pull up one of the barstools at the island.

"How long have you been here?" Jet asks, pushing his finger through a pile of flour on the counter. He brushes the silky powder from his fingertip with his other hand.

"A couple of hours. I'm so sorry Mom interrupted your date! I told her to leave you alone, but she said it was rude for me to be here without your knowing." She snorts. "Typical Mom. Shit's hitting the fan, and she's worried about etiquette."

Jet half-smiles. "No kidding. Don't worry about it. Any of it. Stop apologizing. You can stay here as long as you want to. Or need to. You know that, right?"

She nods but can't verbalize her response as her eyes fill again. Before she's overcome, she sniffs and frantically starts cleaning up the mess. I stand and work on the area closest to me, sweeping Jet's fingered pile of flour into my palm and dumping it into the trash. I replace the lid on the canister and line it up with the smaller sugar, sea salt, and cinnamon jars.

Jet sloughs off his coat and carries it into the mudroom. When he returns, his sleeves are rolled to his elbows, and he's carrying a broom and dustpan. "Mom says you got as far as Denver, and you turned back. What happened? She said you argued, but..."

Keeping her eyes down on the crusty cookie sheets she's collected in a pile to throw in the sink full of sudsy water, Cyndi says, "They don't get it, you know? Nobody in this family does. Everyone's perfectly paired up, and I'm the idiot screw-up who ruined the Knox family's undefeated marital record." Her chin puckers. "But what am I supposed to do? Be miserable for the rest of my life, so Mom and Dad have something to be proud of?"

"They're proud of you."

"No, they're not. And they've made it clear the past few days. They're disappointed. Beyond disappointed. The words, 'crushed,' 'devastated,' and 'heartbroken' have been tossed around liberally."

Obviously at a loss for how to respond, Jet sweeps crumbs, sugar, and flour into a small pile in the center of the floor.

Bent over to collect the debris in the dustpan, he says quietly, "So, it's really over then? Between you and Justin? You're never ever getting back together?"

I shoot him a warning look for sounding like a pop star and jump in. "Your parents will get over it. They will. They love you. It's just hard to adjust to change. Especially if they had no idea things were falling apart. This seems sudden to them, no matter how long it's been coming for you."

"Yeah," she says, scraping at a piece of stuck-on cookie with her thumbnail. "I guess. But my breaking point was in Denver, when we were waiting for our connecting flight, and Mom said..." She pauses, closing her eyes to collect herself as she quotes, "'You can't be a sponge for the rest of your life, Cyndi. You can't live with your father and me while you support two children on your own. That's not going to happen, so get that idea out of your head right now.'"

Jet and I audibly inhale.

She opens her eyes. "That's when I got up without a word, took Mikey from her, and walked away with our stuff. She called after me, but I kept walking, following the signs to the nearest ticket counter, where I could get a flight back here. Maxed out my credit card, and my checked bags might not get here until Easter, but I don't care. I won't be abused like that. I can't let Mikey watch me take that. He saw me take that— and so much worse—for so long..." She folds her arms on top of the baking sheets and rests her forehead against them, her shoulders shaking as she breaks down again.

Without hesitation, Jet and I abandon our cleaning and circle the island from either side, where we flank her, massaging and patting, like our hands can rub it all away. But they can't.

And a cookie sure as hell isn't going to fix this.

## EIGHTEEN

## DYSFUNCTIONAL FAMILY

Later, in the bathroom, Jet says through a mouthful of foam, "I'm gonna kill 'im."

As he bends his head over the sink to spit out the tooth-paste, I stare at his smooth neck. "No, you're not."

He cups water in his hand to rinse his mouth, spits again, and says, "Yeah, I am. I'm going to fly to Germany, wrap my hands around his thick neck, and shake him until—"

"Jet!"

He dries his hands and face on the towel hanging next to him on the wall and plunks his fists on his hips. "You're right. I'm not."

I laugh. "Really?"

"No."

"I realize that, dork. And it's perfectly normal to be mad."

"I'm more than mad, Maura."

"Okay. Homicidal."

"That's more like it."

"But you have to be an adult here. She says he never hit her."

"Oh, that makes it okay, then."

"Did I say that?"

"No, but you're implying that mental abuse is less serious than physical abuse, because you can't see the bruises. Screw that."

I pull on his arm until his hand falls from his hip and twine my fingers through his. "Hey. I don't think that at all. I'm only saying, you can't fight your sister's battles for her. She's done a decent job of fighting for herself so far. The only legal recourse for this is divorce. Which she's doing."

"I liked that guy. I thought he was nice."

"Some people are good at hiding their worst selves."

"I feel tricked. And I'm so pissed at Mom and Dad right now…"

Oh-ho-ho! What's this? Dissension in the Knox ranks? It's not nice to revel in something like that, but my internal jerk rubs her hands and cackles. On the outside, I try to remain passive as he edges past me toward the bedroom. I flip off the lights and follow him while his rant continues.

"How can they consider *letting* her go back to him, much less pressure her to do it?" After checking his phone one more time, he slides his legs under the covers and plumps his pillows behind his head. He settles on his back and folds his hands over his midriff. Blinking at the ceiling, he says, "I'm sorry our date was ruined."

"It wasn't ruined. Cut short, maybe, but not ruined." I nestle against his side, and when he doesn't readily participate in the cuddling, I arrange his arm around me.

He allows himself to be posed while he stares at nothing in particular above us.

"I'm sorry things are such a mess with your family. It seems like you guys aren't familiar enough with dysfunction to know how to handle it. Which is a good thing, most of the time. But in times like this, it's hard."

"We're no strangers to problems. But we all know our positions on the team, and as long as nobody steps out of line, we're good."

"Ah. I see. And this isn't the first time Cyndi's stepped out of line?"

"She's definitely the rebel of the bunch, but she's done nothing wrong here."

"I agree. In your parents' eyes, though…" After a pause, I pat his hand and say, "You two are closer than I realized."

"She can count on me to help her out and not be a dick. That's how it's always been."

"That's nice. And so important."

"But that's why I'm so frustrated! Why didn't she tell me sooner? Why didn't she leave that jerk earlier? She knows she could have come here. Or does she? Maybe I haven't been there for her, like she thinks I'm too busy, or something."

"Maybe she wanted to see if she could fix it herself. It might not be about you at all. Imagine that."

Either that goes over his head, or it's not as funny as I'd hoped, because he doesn't react to it at all. Instead, he continues that thousand-yard stare I've seen so many times in candid shots of him on the bench when the team is losing, and everyone else is scrambling, looking at the sideline tablets, studying defenses and offenses, trying to find a weakness in the other team to capitalize on. That's when you'll find Jet, alone, knit hat pulled down on his forehead, legs spread, hands dangling in his lap, in a trance.

Amused after a particularly long camera shot of one such "session," I asked him the next time I talked to him what goes through his mind at times like that.

He laughed and said, "You're not going to believe it."

"Try me."

"Pretty much nothing. That's why I look so... dumb. I'm honestly trying not to think about anything. It's scary how easy it is."

"Like meditation?"

"Good spin. Yeah. It's like meditation."

I assume he's "meditating" now. Or at least, clearing his mind of any homicidal thoughts toward his soon-to-be-former brother-in-law and his parents. I close my eyes and leave him to it.

———

The next morning, as I'm walking down the hall to get to the stairs, I hear sniffles. And sobs. Passing by Cyndi's room, I spy the Knox family rebel sitting on the side of her freshly made bed. The conflict-averse side of me screams instructions to keep walking and pretend I didn't see or hear anything. The actual human with a heart backtracks and says, still from the relative safety of the hallway, "Hey."

She looks up as if it never occurred to her that someone might witness her despair with her door flung wide open. Swiping the tears from her face, she snaps to attention on her feet and straightens the already-made bed, repositioning the pillows until they're exactly where they started. "Oh, hey. I... I thought you were downstairs and I was alone up here."

"Nope. I'm the late sleeper, and Jet's the early bird. Where's Mikey?"

She smiles. "With the early bird. Jet came in here and got Mikey and told me to sleep as long as I wanted. But I can't sleep. I haven't slept much at all for... a while. Maybe my body's forgotten how."

I venture farther into the room so my voice doesn't carry down the hallway or the stairs when I say, "You know, Jet means it when he says you can stay here as long as you want."

"I can't, though. Being a sponge isn't my thing."

"Nobody thinks you're being a sponge."

"Mom does."

"I'm sure she said that before thinking."

"That's when people say what they really think, though. And I would *feel* like a freeloader, which wouldn't work for me. I'll figure something out."

"You don't have to rush to figure it out, though. That's all I'm saying."

"Thanks. But I need my own space. And you guys do, too. Pretty soon, you'll be newlyweds, and... and how can you fully enjoy that with your husband's sad-sack sister moping around with her loud-mouthed toddler? Plus, in a few months..." She gestures down to her still-flat belly.

"Don't worry about us."

"I do, though. This isn't fair to you. And, if I'm being honest, I worry about me, too. You guys are so happy." Her voice catches. "I don't remember there ever being a time when Justin looked at me the way Jet looks at you."

"I'm sure there was. You just never noticed it. *I* never notice it. Thank God. I'd tell him to cut it out."

She releases a wet snort. "Well, he does. You could be talking about something as boring as the weather, and the look on his face... You might as well be reciting Shakespeare. He hangs on every word. If it wasn't so adorable, I'd tease him about it. But I'm sure he gets enough of that from Keith and David." She sighs. "Anyway. As wonderful as it is for you, it's hard for me. It's a painful reminder that I don't have that. Maybe I never did. And if I did, I lost it, which might be worse."

I've got nothing. What do I say to that? What she's saying makes sense. It would be horrible to be so dependent on others for financial and emotional support while also facing every single day the evidence that romantic love does exist but not for you right now.

I step up to her and pull her into a hug. "Your brother would do anything for you."

"I know," she muffles into my shirt.

"I don't think you do. Nothing is too much to ask."

She pushes away and pats my upper arms. "Don't worry. I'm not going to test that theory."

"I'm not worried. Until he says we're taking Mikey on our honeymoon. Then I might flinch."

She laughs. "Oh, geez. If that even comes up in casual conversation, you get him back to the doctor for another head scan."

"I will. And I'll leave you alone now. Gotta make sure those two Micahs aren't getting into trouble."

She chuckles. "I'll be down soon. It upsets Mikey when I cry, so give me a minute."

"Take all the time you need."

I return to the hallway and close the door behind me, but instead of continuing immediately on my way downstairs, I linger against the opposite wall, trying out my own version of Jet's "meditation stare."

Nobody has the perfect life or relationship, but glimpsing my life through Cyndi's eyes is humbling. She doesn't know about the building panic with each day that brings me closer to the wedding, not to mention the job fair. She has no idea my dining room is strewn with art supplies and creepy gold men. All she knows is that her brother loves me, and I love him, and she'd give anything to have that one thing for herself right now. Because when you have that, everything else falls into place, right?

Ha!

———

"Dude. You're doing it wrong. It goes like this..."

From his belly on the terra cotta tiles in the sun room, Jet reaches into the bucket of olive and tan plastic soldiers and pulls out a handful, which, for him, is about twenty of the things. His tongue poking from the corner of his mouth, he sets them precisely in a grid, four by four along the floor's grout lines, then positions another one in front of the block, facing the "company." The leftovers go back in the bucket.

Mikey sweeps his arm through the formation, knocking down most of the figures.

Jet groans but quickly ad-libs with, "Take cover, men! It's the dreaded Mikey Monster!"

The toddler giggles and continues his carnage, swiping swathes of troops from their positions.

His uncle grabs the figure with the walkie-talkie. "Breaker one-nine... *Crssh...* We have a Mikey Monster at ten o'clock... *Crssh...* I repeat, a Mikey Monster... *Crssh...* Everyone take cover and hold positions. Wait for further instructions. Over. *Crssh.*" He hurries his man to a spot behind a chair leg before poking through the downed troops, looking for someone specific. When he doesn't find him, he dumps the nearby bucket and searches through the pile.

"Ah-ha! Um, medic! Over here! Agh! My leg! Can you save it?"

Mikey blocks Jet's way to the injured man, shrieking gleefully at his treachery.

"Hey! You have to let the medic treat the wounded. It's, like, a rule, or something."

"Mikey Monster! Arrrrrrgggh!"

"Yeah, yeah. I guess Mikey Monsters don't care about rules of engagement; I'll give you that. 'Someone cover me!'

"Breaker one-nine... *Crssh*... We have a request for assistance and cover fire from Medic Knox... *Crssh*... Fire at will." Spit flies as Jet rains machine gun rounds at the Mikey Monster.

Mikey joins in the sound effects, obviously enjoying that role more.

I clear my throat from the doorway. "Um, don't you think that's a tad bit violent?"

Jet jumps guiltily and snaps his head in my direction. "Oh, hey. Uh, no. Maybe. But this is what he wanted to do." He pushes himself to a sitting position and wipes some lingering spittle from his lips. "Wanna play?"

I laugh. "No."

"Aw, c'mon. It's fun!"

Mikey holds a soldier aloft. "Daddy!"

Raising an eyebrow at Jet, I cringe. "Now look what you've done."

He winces. "Yeah, he keeps calling them 'Daddy.' When we were looking through the toy closet, I tried to distract him with some other stuff, but he wasn't having it. So, Army men, it is."

"Air Force, though, right?" I say with a smirk.

Jet rolls his eyes. "He's two. Like he knows the difference."

Mikey scrambles to his feet and runs to me, offering up his "Daddy." "Hee-yuh. You pway."

Jet snickers. "Good luck saying no to that."

He's right; I can't. I take the action figure and find a clear space to occupy on the floor. "Let's do something less intense, though. Like... basic training? Or shining our shoes? Peeling potatoes?"

"Bo-ring!" Jet intones, re-setting his rows of soldiers.

"Bo-ring!" Mikey echoes, making Jet giggle.

Okay, they're right. That is boring. But we have to do something that doesn't involve death and destruction. With the guy in my hand—a paratrooper—I knock down one of Jet's men and jump on top of him. "Tickle fight!"

"What? No!" Jet howls. "There are no tickle fights in the military."

"Wanna bet?"

Mikey grabs a man in each hand and has them join the plastic dog pile. "Tick-uh, tick-uh, tick-uh!"

I smirk over his head at Jet. "See? Mikey approves."

Jet rolls his eyes and raises his hands. "I'm out."

"Oh, I see. You're one of those kids."

"What?"

"The kind who has to have everything his way, and if people aren't playing 'right,' you pick up your toys and go home."

He laughs. "I'm not! But you're making a mockery of our servicemen and women, and I... I can't support that."

"You're ridiculous."

"You are." He props his elbow on his bent knee and observes his nephew, who continues without us, as if our participation has always been superfluous. A dopey smile spreads across Jet's face as he watches the gleeful play and hears the youngster parrot some of the walkie-talkie chatter he used before I interjected myself.

I could watch him watch Mikey all day, but I have serious matters on my mind. I sober and lower my voice. "Hey, so, I've been thinking."

Jet blinks and turns a more devilish grin toward me. "How many times do I have to tell you, it's not worth it? Join the non-thinkers like me. We're happier."

I narrow my eyes at him.

"Sorry." He clears his throat. "You've been thinking…"

"I was talking to your sister before I came down here." I glance nervously at Mikey and swallow, hoping I'm not about to commit to something I'll end up regretting.

Jet waves off my perceived reticence to talk in front of the child. "As long as you don't say his name or one of his favorite foods or activities, he won't care what we're saying. Spell stuff if you have to. Worked on me until I was, like, twelve."

"You might have been a little behind the curve, Champ."

"Whatever. Talk."

Mikey gets up and wanders over to a pile of die-cast cars still sitting out from earlier.

"See? He's bored with us. What's on your mind?"

"Your sister needs her own place to stay."

His jaw tenses. He rubs his neck and chin and rolls his head backward as if relieving a cramped muscle. "I know it's unexpected and not what we planned, and I have no idea how long she'll be here, but we have to make the best of it. I told her she could stay as long as she needed to, and I meant it."

"I absolutely agree with you."

Everything about him relaxes. "Oh. Whew."

"But she doesn't want to be a permanent house guest. She wants her own space, where she and"—I jerk my head toward the "zoom-zoom"ing little guy—"can establish their own routines, and she can have some privacy, somewhere where *she* calls the shots, where she doesn't have to ask people not to feed her kid hot dogs for every meal. Or worry about someone happening by her room while she's having what Colin would call 'a bit of a weep.'"

"She was crying?"

I nod. "Do you blame her? This is hard stuff. And she feels abandoned by your parents. And she's all hormonal and stuff."

"Oh, man. That sucks. I feel awful for her." He moves to rise from the floor. "Do you think I should go up there and check on her?"

I grab the toe of his sock. "No! You shouldn't. And that's the point. She needs to be able to have a moment without an audience and without feeling bad that she's making people worry. She'd have that in her own place."

He clears his throat. "Ah. Yeah. Well. She can't afford that. And I've already tried to give her money, but she won't take it."

I pick at my jeans. "She could—I don't know—move into my duplex. Or something. Temporarily, even. At least she'd have some privacy and wouldn't feel like a perpetual house guest."

"Where are *you* going to..." He grins but catches himself and nods more soberly, as if he's truly considering all the pros and cons. "I see. Yes. That might work."

"You're such a goober."

He laughs. "Have you talked to her about this?"

"No. Before I suggested it to her, I wanted to run it by you. You know her better than I do. Do you think she'd like the idea, or would it make her uncomfortable?"

"I don't know. Overland Park is pretty far away. She might want to be closer to us than that."

I snort. "She's not going to find her own place anywhere around here. Nowhere she can afford. My neighborhood, on the other hand…"

My sarcastic tone pulls him up short, and he says warily, "Your house is super-nice."

"Mm-hm."

"Not exactly kid-friendly, but…"

"We'll move most of my stuff out of there. Leave the furniture, of course, because I won't need it here, but none of my movie stuff stays there, at the mercy of the M-I-K-E-Y M-O-N-S-T-E-R."

"Of course not. So, what's the timetable on this? I'm ready. You want to make the swap today?"

I shake my head and laugh at his eagerness. "I figured we'd ask her, first, if it's something she'd like."

"Oh. Right. I guess that makes sense. She might feel weird, since you pay the mortgage on that place."

After a deep breath, I say, "Well, if you're serious about 'what's mine is yours and blah, blah, blah…'"

"I am!"

"Then the duplex—and its mortgage—is yours, too. Under that theory. Not legally, yet, but…"

"Oh, yeah!" I've never seen someone look so happy about acquiring that much debt with two words.

"If she still balks or feels like a charity case, she can pay us rent after she gets back on her feet. I don't want her to think we're kicking her out of this house or trying to get rid of her."

He scoots along the tiles on his butt until he's knee-to-knee with me, scrunching us both into smaller balls until we're close enough to touch foreheads. "It's mega-nice that you're willing to do this for her."

I shrug. "She's sweet, and I like her."

It's also a relief to contribute a substantial piece of material property toward what's, until now, felt like a lopsided partnership, but I don't say that. Making this about money would cheapen it, ironically.

He nudges my nose with his. "I get this is a big sacrifice for you, though, giving up your own place before you have to."

"I'm excited not to live out of suitcases anymore."

"I'm excited for all of it." His lips brush mine, and I have to admit when he talks to me and looks at me like that, it's easier to be a believer.

"Mikey Monster!" Thirty pounds of chub collides with us, pushing us sideways.

Jet grabs his nephew and lays him in his lap like a dulcimer, strumming his tummy. "Tickle torture!"

"No!"

Heeding the toddler's pleas, Jet stops.

"Again!" Mikey begs.

## NINETEEN

## MOVING DAY

How have I gone my entire adult life with so few material possessions worth dragging with me from my old home to my new one? Sure, my movie collection fills several dozen boxes, and I've carefully packed my screenplays into sturdy, impervious rubber totes, not sure how long they'll have to be in storage. My framed posters cuddle back-to-front, separated by plenty of padding in large, flat boxes. And the damn Oscar statuettes and art supplies, they've made the trip, too. But those are the only crucial things, other than my clothes. In fact, I so grossly overestimated my belongings that the truck we rented—the smallest one available—was overkill for my move. How anti-climactic!

Not that I'm complaining. Moving sucks.

For the hundredth time, Jet checks, "Is this everything?" as he grasps the strap to pull down the back gate on the truck.

I rack my brain, sure I'm forgetting something important, something huge. Like an heirloom piano I forgot I had. But no. Not even my car is going with me. It'll stay here for Cyndi to use. My new (to me) car awaits in its stall in Jet's pristine garage.

He doesn't seem bothered that this seems more like a move from a college dorm than from a full-sized, alleged grownup's home. In fact he's been so giddy today, I've had to resist the urge several times to tell him to tone it down.

He jumps from the truck's back bumper and latches the lock, pulling on it a few times to ensure it's secure and won't fly open on the highway. Turning to me, he brushes his hands together. "You want a minute alone with your house, you know, to say goodbye?"

I should, shouldn't I? But the thing is, my hesitancy to move in with him has never been about this actual structure. If I'm being honest, I've never loved it. It was like many of my former boyfriends: convenient, comfortable, and cute. But nothing special. Plus, I'm sure I'll be seeing it around, and it won't be weird seeing someone else with it, because it was always meant to be a mere placeholder in my life.

I shake my head. "No. That seems a tad dramatic for my taste."

He chuckles. "All right, then. Let's go."

On the way to his house, we discuss the logistics of getting Cyndi moved in by next weekend. My precious built-in shelves will have to be torn out to make the second bedroom into a space fit for a toddler. One wall of shelves is staying to house books and toys, but the rest are gonzo. The newly exposed walls will require repainting, so Jet plans to spend most of his upcoming week with the contractors he's hired to execute the "explorer" theme Mikey wants.

As Jet eagerly describes the design, complete with a world map that covers an entire wall and a bed made to look like a cabin, I smile over at him, touched by his enthusiasm. "Mikey's going to love it."

He bounces in his seat as much from excitement as from the truck's worn-out suspension. "I hope so. I just want everyone to be happy, you know?"

"I do."

"Mostly you, though. Are you happy?"

I snort at his cheesy romance-hero question. "Yes! Duh. Why wouldn't I be?"

He brakes at the light at the end of the exit ramp and looks over his left shoulder to make sure he's clear to continue his right turn. Avoiding my eyes, he says, "You're not a fan of change, that's all."

I stare at his profile long enough that he feels compelled to glance at me.

He smiles shakily. "You know. You like to do things the same way at the same time every day. It's cute."

"That's not cute; that's anal. Which I'm not. I'm spontaneous."

He snorts. "Okay."

"No, not 'okay,' like you're humoring me. I am! I'm as laid-back as they come. That's why Greg and I don't get along. He's too rigid and thinks there's only one way to be."

"Maybe you two are more alike than you realize, though, and *that's* why you don't get along."

"Screw you."

He laughs. "I'm not saying it's bad."

"It's more than bad; it's horrible. I don't want to be anything like him."

"You might not have a choice. DNA is a bitch."

"You need to shut up right now."

"Maura, don't be mad at me."

"I'm not. Yet. And anyway, look who's talking, Mr. Planner. Your life is so regimented, I'm surprised you don't have your shits penciled in."

"'Shits penciled in!'" he wheezes. "Good one! You know, now that you mention it, I don't write it down, but I usually do go at the same time every day."

His refusal to get defensive at my baiting only irritates me more. "Why am I not surprised? And FYI, I don't want to know when that is. Let's leave some mystery in our relationship."

"You'll figure it out by yourself, I'm sure. You're smart."

"Anyway, I rest my case."

He laughs. "I've never denied that I like routine, and that I need to know what the plan is—in life, on the field... all the time. You're the one who seems to think it's the worst thing in the world."

"Not the worst thing in the world. But tedious. In fact, after our first date, I almost never answered another call from you, because you were so focused. And that's not me."

"Nobody said we had to be alike. How boring would that be? Anyway, sometimes people who don't have long-term goals go overboard with *daily* stuff so they can feel like they're in control of something."

"I had no idea you were such a psychologist."

"I'm not. Rae pointed it out to me once. And she's right."

"I'm going to kill her. And you! Psychoanalyzing me behind my back."

He waves off my threat and indignation like pesky gnats. "Whatever. You know, like your movie collection. It was hard for you to pack it all up."

"It wasn't hard, *emotionally*. I simply wanted to make sure they all stayed in order, so it'll be easy to unpack them someday. Whenever that is." I mutter that last part and turn my attention to the passing scenery.

"Right. Like that."

"Like what?"

He blows air through his lips, making them flap. "Never mind. Sheesh. I didn't mean to start a fight."

"We're not fighting! You're mistaken about a part of my personality, and I'm correcting you. That's not fighting. That's me being right about you being wrong." I cross my arms over my chest.

When *will* I get to unpack my movies? Not that I'm worried about it or need an exact date. It would simply be nice to have an estimate. You know, so I know.

Oh, my gosh.

Who am I?

———

The text comes through while we're standing at the truck rental return counter, waiting for the clerk to stop asking Jet how much the Lombardi trophy weighed, and if Jet has his ring yet, and when he does get it, does he plan to wear it or stick it in a safe somewhere, and how much will he have to get it insured for and blah, blah, blah. When fans start talking about jewelry insurance, it usually means they're running out of questions, so I don't feel too rude checking the message that's pinged in my purse.

It reeks of a premeditated exit plan when I read it and immediately say to Jet, "We have to go."

As if in on the plot, he immediately replies, "Okay," and hastily says his goodbyes to his fan without asking what's up.

In the car, he sighs. "Nice save. Why does everyone want to talk about how much the ring costs?"

"I wasn't bluffing." I fasten my seat belt. "Deirdre's in labor."

His face relaxes into a dopey grin. "Well, how about that? You're about to be an auntie."

"Please don't call me that."

"Auntie Maura. Oh, my gosh! We need to go shopping. We have a few hours, right?" He jabs at the start button on the car and throws it into reverse to exit our parking space.

"I guess, although I figured we'd go to the hospital now and hang around the waiting room with my parents."

"That's miserable. Trust me. I did that with Gidget's first kid. Longest day of my life. Until this past Super Bowl Sunday." Turning out of the lot after waiting for a line of cars to pass, he points the car toward his—*our*—house. "Let's go home, clean up, run out to buy some cool stuff for your new niece, and *then* it might be time. Or not. Might not happen until tomorrow. Babies take a long time to be born. Especially first ones."

Tomorrow. The time I was going to use to get caught up on all of my Oscar statuettes. Seems a bit selfish to worry about that, though, considering my sister-in-law is ushering human life into the world as we speak.

"Let me call my mom and see what their plan is."

Of course, considering this is their first grandchild—and Greg's kid, to boot—my parents are on their way to the hospital right now. But when I question whether I should do the same, Mom laughs. "Why? It's going to be a while. I want to be there for your brother at the exact moment, but it's not necessary for you to be here. And certainly not Jet. That would be chaos."

"Oh. Okay. I thought— Never mind."

"I'll text you as soon as she's born."

"That works. We'll, uh, be waiting, I guess."

"How'd the big move go today?"

"The big...? Oh. Yeah. Great. Pretty easy."

"What you're doing for Jet's sister is wonderful. She'll get much more use of that place than you have been lately. I'm sorry Cyndi's going through such a hard time. She seemed like a nice person when I talked to her in Dallas. But it's a blessing she's given you this motivation to merge house-holds with Jet before things get too hairy with the final wedding preps. Nobody wants to come home from their honeymoon and have to pack and move. You'll be all good to go. And it's good that you and Jet get some real-life, perma-nent co-habitation under your belts before the wedding. I suggested the same thing to Greg and Deirdre, but they were so stubborn, and neither one wanted to give up their houses until the last second. They'd probably still be living in two places if both of them hadn't sold at the same time. Silly kids."

"Yeah. Are you okay, Mom?"

She laughs. "Yes! Yes! I'm— Well, I'm a bit nervous, to tell you the truth. I've never been a grandma before."

I smile tenderly. "You'll be great at it, though." Before she can humbly shrug off my prediction, I say, "Let me know when the newest Richards makes her debut."

"Richards-Snow, Mo. Don't forget that in front of Deirdre."

Never. If for no other reason than I don't want to hear the lecture—*again*—about why *I* should keep *my* maiden name—or at least hyphenate it with Jet's.

I disconnect the call.

Jet glances expectantly over at me, as if he's been awaiting my direction and not driving home this whole time. "Well? What's the plan?"

"Waiting to hear from my mom."

"Sweet. What Greg and Deirdre's kid needs is a huge, pink teddy bear. And we know better, but we'll tell them it needs to go in the crib. That way, we can watch them get all purple-faced while they explain to us how dumb we are."

I giggle at his plan. "It's so obvious you have siblings. You're always coming up with new ways to torment people."

"It's fun! Especially because Greg and D take themselves so seriously and haven't caught on yet. Guaranteed reaction."

"That's another difference between you and me: I do what I can to *avoid* their sanctimonious rants."

"Not me. I nod and make my eyes real big and let my mouth hang all slack"—he demonstrates, making me laugh harder—"and act like if it wasn't for them, I'd be doing everything in life wrong."

"Jet!"

"They already think I'm an idiot. Might as well have fun with it."

"They think everyone's an idiot."

"Right. I wasn't taking it personally." He pulls into his —our—driveway and hits the button on the opener clipped to the sun visor. As he waits for the garage door to fully open so he can slide the car into its empty stall, he says, "But that doesn't mean I'm not going to get my digs in where I can. Everything we get that kid is going to be cringe-worthy. 'Oh, I didn't realize you were only dressing her in unisex garments made from all-natural fibers; here's a polyester Chiefs cheerleader uniform. In multiple sizes, so she never outgrows it. I'll be hurt if she doesn't wear it for every game!'"

When I say nothing, he looks over at me, his grin fading. "What?"

"I love you so much."

He laughs and ruffles my hair. "I love you, too. Now, hit the showers, Richards. We have some serious spite-shopping to do."

## AUNTIE MAURA

A half-day passes before we're allowed to lay eyes on the child. Through a window. I expected her to be one of the squalling, red-faced ones who keeps rubbing off her hat and scratching at her face with her razor-like fingernails, but in the middle of a few other fusspotts, she lies in her see-through bassinet, placid, awake, and beatific. Maybe they put someone else's baby in the wrong cradle.

I study her more closely, looking for genetic similarities. That's Deirdre's nose, all right. And Greg's big lips. And those eyes... They're still a bit puffy, but I'd recognize them anywhere. I see them every morning in the mirror.

"Don't let them change you, Meleah," I murmur to the glass. "You're wonderful exactly as you are."

Jet sidles up to me and nudges my upper arm with a warm paper cup. "Here ya go. Which one is— Oh. For real? She seems so chill."

I smile and take the coffee from him. "Right? I love her."

"She's tiny, too. Dang." He squints through the window at the index card that lists her vitals. "Six pounds, flat? Holy smokes. I didn't know full-term babies came out that small. All of my nieces and nephews were eight, nine pounders."

"That's because your people are huge."

He looks me up and down. "You're no wood sprite, Richards. And neither are your brother or Deirdre." Sipping his coffee, he returns his attention to Meleah. "She's a cutie. When do we get to hold her?"

While he and Greg transfered our many large, obnoxious gifts from Jet's car to my brother's SUV, I headed straight up to Deirdre's room with the makeup bag we also brought to save Greg's ass, since he forgot to pack it in D's overnight duffel before they left for the hospital yesterday.

My sister-in-law practically snatched it from my hands and began furiously applying foundation, peering into the tiny mirror on the bed-straddling table in front of her.

"Oh, thank God. I've been putting off visitors, because I look like death!"

"You just gave birth." I looked around the room. "Speaking of, where's the baby?"

"I told the nurse we had people coming, so they took her back to the nursery. You can see her through the viewing window."

"Ah. Well. Okay, then." I stifled my smirk while texting Jet to tell him to meet me by the nursery window, preferably with coffee. The bad news wasn't something he deserved to learn in a text message.

"I'm not sure we're going to get a chance to hold her. Ever," I say now that we're face-to-face.

He frowns. "Uh, that's not cool. I didn't come here to drink crappy coffee and make small talk in a dim, cramped hospital room. I came here to hold a baby."

I pat his arm. "Sorry."

"Are you serious?"

I merely shrug and sip more of my crappy coffee.

He snorts. "Whatever. I'm holding that baby." He stabs his finger against the glass, earning a dirty look from a nurse who double-takes and blushes when she sees who's doing the tapping. With a sheepish wince, he waves an apology.

When she walks toward the doorway and swipes her ID to unlock it, we hurry to meet her.

"Hi, there," Jet says to her head and shoulders through the gap in the door.

She bites her lower lip and smiles. "Hi. Are you...?"

"The lead singer of that British boy band everyone loves? I get that all the time, but no."

She giggles. "No! You're Jet Knox, right?"

"If I say, 'yes,' will you let me hold Meleah Richards-Snow?"

Frowning, she shuffles her feet and comes the rest of the way into the corridor, letting the door click softly behind her. "No. I wish I could, but that's against hospital policy. You know her parents, I take it?"

"They're my brother and sister-in-law," I say, wishing I didn't have to claim them.

The nurse blinks at me as if noticing my presence for the first time. "We'll be happy to bring the baby to the room at her parents' request."

"Thanks." I grab Jet's arm. "Let's go."

He holds firm, so there's no way I'm moving him, but he says lightly with a self-deprecating chuckle, "Aw, man! All right"—he leans down to read the nurse's badge—"Shayna. I get it. I don't want you to get in trouble. But"--he edges closer to her and says from the side of his mouth—"that kid's mom is kinda..." He circles his finger near his temple.

Shayna's face closes off, and she sounds like she's reading from a cue card when she says, "Dr. Richards-Snow is one of our resident cardiologists."

"Yes! Oh, that's right. She works here."

"She's highly respected."

"Yeah. Absolutely. Nice lady. Great doctor. But, uh, she doesn't want anyone to hold the baby."

"We have to honor the parents' wishes."

Jet covers his heart with both hands, nearly spilling coffee down the front of his coat. "And that's so awesome."

Her mouth twitches upward. "I don't know if it's awesome, but it's protocol."

"Right. And totally understandable."

"It's more and more common, especially during cold and flu season, for parents to restrict visitors to the viewing nursery."

I sigh. "Jet, come on. It's not happening."

He frowns and slumps. "Okay. Fine."

Shayna clears her throat. "You know, if you ask Dr. Richards-Snow nicely, she might change her mind. You seem like you *really* want to hold her."

"I do! So, so much!"

"And... you're Jet Knox." She blushes more deeply.

I laugh and roll my eyes. "Wow. This is—"

But Jet rests his hand on her arm. "You're right, Shayna. I'm going to beg her. Like this." He pooches out his lower lip and opens his eyes wide while also knitting his brow. In my opinion, he looks deranged. Or constipated.

Shayna, on the other hand, giggles and says coyly, "I dare her to say no to that," before unlocking the nursery door and sliding through it. "And if it'll help, I can call down to the room and gently suggest the baby is almost ready for another feeding. That will at least get her in the room with you. Maybe?"

Jet flashes her a grin and a thumbs-up. "That would be amazing, Shayna. You're a rock star."

What the hell just happened?

––––––

An hour later, during the freezing walk to the car, I grab his hand and huddle up next to his arm, using him as a wind-break. He wraps his arm around my back and pulls me closer. Squinting into the eye-watering wind and spitting mix of drizzle and snow, he nevertheless can't stop beaming.

"You're something else," I say loudly to be heard over the gusts.

"Is that a good thing or…?"

"Mostly good. When I agree with you."

"I told you I was going to hold that baby. And I did."

"You always get what you want."

"Not always. You make me sound like a jerk."

"Maybe not a jerk. But you charmed that nurse into being part of your plan to bully Deirdre into letting you hold Meleah."

"I didn't bully anyone. I begged. I pleaded."

"Was that a real tear you squeezed out when you told her how amazing it was to hold such a new example of the gift of life in your hands?"

He laughs. "Of course, it was real. You saw it."

"Yeah, but were you actually crying?"

Instead of answering verbally, he pulls down the corners of his mouth and rolls his eyes toward his forehead, then bobs his head from side to side and shrugs.

"Oh, my gosh! How many times have you fake-cried with me to get your way?"

"I don't have to fake anything with you, Beautiful." His hand slips down and punctuates that statement with a sassy tweak to my butt.

Laughing, I push him away with both arms. He skids on the slippery blacktop but catches himself on the back of a Buick. "Hey!" he says with a chuckle, shaking the sleet from his hands.

I speed-walk, forcing him to jog to catch up to me. "You know, what you did up there is classic sociopath behavior."

"Oh, come on!"

We arrive at the car, but Jet doesn't press the button on the key fob to unlock it, so I'm stuck between the Audi and its stranger neighbor, jogging in place to stay warm. He backs me up to the cold metal and glass, folds me in his arms, and says down into my face, "I can't help it that I'm charming as hell and know how to get what I want."

"Said every psycho ever." I soften that with a smile and a peck on his chilly lips.

"Right now, I want you."

"Yeah. I can distinctly feel that going on. But your goober-ish, 'I'm-Super-Bowl-MVP-Jet-Knox' routine isn't going to work on me."

The memory of him holding my new niece in his massive, freshly scrubbed hands and looking down at her like she was the first baby he'd ever seen in his life? Slightly more effective. But how predictable is that turn-on? I thought I was better than that. I'm not. Turns out, I'm like every other ovary-bearing being, and that stuff turns me to liquid. How disappointing!

"No, you're a tough nut to crack," he says, oblivious to my

usual turn-on giveaways, thanks to my bulky coat. "But that's what makes you so much more fun."

He lowers his head and kisses me, and suddenly the nasty weather around us means nothing. In fact, I'm pretty sure the clouds of steam billowing from our bodies conceal us from view, so offending passersby isn't much of a concern, either.

Perception and reality are two different things, though, so I eventually break off the kiss and say, "You have to stop doing that to me in parking lots."

"Never."

Now that's a promise that could keep a girl interested for life.

## TWENTY-ONE

## BUNKER HIDEOUT

The thaw has begun outside, but for the first time ever, I'm dreading the end of winter. More accurately, if we could skip spring and magically arrive in summer, that would be fabulous.

Unfortunately, life doesn't work that way, so here I am, enduring yet another visit from my future mother-in-law as she seeks to club into submission those final wedding plans. The only thing saving this from being totally unbearable is that Cyndi is hiding out in her own place now, away from Gloria, who would never venture as far as Overland Park without an escort. And neither Jet nor I are about to accompany her there. Cyndi gets to control whether she sees her mother, and so far, her absence at Jet's is a resounding, "Screw that!"

I wish I had that option this time around. I live here now. There's no escaping.

That's not entirely accurate, I guess. On a nightly basis, I slink to the basement and shut myself away in a windowless room, where my nightmare Oscars statuette project has been relegated. As soon as Jet returns from wherever he's been all day—posing for photo ops or volunteering or flitting here and there, simply being Jet Knox—and after we've eaten a digestion-wrecking, tense meal full of awkward silences and more awkward questions from one of two categories—"Are you ready for the wedding?" and "Where's your baby sister?"—I'm out. Therefore, much headway has been made on my silly art project. Not nearly enough to get me caught up, but more than I've done in the past two months combined.

Jet must have imagined this space as an office, a place he could go to write his memoirs or, more likely, watch porn in peace. Or maybe he (and Gloria) simply ran out of inspiration when it came to this room. It's about as blah as they come, with white, unadorned walls, dark gray carpeting, and a long desk that doubles as a work counter. (Perhaps Jet planned to take up scrapbooking someday?) Despite the recessed lighting, the space is shadowy, and its lack of windows makes it a claustrophobic's nightmare.

Like every other room in this house, though, it's huge. That it has almost nothing in it adds to its depressing vibe. *Had* almost nothing in it, that is. Stacked all along one wall are my boxes and boxes of movies. And adding to the creepiness are these little gold men.

But it's better to be down here, accomplishing something, than sitting upstairs, listening to Gloria lament about what a disappointment Cyndi is. It's not my place to correct her, but I find it hard to stand by while she blathers on and on. Jet occasionally defends his sister, but he seems determined to get through this visit—and life—without angering his mother, no matter how angry he may be at her.

It's weird. These Knox people are a case study in repression and denial. With one exception, of course. Gloria is allowed to say whatever's on her mind, whenever it suits her. I guess that creates a certain balance in the system.

No, it doesn't. It sucks.

But they're not my family—yet. And even when they are, I'll always be viewed as an interloper. I'd better get used to biting my tongue—or making myself scarce.

With my clean forearms, I push my hair from my face and survey the mess around me. Paste, gluey paper, and gold foil sheets litter the work top in front of me. My sticky hands look like something from a medical journal article about a rare skin disorder. What the hell was I thinking with this damn project? Theme and budget, that's what I was thinking.

There's definitely more style than substance to this spring's job fair, so I can't give up now. The Giggler has high hopes, thanks to my enigmatic answers to her frequent chuckle-punctuated queries. My latest, "You won't be disappointed..." was a mistake. Because she likely *will* be. Hasn't everyone who's ever heard that phrase raised their hopes so high at the utterance of it that they have no choice but to be dissatisfied with reality? Anything less than a complete recreation of the Dolby Theatre, including palm trees, in that tent is going to be a letdown for my boss, I'm afraid.

*Hmmm... palm trees. I wonder how much it would cost to rent a couple of those artificial ones. Or maybe I can find a way to make them. Must consult Pinterest later.*

I blow my bangs off my forehead when I remember I don't have time to make the things I'm already making, much less flora and fauna replicas. "You're a dunce, Maura," I mutter, returning to my furious gold foiling and pretending I don't notice it looks like shit. Talk about repression and denial...

Several minutes later, a startling knock sounds on the door

behind me, and I whirl on the visitor, praying, *Please don't be Gloria. Please don't be Gloria.*

My prayer is instantly and positively answered in the form of my two favorite guys.

"Getting high down here?" Colin inquires, waving the glue fumes from in front of his face.

Jet coughs. "Oh, man. Maybe a windowless room wasn't the best place for you to do this."

Now that they mention it, I am a bit dizzy, but it's not an unpleasant sensation.

"Hey, guys! Welcome to my laboratory." I pull up a stool and sit, resting my feet on the top rungs, stretching my arms over my head, and arching my back.

Colin surveys the line of finished statuettes along one wall, arranged similarly to the little plastic soldiers Jet and Mikey like to play with. "Are you building your army? Because something tells me they're going to be rather ineffective. Unless, that is, you know dark magic and can bring them to life."

"If I had any magical abilities, they'd be done."

"You're making headway," Jet says, his tone and faraway stare saying exactly the opposite of his words. He blinks. "Well, anyway. I better get back upstairs. Mom was trying to figure out when to schedule my final tux fitting. I guess the one I already own isn't good enough, so she's ordered me a new one."

I smile thinly. "Good luck."

As soon as he's gone, I grab a rag from the desk and try to wipe the worst of the glue from my fingers.

"Don't stop on my account," Colin says, leaning against a wall. "I haven't heard from you in yonks, so I thought I'd drop in. Rude, I know. But I was at a bar in the area with a couple of the old guys who sometimes accompany their ladies to the salon…" As he trails off, he looks around. "Wow. This… I've never been down here before."

"Creepy, huh?"

He shrugs. "Massive. Like a whole other house. We passed about thirty bedrooms to get here. And a full kitchen. And a workout room. I was starting to get a bit nervous that Jet had you chained up in a dungeon."

I laugh. "Close. No chains. And I'm down here voluntarily, if you can believe that."

"I believe it, considering who's upstairs."

Since the rag is only spreading the paste around my fingers, I hop down from the stool and motion Colin to follow me to the attached bathroom, where I turn on the taps at the sink with my elbow.

"Incredible," he says under his breath as he reaches the threshold of the marble and glass room.

"Right?"

"This house is like the TARDIS on *Doctor Who*."

"Bigger on the inside," we say together, laughing at the oft-repeated line.

Squishing soap between my fingers, I stare at the water rushing from the faucet. "A blue telephone box would be an aesthetic improvement."

"Any headway on renovation plans?"

"Ha!"

"I'll take that as a no."

"I haven't brought it up again. With all the wedding stuff and Cyndi's drama and this job fair crap, it seems like an unnecessary stress to add to the mix. This place is ridiculous, but it works. It seems pretty ungrateful to complain about such a nice house. 'Choose your battles...' and all that rot." I smile bravely at him in the mirror. With the majority of the stickiness rinsed from my hands, I turn off the water and dry my fingers and palms on the plush towel hanging on the wall. "Anyway! I'm glad you stopped by. I feel so isolated lately, like all I ever do is go to work or talk about weddings." I roll my eyes. "I'm losing my mind."

He nods. "Okay. Well, I won't make you talk about your upcoming nuptials, then. However..."

I narrow my eyes at him.

"...I will be calling to make an appointment with you later this week, because I'm ready for a big-boy job."

I laugh. "Oh, you are, are you? Did the sexist old codgers finally manage to shame you about working in a beauty salon?"

He wags his finger. "On the contrary. No. It's time to move on. The owner of the shop is taking more and more of my tips—"

"You get tips at the front desk?"

"The ladies like me, what can I say? But the owner's cut keeps getting bigger and bigger. That's not on."

"No, it's not." I cross my arms over my chest. "And I'm not sure that's legal, but I'd have to look it up."

"Don't bother on my account. I've been there long enough, anyway. Time for new challenges."

"The Blue Rinse Brigade will be crushed."

"I'll still keep in touch." He steps aside while I edge past him to start the cleanup process in the room. I cap my adhesives and toss my paste brush into a glass of murky water to soak overnight—or as long as I'll be away, which we all know will be longer than a day. Or seven.

Without warning, I whirl on him and ask, "How do you stay married?"

His mouth drops open but snaps shut again as he considers my out-of-the-blue question."

"I mean, what's the secret to a happy, successful marriage? Because I've been racking my brain, thinking of all the people I know who have been married forever, and I can't seem to find a common thread."

He scratches the side of his nose. "Hm. Well, I'm not sure I'm the one to ask, either."

"You and Emily were happy!"

"Of course, we were. But we weren't exactly put to the longevity test, now, were we?"

I look down at my feet, contemplating the sadness of someone taken so young, when her life with her soul mate was only beginning.

This, naturally, leads me to think what it would be like if something truly horrible happened to Jet in the near future. Lord knows he puts himself in enough physical danger every day, and I'm not just talking about football or training. He could be in a fatal car accident. Or stalked and killed by a weirdo "fan." Or…

"Hey, there. You okay?" Colin grabs my arm, and the pressure between his fingers and my skin tells me I'm not as stationary as I'd thought. In fact, I continue to yank away, pulled down by gravity, he cries, "Oy!"

I take a step back to catch myself and slam into the wall behind me.

He grasps my elbow in one hand and my hand in his other and gently pulls me toward the door. "Let's get some fresh air."

A few steps down the hall, and I already feel better. My ears stop ringing. The tingling in my cheeks and lips subsides. In the gaming area, right outside the basement kitchen, he helps me sit in one of the bizarre, legless console chairs that rest directly on the floor.

"There. Now, breathe for a while. And when you're ready, tell me what's on your mind."

Not too much time passes before I am ready. Extremely ready to say everything that's been rattling around my head while I've obviously inhaled too many fumes.

"What the heck is my role here? Where's my place? And why do I suddenly care about roles and places?" I pick at the plastic ring that encases the cup holder in the seat's arm. "Obviously I'm more than a girlfriend, but I'm not yet a wife. I'm a live-in fiancée, but I still feel like a guest, like I have no say in any of the decisions required to run this place. Not that I want to make any decisions. I don't. And when important things are discussed, I'm forced to listen, but I don't feel it's my place to weigh in with my opinions. So I sit there. Like a vacuous lump. This is how it starts. It's why all famous people's spouses have that faraway look in their eyes. We've learned to go to our happy places and wait until we're needed. For whatever. In my case, I'm sitting on a shelf, waiting for baby-making."

"Does Jet say that?"

"No!"

"Then why do you assume that?"

"Because everyone else is thinking it. I'm in this weird pre-marital limbo. Like, 'Oh, that's Jet's future wife. She'll come in handy later. For now, she's merely for decoration.'"

He tuts.

"It's not that I want to constantly have a voice in his

professional matters. I wouldn't know where to start. And his family— It's so complicated and ugly right now that it's better to stay out of it. But I do have *some* thoughts on things."

"I'm sure Jet would like to hear them."

"I tell him sometimes. But I'm constantly weighing my words, like I can't be relaxed, or I can't be... me." I sigh, trying to find the perfect explanation. "It's like everything I say or do holds too much significance, because I say so little. When I do speak up, it's like, 'The Maura has spoken.' I'm not allowed to have any throwaway conversations or remarks. Does that make sense?"

He shrugs. "I suppose. As long as it makes sense to you, though, who cares?"

"I care. Because I have to articulate this to Jet so he'll get it. And not be so... so... *Jet.*"

Colin laughs. "Oh, dear."

"Everything I say sets off an action list. Like, almost immediately. Except for the things I do care about, like, 'I don't want a big wedding,' or 'I don't like this house.' He can't fix that stuff right now, so he concentrates on all these other petty things. Like... like..." I grasp for an example. "The closet!"

"Closet?"

"I said something the other day about it being weird that the master bedroom in such a ginormous house had such a small closet. Now, he's commissioned some organizational guru to come and revamp our 'master closet system.' All I meant was that the closet was relatively small and maybe we should both get rid of some stuff. Do we need a hundred Chiefs t-shirts and sweatshirts?"

"Perhaps not. But we all tend to collect possessions over

the years, so it's not a negative reflection of your personality or lifestyle that you have—"

"I'm not worried about the shirts."

"Oh. Right. Hang on. I got distracted." He runs his hand through his hair. "Before the closets, you were saying…?"

I collapse backward, which makes the seat rock and nearly throws me to the floor. Arms and legs flailing, I recover ungracefully. When I'm stable again, I grip the chair's arms and stare at my white knuckles. "I don't know. I've become disgruntled, which is so unlike me. I've rarely cared enough— about anything—to be unhappy, much less about such petty bullshit. It's a sin to find any fault at all with my life." I smile shakily and gather my hair into a bundle at the base of my neck. "You know what? It'll be fine. It'll all be fine."

"Of course, it will," he says quietly.

"The job fair will eventually be over, for better or worse." I wince at my use of those four particular words. "The wedding will also come and go. My mother-in-law will simply go. And hopefully stay away for months at a time. Come June, I'll be sitting by the pool, wondering why I let all this get to me."

"That's the badger!"

"Thank you for listening to me whine about my petty problems."

He waves me off. "Not at all. And they're not petty. They're quite valid, in fact."

"You never did answer my question, though. About the key to a happy, successful marriage."

With a snort, he stands and offers me a hand up from the low, rocking chair. "Because I don't have an answer."

"Damn." I stumble to my feet and sniff the last of my emotions away.

"But I'll think on it. And by the time you walk down the aisle, I'll have some stunning advice. Surely."

"I'm counting on it."

"It has nothing to do with closets, I can tell you that much."

That much I already knew.

## TWENTY-TWO

## BOXING RING

"Make Jet the bad guy."

That was Rae's simple advice.

"Doc does it to me all the time. He tells me what needs to be done, and I have to tell the player."

"How does that relate? At all?"

Her sigh came down the phone line so hard, calls were dropped throughout the greater metro area. "You tell him your wants and needs, and he passes along the info to his mother."

"Put him in the middle, you mean? No. That's not fair."

"Oh, boo hoo! It's about time that guy learned that life's not fair sometimes. And his mom is a—"

"Careful now…"

"—scary dragon lady. He's helped create that monster, so now he's going to manage it. He knows exactly what to say to manipulate her."

"True. But I don't want to manipulate her.'"

"Yes, you do. And it's his mom; let him do the dirty work."

"I don't know."

"I do. It's the only way it's going to work, the only way you're going to keep your sanity."

Put like that, how could I argue? At the same time, I'm mindful of the influence I have on Jet, so I've decided I will only use this power when we are in full agreement about something. I won't make him stand up to his mom for me (like the coward I am) when he's indifferent or has an opposing view. Then it'll be all me. In other words, nothing will be done about it. But I'll have to be okay with that.

Which puts me back at Square One with the wedding.

Sigh.

It does give me leverage, however, with one aspect of the planning. His mom needs to go home. We have the technology for her and Mags to coordinate and communicate long-distance. All of the major decisions have been made and are well in the works. Nothing needs to be done, at this point, on location. We all need to go to our separate corners for the next few weeks so we can bear to be in each other's presence on the happiest freaking day of my life. *Blink, blink*

And I fully planned to pull Jet aside as soon as he joined us after his latest team meeting this evening. Before I can utter a syllable to that effect, however, he thrusts his fist into the center of the living room and says, "It fits!"

Oh, Lord. The ring. *The* ring. From here, I can tell it's as gaudy as I expected, but I smile supportively. "Hey! Look at that. It's… bling-y."

He walks it in my direction, but Gloria shoots from her seat by the fire and arrives at my side before he does. She holds out her hand. "Oooh! Let me see!"

He hesitates, looking from me to her. I don't care if she holds it first; I'll have a lifetime to look at it, after all. But he slides it off his finger and holds it out to me, so I cup my hand under it and receive its substantial weight in my palm.

"Wow. It's heavy."

"Right?"

"Let me hold it," Gloria demands, bumping into my arm and craning her neck.

"In a second." I hold up the jewelry to the light so both of us can see it and examine its brilliance. Sure, it's not my style, but I have to admit, it's an impressive piece of craftsmanship. "I can't believe they got these done so fast. I'd heard it takes months."

"Our design was pretty simple, I guess." Jet edges closer and points to the team's arrowhead logo in rubies, gold topaz, diamonds, and onyx. "Except for that part. That's what I keep staring at."

"It's beautiful," I say into his sparkling eyes. "And it fits."

"Yeah. It totally fits."

"I'm so glad you like it."

"Thanks. You know, it's not something I'll wear every day, but…"

"Can I see it now?" Gloria huffs while simultaneously reaching.

I step back to bring the ring closer to her grasp, which puts me directly in the path of her own ring-bedecked fist. More accurately, it puts my jaw right in its path. Skin rips as the prongs on her chocolate diamond anniversary monstrosity scrape painfully across my face. The contact barely slows the velocity of her hand and doesn't deter its intent at all. As soon as she snatches Jet's new ring from me, I slap my palm to my stinging cheek.

"Mom! You slugged Maura!"

"Oh, I did not!"

She's so confident of this—or in denial—that she doesn't bother to verify her claim with a glance. She only has eyes for her son's bling, which she's placed on her thumb and is inspecting from every angle.

Jet pulls my hand gently away from the scratch. "It's not bleeding. Just raised. I'll go get some ice."

"No. Don't. It's fine." The last thing I want is for him to leave me alone with this lunatic. The second-to-last thing I want is for him to make a big fuss about the whole thing.

Finally, Gloria looks my way, but only long enough to say, "See? She's fine."

Eyes watering, I finger the welt along my jawline. With a little alcohol and a lot of makeup, I might only get the occasional question about it at work tomorrow. And hopefully nobody will assume I'm yet another NFL player's domestic abuse victim.

"Give it back," Jet says to his mom through clenched teeth, wiggling his fingers at her.

Ignoring his request, she pulls her hand away and sticks her thumb aloft. "That logo is spectacular. Now, you *did* insure this thing already, right?"

"Forget the damn ring for a second!"

"Jet! Don't talk to me like that!" The Knox pout emerges as she slides the ring from her thumb and holds it out to him.

Instead of taking it, he nods toward me. "Give it back to Maura."

"But she was finished—"

"No, she wasn't. You grabbed it like... like... a bratty kid."

Gloria gasps.

I nearly have to bite through my tongue to avoid giving into the urge to confirm that I *was* finished looking at it.

That's not the point, anyway. And I don't want her to think I'm taking her side over Jet's.

She sighs and plants the lump of gold and gems into my reluctant hand. "There." Retreating a few steps away, she mutters, "I hope I didn't injure your palm there."

Jet's eyes widen, and I can hear his breath exiting his nostrils at a velocity that could extinguish the gas log, if he were standing directly in front of it. "Mother!"

"What? She's overreacting, playing the victim for your benefit." She waves her lethal meat hooks through the air, fortunately far enough away that no part of my face is in danger of further disfigurement.

The physical injury isn't that big of a deal; it was an accident, I'm sure. But her refusal to acknowledge it, and now her accusation that I'm playing it up, when the opposite is true, and I'd prefer we all shut up about it and move on, astounds me. And not in a good way. In a way that awakens a rarely utilized part of my personality.

"Excuse me?" I tighten my fist around the ring until it bites painfully into my palm. With my other hand, I shield the burning scrape on my face from the open air.

Jet continues to flare his nostrils like an antagonized bull. "The least you can do is say you're sorry, Mom. Geez."

She rolls her eyes. "Sorry."

"Like you mean it!"

She flutters her eyelashes and purses her lips. "I'm sincerely sorry if I accidentally hurt you."

"'If'? There's no 'if' about it!" Jet throws his hands up. "The evidence is on her face!"

Gloria looks down at her ring-weapon as if to check it for damage or—pieces of my skin. She rubs the pad of her thumb across it and shrugs. "It's not even that sharp."

"You are unbelievable," Jet growls.

"Son, don't be mad at me. All I wanted was to see the ring I sacrificed so much throughout the years to make possible. Do you know how long I've been waiting for this moment? Do you understand the money your father and I spent? The time we devoted? The number of nights I lost sleep, worrying about everything that could happen to you out there on that field?"

"I'm well aware of all of that, and I'm grateful, but—"

"Are you? I don't think you are. I don't think you *can* be. You have no idea. You can't fathom that level of devotion. And you take it for granted. As you should. Because this is what parents do. I've been with you since your first pee-wee game, where you lost your front teeth on that other kid's helmet, in the victory dog pile at the end. I've seen you through every injury, sometimes by your bedside, other times worrying long-distance. I have watched every. Single. Game. Seen every single touchdown. And every single tackle. So, excuse me for being a bit caught up in the moment—and disappointed—when you bring home that ring, and you let someone who's come into the picture so recently see it before *me*."

"Mom—"

"It'd be one thing if I weren't here, if I were home in California. But it's heartbreaking that I was standing right here, and it never crossed your mind that *I* had earned the right to hold it first." She blinks her moist eyes.

Oh, for the love of…

Throughout her soliloquy, I've squeezed the ring harder and harder, but now I drop it into my fingers, grasping it lightly, and hold it aloft, pinched between thumb and forefinger. "Here, Gloria. I'm sorry. Nobody meant to hurt your feelings."

She looks through my offering. "Nobody ever *means* to. But you do. 'Who cares what Mom wants?' 'Who cares how Mom feels?' I should be used to it by now."

Jet rests his hands on his hips. "You know that's not true."

"It is," she persists through her sniffles. "She was the only one you wanted to see in the locker room after the Super Bowl, and now you think that ring is *hers*."

"It's neither of yours; it's mine."

"It's as much mine as it is yours."

I shake the ugly piece of jewelry in the air, between the arguing pair. "Take it already."

She crosses her arms over her chest and turns up her nose as she angles her face away from both of us. "No. I don't want it now. It's obvious he's chosen you over me, which I suppose was inevitable. I didn't think it would come to this so soon, that's all." Lowering her chin and deigning to look at us once again, she releases a tear or two for good measure.

Hearing nothing from Jet's direction, I glance at him to gauge his reaction and hope it will give me some clue as to what to say or how to act. But his slack jaw is no help. And then I see the heartbreak in his eyes, the betrayal, and the misplaced guilt, and something in me snaps.

How dare she?

How dare she?

How could she take such a joyous, proud moment for him and make it all about her? If she were truly as devoted as she claims, she would recognize that nothing about Jet's Super Bowl experience has been anything like it was in his dreams. He's been sick, hurt, and worried for weeks on end, when he should be on top of the world, reveling in his success. And now, he's not allowed to show off his fugly ring the way he wants to, without her ruining it?

No.

No way.

Uh-uh.

Eff that noise.

Before I realize what my muscles are doing, I'm pulling back my arm. Then it's snapping forward, and the ring is flying through the air. And Gloria's red eyes are widening as she sees it coming straight for her head. Then they're closing, squeezing tightly shut. She ducks slightly. Her shoulder turns reflexively inward nanoseconds before the ring hits her—hard —on the meatiest part of her upper arm and drops to the hardwood with a sickening *clunk-ping*.

"My ring!" Jet rushes forward and scoops it up like a fumble recovered at a key moment in the game of all games.

As soon as it left my fingers, I regretted it. And if I could have arrived before it did, I would have run to shield Gloria from the impact. But even a science idiot like me knows physics only works that way for superheroes. So now I have to own it. And it's not as hard as it should be. Because, while I shouldn't have thrown it, I'm only sorry I did because this is sure to be a big, hairy deal. I'm not sorry it hit her, and I don't regret the sentiment behind the throw. She deserved it.

"You want the ring, Gloria? There you go."

On his knees near his mother's feet, Jet blows on the jewelry and rotates it in his fingers, checking for dents or missing gems. "You two! Stop it!"

"I can't believe you did that!" she says, glaring at me.

"Believe it. I've about had it with you lately."

"*You've* had it with *me*?"

"Yes!"

"Well, that's rich! I'd say I've been mighty tolerant of your pouty silences and nightly disappearing acts, not to mention your complete lack of cooperation in planning the most important day of your life. What have *I* done, other than *everything* to ensure you have the wedding day of your dreams?"

"Ah, yes. The wedding. Heaven forbid we have one conversation without mentioning that fiasco."

"Fiasco?"

"You heard me."

"Well, I never! From where I stand, I've been the only thing keeping it from becoming a fiasco!"

"And the wedding day of *my* dreams? Since when is this wedding about *my* dreams?"

"From the beginning! Although I've had to be a mind reader at times, since you're so closed off."

"I'm distant because what *I* want is irrelevant."

"Not true!"

"All I want is to marry your son. Period. I don't care about dresses and cakes and dinner menus and balanced bridal parties. I. Don't. Care."

"But all of that comes with marriage."

"No. All of that comes with *weddings*. Big, extravagant, obnoxious, publicity-snatching weddings."

"Are you saying you don't want a wedding? Because it's a little late in the game to be making *that* decision. You should have spoken up months ago!"

"I didn't care enough one way or the other. Until you took over my life with it."

"If it weren't for me, nothing would get done!"

"And that would be okay."

Still kneeling on the floor, ring in hand, Jet looks much like he did the times he proposed to me. Only this time, he's not doing any of the talking. And his mouth hangs open, while he waits for his mom's next rebuttal.

"Did you know about this?" she asks him.

He swallows loudly. "Uh. Well. Maybe. We may have talked a couple of times about how we'd be happy with a smaller ceremony. Or with eloping."

"Eloping?"

"We never discussed it seriously."

"All this time, I've been wasting my time and energy on something you two don't even want?"

"Kind of," he says, heaving himself to his feet.

"Yes," I answer more definitely. "But we knew *you* wanted it, Gloria, so we've gone along with it."

"Me? It hasn't been for me!"

"I beg to differ."

"You can beg and differ all you want, Missy. It's the truth. I thought I was giving the two of you a gift. Now I feel like a fool."

"Mom, it's not—"

"No. I see now. I see. The conversations the two of you must have had the past few months…"

"It hasn't been like that."

"Hasn't it?"

"No!"

"It seems like it has to her." She nods disdainfully at me.

I roll my eyes. "I haven't said a word against you or about you to your son."

"Interesting qualification there."

"I may have confided in a friend that I'm overwhelmed by things, but I haven't ridiculed you. I've been trying to get through this without hurting anyone."

"Well, you've officially failed."

"Guys, guys, guys. Please!" Jet pockets his precious ring

and inserts himself between us. "Everyone calm down. C'mon. This is— This is dumb."

I blink and stare at him, waiting for him to explain that statement. But he doesn't look at me. Instead, he turns to his mom. "I'm sorry, okay? I wasn't trying to make a statement about who I appreciate more for supporting me. I just— Maura's my girl. My best friend. And she's going to be my wife. We share everything. This is how it's going to be from now on. You understand that. You have to."

"If you don't want me here, all you have to do is say so."

"No, Mom! That's not it! Not at all! I'm glad you got to see the ring first."

"Second."

"Whatever. And you're right; you've been amazing my whole life, and I *have* taken that for granted, because you're my mom. I'm sorry."

"You'll understand how deeply it hurts someday when you're a parent."

I snort and chuckle to keep from throwing up. The noise finally turns Jet's attention back to me. "C'mon, now. Let's—"

"No." I storm past both of them. "I'm finished standing here while you apologize for things you have no business feeling sorry about."

"There she goes," Gloria taunts. "Downstairs to her arts and crafts. Or whatever she does down there."

But I don't descend the stairs. Rather, I take them two at a time up to the second floor, in search of a first aid kit.

———

Upstairs, I tell myself my burning eyes are from the sting of the alcohol-soaked cotton swab I dab along my cut jaw. No blood has spilled, but the first couple of layers of skin are gone, so the red line is right under the surface, angry and highly visible.

Jet appears in the mirror behind me, hands in his pockets. Keeping my eyes on my ministrations, I say, "I'm sorry I threw your ring."

"Are you okay?"

I should focus on the physical interpretation of his question, but it takes too long for me to answer, which gives my brain too much time to ponder the deeper meaning. I use the excuse of throwing away the swab and replacing the cap on the alcohol to keep my face averted, but a sob breaks loose, and my shoulders shake. I can't muster the muscle control required to lift the brown plastic bottle onto its top shelf in the medicine cabinet.

As quickly as the breakdown starts, I stifle it, so by the time Jet steps up behind me and wraps his hands around my upper arms, the alcohol is in its place, and I've swallowed my emotions. I shrug him off. "I'm fine. It's only a scrape."

"I'm not talking about your face."

I root through the tubes of ointments until I find the stuff Jet uses on his turf burns. Twisting off the cap, I squeeze a healthy dollop of the clear, greasy salve onto my index finger and smear it along the burning line that requires no mirror to locate.

He pulls gently on my shoulder to turn me to face him. I keep my eyes pinned to his chest.

Without a word, he takes the metal tube from me and dabs another layer of the medication from my chin to my ear. I close my eyes and focus on my anger. Must stay angry.

"Don't be mad at me, Maura. Please."

I shake my head and grind my teeth. "I'm not mad at you."

"It seems like you are."

"I'm not."

The cap disappears from between my fingers. A few seconds later, metal scrapes glass, and the cabinet clicks closed behind me.

"Don't cry."

"Stop bossing me around."

He laughs but it's the saddest sound I've heard since his ring hit the floor. His lips graze the tears I didn't realize had rolled down my cheeks. Then they nudge my lips. I nudge back. Barely. Only enough to let him know I'm telling the truth, that I'm not mad at him. At all.

He pulls me to his chest, and I turn my head so my uninjured cheek rests against his shirt. After a prolonged embrace, his voice rumbles through to my ear. "Don't leave me. Okay?"

I immediately and reflexively reply, "I won't. Don't worry about that. Ever."

"Okay. Just checking."

## TWENTY-THREE

## CONTINUED TENSIONS

The house is eerily quiet and empty the next morning. For the first time ever, I actually miss the crowded, noisy version of this place. At least that's normal. This is... weird. And it feels like we're poised for something awful, like a city that's been evacuated for a hurricane.

I find Jet in the kitchen, drinking the leftover milk from a recently devoured bowl of cereal. Torzi oversees from his master's lap, sniffing and licking Jet's hands. Lowering his bowl, (a mixing bowl is still a bowl, right?), Jet smiles weakly up at me while I pour a cup of coffee for myself and lean against the counter.

"'Morning, Beautiful."

I blow on my steaming drink. "Howdy, Champ."

He nudges the dog into the next seat over so he can rise and set his bowl and spoon in the sink. Then he joins me in front of the coffeemaker.

While he dispenses his next serving, I sip a bracing, scalding mouthful of my first. "Where is everyone?"

"I gave Beau and Helen the day off. Figured it would be

less awkward around here without extra people milling around."

"Oh. And your mom?"

"Packing."

I cough to keep my latest swallow from slipping down the wrong pipe.

He faces me, curling his hands around his mug. "You okay?"

I swallow and nod. "Yeah. Your mom's leaving?"

With a warm finger, he gently turns my head more to the side so he can get a better view of my now-faded and makeup-covered—but still visible—scratch. Distractedly, he says while studying the wound, "Yeah. It was her idea. I'm not kicking her out or anything."

"Oh. Good." His scrutiny is unsettling, so I return my head to a more natural angle and continue drinking.

This is where I should say I'm sorry for my part in this ridiculous family drama, but I can't bring myself to utter the words. Because while I do regret losing my temper and revealing as much of my feelings as I did last night, not to mention launching a twenty-thousand-dollar ring across the room, I don't regret beaning *her* with it. And I'm not sorry she's leaving.

I have to admit, though, her departure isn't as satisfying as it would have been without the brouhaha and boo-boos.

Smelling of coffee, Jet leans down and kisses my wounded jaw. "Hey. Why don't you take the afternoon off? We'll have the place to ourselves for the first time in forever." He sets his cup on the counter behind me and pins me in place with one arm on either side of my hips. "I'll be back from the airport by noon. Meet me here?"

I pull my head back. "I can't. I don't have any time off that's not already spoken for."

"Forget those other days."

"They're for our abbreviated honeymoon."

He groans at the reminder of the bad news I finally mustered the nerve to deliver a couple of weeks ago. "Fake like you're sick."

"No!"

Between tiny, sucking kisses along my neck, he says, "Has anyone ever told you your work ethic is sexy?"

"No. Because my work ethic generally sucks, when I'm not worried about being fired."

He presses against my leg. "You work so *hard*."

"Jet."

"Fine." He laughs into my neck.

"I want to."

"Yeah, I know."

"But I have to go to work."

"Well, you don't *have* to." He stands at his full height and looks down into my face.

Firmly, I say while maintaining full, intense eye contact, "Yes, I do."

He opens his mouth to rebut me, but my tone and expression are non-negotiable, so he sighs and relaxes, moving his hands to my shoulders. "Tonight, then. You're mine."

I should be ashamed at what a turn-on those macho words are. But I'm too turned on to be ashamed. Funny how that works.

I have a reputation to maintain, however, so I place my coffee cup next to his, yank on the front of his t-shirt, and stare at his mouth when I say, "No, sir. You're *mine*."

"I can live with that."

I grab his lower lip in my teeth and suck it into my mouth. He grins—or tries to—then lifts me onto the counter with both hands wrapped around my waist. I giggle, letting go of his lip and giving him the opportunity to take control of the kiss. Which he does. Like the play-maker he is.

I'm vaguely aware of Torzi's jingling tags and clicking nails as he exits the room, but everything else disappears, especially after I slide our coffee mugs farther away from us to prevent sloshing anything on my clothes.

Jet's hand slides up my thigh and under my dress, but his probing fingers eventually bump into an impassable barrier.

"Tights? Seriously? Why?"

I smirk into his face. "It's still technically winter, Knox."

"You need to start wearing thigh-highs, Richards."

"With garters?"

His pupils expand. "Yes!"

"I'll look into it."

He rubs me through the silky layers between my legs. My eyes flutter closed as I lean in for another kiss. I can get used to tongue for breakfast.

"Ahem!"

Still connected by the lips, we freeze and stare into each other's wide eyes. As long as we don't move, this won't be happening. His hand retreats ever-so-slowly from its warm, moist burrow, sliding down my thigh the way it came and resting on my knee, where he pretends it's been all along. Our mouths separate with a wet click, and we both immediately run the backs of our hands across our respective sets of swollen lips. I clear my throat. He clears his.

When he doesn't withdraw completely from me but merely says over his shoulder, "Good morning, Mom," I figure he has a pretty big reason for staying put.

"Oh, don't mind me," Gloria says breezily. "I'll be out of your way soon enough."

If I weren't so humiliated, I'd roll my eyes. Jet tilts his head back and says toward the ceiling, "I thought you'd be upstairs for a while longer."

"I can be, if you guys need to finish up. You can text me the all-clear."

I snort. Because that's actually funny. Of course, she's not trying to be humorous. At all. So I sound like a major smart-ass.

However she interprets my noise, she chooses not to acknowledge it. "There wouldn't happen to be any coffee left over there, would there be? I'd check myself, but..."

Jet opens the cabinet next to my head and pulls down the first mug in reach. He side-steps to the machine and presses the button to dispense a serving for his mother into *my* "World's Greatest Mom" mug from Torzi. By the time the cup is full, Jet's recovered enough to turn and face Gloria. Unfortunately, this leaves me exposed, so I hop from the counter and smooth my skirt over my hips.

A nice, normal person would look away. She stares. And smirks. Like this whole thing has merely reinforced what she's suspected about me all along. I defiantly return her stare. If she doesn't have the good manners to exit a room and come back later when she walks in on two consenting adults going at it on a kitchen counter, then she wasn't raised as well as I was. Or something.

Receiving her coffee from her son, she reads the black words on the white background and tsks. "Well, we all know *this* isn't true, don't we?"

"Mom."

"No, no. I stand corrected after last night. I thought I was at least in the running for this title, but apparently that's all been a big delusion."

My eyes desperately seek out the clock on the microwave, but before I can announce it's past time for me to be leaving for work, she sighs pitifully and continues, "Oh, and don't worry about taking me to the airport. I'll call a cab. Or get one of those Boober things."

"It's Uber, Mom, and—"

"Sorry. I must have breasts on the brain."

"Just stop it, okay?" Jet explodes.

"Do not raise your voice at me, Mister. I let it slide last night, but you will not disrespect me like that again."

"I'm not disrespecting you. I'm trying to get a word in."

I edge toward the mudroom and garage beyond. But they're so. Far. Away. "I'll be, uh—"

"No." Jet halts me with both his voice and by utilizing his inhuman reach, grabbing my hand and pulling me back to his side, where he holds me with an arm around my waist, his hand on my hip. "No. I need you to hear this."

"But I'm late—"

"This won't take long." He lasers a glare across the room at Gloria, who laconically sips her coffee and waits. "This is stupid. We're family. But lately we've been acting like anything but. The thing with Cyndi... And now this. It's gotta stop."

She merely blinks at that demand, so he takes a deep breath. "Mom, I'm taking you to the airport, like I always do."

"A few days earlier than planned, but..."

"Yeah? And that's your choice, too."

"I don't think so. It would be a tad awkward for me to stay now, don't you think?"

"Yeah, it would be. Because you've made it that way."

"I'm not the one throwing things at people."

I blush.

Jet squeezes me tighter, as if he can sense I'm about to bolt. "She was provoked."

"Oh, so everything is my fault? I see. It's my fault your sister is divorcing her husband; it's my fault your fiancée has no self-control. Let me guess: it was my fault you got sick before the Super Bowl and concussed during the game, too?"

"You punched Maura and refused to apologize!"

"My ring inadvertently *grazed* her. And look! It's fine today! Exactly like I said it would be. I'd also like to remind you that I did apologize, but I see we're being selective in our memories this morning."

"Blame the concussions, I guess."

"No! I will not. You are willfully making me out to be the villain and ganging up on me. And I won't stand for it."

"Oh, c'mon now."

"I have given this family *everything*. And this is the thanks I get." Her face crumples.

Cold air hits the spot were Jet's hand was resting on my hip, as he crosses the kitchen and hugs his mother. She holds her coffee cup aloft in one hand and rests her other one—chocolate diamond weapon-ring glinting—on his back.

"I'm sorry, Mom. Shhh. Don't cry. Please."

"It hurts to be so misunderstood!"

"I know, I know. I'm sorry."

As I'm softening toward her, wondering if I've gotten this all wrong and feeling horrible for my part in her misery, she glowers over her son's shoulder at me with eyes drier than the turf in a domed stadium on game day.

Oh. My. Gosh.

———

I can't get those eyes out of my head. For one thing, it's always been somewhat creepy how much Jet looks like his mom, especially around the eyes. But this morning in the kitchen, I got a glimpse into the future, through those eyes, and it was a terrifying sight: two Knoxes manipulating their way through everything, dragging me along for the ride. From weddings to houses to babies to career moves—all his, of course—to family visits, I won't have a say in a damn thing. Ever. Oh, they'll let me think I do. *They* might convince themselves that I do. But I won't. Not really. There won't be room for what I want after those two launch their more definite plans.

At work, I daymare between appointments, imagining scenario after scenario, always with me standing meekly in the background, watching the two of them scheme, and dealing with the constant cycle of confront, cry, console, and cave.

My current imaginary argument with Gloria and Jet is about relocating to New York for him to take a broadcasting job after his playing career is over. We're all a few years older but none-the-wiser, *plus* I have about a half-dozen kids hanging from me while I try to conduct my end of the discussion. Everyone's crying but me. I'm trying to comfort the children and determine if Jet's tears are real or a ruse to get his way. I already know Gloria's a big, fat faker.

Colin pokes his head through my open office door. "Hey, kidder. Ready to make me a man? Hang on. That didn't sound at all right. What I meant was—"

"I don't want to move to New York."

His face whitens and falls as he more fully enters the room. "You're moving to New York?"

"Not now. But eventually. Probably. Or Connecticut.

"I've heard Connecticut's nice."

"I'm sure it is, but I don't want to live there."

"They don't have a team, do they? How can Jet be traded to Connecticut?"

I motion for him to shut the door. "Shh! He's not being traded. Good God. All I need is for that stupid rumor to start."

He clicks the door closed and sits in the chair across the desk from me. "No. Sorry. I'm a bit lost, as usual, though. What's happening?"

I grip the edge of my desk, suck in a huge breath, and steel myself to say, "I don't think I can do this."

"This?"

Clamping my lips together, I search for a way to say it that won't bring on a panic attack. Finally, I land on, "The WAG life might not be for me."

"What? Oh, come on now, Lady Maura. You were made for it! You have the perfect personality."

"You mean 'no personality'?"

"Who says that?"

"I do."

Oh gosh. Why'd I have to utter those two particular words? I blink furiously. "Anyway, we're here to talk about your life, your future, your prospects. Which are many!" I swallow and sift through the papers on my desk, flipping one so it's right-side-up for him and sliding it across the surface. "This one would be perfect."

"Whoa, whoa, whoa. Hang on a mo."

"No."

"Okay, we have to stop rhyming."

In spite of my misery, I chuckle.

"There's a smile. Now, what has you in such high dudgeon?"

"I'm not in a 'high dudgeon.' At all. More like… resigned."

"Then what has you so resigned? It's Gloria, isn't it? Now, there's a misnomer if I ever heard one. From where I sit, she sucks all the joy out of a place. What's she done now?"

"She's opened my eyes, my friend." When he merely tilts his head, I tap the paper. "Never mind. Let's talk jobs."

"I can't possibly discuss employment with you so obviously distressed. That's not on."

"I'm fine. I shouldn't have said anything."

He snatches the paper from the front of the desk, and, jaw tight, reads through the listing for an admissions clerk at the University of Missouri-Kansas City. After what could only be a skim-through, at best, he folds the sheet and shoves it into his inner coat pocket. "This will do."

"You can't have possibly read that."

"I don't need to. I trust you with my life."

"Then trust me when I say you don't need to concern yourself with my stupid problems."

"Tell me what the devil is going on." His eyes as cold as English stone, he waits for me to comply.

For the first time in our friendship, I get a true glimpse of the former cop, and unbelievably, it's intimidating. I wouldn't want this guy interrogating me at a police station or testifying against me in front of a room full of powdered-haired judges and attorneys. Then again, I *would* want someone this fierce on my side. And he *is* on my side. But…

"You can't fix this."

Saying it out loud almost wrecks my composure. Those four words are so terrible, so hopeless. Yet, they've been circling my brain all day. I've told them to myself a million times.

He leans forward, resting his forearms on the desk, his somber face pushed toward mine. "Bloody well try me."

I shake my head. "I have to figure this out for myself."

"Brilliant. Then what are you going to do?"

I shrug.

He stands. The tendons stand out in his jaw and neck. "Quitting isn't figuring it out."

"Now you sound like Greg."

"Well, bugger me. I suppose I'll have to live with that this once."

In an effort not to cry, I laugh. "Why are you so mad at me?"

"Perhaps because I get the feeling you're about to make the biggest cock-up of your life."

I wave off his dramatics. "Oh, now... I've made lots of big mistakes, so I'm sure whatever I decide here won't be the biggest one. Never forget the haggis. Now *that*..." I shiver. "Anyway, you should be proud of me for recognizing what a disaster this would be and getting out before it goes too far."

"You don't think you're already past that point?"

"No. I'm not. There's no signed certificate, no kids. Just two people who can say, 'See ya,' and be done with it."

"You can't possibly believe that!"

"Why not? What do you know about what I believe? You're not there every day. You don't see how manipulative they both can be."

"Tell me, then! I already know about Gloria, but I've never witnessed Jet bully you into doing something you don't want to do."

"He doesn't do it with me... yet. But I've seen him charm others to get his way."

"All in fun, surely. To get a table at a crowded restaurant, perhaps?"

*To hold a baby.*

I blink away the image of Jet cradling newborn Meleah in his arms. "It's only a matter of time before we reach a point that he feels the need to turn those powers of persuasion on me. I'm already a lame excuse for a human being; soon, I'll be nothing but a walking incubator whose sole purpose will be to push out the next Heisman winner."

"You have control over that."

"No, I don't. I have control over nothing."

"Then grow some twiddle-diddles and take control already!"

I shoot to my feet. "I've tried, okay?"

He blinks.

"I've tried. I said, 'I don't want a wedding.' Crickets. I threw a Super Bowl ring at Gloria. Tumbleweeds. Nobody gives a shit what I want."

"Jet gives a shit."

"He cares more about keeping the peace with his mother."

"He loves you. And you love him."

I groan at the ceiling. "Colin, this isn't a chick flick where that's enough to magically make everything else that's so broken work."

"Then there's your problem."

"That's what I'm trying to tell you!"

He shakes his head. "No. What I mean is..." He sighs. The paper in his coat pocket pops and crinkles as he shifts from foot to foot, staring down at the floor. Finally, he looks up. And *he's* crying. Good God. What the hell is going on?

In response, my eyes immediately fill. I can't stand to see a grown man cry. Can't stand it. Gets me every time. On TV, in movies, and definitely in real life. Can't. Handle. It. And he knows it. I'm about to call him out for being yet another manipulative crier, but all I manage is a wobbly, "Come on!"

My defiance seems to spur him to miraculously recover his stiff upper lip. With a sniff and an angry jab of his forefinger at me, he says, "You begged me to tell you the secret to a happy marriage, and I was at a loss, because I couldn't think of anything universal that was also profound enough."

I tap my foot and swallow more tears.

"But you know what? It doesn't have to be profound. In fact, most of what people say about marriage at weddings is a load of bollocks, and we all know it. Still, we smile and sniffle and think, 'What a lovely sentiment.' But the couple who's still together in five, ten, fifteen, fifty years… you know what they have that failed ones didn't? Fortitude. Follow-through."

"Great. Two of my best strengths."

He ignores my sarcasm. "But most of all? They never say love isn't enough. They know love is *everything*. They don't allow each other or anyone else to downplay it. They don't allow anything to distract them from that one basic thing. Not even death." He swipes his hand across his eyes. "*That's* the secret. Take it or leave it, if it's not convenient and doesn't fit into your plans to chuck it all. But you will be sorry. Love shows no mercy when you deny it."

He yanks open the door. I rush to catch up to him. "Colin, wait."

He pauses, but when I arrive at his side, I realize how crowded the outer office is, and as people do in waiting rooms, everyone has snapped their attention to the open door, wondering if their turn is next. Our blotchy faces and the obvious tension between us also earn the harder-to-get looks from the receptionists and other mingling staff. As a hush descends, I bite back my original thought and say, "Good luck on your job interview. I'll give them a call and let them know you're coming."

He lowers his chin and looks through the top of his eyes at me. "If you screw this up, I will never forgive you," he growls before departing.

Some people watch him leave, but most keep their stares trained on me, waiting for my reaction to such a dramatic declaration from a client.

I roll my eyes to clear the tears and shoot my audience a shaky smile. "We take job hunting extremely seriously here. So, uh, who's next?"

## TWENTY-FOUR

## SOZZLED ROMANCE

To say the stakes are high would be a huge understatement. Here I am, not only on the verge of losing the love of my life (let's be painfully, if not melodramatically, honest), the day after I've promised him I'd never leave him (don't forget that gem), but my best friend in the whole world has also vowed to give up on me if I follow my gut and throw the ball away to avoid the sack. And on a more practical level, walking away now would leave me—or a single, pregnant mother and her toddler—homeless.

Doing nothing and allowing things to continue on the current path—usually my strategy of choice—is also not an option. Because I will lose my mind. Maybe not now. But a few miles down the road? Crazy Town. And farther, Divorce-field, Depressionville, and Lonely Mountain. Nobody wants to visit those places, much less live there.

My mood is bleak, the blackest it's ever been, when I pull into the garage. It doesn't improve when I stumble through the dark house, wondering why the heck Jet has all the lights either dimmed or turned off. Things worsen when I jump to the conclusion that he must have a migraine, and I rush up the stairs, calling his name while simultaneously scrolling through my phone to find Doc's number.

I slow down to prevent crashing loudly into the master suite, but when I open the closed door, the only thing that greets me is chaos. Clothes everywhere. Every single article from what used to be the closet covers the surface of the bare California king mattress, plus most of the floor. In the closet's place is a ragged, gaping hole, surrounded by more dismantled wall and bare studs.

I spin around in a circle and drop my purse when I hear Jet's weak voice calling from one of the bedrooms I passed. Which room takes me a while to figure out, but finally, I swing open the correct door... to be greeted by a naked man, lying on his side on the bed with a football covering his most interesting stretch of flesh.

"What are you doing?" I pant.

"Waiting for you," he replies, oblivious to my panic. He tosses the football at me, revealing an enticing sight, indeed. "Wanna play?"

The ball bounces off my unresponsive hands.

"Aw, man. That was right in your breadbasket, babe. You gotta catch those."

I take in the bottle of wine and fishbowl glasses on the nightstand, plus his purple-around-the-edges teeth. "Have you been drinking?"

"A teensy bit. I got bored waiting for you to get home."

"Traffic was a night—"

"I don't care. Come here." He sits up and holds his arms open to me.

"I thought you were sick. The lights. And what happened to our closet?"

"We're having a bigger one built. I told you that."

Did he? Instead of admitting that I may have not been paying attention during that conversation, I cover with, "Oh. I didn't realize that was happening today-ish."

"No time like the present, right? Speaking of, you need to get rid of those clothes and get over here. Tights, be gone!"

I abandon my phone, kick off my shoes, and approach the bed, but I don't make any other moves to undress.

As soon as I sit on the end of the mattress, he swoops in behind me and thrusts a glass of wine at my hand. "What's the matter, babe?"

"I thought you were sick," I repeat with a thick throat. I sniff the wine but don't drink it. Half-standing, I set it on the dresser, then return to the bed.

"Aww. Didn't you see the signs I made?"

"What signs?"

"The ones on the walls downstairs. And up the stairs. And pointing to this room. Because I knew it was kinda weird I wasn't in our room."

"No. It was dark. And then I was looking in my phone for Doc's number."

"I'm not sick." He pokes me in the back as proof.

In spite of myself, I laugh. "Get that thing away from me."

"Oh, you know you love it." He slides my cardigan from my shoulders and unzips the back of my dress. "You love me. And I love you."

I whirl on him while he unhooks my bra.

"Hey, I'm not done yet," he says.

"Stop."

"I don't want to." He reaches again, but I jerk away. Annoyance creeps at the edges of his playfulness. "What's wrong?"

"I love you, Jet."

He swallows loudly. "Why does there sound like there's a 'but' coming?"

I shrug the rest of the way from my dress and kick it free of my feet before practically tearing off my tights and panties.

"Whew. Now this is more like it." His pulse becomes visible in the vein in his neck while we stretch so we're pressed front-to-front on our sides. "You had me worried for a minute."

"I'm sorry," I say, threading my arms between his biceps and flanks. "I love you. There's no 'but.'"

His hand slides down, and his finger trails a lazy line from my lower back along the place where the good Lord split me. "Oops, I found one. A nice one."

I smile, but as soon as he's otherwise occupied, the tears flow. Silently. And as Jet makes love to me, I remember Colin's words and know it *is* already too late. I've promised never to leave Jet. Maybe I didn't do it in front of a bunch of people in a church, but it still counts. I made a vow. A commitment. God heard it. Jet heard it. I meant it.

For once in my life, I'm not going to flake.

That leaves me between the proverbial rock and a hard place. Or at the moment, between a mattress and a hard body. Which is not the *worst* place to end up, considering how my day started and where it went from there. I certainly didn't expect this, that's for sure.

Jet returns to the pillows, but his satisfied grin fades when he spies the rogue tear near my ear. "Was it that bad?"

I laugh and kiss his chin. "No. It was wonderful. Exactly what I needed."

He dabs the tear with his thumb. "Oh. Good. Because I

brought my A-game. But I'm kinda drunk. So, you never know."

Desperate to maintain contact, I pull him on top of me again.

"I can't go again for a while, babe."

I roll my eyes. "I know that, *babe*. I just want to be close to you."

"Awright. As long as you're not expecting anything exciting."

"Exciting is overrated."

"You okay? You seem sad, or something. Like, even when you're smiling, you're not smiling. Does that make sense? Gosh, wine is the worst! One minute, you're fine; the next minute..." He rolls away from me. "I gotta move over here. The room's spinning. I'm afraid I'm gonna barf on you."

"Sexy."

"I know, right? Best pillow talk ever." After settling on his back, pulling the covers up to his chest, and dangling one foot off the side of the bed to place it on the floor, he grins with his eyes closed. "Ah. Better."

"You're such a lightweight."

He groan-chuckles. "Tell me about it. But in my defense, that was a super-nice bottle of wine."

"You drank a whole bottle?" I do a double-take at the half-bottle on the nightstand. "What's that over there?"

"The second one. Jackson has a wine cellar. He gave me two fancy-schmancy French wines after we won the Super Bowl. I've been saving them for a special occasion."

"And that would be today, because...?" I look around, finally locating the empty glass container on the floor next to the bed.

He opens his eyes, widening and narrowing them as he

struggles to focus on my face. "Because. I decided, 'Screw that. Every day should be a special occasion.'"

"Good attitude."

"And I love you. And that's special."

Risking a regurgitated wine shower, I cuddle up to his side and rest with my ear on his pec. "You're adorable when you're drunk."

"I don't feel adorable. I feel stupid. And sleepy."

"Then sleep for a while. I'll wake you up to feed and rehydrate you."

He pats my back, slightly harder than is comfortable, but I stifle my grunts. "Aw, babe. You're the best."

———

It's not until a couple of hours later, while I'm buttering a skillet to make grilled cheese, that I realize something—or someone—is missing.

"Hey, where's Torzi-boy?"

Jet, slumped over on the island, straightens enough to jam his cheek against his fist and rasp, "Spending the night with Jacob."

"Oh, how sweet."

"Jake's gonna take him to get his hair fixed tomorrow, too. Finally."

"Excellent. No more Torz-Bob Square Head."

Jet half-smiles and snorts, then collapses onto his arms again. "Wake me up when it's ready."

"Drink more of that water," I say, dropping a piece of bread into the pan and topping it with two slices of cheese and another piece of bread.

He grunts an unintelligible retort.

"Don't make me call Rae to come give you an IV."

Slurping drool, he rises and grips the sweating water glass in his hand. With it pressed to his lips, he pauses. "An IV would be amazing right now."

"Athletes are so weird."

"I'm never drinking wine again."

"Good call."

"Please, don't tell anyone I got this messed up on red wine."

"Could have been worse, like white wine spritzers. Or appletinis."

"Is that sandwich ready yet?"

I flip it. "Nope. A few more minutes."

"Minutes?"

"Seconds. Geez. You're such a baby. Keep drinking."

He glugs more water. "This is actually working."

"I'm kind of a wine-drunk expert. Unfortunately. It's not fun."

Swiveling to face me, he smirks. "Yeah? You need to tell me some stories to distract me and make me feel better."

While I debate complying, I lift the edge of the sandwich to check the color of the bread underneath. A little longer...

"No," I say in answer to his request for tales from my Drunk Files.

He laughs. "It's okay. Rae's already told me one story."

I whirl on him. "She didn't!"

He nods but quickly stops and grabs the edge of the island. "Oooh."

"Yeah, keep your head still. I'll get some aspirin for you as soon as you get something in your stomach."

"Anyway. Rae said one time, in college..."

*Oh, boy. Which time...?*

"…you and her smuggled some Boone's Farm back to your dorm…"

*Still not specific enough.*

"…and it was, like, one of those huge jugs with the little handle, like moonshine…? And you pretty much drank the whole thing by yourself and passed out."

*Lame. And describes a typical Friday night back then.*

He adjusts himself on the stool and scratches between his legs.

*Nice.*

"Anyway, so she was watching TV…"

*More likely, porn. But we'll stick with her version for now.*

"…and she says you suddenly woke up and bolted from the bed, but you couldn't get the door open, so you were, like, whimpering and leaking bright purple barf from the corners of your mouth, and getting it all over the doorknob, so she couldn't help you, because she didn't want to touch that…"

*Plus, she was laughing too hard at me to help. And she was watching porn. I remember the freeze-frame on her laptop. It's burned in my brain forever.*

"You finally got the door open, and you ran into the hall toward the bathrooms, but you were puking the whole way, so there was, like, this purple trail behind you. And then…" He wheezes and slaps the granite countertop, as if he had been there to see it. "…then, when you were almost to the bathrooms, you ran into some guy you had a huge crush on. Ted? Todd? Tim? Tom? Something with a 'T.'"

*Brayden. Brayden Hutchens.* "Never mind."

"Anyway, you collided with him, and you guys fell to the ground, and he was squealing, 'Get her off me!' and you kept saying, 'I'm so sorry! I'm so sorry!' but you were so wasted you couldn't get up, and you kept dry heaving into his face!

And with every spasm, he was, like, terrified, and letting out these little screams."

He throws his head back to laugh, which upsets his equilibrium. Grasping at the front of the stool, he maintains his balance for a second, but his weight pulls him backward, upending the stool and depositing him in a heap on the floor.

Lips pursed as I try not to laugh, I scoop the sandwich from the skillet and slide it onto a plate, which I walk to the island and set at his place.

"You deserve that," I say, nodding down at him.

He's too busy giggling to reply—or get up.

I right the stool and offer him my hand. After a few seconds, he composes himself enough to accept my help. As soon as he's on his feet again, I yank my hand away.

"I'm going to kill Rae."

He wipes his damp eyes as he straddles the stool again and bellies up to his plate. "Oh, shit. That's the funniest story ever."

I rest my hands on my hips. "How long have you known that?"

He picks up the sandwich, inspecting both sides. "Forever. Like, she told me before we started dating, when I was trying to get more information about you."

"Probably trying to scare you away from me."

"Didn't work."

"Obviously. Because you're warped."

"No, because we all do stupid crap when we're kids. If you were still stumbling around, drunk on Boone's Farm, spraying vomit everywhere on a typical weekend, that would be something else. But college? Geez. That's just funny."

"I can't believe you never told me you knew about that."

He shrugs and bites into his grilled cheese. Shifting the food to one cheek, he muffles, "I sorta forgot. Until now."

I ruffle his hair. "Let's try to forget it again."

Holding his sandwich aloft, he stares at it before taking another bite. "This side's kinda burnt, Beautiful."

I grip the iron skillet and lift it like I'm going to bop him over the head with it.

He laughs. "It's good, though. Thanks. I feel so much better already."

## TWENTY-FIVE

## GEEZER

Two weeks. That's all that stands between me and what's supposed to be the happiest day of my life.s

"Maybe if you didn't have such a bad attitude about it," Rae said to me the other day at lunch after her final tux fitting, "it wouldn't be so bad. What's the big deal, anyway?"

I had no decent answer for her, so I admitted she was right about the attitude, but the whole experience is tainted. Especially now that Gloria knows my true feelings about everything but continues to move forward, as planned. Email is the only method of communication between us nowadays, and she prefaces every message with, "I know you don't care, but..." or, "I hate to bother you, but..." or, "I hope it doesn't stress you out for me to tell you this, but I think you should know..."

Meanwhile, I'm keeping my eye on the prize: a lifetime with Jet, including a tropical honeymoon to kick it all off. The other minor inconveniences are gnats buzzing around the fruit bowl of my life. Eventually, the gnats will die (they have a short life span, after all), and I'll be left to enjoy my fruit salad in peace. Until the next gnat comes along. I need to invest in a good fly swatter. Still researching the best models.

One of those gnats, unfortunately, is the looming job fair. Everything is set—except the damn statuettes. And like everything else in my life right now, I'm in too deep on that project to abandon it. I have twenty Oscars done. Twenty! It's amazing I've managed that many. But I have twenty-one to go. It's taken me three months to do those twenty. Forget finishing before the wedding.

Abandoning that goal still only gives me six weeks to do more than half of the job. Four weeks, actually. Because for the next two weeks, every spare minute I have outside of work is dedicated to the wedding. Fittings and bachelorette parties (yes, plural) galore.

Plus, surprise of all surprises, Gloria signed me up to pose for a photo spread in a local magazine. Some bridal article set to publish in June. I may have said some bad words when I read that particular email. The kicker was when she wrote, "We have to do your hair and makeup run-through at some point, anyway. This photo shoot will work perfectly." Because I want the stylist to be *practicing* the look for a spread that will be on newsstands in every local grocery store, pharmacy, and gas station in the greater KC area. Right.

No matter what I want, it's happening tomorrow, and I'm sure it'll kill my entire Saturday, despite reassurances from Gloria that it'll take "an hour or two, tops." It takes an hour to get into the damn dress; I guarantee it's going to take double that to make me photo-worthy. Mags will have to be there to oversee everything, too, especially the handling of the dress. Ay-yi-yi.

Honestly, I'm trying not to think too much about it. I'm going to show up at the studio, do what I'm told, and hope my attitude in relation to this whole experience doesn't show up in the photos. Can you PhotoShop panic and loathing from someone's eyes? Didn't think so.

As for my usual quality time with Oscar, evenings are occupied more and more often by babysitting duties. Every day this week, Jet and I have had Mikey, as Cyndi struggles with the most severe case of pregnancy sickness I've ever heard of. I've not witnessed it in person, thankfully, although I have seen the effects of it on the poor woman. She looks terrible! Since we all know Jet can't be trusted alone with his nephew, Oscar and I don't have time for each other. Bathroom escapes, hot dogs, and Daddy soldiers must be avoided at all costs.

Maybe my lack of quality time with Oscar is for the best, though. Maybe I need to focus on one stressor at a time, get through the wedding, refresh on the honeymoon, and come back with gusto, ready to be a statuette-producing machine. Yeah. That's how it'll go down. I'm sure of it. Twenty-one figures in four weeks? No problem. I'll crank out one—or two —every weeknight and have time to spare. If push comes to shove, I can pull an all-nighter on a weekend.

With that settled, I officially shove Oscar *and* the wedding *and* the magazine shoot to the back burner and concentrate on being present with Mikey and Jet. We've just said goodbye to Greg, Deirdre, and Meleah after a short "play date," during which my brother and sister-in-law struggled to stay awake and barely uttered a coherent sentence between them. Meleah was bright-eyed, though, and had a grand time flirting with her future Uncle Jet.

After an hour of telling Mikey to be gentle with the baby and silently laughing at my brother's droopy lids, I showed mercy on the new parents and announced our departure.

In the car, Jet turns to me. "Now what? I told Cyndi we'd wear this kid out and bring him home ready for bed."

"That was a dumb promise."

"Right?"

"Jump Zone!" rings out Mikey's vote from the backseat.

Jet bats his eyelashes at me.

"No. Are you kidding? Last time we took him there, it went on your 'never again' list, right underneath red wine."

He sighs. "Oh, yeah. It *was* bad, wasn't it?"

"Horrible."

As if the crazed kids in the ball pits, bounce houses, and room-sized trampolines weren't obnoxious enough, the parents who swarmed Jet and wouldn't leave him alone to play with Mikey were ridiculous. "Sign this," "Pose for this selfie," "Show me your Super Bowl ring" (as if he'd wear it out to somewhere like that). It was such a hassle, we gave up and left after a mere thirty minutes. Which made for an irate toddler.

Jet rubs his chin. "Who else's house can we crash? Rae? Does she like kids?"

I snort.

"What about Colin?"

I consider it while Mikey chants, "Jump Zone!" over and over less than three feet from my ear.

Colin and I have patched things up since his last visit to The Career Center. In fact, our conciliatory texts crossed paths through cyberspace and arrived at nearly the same time (typical).

I typed, *You were right, as usual. No quitting here,* and he tapped, *Sorry I was such a knobhead yesterday, mate. I'm here for you whatever you decide.* Our *LOLs* landed simultaneously, followed by *Great minds* from me and *I'm so glad I don't have to choose between you and Jet* from him.

Despite our reconciliation, I hesitate spending too much time around him *and* Jet so soon. Jet has no idea there was ever anything to reconcile, and I'm a bit nervous about it coming up tonight. On the other hand, not acknowledging it at all could be equally awkward.

"Jump Zone! Jump Zone! JUMP ZONE!"

"Let's go to a really cool guy's house!" I decide impulsively, unable to think, much less obsess about every detail and eventuality. I'll take my chances with Mikey providing enough entertainment that there won't be any opportunity for tension.

"Colin's?" Jet asks, raising his shoulders toward his ears as he anticipates my answer.

"Yeah. Let me text him and at least warn him we're on the way, though."

When Colin's acknowledgment and, *Come on over! I'll even put trousers on!* comes through, Jet claps. "Yay!" While backing from my brother's driveway, he says into the backseat, "Colin's so fun, Mikey! He can make all these noises with his mouth, and he— Well, you'll see. You'll love him."

———

"I love this kid."

Well, that's unexpected. I knew Mikey would love Colin. Everyone loves Colin. And since he's a big kid, himself, so it stands to reason that kids would love him. But this is the first time I've seen my friend interact with a child, so I wasn't sure the feeling would be mutual.

To be honest, I never pegged Colin as a huge fan of kids. It's not that I thought he didn't like them; I figured he was like me, though: undecided and untested. But he's seemed perfectly relaxed—and extremely amused—by his unexpected pint-sized guest. He doesn't condescend to him. He talks to him like he does everyone else. If Mikey understands what he's saying, great. If not, Colin shrugs and figures the toddler will catch on eventually, but he's not going to "dumb it down" for him. Mikey loves it.

He loves it almost as much as the sound effects Colin can make. "Beat box!" he begs now, immediately getting into his "dance crouch" when Colin imitates a hip-hop DJ, complete with turntable scratching. I marvel not only at the noises coming from my friend but at how entertained he's kept such a young child with absolutely no toys at his disposal. Jet claps and laughs at the show.

Mere minutes later, Mikey gives out. He climbs into Jet's lap and rests his head on his arm. "Mikey west."

"Now, this is a first," Jet says with a laugh, tickling his nephew.

Mikey smiles around the thumb he's jammed into his mouth, but he maintains his far-off stare.

"Maura says your sister's been ill?" Colin says. "Morning sickness, or some such, except 'round the clock?"

Jet absently rubs Mikey's back, making the boy shiver and squirm. "Yeah. It'll pass, I guess. She had a similar issue with this guy. Things haven't been easy for her lately, either."

"Aw, bless." Colin clicks his tongue. "It's a shame." Suddenly, he smiles and nods at Mikey. "Someone's not going to be awake much longer."

I rise from the couch. "We should get him home before he sleeps too long, wakes up, and gets his second wind."

Jet agrees, standing and tossing Mikey over his shoulder, much to the little guy's delight. "Unca Jet!"

Jet turns in a half-circle. "Did you guys hear that?"

"Unca Jet!"

"I could've sworn I heard my name. Huh. I must be hearing things."

"Unca Jet!"

"Oh, my gosh! It's this sack of potatoes! It's talking. Get it away from me!" Without warning, he lobs the giggling toddler at Colin, who catches him in both arms without missing a beat.

"I've got him. I'm not afraid of talking veg. They're quite tasty." He munches along Mikey's back. "Mm. Delicious! Could use some salt." With remarkable realism, he imitates the sound of a shaker, then munches again. "Much better." Setting the child on the ground, he says, "All right, hero. Off you go. You've worn this plonker out."

"Bye, Plonker!"

Colin bends at the waist and rests his hands on his knees while laughing. "Did you just call me 'Plonker'?"

"Plonker!"

"Excellent."

"That's not a bad word, or anything, is it?" Jet checks.

"Nah. A bit of a mild insult, like 'moron.' And nobody around here's going to know, anyway."

"I don't want to get in trouble with my sister for teaching him anything too colorful."

"You can blame me, mate."

"I will." Jet grabs Mikey's hand and pulls him toward the car. "Say goodbye to your new friend, bud."

"Bye, Plonker!"

"Take care, Geezer."

I hug Colin and say near his ear, "I owe you lunch. Call me next wee— Oh. Wait. I can't next week. I have a huge list of wedding errands to run on my lunch breaks."

He pats my back. "We'll catch up after you return from your honeymoon. I'll want to hear all about it. Well, most of it. And I'm sure I'll have lots to report on the new job by then, as well."

"Okay. See you around."

"See you at a certain wedding, I'm fairly certain." He taps his lips with his forefinger. "I'll have to check my calendar, but I believe it's two weeks from tomorrow. Two very important people. Ringing any bells?"

I stick out my tongue at him. "Nope. I hope it's a good time, though. I'll probably skip it. Stay home and watch a movie."

He waves us off from his front stoop, blowing kisses like someone saying goodbye to their loved ones as they pull from port on the Titanic.

"What a ham," I mutter around my chuckles.

"Plonker!"

Jet sighs. "That so sounds like a bad word."

## TWENTY-SIX

## THE SLEEPOVER

Mikey passes out in the car, of course, so when we arrive at Cyndi's, Jet carries him into the house, fully prepared to help put him to bed. But as soon as we enter the living room, we find Cyndi crying on the sofa. It takes only a few seconds to determine there's nothing seriously wrong, but when Jet asks, "What can we do?" she presents us with a much bigger challenge.

"Can you, I don't know, take Mikey home with you? Can he spend the night there?"

"Sure!" Jet immediately says, gently bouncing the stirring boy and transferring the snoozer's head to a more comfortable position on his shoulder. "Yeah." He glances at me, suddenly looking and sounding much less certain. "That would be cool. I think. We could handle that, right?"

Cyndi is so green and so distraught, there's no way I could refuse her, despite having no idea how to take care of a toddler for longer than a couple of hours. "We'll figure it out. Don't worry," I say. "Help us pack a bag for him, maybe?"

She nods and drags herself from the couch, leading us into Mikey's room.

Jet mouths behind her back and over Mikey's, *"Oh, my gosh. What the fuh—"*

"Thank you so much for doing this." She turns abruptly at the threshold to the bedroom, looking adoringly up at her older brother in the process. "I'm sorry. Were you saying something?"

He grins. "No! I mean, I was whispering to Maura, 'What fun!' Because this is going to be so much fun. Right, Maura?"

"A ton of fun."

Cyndi opens the dresser, rooting through the clothes in the drawers. "I don't know what I would do without you guys. He's a good kid—you know that—but he's at that age where you have to keep an eye on him at all times, when he's awake. He's a good sleeper, once you get him settled, but I'm afraid tomorrow morning—"

"Don't mention it, Sis."

"I can't do anything right. I was a horrible wife, I'm a bad mom, and... and..." She presses a pair of footie pajamas to her eyes and breaks down.

"Oh, geez. No. Don't think that. Or cry. Or..." Jet wraps his free arm around her shoulders and squeezes. "It's okay. We're here, and we'll—"

Without warning, she bolts for the door, zooming across the hall to the half-bathroom.

"...take care of everything."

Mikey whimpers and wakes more fully. Looking around and not seeing his mom, he ratchets from whine to wail in record time.

Jet pats his nephew's back and mutters, "So much fun."

———

After a harried couple of hours of "appease the kid," we're finally in bed. Jet decided Mikey could sleep by himself—"He does it at his own house, why not here?"—so we've put him right next door to the room we've been sleeping in while they remodel our bedroom, which went from a closet re-build to a complete bedroom overhaul in one workday. (Don't get me started.)

Before we left him, we lined the entire perimeter of the king-sized mattress with pillows, *and* we placed pillows all along the floor around the bed. Then we high-stepped through the cushioning for several trips back and forth for drinks, night-light adjustments, stories, and kisses. More kisses. "All da kisses, pwease!"

He's been quiet for a few minutes now, so it feels safe to get comfortable. As comfortable as I can get in this unfamiliar room, that is. Jet offered to reassemble our bed in here for the duration of the remodel, but that would have made this space one big mattress. It didn't seem worth it. Now, I'm second-guessing my decision.

A few inches too long for this bed, Jet tosses and turns next to me, inadvertently elbowing me in the shoulder blade. "Oh, geez. Sorry!"

"It's okay," I reply, reaching behind me and rubbing the assaulted spot.

"Here." He takes over rubbing the wing-like bone, which leads to lower rubbing and kissing and...

"Hey," I say before he goes too far. "Your nephew is right next door."

"So? He already got his share of kisses; it was starting to make me uncomfortable."

I laugh. "That's not what I meant. He might hear us."

"He's out of it. Exhausted after being such a dick—tator."
He rolls me over to face him. "Damn. Kids are hard work."

"They are."

"Like, from Day One. Greg and D looked like zombies. Like
they haven't slept at all since they brought Meleah home."

"They probably haven't."

"Oh, my gosh. I need sleep, Maura. Lots and lots of sleep."

"Me too."

He sighs, touching his nose to mine. "But then. Then I
hold her and think, 'Wow. This is amazing. They made her.'"

I blink my stinging eyes. "Yeah, well... I try not to think of
them making babies."

He smiles at my joke but quickly sobers. "And then, *then* I
see you with Mikey, and—"

"Then you *really* understand how we might be better off
playing the rich aunt and uncle who spoil their nieces and
nephews rotten?"

"No! You're so good with him."

I scoff. "I have no idea what I'm doing!"

"He doesn't care."

"Because it usually works to his advantage."

He nuzzles my neck. "You try. That's all that matters."

"I also know I only have to try for a finite amount of time;
then I get to send him back to someone who knows what the
heck they're doing."

"Nobody knows what they're doing, especially with their
first one."

His lips trace lower, and his hands creep up the inside of
my shirt. "But I never want to be too tired to do this"—he
kisses my collar bone—"or this"—he palms my breasts—"or
this..." He disappears under the bedspread.

"Me neither," I manage to say, my eyes rolling back in my head.

I giggle when he bites the waistline of my underwear and yanks them downward with his teeth. I arch my back to make his job easier, and he soon reemerges, his hair standing up as he shimmies from his boxer briefs. I cover my mouth with one hand and point to his head with the other. He crosses his eyes and sticks out his tongue to complete the crazed picture, laughing as he throws off the covers and collapses on top of me, falling into a long, un-silly kiss.

Millimeters from coupling, we stop when we hear a THUD from next door, followed by a thick, pregnant silence, and culminating in a crescendoing tornado-siren sound effect that would put Colin's skills to shame.

Jet scrambles to his knees. "Shit!" he hisses, hopping from the bed and fishing his underwear from the tangled sheet and comforter at the foot of the mattress.

"UNCA JET!" Mikey bellows tearfully through the wall. "I fallded!"

"Stay right there," Jet says to me, hitching his underpants into place. "Don't move. I'll be right back."

"What if he's hurt?"

"I'm sure he's fine. He's talking. Just give me a sec." He smooths his hair down and calls on his way out of the room, "I'm coming, buddy!"

Yeah, I was about to, too. But whatever.

I fall back into the pillows and do as I'm told, but as the murmured negotiations drag on next door, my libido wanes, sputters, and dies. I'm fully dressed, and I've remade the bed by the time Jet peeks around the door frame to make sure I'm decent before carrying an eye-rubbing Mikey into the room on his hip.

"Slumber party!" he says, tossing his nephew in the spot to my left, normally occupied by him. He slides under the covers on his side of the bed and nudges Mikey closer to me. "Move over, bed hog."

Mikey continues digging at his eyes with his fists but smiles. "I not a bed hog!"

Torzi, summoned by the commotion and encouraged by the open bedroom door, flies onto the foot of the bed, spins about a hundred times, and lies down on my feet. I try to gently push him away, but he growls and bares his teeth, so I back down.

"What happened, Cutie?" I ask Mikey as he takes over my pillow, head-butting me in the process. "Ow."

He sniffles, seeming to remember he's supposed to be distraught. "I falleded off da bed."

"I heard that. But the pillows were there, right? It didn't hurt, did it?"

"Naw. But I was skeered."

"Oh."

"I miss Mommy."

Heart. Melting.

"And I wike snuggles."

"I like snuggling, too," Jet grumbles.

Mikey grabs my upper arm like a koala on a eucalyptus tree branch. "Mo-Mo's turn," he says with a yawn into my ear. "Unca Jet's turn later."

Jet turns off the lamp over his head. "That's okay, Buddy. I'll be fine over here."

———

For the umpteenth time, I startle awake when a pudgy, not-so-fresh-smelling hand lands on my face, followed by murmuring, fidgeting, and readjusting until Mikey plays the part of the crossbar in the capital H the three of us form on the bed. I sigh and rise on my elbows to see how Jet's faring. Only... Jet's not here.

"Son of a..." In his place are four pillows, two long and two high, anchored under the bedspread. I'd like to punch Pillow Jet.

Instead, I fashion a similar Pillow Mo-Mo and slink from the room, putting my finger to my lips when Torzi raises his head to watch my escape. For once, the dog obeys—maybe he can smell how close I am to the edge—and rests his head on his paws with a long-suffering sigh.

As I make my way down the hallway, I poke my head into each bedroom, looking for that traitorous fiancé of mine. I find him passed out on his belly on the middle of the bed in the room closest to the stairs, the one his parents usually occupy when they're visiting. I sneak up to his bare foot and lightly run my fingernail up his arch, hoping to simulate the sensation of a crawling bug.

It works.

He kicks his leg and shoots into a sitting position, slapping at his foot. "Guh!" he grunts, searching the bedspread for the "insect."

When I snort, he looks up. "Did you see it?"

"See what?"

"Something was crawling on me. On my foot."

I shake my head. "Nope. Must have gotten away. Scurried. Like you did. From the other room."

He stops his hunt for the phantom bug and rubs his face. "I couldn't take it anymore. He kept kicking me. Look!" He turns and lifts his right arm, giving me a good view of his scratched-up flank.

"What the heck?"

"The kid's toenails."

"Ew."

"Tell me about it."

"His fingernails aren't short, either. I kept getting smacked in the face and head-butted in the ribs."

"Gonna sign him up for a mani-pedi today."

I laugh and join him on the bed, copying the position I originally found him in. Face buried in the pillows, I ask, "Why didn't you take me with you when you left?"

He stretches out alongside me. "You seemed pretty out of it. I didn't want to wake you up."

"That must have been during the only five minutes I slept."

"If it makes you feel any better, I haven't been in here long." He tugs at the covers under me. "Here. Get under the blankets."

I don't move. "I can't. It's almost time for me to get up, anyway."

"It's Saturday. Sleep in."

"I have that stupid magazine shoot. I'm meeting Mags at nine o'clock."

He kisses the back of my neck. "Shoot."

"Yep. The shoot."

"No, I mean, like, 'darn.'"

I shift to my hands and knees, before I really do fall asleep, and crawl toward the side of the bed, where I sit, slumped. "I'm sure I look awesome, too."

"You're beautiful."

"You're a liar."

He heaves himself to his feet and shuffles to the door. "You're the most gorgeous woman on the planet. And you'll look even better after some coffee."

"After you drink some, or I do?"

"Both."

Feeling like a sloth, I follow him downstairs. "Make it happen, Champ."

## TWENTY-SEVEN

## PHOTOSHOOT

The "most gorgeous woman on the planet" has a cluster of zits on her cheek. And dark circles under her eyes. And dry, winter skin. And lank hair. There's not an airbrushing computer program in existence that can save me. The look on Mags's face when she meets me in the weekend-deserted lobby of the magazine's offices confirms that fear, too.

"Is everything okay?" she asks as she leads me to the studio where the photographer is already setting up. He doesn't even glance at us as we pick up the garment bag containing the wedding dress and follow his assistant to the deserted green room we're using today as a dressing room.

I wave off the wedding planner's concern. "Sleepover with Jet's nephew."

"You pulled an all-nighter? I wish you hadn't done that."

Rolling my eyes, I robotically remove my clothes and don my trousseau, with nary a smidge of self-consciousness at being naked in front of a near-stranger. Sleep deprivation is good for something: apathy. "It wasn't an all-nighter, and it wasn't a planned thing. It sorta worked out that way, that's all."

And it continues to work out that way. When I left, Jet had recently ended a call with his sister, who was still in no condition to take care of anyone but herself.

"Are you sure you're going to be okay?" I asked him on my way out the door.

Jet looked through the doorway at Mikey, secured in a booster chair in the kitchen, scarfing down pancakes and finger-painting with his syrup, and winced. To me, he flashed a quick, nervous smile. "We'll be fine. Maybe we'll call Colin to come over and play." Louder, he said toward the kitchen, "You want to hang out with Plonker today, Mikey?"

"Plonker!"

"See? It'll be great."

"Assuming Colin's available."

"I'll bribe him with Newcastle."

"Babysitting and beer. Great combination."

"Don't worry about anything. Go and have fun at your photo shoot."

"Ha!"

"No, seriously. They're fun. You'll see."

So far, I'm having almost too much fun to handle.

Standing guard at the door, Mags murmurs, "The stylist will be here in about thirty minutes. It's amazing what she can do with contouring. Let's not panic yet."

"I'm not panicking," I say, grunting as I pull at my stockings and straighten my shapewear. Is she kidding? I'm too tired to panic.

Mags steps forward and helps me dive into the dress. Then, tightening the corset-like stays in the back, she mutters something under her breath I don't catch and don't care to ask her to repeat. Everything I say and do here can and will be used against me when it's inevitably relayed to Gloria later in full detail. The less I interact with the wedding planner, the better. I'm merely the mannequin. Silent and compliant.

When the stylist arrives, she and Mags exchange a glance that's not lost on me, so I do say, "Sorry, okay? I don't *mean* to be this beautiful. I woke up this way."

They chuckle nervously at my sarcasm, and the stylist gets right to work, covering me in a black cape to protect my dress from makeup dust and hairspray. Mags leaves to check on the photographer's setup progress in the studio. As soon as she's is gone, the stylist, who introduces herself as Shelli, warms considerably.

"It's not that bad, darlin'," she reassures me. "You have a natural beauty that we're going to play up. Some women need so much makeup. You don't. There are a couple of problem areas here—those under-eye circles are pretty wicked today—but they're no match for me."

"Great," I manage as she slops foundation onto my cheeks, nose, chin, and forehead, then vigorously swipes a triangular sponge across my skin to blend it all together.

"So, Jet Knox, huh? Lucky girl."

Since I'm relying on her to make me look good, it would be foolish to be rude, curt, or cool in my reply. Therefore, I smile and say honestly, "I am."

"He's a hottie. Hope you don't mind me saying it."

"He's a nice guy, too."

"Of course! Seems like every time I turn around, I'm reading about something else he's done for a charity or whatever. Stays busy year-round with that stuff, sounds like." She clamps her lips together to demonstrate how she wants me to hold my mouth while she works around my nose and chin.

Since I'm limited to humming my responses, I simply agree, "Mm-hm."

"Did he really pay for an entire gastrointestinal surgery for a kid? He was asked to donate one of his jerseys or helmets or something for a silent auction to help the family, and he was like, 'I'll pay for the whole procedure'?"

I nod. "Mm."

"That's pretty awesome. And were you were all, like, 'Hey! That's my shoe fund!'"

My eyes widen, and my brows knit. "Mm-mm."

"Kidding! I'm sure you're generous, too. Of course, it's easy to be generous with someone else's money, right? And when he has that much of it... You're not going hungry so some kid can get his guts fixed." She steps back and examines her work. "You can relax your mouth."

"It's hard deciding who to help. He— *We* want to help everyone. But we can't."

"Some people figure that means not helping anyone, though. And that's not right."

"No. It's not."

She moves on to my eyes. "Daytime wedding, right? We're not doing smoky eyes, or anything dramatic like that?"

"No."

"We're going to channel spring. Dewy and light and fresh."

I close my eyes, placing myself in her hands. This is so not my territory. I couldn't second-guess her if I wanted to. Anyway, she acts like she's making this up on the fly, but I'm sure she received her orders months ago from Gloria, via Mags. She's hardly waiting for instruction from me.

She hums as she brushes eye shadow along my lids. While she pokes the eyeliner into place a few minutes later, she says, "What's the scoop on Keaton Busch? I heard he's playing arena football now. Paid a huge fine and did some community service to avoid jail time?"

"You know more than I do," I reply.

"Oh, I see. You aren't allowed to talk about it. Gag order or something?"

"No. I don't know anything."

"Right. I get it."

I sigh. "Tell me about yourself. Do you specialize in wedding styles?"

She goes on a forty-minute spiel about her entire life—basically—but it keeps her off the topic of hot NFL guys and what I may or may not know about them, so I'm okay with it. It also requires almost zero input from me, other than an occasional "Hm" or "Ah" to prove I'm still awake. Which is getting harder and harder to be by the second, considering how tired I am. It's also less awkward to have someone inches from my face if I keep my eyes closed. When she moves on to my hair, my lids stay down. There's much tugging and what feels like teasing, but the updo Gloria showed me months ago requires quite a bit of volume and lift, so I suppose back-combing is to be expected.

The door to the green room squeaks open. "The photographer's ready for us whenever," Mags announces.

"Just... about... done," Shelli replies, twisting a hank of hair and securing it—painfully—to the base of my skull with a bobby pin.

I flinch.

"Sorry about that, girl. Okay. Finito. What do you think?"

I open my eyes, but since there's no mirror in here, I have to judge the final product by Mags's reaction while Shelli digs in her massive, glittery carryall for a hand mirror.

Mags clasps her hands under her chin and smiles. "Perfect. Exactly what we discussed. You nailed it, as usual, Shell."

Wow. The under-eye circles and acne must be mere memories, which is all I care about. Otherwise, makeup is makeup and hair is hair, right?

Wrong.

Mags continues to gush as Shelli slides one mirror into my hands and holds another up behind me so I can get the full view of my Bride of Frankenstein hair. The only thing missing is the gray squiggly streaks down either side, and they're about to pop any second now. Especially when I move my attention from my hair to my face.

"Spring, light, and dewy" must translate to "pastel, pancaked, and oily," in Shelli's mind.

Mags breaks off in the middle of her monologue about how thrilled Gloria's going to be with the results when I rest the mirror in my lap and have to focus on breathing so I don't pass out. "What's the matter?"

I shake my head. "Nothing."

Shelli's shoulders slump. "You don't like it?"

"It's— I'm not used to wearing makeup, that's all," I hastily qualify toward her crestfallen face, stalling as I try to figure out how the hell I'm going to get out of here without any photographic evidence of this disaster. "Not this much, anyway. Which I'm sure is necessary, for the camera, and everything."

"Exactly."

"But on the day of the wedding?"

"Same deal. Maybe less eye makeup, but I went with a light touch already. Like I said, you didn't need much."

Light touch? Ha! Did this woman train with Marilyn

Manson? Lady Gaga? The guys from KISS? *Rocky Horror Picture Show*?

Okay. No time to freak out. Blotting papers. That's what I need.

I search the area, barely moving my head. With every movement, every flutter of air around it, my hair shifts against my scalp, rebelling, pulling its way back to its normal shape, my follicles screaming at their unnatural positions. Finally, as Mags and Shelli explain how easily someone as fair as I am would be washed out by the lighting in the studio, if not for all of this makeup, I spot the pop-up box of tissue paper on a nearby table and lunge for it. Grabbing several sheets at once, I press them furiously against my glistening face, hoping to minimize the fresh-from-the-oven turkey effect.

"No!" Shelli shouts, slapping my hands away from her artistry.

Frantic, I say while trying to turn my back on her, "Listen, I can handle one or the other: big hair or big makeup. But not both. I… I don't look anything like myself!"

"Watch the dress!" Mags squeals, stepping forward to help Shelli restrain me. "Maura! Be still! Calm down!"

I flail my arms at the two of them and try to evade them in the tiny room, but for some reason, I can't move. It's like I'm stapled to the floor or some—

*RIIIIIIIIIP.*

All three of us freeze at the sickening sound.

Mags recovers first, running her hands all over me, as if she's looking for a gaping, bleeding wound. She'd probably prefer that be the case, actually. "Please, tell me that was the makeup cape," she mutters over and over, but it's obvious as soon as she steps back to view the whole picture that she was standing on the dress she was trying to protect.

Freed, I scamper away from her, immediately feeling the draft from the tear.

Mags gasps. "Look what you did!"

"What *I* did? You were the one standing on it. And assaulting me!"

"You were hysterical. And about to ruin an hour's worth of Shelli's work."

"Oh, what a shame!" I turn to the stylist. "No offense."

She narrows her eyes at me. "Ha. Ha."

"Gloria's going to kill us," Mags says with the heels of her hands pressed against her temples.

"Us?" I chuckle nervously. "No, no, no. *You*. I didn't rip the dress; you did."

"Because *you* were being uncooperative!"

I barely register the soft knock before a man's head pokes through the cracked door. "Ladies? Is everything all right in he—" His face falls. "Oh, shit. You have got to be kidding me."

Mags rubs her face. Shelli shrugs and backs away from the two of us. When I assume the photographer is about to lament the ruined dress, he whines, "Nobody told me the bride was that tall!" He stomps away, muttering about Sasquatches and his lighting being all wrong.

The three of us watch after him for a few seconds, but the studio door slamming in the distance seems to be our cue to continue where we left off.

"I have to go in front of hundreds of people looking like this!"

"Not if we can't fix that dress!"

"You looked beautiful, damn it! It *was* my best work, until you messed with it."

## TWENTY-EIGHT

## BAD BABYSITTERS

Still finding pins throughout my hair, I trudge home in disgrace, the photographer's hurtful running monologue ringing in my ears. "I was expecting petite. That's usually what these athletes go for. Makes 'em feel more manly, or something. Or they're harboring latent pedophile tendencies. Who knows? Anyway, I wasn't expecting an Amazonian."

I pretended to ignore him until the name-calling started. That's when I pointed out that Drew McKnight's German supermodel wife, Greta, is six feet tall, a full inch taller than I am.

He'd muttered, "You're no Greta Steinberg."

No. I'm not. I'm so glad he pointed that out. Instead of throat-punching him, I focused on the top of his assistant's head as she rearranged the train of my dress for the millionth time to conceal the huge gash in it. Her hair was so shiny. And lying so naturally and painlessly against her scalp.

I toss the latest bobby pin Easter egg in the trash on my way through the kitchen, hoping the relative quiet in the house means Mikey is back with Cyndi. Colin's car is still outside in the circle driveway, but maybe he stayed to watch soccer. *Or* the cartoons I'm hearing.

"Hey, I'm ho—"

Three guilty faces greet me from the couch. Well, two guilty faces and an indifferent one pointed at the TV. An indifferent one framed by a much different hairstyle. As in, no hair.

I gasp. "What happened to Mikey's hair?"

A fourth face points my way, but the dog doesn't loiter. Rather, he jumps from the couch and rockets up the stairs.

Jet nods at my head. "What happened to yours?"

I couldn't quite brush all of the hair spray—or pins—from my locks after changing into my street clothes, and I just wanted to get out of there, so I gave up, figuring I could come home and shower. It had already taken forever to squeegee the makeup from my face.

I wave off his question. "No, no. You first." After all, he'll find out soon enough from Gloria all about my adventures today.

Jet swallows audibly. "We, uh… Well, it's a funny story…"

Colin jumps in. "We had a bit of a mishap earlier."

"One that required you to shave the kid's head?" I lower myself onto the edge of the nearest chair. "Oh, this oughtta be good."

Colin looks toward his hairline and twists his mouth to the side. "Good? Not so sure you'll call it *that*, but, uh, nobody got hurt, so I suppose that's what's most important."

Suddenly, I don't want to know. I stand and head for the stairs. "You know what? Never mind. I've had one of the worst days in recent memory, which is saying something, so I'm going to go upstairs, wash this can of hair spray from my head, and soak in the tub for, oh, twenty-four hours ought to do it. If anyone needs me… Don't. Don't need me."

Jet stands. "Maura. Uh…" He turns back to Colin. "You mind sitting here with Mikey while I talk to Maura upstairs for a minute?"

Colin loops his arm around the toddler. "It's the least I can do, mate. We'll be fine down here. Right, Geezer?"

Mikey smiles up at his new buddy. "Yeah, Plonker!"

Colin flashes two thumbs up at us, and I try not to worry about the sick tinge of his expression. Or the sweat on Jet's brow.

While I strip for the third time today with an audience and turn on the water to regulate the temperature for a quick shower to wash my hair, Jet sits on the side of the garden tub. "I have some bad news."

Considering the past twenty-four hours, it could be related to any number of things—Cyndi, Mikey, Mikey's hair, Gloria already getting wind of the ripped dress and calling Jet to tell him all about it, to name a few—so I don't attempt to guess. Instead, I brace myself for more unpleasantness. Then again, how much worse can this day get?

Jet picks at the hairs on his knee. "Before I tell you what happened, I want you to know that I'm going to fix it. I haven't figured out how yet, but I will. I promise. Okay?"

I nod and roll my eyes. "Okay. Fine. Spit it out."

He sucks in a huge breath. "Mikey got into your Oscar statue things."

Halfway in and halfway out of the shower, my muscles seize, and I stand motionless, staring at him, processing what he's said and trying to figure out the ramifications. I grip the edge of the tile wall. "Wait. What?"

"We were playing hide-and-seek in the basement."

Wanting to know how many people I'll have to kill, I ask, "Who's 'we'?"

"Mikey, Colin, and me."

"So, two grown men and a child."

"Yes. But—"

"How bad is it?"

"It's, uh… It's not good."

"'Not good'? What did he do? And how did he have time to do any substantial damage with *two* adults supposedly supervising him?" I turn off the water, grab the towel from the stainless steel hook on the wall, and pat dry the wet half of my body. Then I wrap the cloth around me so I don't have to continue this horrific conversation more exposed than I already feel.

Jet steps toward me, but I stiff-arm him like he does to defenders when scrambling for a first down. "Tell, don't touch."

"He got into the rubber cement."

"Oh, my gosh. Did he eat any of it?"

Jet shakes his head. "No. He… He put some in his hair. Like gel."

"Oh." My shoulders relax slightly. "That explains that. Was his hair the only casualty?"

"Newp."

"When you say he got into my 'Oscar statue things' are we talking about the supplies or the actual statuettes?"

"Yes."

My heart pounds. "Which one?"

"Both. All."

I cover my mouth and nose. "Oh, Jet…"

"Yeah. He painted some of the statues with it, too."

I drop my hands. "How many is 'some'?"

"All… of them?"

"And you and Colin? Where were you two during all this? Making out?"

He laughs but quickly sobers. "No. We were down there with him. Looking for him. You know, seeking."

"You let a two-year-old hide by himself?"

"No! Well, sort of. See, it was my turn to seek, but Colin thought it was *his* turn to seek, so we were both on our phones while we were supposedly 'counting.'"

"Idiots!"

"I know! I know, babe."

"Don't 'babe' me! Were you two drinking?"

"No! I wish I could say we were, to give us a better excuse."

"I would kill you."

"Then we definitely weren't drinking. At all."

My knees suddenly weak, I sink to the side of the tub. "All of them are ruined?"

He nods. "Pretty sure. You'll want to check for yourself, obviously. Maybe you can save one or two."

I snort. "One or two. Out of twenty. When I still had more than that left to do." I cover my eyes. "I can't do it. I can't do this."

Tentatively, he reaches out, grabs my limp hand in my lap, and sits next to me when I don't attack him. I let him hold my fingers, because I don't have the will to pull away.

"I'm so sorry. It was boneheaded, like something out of a movie or TV show, where the guys are so clueless, you think, 'How can anyone be that dumb?'"

I uncover my eyes. "He could have been seriously hurt. He could have died!"

"But he wasn't. He didn't. He— He just lost some hair in the deal. And I yelled at him."

"You yelled at him for something that was technically your fault?"

He nods. "Yeah. I was scared. Because I knew he could have gotten seriously hurt, and it would have been my fault. So I yelled."

"Wow."

"I feel like shit about it."

"Well, as long as you feel bad." I laugh mirthlessly.

"Hey, I told you I'm going to fix this."

"How, Jet? How?"

He stares blankly for a few seconds. Finally, he says, "I don't know. Yet. But Colin and I will figure it out."

I point to the bathroom door. "Now would be a great time to get started on that brainstorming session."

Springing to his feet, he darts for the door. "Yes, ma'am."

"In the meantime, I'm going to execute my original plan and stay up here. Only, I might be up here for forty-eight hours. Screw work on Monday."

"Okay. Whatever you want. Can I bring you a glass of wine or food or—"

"Don't come back up here."

"Got it."

He reverses from the room, pulling the door closed behind him. "I love you," he sneaks in right before it clicks shut.

The fact that I love him is the only thing keeping him alive.

———

I've only refreshed the water in the tub once before there's a knock.

"Somebody better be bleeding! And it better not be Mikey," I shout at the skylight with my eyes still closed. I hear the door open and lower my chin to level my intruder with a withering glare.

Jet's worried face enters the room, followed by his entire fidgety body. He holds up his dark phone. "Cyndi's at the ER."

"What?" I bolt up in the water, pulling the plug to drain the tub. "Oh, my gosh. What happened?"

He shakes his head. "I don't know, exactly. She called an ambulance. The hospital called me. Said she was in and out of consciousness. Severely dehydrated. Damn it! I should have made her come home with us last night." He paces the bathroom, his words echoing.

I step down to the mat, drying myself in double-time. "She said she was fine. Needed some peace and quiet and time to recover without responsibilities. You couldn't know."

"She could have recovered here."

"Okay. Let's stay calm and get to her as fast as we can. Which hospital?"

He consults his phone to be sure while I throw on clean clothes and twist my hair into a wet, messy bun on top of my head. "Let's grab Mikey and go."

"Colin said he'd stay here with him."

"Good call." I hobble around the bedroom with one shoe on and search for its mate under the bed. Jet finds it first and thrusts it toward me. Patting his pockets to check for his wallet, he follows me downstairs.

After making sure Colin understands that Mikey cannot be left alone for a single second ("Not even to use the toilet?" "*Especially* not to use the toilet!"), we leave the house, taking the fastest car available to us.

All the way to the hospital, Jet abuses the paddle-shifter next to the steering wheel as he berates himself.

When I can finally get a word in, I say, "Hey. We couldn't know. And she did the right thing, calling 911."

"Why didn't she call *me*? Before it got to that point?"

I don't have an answer for him until much later, after I've thought about it for a while, and we've been directed to sit in the waiting room, on display with the walking wounded, many of whom stare openly at us. Not us. Him. I'm merely the haggard, wet-haired, bare-faced lady who happens to be sitting next to Jet Knox.

I place a hand on his jiggling knee to still it and lean over so he can hear me when I murmur, "Maybe she didn't want to bother you."

He stage-whispers back, "Bother me? 'Sorry to bother you, but I might be dying'?"

"I doubt she's dying. Lots of pregnant women go through what she's been going through. I can't remember the technical term, but Kate Middleton had it."

He sighs. "Why does everyone still call her Kate Middleton? That's not her name anymore, is it?"

"'The Duchess of Cambridge' is a bit of a mouthful. And 'Kate' is too vague."

He considers this, nods, and shrugs. "All right. I get that, I guess."

"Anyway, Kate Whatever-You-Want-to-Call-Her is fine now. Her kids are fine. Don't worry."

"I wish we knew for sure what was happening." The leg bounces again, and he bites at a hangnail on his middle finger.

"The lady at the desk said it wouldn't be long."

Three hours, a hundred autographs, and countless awkward interactions later, a nurse emerges from the security doors, spots us, and signals us forward. One good thing about being instantly recognizable is that nobody has to call out your name to identify you in a waiting room.

Jet practically runs to the guy. "What's up?"

*What's up? I'm so tired, I almost laugh. I half-expect the nurse to reply, "Not much, dawg. Great game down in Dallas. Way to bring it home."*

Instead, he says, more appropriately, "I can take you back to see your sister now."

"Is she okay? Is she going to be okay?"

The nurse couldn't sound more bored if he tried when he replies, "She's fine. I'll explain more when we get there."

"But—"

I grab Jet's elbow. When he looks down at me, I say, "He can't talk about it out in the hallway. Be patient."

Before he can object, we arrive at the glass-and-curtain-walled cubicle where a tired-eyed Cyndi smiles sheepishly at us. "Sorry, guys. I didn't mean to scare you."

Jet rushes to her bedside, but he seems at a loss for what to do once there. He balks at touching her hand, occupied by an IV and lots of tape, so he opens his arms to hug her but can't get the right angle. He settles for a kiss on her forehead. She closes her eyes, and her face crumples.

The nurse says with zero emotion, "Your sister is suffering from hyperemesis gravidarum, extreme nausea and vomiting, which is common during pregnancy. It leads to dehydration and malnutrition, and—if untreated—can have serious consequences for both mother and baby. She's getting fluids in her IV, plus anti-emetics to control the nausea and stop the vomiting and should be good to go soon."

Jet watches as the nurse writes something down on the papers clipped to the large board in his arms. "Go? Like, home? But what if—"

"She'll be sent home with prescription anti-emetics and instructions for staying hydrated, plus dietary strategies to control or prevent nausea. And if her symptoms return or worsen, she should see her doctor—before it gets serious."

"You're coming home with us," Jet says firmly to his sister.

If he expects an argument, he doesn't get one, and the nurse backs him up with, "That's a good idea, for a couple of days, anyway, until she stabilizes, to make sure the prescription is working."

"I'll be fine," she says weakly and on a sigh. "I'm mostly tired. And embarrassed."

"Embarrassed?" Jet smooths her hair from her forehead. "Why?"

Her cheeks redden, and her eyes fill again.

The nurse snaps the bungee-corded pen back in place at the top of the clipboard and smiles sympathetically at her, acting like a human for the first time since summoning us back here. "It happens all the time. Nothing to be embarrassed about. I'll give you guys a few minutes, and I'll be back with your discharge papers as soon as I can find a doctor to sign them."

As soon as he leaves, Jet reaches across the bed and grabs Cyndi's IV-free hand. "Why didn't you call me?"

"Jet..." I slide a chair behind his knees, urging him to sit. And stop haranguing his poor sister. "Dial down the intensity a bit, okay?"

She smiles gratefully at me and pats his hand. "I thought I was okay. Until I wasn't okay."

He nods. "Like being wine-drunk."

Her laugh relaxes his shoulders. "Yeah. Something like that. And then I was so weak, I could hardly dial my phone. I had one call, and I was worried I might not stay awake long enough for the person on the other end to answer. If I called you and didn't say anything, you might think I'd butt-dialed you. If I called 911 and said nothing, I knew they'd send someone right away, faster than you could get there."

Jet turns to me. "She's the smart one in the family."

"Not smart enough to avoid this." She gestures to the beeping machines and cold, sterile surroundings. "So dumb. And I scared you. I'm sorry."

"Stop apologizing. I'm glad you're okay. And the baby?"

"We're both fine." She sniffs and blots her eyes. "How's Mikey? Has he been a good boy for you guys? Where is he, anyway?"

"With Colin," I answer. "And he's been great." Jet looks down at his shoes, so I rush ahead. "He, uh… He… Gosh, I hope you're not mad, but we had to cut his hair."

Her face pales again. "What?"

"Not a biggie. Got some sticky stuff in it that wouldn't wash out, so… Sacrifices had to be made."

"Did you save any of it?"

Not quite sure what she means, I reply, "Well, no. It all had to go."

"Right, but that was his first haircut."

Jet gulps and looks up. I stare mutely at her hopeful expression.

When neither of us speaks right away, she practically whispers, "I wanted to keep a lock, as a memento."

"People actually do that?" her brother mutters but answers more loudly and directly, "Sorry, Sis. It was pretty gummed up."

"Oh, Jet. He's not allowed to have gum."

I squeeze his shoulder before he corrects her. With a regretful head tilt, I say, "We know. And we're so sorry, Cyndi.

And I'm sorry we're telling you this now, but we didn't want you to be shocked when you see him later."

"It's all gone?"

I nod.

Jet acts out shaving his head with clippers, complete with Colin-esque sound effects. "Buzzed."

I kick his butt through the opening in the chair back. "But he looks adorable! And it'll grow back."

"But his baby curls!"

Oh, geez. Baby curls? I figured that was just his hair. I didn't realize that was a one-time thing, and once they were gone, they were gone forever. Jet's hair still curls on the ends when it's wet and he lets it get too long. I assumed it was a Knox thing and would be the same for Mikey.

"Maybe Jet can try to fish a strand or two from the—" He cuts me off with a curt shake of his head. "Or not. Anyway. Oh, gosh. Don't cry. I'm sorry. Oh, sheesh. We should have waited to tell you."

She waves off my profuse apologies. "It's okay. I'm hormonal. And tired. You guys have been so great, and I can't begin to thank you for taking such wonderful care of Mikey while I've been feeling so awful. It's only hair, anyway. I'm trying to do everything by the book, and I'm failing, and I... I —" She gags and retches.

Jet slides his chair back as far as it'll go before it bangs into the wall a few inches away. "Oh, gosh. She's gonna blow again."

"Nothing... in... my... stomach..." she says between heaves. Nevertheless, she holds the kidney-shaped plastic dish under her chin and spits into it. "Oh, gosh. My ribs."

I turn my back to give her some privacy—and settle my own stomach.

"Way to go," Jet grumbles at me, then smiles.

I choke back my own tears.

"Hey. I'm only kidding!"

"I upset her."

"You saved my ass." He grabs my hand. "Thanks." Louder, so Cyndi can hear him, he says, "You okay over there, Sis? How about another IV? They work wonders for me."

## TWENTY-NINE

## CLEANING UP AND MOVING ON

Three days later, Mikey and Cyndi return to their own place, each lighter than they were before, for different reasons. It was touch-and-go when we first brought Cyndi home from the hospital. Every time she saw Mikey, she'd cry about how much he looked like his dad with his new haircut, so Jet and I took turns ushering the shorn toddler from the room and consoling Cyndi, to prevent her sensitive gag reflex from kicking in again.

Then Jet had to figure out how to shuffle his obligations so he could be home to take care of his sister and nephew when nobody else was available, due to work schedules. I tried to pick up the slack where I could in the evening, missing a team charity gala (oh, darn), but my lunch breaks have been booked solid with wedding errands handed down by Gloria, who's been scarily quiet about the photo shoot debacle.

Surely she knows by now. But I haven't heard a whisper— or seen a single email—on the topic. I don't know what's happening with the ripped dress. And I don't care. I'd almost forgotten all about it, in fact, until Jet said in bed after we got

Cyndi and Mikey settled the first night, "I'm almost afraid to ask, but how'd the magazine shoot go, anyway?"

"You're right not to ask."

"Oh."

I almost broke down right there and told him how terrified I was of appearing in front of all of our friends and family—not to mention the countless strangers that will be attending our wedding—with that hair and makeup, but it had been such a long, trying day for both of us that it was easier to push it all down and say, "It's over. That's all that matters."

That answer must have satisfied him, as he was asleep less than five minutes later. Despite my exhaustion, I stared at the ceiling for several more hours.

Now, a week and a half from The Big Day, with some sense of normalcy returned to our household, if not our lives, I find the courage to assess the damage to my Oscars. Tonight's a good night to do so, because Jet's out of the house, so I can't murder him in a fit of rage. All I can do is stand here and stare at the carnage. It's epic.

I nudge the now-uneven rows of papier mâché men with my toe, searching for one—just one—without rubber cement drizzled all over it. Such a thing doesn't exist.

Shaking open the large black garbage bag I brought down here for this heartbreaking job, I take a final, bracing breath and lean over to pick up the first statuette. I examine my whimsical work, ignoring for a moment the damaged parts before tossing it into the bag. And repeat. Eighteen more follow until I'm the room's only remaining human-shaped occupant.

I return to the middle of the room and the island work-space and sweep the remaining supplies on top of my little gold men. I can't face starting over on this project, even if I did have the budget to purchase the required materials. And if I can't fulfill my original vision, I don't want to bother. I'll regroup after the wedding and honeymoon.

Jet said he'd figure out how to fix this, but I haven't heard another word about it since that day. Maybe he's finally learning he can't fix everything. Some things are unfixable. You have to trash it and move on.

Cinching the bag, I tie the handles into a double-knot and heft the sack, marveling at how light it is, like it contains nothing at all.

I turn to leave and catch a glimpse of my screenplay cabinet. It could have been so much worse, right? I may have put hours of effort into these stupid statuettes, on my own time, but at least those two numbskulls figured out what was going on before Mikey set his sights on anything truly valuable. Who knows? Maybe he tried and was foiled by the lock on the display case. And the sound of breaking glass would bring the most clueless morons running.

Which reminds me...

I send a tiny prayer up once again that Mikey wasn't hurt or poisoned during the incident. Rarer and more valuable than any Oscar-winning screenplay is that child. When I consider what could have happened, my head lightens, my vision narrows, and my knees weaken. And suddenly, my ruined art project doesn't matter at all. Not one bit.

I turn off the light in the room and head upstairs.

———

Jet spends more time at my duplex now than he did when I lived there. Which is fine. I get it. He's worried about his little sister. Sometimes I accompany him, but today, I was content to let him go alone. He and Mikey had their final, final, final tux fittings, anyway, so it was a perfect opportunity for uncle-nephew bonding, followed by a quiet dinner with Cyndi and a quick beer with Colin to end the night.

Off the hook for the evening, I venture into the bowels of the basement, pull a random movie from a random bin, and trot back upstairs. I almost exchange the disc for another when I see what it is before sliding it into the player. But, frankly, I'm too lazy to run downstairs again, and a classic like *Rudy*, despite its subject matter, holds some appeal, upon further consideration. It reminds me of simpler times, when football was merely for fun. Plus, I love an underdog. And it's familiar enough that I won't be disappointed when—not if—I fall asleep in the middle of it.

With the film flickering, the fire crackling, the lights dimmed, and a warm, dozing doggy stretched on my torso, it doesn't take long for the one glass of red wine I drank with dinner to soak into my bloodstream and team up with my general exhaustion to send me into a coma-like snooze on the sofa. Every once in a while, I surface enough to hear the movie still playing in the background. Snippets of dialogue and sound effects filter through and fade again as I slip into a deeper slumber, succumbing to both my body and mind's need for oblivion.

During one of my lighter phases of sleep, I become vaguely aware of Torzi stirring, so I pet him and croon, "Shhh..." If he stands or launches off me, it'll wake me for good, and I'm not ready yet. A few more minutes. The movie's almost over. The crowd chants, *"Rudy... Rudy... Rudy!"* I smile but keep my eyes closed. I love this part. I've seen the film enough times, however, to picture it behind my lids.

Then, softly, another voice joins the chant. "Rudy… Rudy… Rudy."

Torzi's tail thumps against my belly, its feathery fur tickling the inside of my elbow. The corners of my mouth lift higher. Jet's knees crack as he crawls up to the couch, stopping with his face inches from mine. "Maura… Maura… Maura."

The dog whines. His tongue laps noisily at the air. I drop my hand from his back so he can edge closer to his master's face and lick him.

"Oh, you want some of this, too?" Jet asks. "Torzi… Torzi… Torzi."

I open my eyes and laugh at the vigorous spit bath Jet receives. Finally, he pushes the dog away. "Okay, okay. You love me. I get it. I saw you licking your balls earlier, too, so I don't feel all that special."

Relieved of the canine's weight when he jumps to the floor, I arch my back and stretch my arms over my head.

"Wild Friday night here?" Jet asks, sitting back on his heels and glancing at the TV, which immediately sucks him in.

"Just Torzi, Rudy, and me," I reply around a yawn. "How'd your afternoon and evening go?"

He shakes his head as if trying to break the irresistible pull of the biopic and turns his attention back to me. "Uh, fine."

"Good. Tuxes all ready for the big show next week?" My heart palpitates and flutters at the reference, so I sit up.

He joins me on the couch. "Yeah. Hey. My, uh, mom called to check in, and she said something about not worrying about your dress, because Mags found a seamstress who fixed it, and you can hardly tell anything happened…?"

I gulp.

He chuckles. "And I was, like, 'Something happened?'

because it was the first I'd heard of anything, so she told me this long, drawn-out story that sounded like something from a Melissa McCarthy movie, and if I didn't know my mom better, I would have thought she was punking me. But she doesn't have much of a sense of humor—or an imagination. What the hell, Beautiful?"

With a loud sigh, I stop the movie, turn off the TV, and toss the remote down the couch on an unoccupied cushion, away from us. "First of all, I'm sure she told you *Mags's* version of what happened."

"Whoever's version it was, it was crazy. Why didn't you tell me?"

I shrug and finger the hem of my red jersey. "I got home, and Mikey's head was shaved, and my statuettes were trashed, and Cyndi was at the hospital, so the stupid photo shoot and the dress seemed unimportant. Then, after a couple of days, the whole thing had faded, like a bad dream, and I figured if your mom hadn't already told you, why bother you with it?"

He grunts. "Uh, because I care?"

"The dress is fixed, so I guess that's all that matters."

His brow wrinkles. "I don't give a damn about the dress. I care that *you* went through something so awful—it sounded awful, the way my mom described it, anyway—and didn't want to tell me."

"I didn't have time."

"Those three hours in the waiting room at the ER would have worked. Pretty sure we would have had plenty of time left over."

"People were staring at us and asking for your autograph, and you were worried, and... It wasn't the right place to get into it."

"What really happened? Maura's version." I turn my head

to look into his eyes, which he rolls. "I don't believe for a second what my mom said about you flipping out on Mags and the stylist, for no reason."

I blush. "That's pretty much what happened, though."

His chin drops.

"Well, there were reasons, I guess. The lady, Shelli, did my hair and makeup, and when I saw the results, I lost it. Because it was awful. And I'd had so little sleep the night before, and I didn't want to be there, and... and... it all— I don't know. I snapped. I felt like I was holding it together okay, at first. I tried to be nice about the whole thing, hinting that I was worried about looking like that on our actual wedding day, but when I went to blot some of the makeup off, Shelli freaked, and Mags stood on my dress, so when I tried to get away from them, it ripped."

"Holy shit."

"Then the photographer was a complete dickhead, griping about how tall I am, as if I have any control over that."

Jet snorts indignantly. "What the hell is it to him?"

"Something about the lighting and assuming all pro athletes prefer women they can tower over or carry around on their arms like ventriloquist dummies? I don't know. I guess Greta Steinberg is the only tall NFL wife allowed."

His laugh carries with it a hard edge. "What a douche. Who is this guy?"

"Never mind."

Putting his arm around me, he pulls me close and squeezes. "Aw, Maura. I'm sorry. That sounds terrible."

"It was." I snuggle against his chest. "But whatever. I got through it, and with everything else going on, who cares?"

"But what about the stylist situation?"

I push away slightly and look up into his concerned face. "What about it?"

"Is everyone clear about what you want next Saturday?"

I understand that he's talking about hair and makeup, but the answer that pops into my head encompasses so much more. And makes me feel so damn hopeless.

When all I can do is shake my head and choke back tears, his jaw clenches. "Tell me. We'll make it happen."

"I don't know," I say, my throat tight. I sniff and shake my head. "I wouldn't even know where to start. And it's too late."

"No, it's not." He pulls his phone from his pocket and searches "wedding hair and makeup," his fingers flying through links and pulling up pictures. "This one? Or this one? Oh, this is nice. The stylist can—and will—do whatever we pay her to do. She doesn't need six months' notice on a hairstyle. You should have everything you want."

Screwing up every ounce of courage to articulate my feelings, I place my hand over his phone to stop his frantic troubleshooting and say, "I want to be married to you."

He grins. "That's a good start."

I blink erratically, and my chin puckers. "But what I really want…"

His smile fading, he waits. His phone screen blackens as it hibernates, and he sets the device aside to give me his full attention.

"What I really want," I start again, stronger, "is to skip the whole wedding."

Reaching for his phone, he says, "Right? Me, too. It's such a pain in the ass. But it's only one day, and then—"

I grab his hand. "No, I mean it. It's not about it being a pain in the ass. I don't… I don't want to do it. At all. Any of it. When I think about it, I feel panicky. I try to picture myself in that dress, walking down that aisle, in that church, with all of those people, and... Well, I *can't* picture it. It's like a movie that keeps glitching at that part. It freezes up, and it never recovers. Then I realize it's because... I don't think I *can* do it."

It seems like it takes forever for that to sink in, for him to fully understand what I'm saying, but when he does, when it dawns in his eyes, he immediately says, jaw tightening, "Then we won't do it."

My full sinuses almost produce a snot bubble when I scoff at his confident declaration. "Okay. Right. We'll call the whole thing off. Never mind that three hundred people have already RSVPed their yeses. Or that many of them have made expensive travel arrangements to attend. Or that I have three bridal showers and a bachelorette party this weekend. Or—"

"Who cares? If the bride doesn't want to be there, all bets are off, right?"

"Yeah, but maybe I can ask Deirdre to prescribe me something. Valium?"

"The idea that you have to be drugged to face marrying me is too depressing for words."

"That's not—"

"Yeah. That's what it would boil down to, and screw that."

"Jet!"

"Seriously. We already have the marriage license, ready to be signed."

Yes, that was one of countless lunch break errands this past week, but still... "That's the least of our problems! Our honeymoon reservations, my vacation time, all of the other non-refundable stuff associated with the actual wedding— cakes and DJs and flowers and—"

He sighs. "Listen, Richards. Are you a free spirit or not?"

"What?" I flick tears from my hot face.

"Do you have it in you to be spontaneous, like you always claim you do, or are you like every other uptight, boring *grownup*, too worried about rules and what other people think to grab life by the hair and ride it the way *you* want to ride it?" He leaps to his feet and demonstrates, galloping in place, thrusting his hips, and smacking "Life" on its invisible ass.

I laugh. "I don't know! It's not about—"

He abruptly stops and yanks me off the couch to stand with him. "It is, though. That's all it's about. And what's the point of having some insane wedding that will be a great time for everyone but us?"

"You want it, too, though."

He shakes his head. "Not if you don't. And if I'd had any idea before now how terrified you were of it, if I'd been paying better attention, we would have had this conversation a long time ago. And maybe you'd already be my wife, and I'd already be the luckiest dumb jock in the world."

"Jet, we—"

He turns me by my shoulders and pushes me toward the stairs, slapping my butt for good measure. "We're out of here. Go pack your bags."

"But—"

"We don't have time to argue. I have a million calls to make, so you'll have to pack for me, too."

I pause at the bottom of the stairs, glancing back at him to make sure he's serious.

He flaps his hand in a shooing motion while he retrieves his phone from the arm of the couch. "Go on. We gotta go no-huddle, Beautiful."

## THIRTY

## ESCAPE

For the third time in less than two years, I'm sitting on the Wise family's private jet. That's three times more than I ever imagined. And for the first time, Jet and I have it to ourselves, rattling around on this thing, on our way to our honeymoon, a week earlier than planned, running—no, flying—from everything and everyone. Our thatched hut in St. Bart's wasn't available, but Jet's favorite travel agent sniffed out an available private island in Belize, so here we go! We'll be there in about three hours.

I'm elated to be free, as if by magic, of the day I've been dreading for months; at the same time, I'm fully aware magic has nothing to do with it, and there will be consequences. I don't need all of the details, but I want to be somewhat prepared for what those consequences will be.

I already know what they are at my job. The Giggler was particularly chuckly when I moved my week's vacation up a week with only a day's notice, but whatever. I'm fairly confident nobody wants to take on the job fair at this late date, so my position is secure at least until that's over.

Now, I need reassurance about other aspects of the plan. "Was your mom mad?"

Jet avoids my eyes and stares through the window as we continue our ascent after takeoff. "I didn't give her a chance to say much. I basically said she could give me all of the information to contact people and cancel stuff, or she could do it herself. Either way, it was happening. She said she'd do it."

"Do you think she will?"

He blinks and focuses on my face. "Yes."

At what price? Holding our wedding rings ransom? We know she has a strange jewelry fetish. I wonder when we can expect to see the bands I assume are in her possession. She's probably stroking them right now, calling them "Precious."

Rather than voice all of that, I simply ask, "Does she hate me?"

"She loves us both and wants us to be happy."

"Hmm." I let that one go and move on to a bigger worry—for me, anyway. "What about your sister? Is she going to be okay?"

"I asked Colin to keep an eye on her and Mikey for us. Told him I'd buy him a six-pack of Newcastle."

"Ooh! Big spender."

He laughs. "It's about all I can afford after paying for a wedding we're not going to have, reimbursing people for nonrefundable travel, and booking this spur-of-the-moment getaway."

My heart sinks. "Never mind. I don't want to know money stuff."

"It's worth it, don't get me wrong." He cups his palm over my knee. "I'll tell you what. If Colin does a really good job, I'll bump it up to a twelve-pack." He winks.

"What about our marriage license? When are we going to make that official? It needs to be signed in Missouri, and—"

"Would you stop worrying so much? It'll all be taken care of when we get back. You know, you kind of suck at this whole 'spontaneous' thing."

His teasing tone leaves no room for hurt feelings, so I stick out my tongue at him and concede the point.

When the plane levels off to cruising altitude, I take off my seat belt and angle myself to better see through the window and watch the clouds below us.

Jet walks to the back of the cabin, where there's a pocket door. He slides it open and looks inside. "Hot damn," he mutters. "I've always wondered what this was."

"What is it?" I ask, joining him and peeking around his arm. A room with a bed, desk, and TV nestles back there.

We exchange mischievous smiles.

He grabs my hand and leads me into the bedroom, bouncing on the end of the bed. "If these walls could talk."

I wrinkle my nose, picturing both Lyle and Brendan Wise and deciding I'd rather not think too much about what the team's owners have gotten up to back here. With whomever. I perch on Jet's knee and hold onto his neck as we hit a pocket of turbulence. He straightens his leg and slides the door closed with his foot.

"Wanna join the Mile High Club?" he asks.

"Uh, yeah! Wait. Are you already a member?"

He laughs and pulls a face. "No! But I'd love to become one with you."

"Totally. In a minute. I'm not done asking questions."

Smiling into my eyes, he blindly runs his hands up the inside of my sweater, fiddling with my bra clasp. "What more is there to know?"

"You were on the phone for a while, but you've only mentioned talking briefly to two people."

"I had to call the travel agent, too, remember? And Brendan, to borrow his ride."

"Okay. That's four calls."

He nips at my lips. "Does it matter? We're here, everything's covered at home, and everything's arranged where we're headed. Let's enjoy ourselves."

I let him pull my sweater over my head and toss it on the floor next to the bed. Then I roll from his lap to the mattress to finish undressing myself so he can take off his own clothes. Since I'm ready first, I pull back the duvet, tuck my legs under it, lie on my side, and ask while watching him, "And that's it?"

"That's all you need to know right now," he answers, slipping into bed next to me and pulling me on top of him. "I have a couple of surprises planned for you."

I brace my hands on either side of his head and grin while shivering with pleasure. "That sounds fun."

"It will be. And then some."

I lean down to kiss him but stop inches from his mouth. "Do you feel weird doing this?"

"I'm feeling a lot of things right now; 'weird' isn't one of them."

"Because it's, technically, your bosses' bed."

"I'm trying not to think about *that*."

"I can't think of much else."

Rising on his elbows, he looks down the lengths of our bodies. "I'll tell you what I'd rather think about, and maybe it will distract you."

"Yeah. Good. Let's do that."

"I'm thinking"—e reaches up with one hand and tucks a

strand of hair behind my ear—" that I'm marrying the most amazing woman I've ever met."

"Pshaw."

He rests his finger against my lips. "And we're going to have an awesome life. This is only the beginning."

I nod and swallow thickly.

"And I'd love to show that amazing woman exactly how I feel about her. If she'd stop talking."

"Okay."

He chuckles at my meek response and pulls my head down toward his. I fall against his chest and into his kiss.

Several bumpy—but exhilarating—minutes later, I hold his face in my hands and open my eyes, seeing that he already has his locked on me.

"Hey there, Beautiful," he says, out of breath.

"I love you," I whisper against his lips.

"I don't have a big enough vocabulary to tell you how I feel about you."

I giggle at his self-deprecating declaration. "Actions speak louder than words, anyway, Champ."

"I'm totally up to that challenge."

———

He promised surprises, and surprises there have been. A-plenty. Starting with the place we're staying. At times it feels like we're no longer a part of the rest of the human race. Our tiny island offers isolation on a scale that my developed-world brain couldn't begin to comprehend until I experienced it. I have to keep reminding myself we're a five-minute boat ride from civilization. Clothes aren't merely optional; they're downright superfluous.

Packing wasn't a complete waste of time, though. We venture to the mainland at least once a day. On my first adventure outside of the United States, I want to be able to say I've had the full experience, including interaction with non-Americans.

Now, on our fourth day here, Jet announces our daily foray into the village will be to "someplace nice," which I assume will be a restaurant. He dresses accordingly in a navy suit with an open-collared white dress shirt and dark brown shiny shoes, and I step into the pale yellow sun dress I brought for this exact purpose.

We dock in the tiny coastal town that's now relatively familiar to us, and he leads me by the hand through the open-air market, where he purchases a large bouquet of gorgeous white flowers and presents them to me. Thinking they're a bit over-the-top and wondering how I'm supposed to keep track of them for the rest of the evening, I nevertheless accept them with a gracious, "Thank you," and we continue on our way through the hot, dusty streets.

After passing the third restaurant, I say, "Yo, Champ. Are we going to eat at some point, or are you enjoying your walking tour too much?"

He consults his phone for about the fiftieth time and replies, "We're almost there. Just up this hill."

I trudge with him up said hill that levels off and dead-ends at a church, complete with steeple, bell tower, stained glass, and a sign that declares it to be St. Paul's Episcopal.

Jet wipes sweat from his brow. "Made it. Finally."

Before I can ask what's going on, he kneels on the flag-stone courtyard in front of me. "Maura, will you still marry me?"

I laugh my happy tears away. "Yes! Get up."

He pops to his feet and kisses me. "Good. Because there's a priest in here waiting for us. And we're later than I told him we'd be. I didn't realize how long it was going to take to find this place." He pulls me by the hand toward the heavy wooden doors.

Inside, after my eyes adjust to the dim interior, I take in the ornate fixtures. It's downright Gothic, and it smells like every American church I've ever been in: wax, furniture polish, cut flowers, old books. I stare at a stained glass window depicting Mary weeping at the feet of Jesus on the cross. It looks like they've both had better days.

Jet follows my gaze. "Reverend Deitz should be around here somewhere. I emailed him from the plane. He was the only one who could marry us on such short notice. And it won't be legal. We'll still have to go back to the courthouse at home and have a justice of the peace sign our license. But I thought this would be nice. Romantic."

"It's beautiful." In a creepy way. I shift my bouquet to my other arm so I can grab his hand and squeeze it. "This is amazing."

Before he can do anything but grin proudly, a man in black with a white square at his throat approaches us with a gentle smile. In a lilting accent that isn't local but I can't place, he asks in English, "Jet and Maura?"

Jet steps forward and shakes the priest's hand. "Thanks for agreeing to meet with us, Reverend. Sorry we're late. It's funny. I could *see* the church from the dock, so I thought it would be easy to find, but since we can't walk through buildings and houses, it took a while to figure out how to get up here."

"No worries. This is my pleasure!" he says, reaching

around Jet to shake my hand, too. "I am glad to share this beautiful day with you."

Ahh… Now that he's said a few more words, I can tell his accent matches his last name. German. Sort of. With a Central-American twist.

He motions for us to precede him into the sanctuary. "Please. Welcome." While he leads us through the unfamiliar building, he asks me, "Would you like to walk up the aisle toward your groom? I am afraid I have no way to provide music for the processional, but—"

"No! I mean, no. Thank you. That's okay."

Jet snickers at my vehement response and says on our way to the altar, "Like I said in my email, we'd like to say some traditional vows in a church to make it—I don't know—official-like, in front of God, and everything. And it would be super-cool if you'd sign something I brought for us to remember this. Our marriage license isn't valid down here, so I brought a wedding invitation for all of us to sign. I've crossed out the church address from back home and wrote this one in."

I stare at him while he rambles nervously, both astounded at the volume of information, as well as the content.

"Maybe we can take a selfie, too? If that's not too disrespectful, or whatever. We can do it outside, even." He stops babbling when we reach the front of the sanctuary, and he waits for Reverend Deitz to reverence the altar.

Not sure if the priest's actions are also expected of us, I mimic him, to be safe. Jet shoots me a bemused look, but the priest turns to us and smiles before I can defend my behavior.

"That would be lovely," he says to all of Jet's suggestions. He nods at my bouquet. "If you would like to set those down on the pew over there, we can get started." I do as he requests, and he asks Jet, "Do you have the rings?"

As I'm about to explain the situation, Jet digs the bands from his front left pocket and places them in the priest's upturned palm. As far as I can tell, they're the real ones, too. Simple, platinum, matching my engagement ring. Once again, I'm struck dumb by Jet's preparedness.

He catches my astounded expression, chuckles, and winks at me. "Didn't think I'd trust those to anyone else, did you?"

Before we can discuss it any further, Rev. Deitz tells us to join hands and face each other.

Suddenly and inexplicably, I'm the nervous one. Jet, having laid out the plan, now appears calm and like he's never been surer of anything in his life. I smile shakily into his beaming face while we do as we're told. He rubs my knuckles with his thumbs and shoots me a cheeky air peck.

The priest says a short prayer, thanking God for bringing us together to celebrate and bless our marriage. Then he hands my wedding band to Jet and says, "Repeat after me while placing the ring on your bride's finger."

The groom recites as he slides the band smoothly onto my hand, "I, Jet, take thee, Maura, to have and to hold from this day forward, for better or for worse, for richer or for poorer, in sickness and in health, 'til death do us part."

When it's my turn, I mostly succeed in making it through the vows, although I have to whisper the last half through extremely tight vocal cords. I push the shiny ring all the way past Jet's second knuckle—this one fits, too—and clear my throat.

The priest pronounces us husband and wife (in God's eyes) and oversees the official "first" kiss. I stifle my giggles when he has to tiptoe to place one hand on each of our heads, even though we each slightly bend our knees, but once his palms have found resting places on our crowns, he says, "Blessings be with you all the days of your life."

Minutes later in the vestry, pen poised to sign the wedding invitation Jet brought as a memento—and probably proof for his mom that we said vows in front of a man of God— Reverend Deitz pulls up short. "Oh, I am so sorry, Mr. Knox. I called you by the wrong name."

Jet waves off the apology. "That's okay. Unless…" His face pales. "Oh, shoot. Does that mean it doesn't count, or something?"

The minister shakes his head and laughs as he scrawls his signature with a flourish. "It still counts. God knows you by all of your names."

"Oh, whew. But not even God calls me 'Micah.'"

And that's how I married Jet Knox.

## THIRTY-ONE

## WELCOME HOME

It's good to be home. Maybe this monstrous house is growing on me. More likely, I'm ready to find out what this "forever" we've been going on and on about and so eagerly anticipating is really going to be like. Unfortunately, we have visitors who will delay "forever" for at least another few minutes.

"Oh, great. The welcoming committee has arrived," I mutter about the two familiar cars in the driveway.

Jet widens his eyes at my ingratitude as he puts the car in park and turns it off. "Geez! For your information, Colin and Rae asked if they could be here when we got home, and I thought it was a nice idea and that you'd be happy to see them, so I said yes."

"Why didn't they ask me?"

He shrugs coyly and exits the car. "Let's go say hi and tell them all about our trip."

I doubt either one wants *that*. But the wedding ceremony is a good story to tell everyone. Romantic and sweet, with a hint of humor, considering how much the bride and groom towered over tiny Reverend Deitz and the fact that Jet forgot to use his Christian name in his vows. We might leave that part out when we tell Gloria; something tells me she won't appreciate it.

In fact, only one thing darkened our "wedding" day, a text from my new mother-in-law that landed on both of our phones as we were walking back to the boat to return to our private island:

*Everything's been canceled. Guests have been notified. I hope you're happy.*

The closed-off expression on Jet's face lasted for two seconds before he replaced it with one of forced jollity. "I'm happy; how about you?"

I took his cue, although I suddenly want to puke. "Ecstatic."

"Good. That's all that matters."

Maybe we both thought more about his mom than we should have on the boat ride, but we kept each other plenty busy with other things once we docked at the hut.

The official story of our wedding day will end at the quaint Episcopal church. And Colin and Rae will be the perfect people to practice on.

Where are they, anyway?

Bickering voices lead us to the back patio.

"It's about to piss down! I say we move them inside."

"Jet texted me from the airport. They'll be here any second. We don't have time to move them."

"I will bloody kill you if you all of our hard work gets rained on."

"Calm down, you dumb Limey."

As soon as we open the door, our two friends cease arguing and turn their attentions to us with wide smiles.

"Hey!"

"Cheers!"

And that's when I see "them." All of them. Forty-one of them, if I had to guess. In fact, I'd bet my life on it that once I have the chance to count them, there will be forty-one, exactly.

"We used my idea," Rae says, picking up one of the statuettes. "Imitation Ken dolls on tuna cans, gold spray paint."

"Hope you don't mind," Colin adds when I'm incapable of doing anything other than gawp at the plastic army.

I laugh. "Mind? I love you guys so much right now!" I high step through the rows of tiny men to get to my friends in the center and pull them to me in an intense group hug.

Jet curls around my back. "Can I get a piece of this?"

Patting me on the shoulder with the Oscar still in her hand, Rae says, "Oh, yeah. Jet bankrolled the project."

"Mikey didn't have the funds in his piggy bank to pay for the damages, so I spotted him."

We separate and I look around, again, in amazement at the answer to my many, many prayers. "You guys!" I finally manage, but my jubilation manifests itself in rogue tears.

Rae groans. Colin clears his throat. Jet rubs my back. "Aw, Maura. It's okay."

"I can't believe you did all this for me."

"In case you haven't figured this out yet, we kinda like you," Rae says. "When Jet told me what happened and that he and Colin were in deep shit and needed to figure out how to fix it, fast, I told him about my plan. He and Colin were going to do it themselves, but let's face it. They're not exactly a dynamic duo. I could only imagine the kind of trouble they'd get into with a hot glue gun."

"Hey!"

"Oy!"

She rolls her eyes at their objections. "Anyway, then you guys eloped, and Colin and I figured we had the perfect opportunity to be the big heroes. We finished the last ones yesterday."

Colin glances up at the overcast sky. "That being said, mates, perhaps we should get these wherever you want to store them."

Jet grabs three in each hand. "Load 'em up in the back of the Hummer. They'll be safe there and ready for transport."

In the garage after the last statuette has been transferred, Rae says, "Well, it's been fun, but you guys must be tired and want to get settled."

"You have a date with Ana Paula, don't you?" I tease.

"Yes. But that doesn't make you any less tired." She ruffles my hair and exchanges an odd glance with Jet, who nods and winks at her. He widens his eyes at Colin.

"Uh, right. And I must be on my way, as well. I promised Mikey we'd go to Jump Zone."

I laugh. "That kid has you wrapped all around his chubby fingers."

"I'm sure it'll be delightful. And anything I can do to help."

Jet claps him on the shoulder. "You have fun with that. Thanks for standing in while we were gone, man." He lifts his chin in Rae's direction. "Tell AP I said hi."

With more hugs and waves, the two of them leave, smiling and looking over their shoulders a few more times on the way to their cars.

Before I can point out their odd behavior to Jet, he turns, pops the trunk on our car, and removes our luggage. Inside the house, he drops the cases at the base of the stairs and says, "Helen will take care of those tomorrow. Leave 'em."

I start to protest, but he puts his finger against my lips and smiles. "Do you realize what time it is?"

I try to guesstimate, based on what time it was when we landed and how many minutes have elapsed since. "Four o'clock-ish? Why? Are you hungry again?"

He laughs. "No. Well, yes. But that's not what I'm getting at." Pulling me to his chest, he murmurs, "Do you realize if things had gone according to plan, we'd be getting married... right now?"

I shiver, but pretend I'm only kidding and laugh at my theatrics. Then I ask, "Do you regret what we did? Maybe your mom was right that we could have come home yesterday and still had the big ceremony and reception today."

"Nah. It's a shame, though, you never got to see me in my tux. I looked spiffy."

"I've seen you in a tux before. And I prefer the suit you wore in Belize."

He shrugs. "Then I guess we made the right choice."

"I'm glad you never saw me in that dress. Or makeup. I kept having nightmares where you lifted my veil and screamed."

He cracks up and hugs me tighter. "Never."

I wrap my arms around his neck. "Mm... It was hideous."

"I guess I'll see for myself what I missed when that magazine hits newsstands this summer," he says to the accompaniment of my groans. He silences me with a kiss that makes me glad we're going to play the part of the pampered Lord and Lady of the manner and make our housekeeper unpack for us.

At the end of the kiss, he pulls me toward the basement stairs and announces, "I, uh, got you a wedding present."

Horror freezes me on the second step. "What? No! I didn't get you anything."

Two steps lower than me, he looks up and squeezes my hand. "You've given me everything." Blushing, he rushes on, "Anyway, I wanted to do something special for you."

"Jet."

He tugs on my hand. "C'mon."

I allow myself to be towed down the stairs and into the chilly basement, bemused by his running commentary. "Now, I know you don't love this house, and I promise when things settle down, we'll seriously discuss looking for something else. Or we'll fix up this place so that you like it better, but in the meantime, I hope this is a good start. Or makes you feel more at home."

Passing the gym, trophy room, and guest bedrooms down here, I smell fresh-cut wood, paint, and new carpeting. And— oddly enough—popcorn. "What have you done?"

"Tee hee! This has been the hardest secret to keep in my entire life."

His gleeful giggle cracks me up, and I'm still laughing when he opens the door to the room I haven't visited since cleaning up the post-Mikey Oscar carnage. If I'd been led here blindfolded, I wouldn't believe it's the same room.

Can lights shine down on several tiered rows of red leather sofas facing an enormous projection screen that covers almost the entire far wall. Red velvet curtains with silver rope pulls frame the screen.

Torzi's head pops up from the nearest of six sofas.

"There you are, fleabag. You're not supposed to be in here!"

While Jet scolds the dog, who's not at all impressed and holds his yawning ground, I continue to survey my surroundings.

A wet bar, including beer, wine, and soda taps sits tucked

in the back corner, next to a theater-grade popcorn machine, currently full of fragrant yellow puffs. On the wall behind the bar is my beloved "Be Kind, Rewind" sign.

Red carpet lines the shallow steps on either end of the sofa rows, but easy-to-clean wood laminate rests under the bar and seating areas. Along the dark-gray walls, staggered perfectly in position with one another, hang my framed movie posters.

Behind us, on the near back wall, towers a narrow, black, built-in floor-to-ceiling cabinet. Jet sees me eyeing it and opens it for me. Inside rests a black box that blinks to life when Jet pushes a button. He grabs the remote from the top of it and navigates some menus that pop on the projection screen. In seconds, the opening sequence to *Becoming Jane* appears on the screen wall.

"I had all of your movies converted to digital for you. But your originals are in a safe over there, along with a backup hard drive of the digitals." He points to something I assumed was merely a wall but now see has a door handle with a keypad next to it.

I want to say something, anything, mostly "Thank you," but I can't, so he continues, "Your screenplays are in the safe for now, too, because the crew couldn't finish the display case I wanted in time, but they'll eventually go in a built-in, in that blank space next to this cabinet."

He closes the door on the hard drive's cupboard and returns to my side.

I turn my back on the in-home cinema of my dreams and squeeze my eyes closed, pressing my hands to my nose and mouth and bouncing on the balls of my feet.

"Oh, no. You don't like it? I was worried I wouldn't be able to match the paint to the shade in your old living room, but I thought I got it right. I compared about a thousand different swatches. And Cyndi helped, because I'm not that good at telling the difference between col—"

I cut him off by throwing myself at him and smashing my mouth against his. He laughs and pulls his head back. "Oh. This is happy you. Sometimes it's hard to tell. I thought I screwed up, or something."

"This is the most amazing thing anyone has ever done for me. And that's saying something, so soon after Rae and Colin made all those Oscars."

"I hate to steal their thunder. No, I don't. This is awesome." He sticks out his tongue and snickers.

I let go of him and plop down on the sofa next to Torzi, who promptly sits in my lap. Jet leans down next to me and presses a button that ejects a footrest in front of me and reclines my section of the seat. As I gaze up at him, he smiles, then softly kisses my lips. Torzi licks our chins until Jet gently pushes him away.

"Welcome home," he says quietly to me, his eyes shining.

The dog permanently vacates the room with a harumph when I pull Jet on top of me, and we make out like giggling teenagers.

———

One more surprise awaits, but the Oscars and home cinema shocks threaten an anti-climactic reveal when Jet shifts his weight off of me on the squeaky leather sofa and says through swollen lips, "Oh, yeah. They finished the bedroom and closet remodel while we were gone, too."

Considering I was never shown the plans and rarely asked for my input on the project, I have no idea what to expect. I haven't had high hopes or a great attitude toward the remodel, and I've shown little to no interest in it, from Day One, since I considered it a frivolous, unnecessary distraction during an already-hectic time leading up to our wedding. Now, though, seeing that sparkle in Jet's eyes as he wiggles his eyebrows, I'm dying to see it.

I hop to my feet and run for the door, shouting, "Race ya!" over my shoulder.

It's hardly a challenge for him to catch up to me, but he lets me lead the way until we arrive, one of us gasping for breath, the other one barely breathing any heavier than usual, in the upstairs hallway. There, he overtakes me and presses his back to the bedroom door, shielding the lever handle from my grasp.

"You meant this to be a surprise all this time, didn't you?"

He pauses. "Maybe."

"And that's why you never showed me the plans, only asked me random questions here and there?"

"Yeah. I like surprises. Don't you?"

"I'm beginning to love them. Step aside, Champ."

He laughs. "Okay." Depressing the handle and pushing back with his shoulder, he remains against the door to allow me entry to the room. "I hope you love it."

"I'm sure I—"

The first thing I see is the taupe tufted wall that serves as the headboard for the bed, which is centered under a dainty crystal chandelier and covered in a deep purple duvet. At the foot of the bed squats a custom-built velvet-covered bench in the same color as the duvet and edged with thin, silver rope. Two matching dark-gray-and-white tables bracket the bed and hold tall glass lamps with wide, round shades. A white wing-backed chair with black piping rests in the corner, by the window. White wall-to-wall carpeting caresses our feet. It's like something straight out of Hollywood. Old Hollywood. In the Golden Age.

While I gape like a fish at the threshold to the room, Jet strides to the closet and throws the doors open. A light automatically comes on, illuminating the racks of perfectly hanging clothing and shelves of precisely positioned shoes.

"You like it?" he asks eagerly.

"It's gorgeous. Simply gorgeous." I cross to the windows and finger the plush curtains pulled back and held in place by black iron scrolls. "It's so... me."

Grinning, he abandons the closet and joins me by the window. "I thought so, too. When I saw the final pictures, I was relieved, because during the reno, I wasn't sure. Especially about that thing." He points to the bench. "But it turned out cool."

"It's brighter in here now, too. Seems bigger, even though we lost some square footage to that massive closet."

"Now when I have to hide in there, I won't get all sweaty and anxious," he jokes. "And look!" He steps to the bedside table on his side of the bed and grabs a remote control. With the press of a button, light-blocking shades drop from the top of the windows, plunging us into almost total darkness, save for the light spilling from the closet. He hits another button, and the chandelier above the bed fades up to a dim, romantic glow that mimics candlelight.

"Huh?" he prompts.

"You are something else. And you're seriously spoiling me."

"It's fun." He sets down the remote and wraps his arm around my waist, pulling me against his side.

"I only have one concern."

His brow furrows as he looks around. "What? What did I forget?"

"I love that this room is so me, but it's *our* bedroom, not mine. Where are *you* in here?"

He squeezes me more tightly against his hip and says seriously into my eyes, "I'm right here, next to you, for the rest of our lives. It's going to be awesome."

It already is.

## THIRTY-TWO

## CONSEQUENCES

Hosting this event is much more my speed than some extravagant, gaudy wedding. It's more exclusive, for one thing, which means I know everyone here by name. And they know me. And the only time I'm the center of attention is when it's my turn in the cannonball contest. As it should be.

Jet and I both still have major guilt about leaving our closest friends and family in the lurch by eloping, so when Jet first suggested we try to make it up to them by hosting a summer barbecue/pool party/movie night/Super Bowl victory celebration, I jumped on the idea. After all, how hard can it be to throw such a laid-back get-together, especially when it's fully catered and staffed by a professional DJ, bartender, and driver to shuttle our guests from the Arrowhead parking lot to our house? Well, it's been slightly more complicated than I anticipated, but it's still more fun than a stuffy wedding.

And now that the job fair is firmly in my past, I've had the time and attention to spend on planning the party. I'm not even all that disappointed that the fair didn't live up to the vision in my head, and my boss wasn't overly impressed with it. Every time I looked at one of those Oscars, I was reminded of the great friends and husband I have, and the low turnout of job seekers didn't bother me much. The ones who did show up loved the atmosphere and complimented the clever theme. And hopefully, they walked away with new career prospects. That's all that mattered. I'll knock the next one out of the park or through the uprights. Or whatever. A sports theme might be more in tune with local interest, anyway.

I have four months to think about it, though, so for now, all of my attention is on enjoying this off-season before football takes over again in the fall.

Another bonus to today's party is that it's way too crowded and hectic and loud around here to have the one-on-one time Gloria's been dying to force on me since the end of March, when I supposedly foiled her plans, single-handedly, for hosting the city's social event of the year. Screw that conversation.

Since things have settled down in Jet's family, he thinks I'm exaggerating the underlying tension between his mother and me. As far as he's concerned, the Knoxes are back to being the all-American sweethearts they're so good at being, and he's once again the golden child who can do no wrong. As his wife, I am, by extension, also golden.

Cyndi's still going through with her divorce while waddling around, single and pregnant, but since all of her siblings are standing behind her, Gloria seems to have resigned herself to pretending it's not that big of a deal to her anymore. "I only want my kids to be happy," she says like a scratched record. "That's all I've ever wanted."

Riiiight.

So here we are, one big happy family and about a hundred of our closest friends, kicking off summer in style.

Well, most of us are. I'm currently bandaging a phantom wound for Mikey in the cinema's adjoining bathroom, but the plan is to get right back to having grownup fun upstairs once Jet and I get the kids settled in for their next movie.

"Show me again where your boo-boo is," I say to my nephew, who's perched on the vanity in front of me.

He points to a slightly reddened area on his knee that may or may not be the mildest carpet burn I've ever seen. I pull the wrapper away from the adhesive bandage and stick it to his rubbery skin.

"Kiss it!" he says with a sniffle.

Laughing, I comply. "Geez. You're a bigger baby than your Uncle Jet."

"*Inside Out!*"

"Hang on. Let me throw away this trash. Do you have to use the potty while we're in here?"

"No! *Inside Out!*"

"Uncle Jet's still working on getting it started. You're not going to miss anything. Let's try to use the potty, so we don't have any accidents during the movie."

"O-tay, fine." He sighs but cooperates while I pull down his shorts and *Finding Nemo* briefs and set him on the toilet. I applaud Cyndi's efforts to potty train him before she has another one in diapers, but I'm not willing to sacrifice my leather cinema seating to the cause.

After the initial tinkle, when I expect him to say he's finished, he grunts and with a red face says, "I have to poo."

"Great. I'll be, uh, over here," I reply, stepping back a bit and leaning against the vanity to wait.

While Mikey pushes and strains—the kid needs more fiber in his diet—the door to the bathroom cracks open. Expecting Jet, I aim a smile at the gap and say, "We're finishing up."

My mother-in-law steps into the space.

"Oh, hey, Gloria."

"How many times do I have to tell you to call me Mom? It's starting to hurt my feelings that you won't."

I gulp. "Oh. Right. Habit, I guess."

"Is everything okay in here?"

In a strained voice, Mikey says, "Hi, Grammy," and waves.

"Hi, precious. Did Maura fix up your boo-boo? Oh, I see she did. Do you need me to kiss it?"

He shakes his head. "Mo-Mo did."

"I'll kiss it, too, when you're finished. If you'd like."

"Naw. Done! I need a wipe."

I exchange a panicked look with Gloria, who waves a deferring hand in the toddler's direction. "By all means. It'll be good practice for you."

Unbelievable. Well, if it makes her happy to see me perform such a degrading job, whatever. Like it's no big deal—it's not, I guess; I've changed Mikey's and Meleah's diapers countless times in the past few months—I step forward and tear off a generous amount of toilet paper from the roll on the nearby stand.

"Bottoms up," I say cheerfully and hold my breath while cleaning between my nephew's southern cheeks. Then I toss the paper in the toilet and let the little guy flush and watch his waste disappear.

"Hooray!" he cheers, pulling up his pants and trying to run from the room at the same time.

"Ah, ah, ah. Not so fast, sir. Wash those hands!" I say.

Gloria intercepts him and holds him so he can reach the basin. The two of us wash and dry our hands, and I try to push all three of us from the enclosed space and into the theater, but Gloria releases Mikey to escape while also blocking my path. Worse, she backs me into the stinky bath-room once more and pulls the door so that it's mostly shut behind her.

"You're so good with him," she says with a simper.

"Thanks. He's a sweet kid."

Usually. When he's not destroying things. Or making me wipe his ass. And anyway, I guess he's only doing what kids do. He looks so much like Jet, especially now that his hair's grown back out, that I can't stay mad at him. Ever. Not even when he stays the night and insists on sleeping in the same bed with us. At least now that we're back in our master bedroom with more mattress real estate, he's not as terrible a bed-mate.

"I expect you and Jet will have your own soon?"

I eye the cracked door with longing and chuckle nervously. "Uh, well, I don't know. We haven't talked about it."

"What's there to talk about?"

Resigned to being stuck in here with her, I spritz some air freshener and turn to the mirror to inspect the tan lines at the edges of my swimsuit, making a mental note to reapply sunscreen before going back out to the pool. As if the conver-sation is boring me, I reply, "There's no rush. We're enjoying being newlyweds. And we both have busy careers, so..."

My mother-in-law snorts. I'd like to ignore it, but I can't. No, this is exactly what Colin meant months ago when he talked about setting precedents. And this, her cornering me and bullying me in private, is definitely not a precedent I care to set.

Into the mirror, I say to her, "Like it or not, I do have my own life, apart from being the—what did you call it that one time?—'CEO of the Jet Knox brand'?"

"That's right. And it should be your main focus, considering it affords you this lifestyle." She motions to the bathroom around us, but I get that she's referring to the whole house and the pulsing party it contains.

I could be as obtuse as she would be in this situation, but playing it straight will likely get us out of this conversation—and this room—sooner, and that's definitely my biggest goal at the moment. Followed closely by ordering an enormous margarita at the poolside bar.

"This lifestyle isn't that important to me."

"Until you don't have it anymore."

"I've lived without it before and could easily do it again. Jet likes it. I could take it or leave it."

"That attitude is a sure way to lose it. And he's worked hard for it, so don't you dare jeopardize it or take it for granted."

I sigh. "Gloria, I don't know what you want from me. I love your son, and we make each other happy, which is what you constantly claim is your only concern, so what's the problem?"

Her jaw tightens, and her green eyes narrow. "You got your way with the wedding; don't deny Jet what he's always wanted: to be a father."

"Nobody's denying anybody anything!"

"This is important, Maura. This is about his legacy."

The door pushes open farther, bumping Gloria between the shoulder blades. She steps out of the way and turns, coming face-to-face with her son. Her furious son.

"What's going on in here?" Jet asks, keeping his eyes firmly focused on his mother.

Gloria laughs, her face relaxing and voice rising an octave. "Maura and I were catching up, that's all."

I roll my eyes at her lie but choose not to say anything

when Jet glances at me before zooming right back in on her. "Really? Because it sounded to me like you were grilling Maura and blaming her for canceling the wedding."

"Oh, that? No! But she was the one most opposed to such a large affair. She admitted it herself when she threw your ring at— Well, let's not bring up that unpleasantness again."

"We had the exact wedding we *both* wanted in Belize."

"Yes, well that's hardly—"

"It counted. I double-checked."

I press my lips together to keep from laughing out loud.

"And what's this about kids? I don't need you to lobby on behalf of my sperm, okay?"

"You've always wanted to be a dad. Don't try to downplay that now to keep the peace with your wife."

"I'm not downplaying anything. She knows how I feel *now*, not how I felt when I was a stupid single guy, looking up to my older brothers and wanting what they had, having no idea how much work goes into being a parent. I like being an uncle. It's fun. But I also like sleeping in sometimes. And doing whatever I want, whenever I want to. Someone who feels like that isn't ready to be a dad."

"It's different when they're your own. And if you get too set in your selfish ways, you'll never be ready."

His nostrils flare. "You know what, Mom? It's none of your business."

"Excuse me?"

"You're excused." He steps aside and motions her past him. "The kids need another grownup to supervise the movie. I bet they'd love it if it was you."

"But, Jet! I was only trying to—"

"Please go, Mom."

She aims a final glare at me, to which I wince in reply, as if to say, *"Don't blame me. I'm just standing here."*

Jet's jaw drops. "Hey! Don't give Maura the stink-eye! You're the one being ugly."

With a toss of her head, she disappears into the crowded theater, where she's greeted by several delighted voices saying, "Grammy!"

Despite how angry she's made me, I hope the warm welcome takes the sting out of what happened here with her son. I only want her to be happy, after all.

————

Jet's happiness is more important to me, though. Although he shrugged it off at the time, and we rejoined the party upstairs, I can tell he was "playing on" for our guests, because that's what you do when you're Jet. You play on. You play through the pain, especially in a packed stadium of cheering fans.

I notice him sitting with his feet in the water, separated from the rest of the revelers after nightfall, when the guests with kids have departed, so I join him, lowering myself to the side of the pool and dunking my feet next to his. Since we're left with only the hardcore partiers, I'm confident nobody will notice our absence.

He looks over at me and smiles. "Hey, babe."

Hm. I may be too late.

I smile back like nothing's wrong. "Hey. Taking a breather?"

"Coolin' off my dogs," he says, swishing his feet back and forth in the water.

I rub toes with him. "A great party in the books."

"I guess so. Most people seemed to have a good time."

"People are *still* having a good time." I look behind us at Rae and Ana Paula, laugh-singing karaoke. "Just out of curiosity, when do you think they'll stop having a good time and go home?"

He smirks. "When we tell them to get out."

"Oh."

"Not too much longer."

"I'm not in any rush; I was just wondering." I braid my fingers through his, and looking across the placid surface of the deserted pool, I drop casually, "I'm sorry about what happened earlier, with your mom."

"Why are *you* apologizing?"

"Because someone needs to, and I'm not holding my breath that it'll be her."

"I don't want her fake apologies, anyway. I want her to stop treating you like that."

With false confidence, I say, "She will. I was doing fine until you busted in. How long did you eavesdrop, anyway?"

I nudge him, but he remains serious when he answers, "Long enough. I heard enough." I lean into his side when he wraps his arm around my shoulders and cups my farthest upper arm in his hand.

"You gonna be okay?"

"Of course." He grins. "It's only one bad series of plays in an otherwise great game."

"Good attitude. A bit oversimplified, but I'll give it to you."

His eyes widen and twinkle, and his jaw sets as his grin morphs from happy-go-lucky to nefarious. "You're askin' for it."

"Whatcha gonna do about it?"

He tightens his hand on my arm and leans forward, tipping

us both into the deep end of the pool. When we surface, I slosh water into his laughing mouth.

"Everyone in the pool!" he yells, prompting a free-for-all of drunken divers.

I quickly swim to him and cling to his shoulders, blinking at the frenzied splashing around us.

"Maybe this will sober some of them up and get them the heck out of here," he murmurs next to my ear.

I'm not so sure about that, but it's worth a shot.

## THIRTY-THREE

## ROOKIES

Ball caps and sunglasses afford us as much anonymity as we've had in months. The two kids who aren't ours serve as decent red herrings, too, although anyone who gets close enough to hear us can tell right away they're not ours. Or we're the most bumbling rookies on the planet.

"I don't like using the carrier," Jet complains next to the car while I slide four-month-old Meleah into the contraption hanging from the front of his body and thread her legs through the holes.

"Do you want to steer that yacht of a stroller around the entire zoo?" I ask, nodding toward the folded up monstrosity in the trunk.

"No."

"Then the carrier, it is." I situate a Royals cap on Mikey's head to match the ones we're wearing. He immediately takes it off. I try again, this time arranging it backwards, which is obviously more acceptable, since he leaves it alone.

"Every time I bend over in this thing, though, I feel like she's going to spill out of it."

"She will. Jet. You can't bend over."

"Oh. Then what's the point?"

I level an incredulous look at him but doubt he can read it through my sunglasses. "Your hands will be free to help with Mikey and take pictures and stuff."

"I wanna ride da twain!" Mikey shouts for the entire zoo's information.

Jet ignores him and sighs at me but waits for me to finish reassuring Mikey we'll ride every single ridable thing here, as long as he stops yelling. Then Jet says about the carrier, "Fine."

"I'll wear her, if you don't want to."

He turns away from me to keep her out of my grasp. "No. I like her. She smells good."

Yeah, now she does. She didn't smell good when we first arrived, and I had to spend the first few minutes of our babysitting adventure changing her diaper on the front passenger seat of the car with Jet muttering in the background about Corinthian leather.

Tucking his chin, he looks down on Meleah's fair head. "What's she doing right now?"

"Dozing. And your massive head will provide plenty of shade, so we may have to only reapply her sunscreen four or five times, as opposed to every half-hour, like Deirdre instructed. Let's go."

We set off from the car while I'm still digging in the back-pack, making sure I have the aforementioned SPF 100, plenty of diapers and wipes, a change of clothes for each child, breast milk bottles in the insulated pouch, binkies, animal crackers, quarters for petting zoo feed, bottles of Gatorade Jet purchased at the gas station on the way here, and...

"Ugh." I stop in my tracks when I realize the magazine I've

been pushing to and fro in the pack is the stupid bridal issue with my picture in it. Leave it to Greg to find a way through his sleep-deprived haze to still get a dig in on me. Nice way to thank me for taking his kid off his and Deirdre's hands for the day.

I pull the publication out and say to Jet, "We need to find a trashcan."

He glances over his shoulder at the glossy booklet in my hand and does a double-take. "What? No!"

"Yes. It's in the way, and I'm sure I look hideous in it."

"I bought that at the gas station. And you don't look hideous in it; you look hot. In fact…" He snatches the magazine from me and flips to the two pages I'm spread across. "We have that dress at home somewhere in storage, right?"

"Yeah." Had to pay for it, anyway, so Gloria had it shipped to our house while we were on vacation and Helen—helpful, sweet Helen—lovingly placed its box high on a shelf in our closet. It taunts me up there daily.

"You should totally wear it for me someday."

I roll my eyes. "Whatever. The magazine's in the way right now, though."

"Hang on." Jet backtracks to the car, still in view, and tosses the book on the front seat, before returning to us at a jog and beeping the car locked over his shoulder.

"You can't jog with the baby in the carrier!" I admonish when he's still several yards away.

He slows to a smoother trot and catches up to us, pointing at the harness. "This thing is useless."

Inside the gates, next to the gazebo, we study our fold-out map of the park, looking for our first target. Mikey, already familiar, thanks to his many recent forays here with "Plonker," tries to run ahead. I zoom after him, grab his hand, and drag him back, suddenly understanding the attraction of those kid leashes I've shaken my head at for years.

"Mikey, you have to stay with us," I tell him. "I mean it. No snow cone if you run away."

He blows raspberries. "You're mean," he says with a pout but stays by my side.

I turn to Jet, who's folding the map and sliding it into his back shorts pocket. "A little help here?"

He shrugs. "I can't bend down to talk to him, so you're on your own. Mikey! Don't be a jerk, all right, man? This is going to be fun, but everyone has to be nice. Say you're sorry."

"Sorry, Mo-Mo."

I pick him up and rest him against my hip. "It's okay, buddy. I'm sorry, too. I get scared when you run away, though. Let's go over here and look at the otters. They're funny."

———

A couple of hours later, we've ridden a train, two trams—one on land, one in the air—and a boat, and we're so far away from the entrance to the zoo that merely thinking about what it's going to take to get back to the car is almost too much for me to bear. We've also discovered the map isn't for finding exhibits; it's for quickly locating bathrooms. We've seen every single bathroom from one tip of the park to the other. Now, we sit on a bench, listlessly watching Mikey point and gab at the chimps.

Jet leans back with his legs straight in front of him, feet crossed at the ankles, elbows hooked over the backrest. Meleah takes her third nap against his chest in the carrier. The kid's not going to sleep a wink tonight, at this rate. Mikey, on the other hand, will be comatose. So will Jet and I. Three out of four is a pretty decent average.

Jet yawns and wipes his eyes underneath his sunglasses. "I haven't been this tired since the flight home after the Super Bowl, when Doc kept waking me up to check my pupils."

I laugh. "Oh, come on. This can't be as taxing as, say, practice or training camp."

"Not physically, no. But mentally? I'm exhausted. They have to be kept alive. All the time."

"Yes. That's the one requirement with parenting and babysitting."

"And the poop. How do such little bodies produce so much poop?" He jerks his chin in Meleah's direction. "This one, especially. She's the poopingest person I've ever met."

"She's Greg's kid. What do you expect? Of course, she's full of... it."

He laughs. "I'm glad you've volunteered for diaper duty. You're a trouper."

I smile back into his face. "Pretty sure I permanently have that smell trapped in my nostrils, but anything for the team."

"Good news is, in a couple more hours, we get to take them home. And go to a different house, where they aren't. And do whatever the heck we want to do."

"Sleep, basically."

"Yeah, but that's more than your brother can say." He pulls his buzzing phone from his pocket but almost immediately puts it away again after skimming the incoming message. "Mom says don't forget to take pictures today."

I wince. "I haven't taken a single one."

"I did. One, at the very beginning, when the llama licked Mikey, and he freaked out."

"Oops."

He shrugs. "Whatever. She'll get over it."

And those are his five most commonly used words when referring to his mother lately. She regularly has to get over things, where he's concerned. It would be more, too, if I didn't keep his apathy in check. She'll never know that, of course, and I don't need or desire credit; I simply want to keep the peace between the two of them so I'm not outright blamed for the things that don't go her way.

Now, I snap a few shots of Mikey prancing back and forth, doing his best monkey impression. And I'll try to remember to get a few more on our way back, maybe on the sky safari. I'm sure we'll be taking that again, considering it was such a hit, and it will give us a much-needed reprieve from walking.

Meleah sighs contentedly and farts. Jet chuckles. "Geez. Real ladylike. Just like your aunt."

I shoot him a fake dirty look for his technically accurate assessment. "Better out than in. And you can shove 'ladylike' up your—"

"Animal cwacker!" Mikey yells, running up to me. I root through the backpack and hand him the fifth packet he's eaten today. I hope he eats some broccoli, or something, for dinner tonight.

He runs back to the observation window with his snack and sits cross-legged in front of the glass to continue watching the chimps as he chomps.

Jet shakes his head at him. "That kid."

"He's something else," I say with a tender smile.

"Cyndi's going to have her hands full in a couple of months, that's for sure." He sighs and sits forward, his back comically straight as he draws his knees up and perches on the front edge of the bench. "Speaking of, has she seemed okay to you?"

I consider his question and think about my recent interactions with his sister. "Yeah. In fact, she seems really happy."

He rubs his chin and frowns. "I know."

"Is that a problem?" I laugh at the concerned set to his mouth and crinkled brow.

"No! But with her divorce being final last week, I would have thought... I don't know. That she might be kind of *sad* about that."

"I'm sure she was."

"But she didn't mention anything to you?"

"No. The more she reveals about Justin and the way things were before she left, I guess it makes sense that she's relieved to be moving on."

His jaw tenses. "Asshole."

To distract him, I switch gears. "What's the deal with her mystery Lamaze partner? Any idea who that could be?"

"All I care about is that it's not me. No thanks," Jet says with a shiver, despite the steamy air around us. "Probably a friend from work. She's always been popular. Outgoing."

"Why would she be so cagey about it, if it were only a friend, though? I think she's found someone. That would be another explanation as to why she's not so broken up about her divorce."

Jet wrinkles his nose. "When would she have time for dating? She's up at the butt-crack to go to work at the bakery, and by the time she gets home during Mikey's afternoon nap, she's bushed."

I shrug. "I don't know. Something's up."

"Nah. With Cyndi, what you see is what you get. She's always been happy-go-lucky. This is the first time you've seen it, because you met her at such a sucky time in her life."

"I'm relieved she seems to have settled in. Things are

about to get pretty crazy for you." Not that I mind picking up his slack once training camp starts, but he'll be distracted and torn if he feels he's not as available to his sister as he needs to be.

He nods. "Yep. This is our last hurrah for a while."

"And we spent it at the zoo with other people's kids."

He grins. "What can we say? We're team play—" He sniffs. "Aw, man! She pooped again!"

I laugh and hold out my arms. "Give her here."

With a dramatic cough, he readily relinquishes the infant.

I'm pretty sure my multiple encounters with changing tables today qualify me for an award. MVP is already taken in our house. That's okay, though. I'm more than satisfied with Rookie of the Year.

———

# ACKNOWLEDGMENTS

Heartfelt thanks go, as usual, to the beta readers who read a rougher draft than I usually provide and returned excellent feedback to guide rewrites and edits, when I was finally ready. Lynda G., Natasha Walsh, Heather McCoubrey, Erin Baker, Hans Campbell, Kaley Stewart, Bethany Dodson, Denise Parente, Elizabeth Jenkins, and Nicole Ford were on it, like always, and provided timely comments. They were *not* the holdup in the process. They were awesome. And while some of them said, "Don't change anything!", they know me better than that. I hope they approve of the changes I did make. Thanks, guys! You are, seriously, the MVPs of my team.

Finally, but not least of all, thanks to my family and friends who put up with me. Creative people are often not easy to love, and I am painfully aware of this. Thanks for loving me, even when I make it hard for you to like me.

# ALSO BY BREA BROWN

The *Secret Keeper* series:

- *The Secret Keeper* (Book 1)
- *The Secret Keeper Confined* (Book 2)
- *The Secret Keeper Up All Night* (Book 3)
- *The Secret Keeper Holds On* (Book 4)
- *The Secret Keeper Lets Go* (Book 5)
- *The Secret Keeper Fulfilled* (Book 6)

The *Underdog* series:

- *Out of My League* (Book 1)
- *Rookie of the Year* (Book 2)
- *Opportunity Knox* (Book 3)

The *Nurse Nate* series:

- *Let's Be Frank* (Book 1)
- *Let's Be Real* (Book 2)
- *Let's Be Friends* (Book 3)

Stand-alone novels:

- *Daydreamer*
- *The Family Plot*
- *Plain Jayne*
- *Quiet, Please!*